Where the Light Enters

Kathy Miner

About the Author:

Kathy Miner lives in Colorado Springs, CO, with her family and critters. She welcomes comments, questions and conversation about her book, and can be contacted on Facebook at Kathy Miner Books, via email at kathyminerwriter@gmail.com, or you can visit her website at www.authorkathyminer.com. You can also sign up for her monthly newsletter.

Gratitude and Acknowledgments

If ya'll ever need your faith in humanity restored, you should write a book. So many people have been so generous with their time, knowledge and encouragement, and I am humbled to thank the following people for their support and involvement:

Stacy Bender, you gave me a lovely morning with the real-life Ben, and the opening scene of this book was born out of that fear-and-love experience. I hope to keep learning about horses from you for many years to come. Julie Cook, you reminded me at a crucial juncture that exercise and smokin' fast writing go hand in hand – if I hadn't spoken to you that day, I don't know when I would have finished this book! Josh James, you shared your experiences with the U.S. Marine Corps, even when your memories were painful. I thank you for your honesty and courage, and honor you for your service to our country. Dorman Gray and Andrew Weber, both of you saved me hours of research with your quick responses to my desperate Facebook posts, and I am deeply appreciative! David Perry, you never once failed to throw encouragement my way when I asked for it. I appreciate that so much, and I thank you as well for your excellent information on hunting.

My proofreaders/beta readers deserve so much more than my humble thanks; it just doesn't go far enough to say that this book would be much, much less without their time and attention. Laura Martin, Candice Moriarty, Annette Milligan and Tammy Themel, you are all my long-time friends. I value your input and suggestions for my writing, but not nearly as much as I treasure the friendships I have with each one of you. Kim Bender and Nan Anders, sister and mom-in-love respectively, thank you so much for your thoughts and on-going support. Ray Hjelt, I am thrilled you had both the time and willingness to offer such a valuable, thorough critique. You made this a far better book and changed me as a writer in the process.

Max and Phyl Miner, I just can't put together words big enough to express my thanks to you. You have cheered, helped, advised, brainstormed, critiqued and just plain listened for hours without number, and all I can give you in return is my love and gratitude. Mom, your critique was nothing short of brilliant. I had to stomp around and grump at everyone for a week before I could take your excellent advice, but I'm so glad I did. You made this book as well as the next one so much better.

Rob Anders, you show me every single day what love looks like. You came into my life just as the storm clouds gathered, and you have stayed through the tempest. Here's hoping these glimpses of sun we've been catching mean better weather ahead. Thank you, for your strength and steadiness, your brilliance and wicked sense of humor, and most of all, for choosing each day to share my life.

Jesse, Casey and Kaya Reynolds you are my babies always, no matter how tall you boys get or how much you protest, baby girl. The three of you are the source of the joy, heartbreak and hope that I try to share with every word I write.

Kristy Zeluff, sister and soul mate, first and last it will always be you. I can't even offer the words "thank you" because it's so much bigger than that. You sent me a card once that said, "Growing up with you made the stars sparkle brighter," and I get that. This whole adventure is that much more magical because we're on it together.

Dedication

For my cousin, Sondra Houtkooper, and my friend, Michelle Linn, who have both survived the most terrible of losses. I remember your sons with love, and will speak their names here and always:

In loving memory of Matt Houtkooper and J.W. Linn, two beautiful young men who left us for the arms of the angels far, far too soon.

ONE
Naomi: Woodland Park, CO

Naomi drew in a deep breath of air, and could hear her whole body shaking on the exhale. Trying to ignore the two men watching from the fence around the corral, she took one step, then another, towards the big chestnut quarter horse waiting in the center of the ring.

Big Ben shifted to the side as she approached, watching her with one narrowed eye, ears tilted forward, nostrils flared. Nerves shivered along his glossy red coat, from neck to flank. She could both see and *feel* his tension. He was ready to bolt. And so was she.

Naomi stopped walking. Her shoulders slumped, the halter and lead rope she carried now dragging on the ground. "It's not going to work. He knows I'm scared." She blinked hard, angered by the tears pressing on the backs of her eyes. Damn it, she would not cry. "He's so much bigger than Dilly."

At the fence, Martin turned and walked away, trying – and failing – to hide an eye-roll. She could *feel* his frustration and impatience as clearly as she could detect the horse's wariness, and frankly, she could do without the editorial. Ignacio, the other man, tilted his head to the side, his expression gently curious.

"Dilly bit you. Twice."

"I know." Naomi rubbed her upper arm where the second bruise was still healing. "She was just being snotty. That's her way."

"That's right, it is. Ponies can be mean as snakes." The man nodded at the chestnut. "Big Ben here never bit a soul in his life. He's as sweet as they come."

"He could squash me like a bug."

Martin had circled back to the fence, and didn't bother to hide the eye-roll this time. "This from the woman who has a dog the size of a Sherman tank."

"Hades is a cream-puff," Naomi snapped. "He would never hurt anyone." Unlike the enormous Ben, who was clearly waiting to bite a chunk out of her and trample the rest to a smear of goo.

From his position outside the arena, Hades, hearing his name, lifted his massive head from his paws and gazed at her. She didn't need to meet that gaze to *feel* his love. The big Rottweiler chuffed a soft, encouraging sound, then yawned and returned to his nap.

"Huh." Martin radiated skepticism. "I'd like to see what would happen if someone made a move towards you Hades didn't like. Bet he'd make quite an impression, and 'cream puff' wouldn't be it."

"Martin, I could sure do with some more wood split. We're running low, and it's certain we'll see more snow before the end of the day."

Ignacio didn't look at Martin as he made the request. Martin stared at Naomi a moment longer, then made a low, disgusted sound and headed for the far side of the house. Persephone bounced along at his heels, a golden fairy in dog-form, the embodiment of joy, excitement and love, love, love. Naomi felt her upper lip twitch into a sneer. There was no accounting for taste.

When Martin was out of earshot, Ignacio spoke again. "Naomi, stop glaring holes in Martin's back and look at me."

Naomi shifted her attention. Ignacio' eyes were ageless and patient, his face so weathered he could have been forty or eighty. She could *feel* his awareness touch hers as he used an intuitive skill remarkably like her own to settle and calm her. From anyone else, the touch would have been intrusive, but from Ignacio it was like the wind brushing her face or the sun warming her shoulders. She felt tension seep out of her muscles and sighed softly in relief.

"Move back to the fence and drape the halter and lead over it." Naomi obeyed his instructions, and he went on. "Now just lean against the fence and relax. Close your eyes."

Naomi squinted at him, then glanced at the still-tense Ben. "It would be easier to relax on the other side of the fence."

"Yep. And you'd never connect with this pretty boy, which would be a darn shame. He's been lonely and sad since...well, since before."

Before. It had been nearly a year since the plague that had wiped out the world they'd all known, and people still had to let sentences trail off uncomfortably or cut themselves off mid-thought. No one named their dead, not in casual conversation.

Ignacio had lost his wife of many years, four of his five children, and all but one of his grandchildren. He lived here, on the ranch that had been in his family for generations, with his sole surviving daughter and four-year-old grandson. Naomi had been coming here with Martin for the last couple of weeks to start learning about horses – how to handle, care for, tack and ride. The results so far had been mixed; she did fine with little Dilly, the Welsh Pony, bites and all. Big Ben was a different story.

Ignacio nodded at her. "Come on now. Close your eyes. Relax your body. Horses read everything about us in an instant. Give him a blank slate for a minute, and we'll talk this through."

It took more courage than Naomi cared to admit to do as he asked. She shut her eyes and lifted her face to the feeble, late-winter sun. She knew Ignacio was right; Big Ben's discomfort was a mirror-image of her own. She had to get her feelings under control or she hadn't a prayer of ever being at ease around Ben, much less riding him. She rolled her head from side to side to release the tightness in her neck and shoulders, then took another deep breath. This one didn't shake on the exhale.

Ignacio spoke. "You could see that Ben was about to bolt. Tell me why."

Naomi frowned, eyes still shut. "He knows I'm scared. I said that before."

"No." Ignacio's patience seemed to come from his very bones – Naomi had yet to see his temper so much as wobble, whether the uncooperative student he was working with was equine or human. "Why did he get so uncomfortable? Here's a hint – think about how you were moving towards him. What did that tell him?"

Naomi went back over the moments in her mind. "I was moving too tentatively. He thought I was creeping up on him."

"That's right. Ben isn't like Hades or Persephone. They're predators. So are humans. Ben's a prey animal, and when you're not too busy being afraid, you'll be able to *feel* the difference. Pretend it's little Dilly here, keep your eyes closed, and just *feel* what he's feeling."

Ignacio was one of the few people who seemed completely comfortable discussing the changes so many of them had gone through in the wake of the plague. For him, the increased intuitive *knowing* many people now experienced was just an enhancement, a deepening, of a skill he'd possessed all his life. Naomi envied him his ease with the topic; too often, she felt like an awkward teenager, constantly worried about committing a social faux pas. At least she wasn't alone. In this strange new world, no one had figured out the rules yet.

Ignacio nudged her attention back to the task at hand. "Come on. You connect with your dogs as easy as breathing. Think of this guy as a really big dog."

Naomi snorted her disagreement. She'd learned the hard way with Dilly that horses and dogs were definitely not the same, at least not when it came to creating this connection. She had earned that first bite when she'd tried to reach out to the pony a little too enthusiastically. Animals, she now knew, were even more sensitive to intuitive intrusion than people.

She and Dilly had never achieved a solid connection. Naomi picked up fleeting impressions from her, sudden flashes of panoramic vision in washed-out shades of blue and yellow, usually accompanied by a heightened sense of Hades as a threat to be monitored. She didn't know if the insubstantial connection was due to her inexperience with horses or if it could be attributed to Dilly, who loathed all living creatures with the occasional exception of Ignacio.

"Naomi. Stop thinking. Just *feel*."

"Ugh. All right." She heaved a disgusted sigh and frowned in concentration. With her eyes shut, she was more aware of the sounds around her: the hush-hush of the rising wind, bringing the scent of snow with it; the distant warning cry of a crow; and the soft rustles as Ben shifted his weight restlessly. She dropped to a deeper level of concentration and gently – don't be tentative, she reminded herself – gently and confidently extended her awareness.

She became aware of the horse's perplexity first. This human was a puzzle – some of them were, he had learned – but this one was more confusing than most. Confident one minute, fearful the next. What was she afraid of? What was wrong? Should he be afraid? He didn't understand her, and he certainly didn't trust her.

Beside her, Ignacio clucked softly, and Naomi *felt* Ben's attention shift. She was still connected enough to grin in delight at the wave of *love* that washed over her. What a sweet boy, what a huge, giving heart he had. She explored his emotional landscape while he communed with Ignacio, relaxing more and more as she took these first steps towards knowing him. He reminded her of Hades quite a lot actually – generous of heart, a gentle giant. She heard the soft thump of his hooves coming closer and decided to keep her eyes closed. His size was overwhelming; his energy was beautiful.

"Good, good," Ignacio murmured softly, and she knew he was speaking to both of them. "That's right. You two are meant to be together, I knew it from the start. She's not sneaky, boy. She used to love horses, a long time ago – she just needs to remember that feeling. And she just wants you to like her, maybe a little too much."

Naomi's lips twitched in amusement – she hadn't realized the truth of that until Ignacio said it. He was right on the money. As a little girl, she hadn't wanted riding lessons as much as she'd wanted to be a horse, to move with power and grace, to be both beautiful and strong. Macy's adoration of horses was so similar – even at ten, she still galloped everywhere she went.

Naomi gasped and curled forward around the sudden stab of pain in her chest. God, how she hated the unexpected cuts. The constant, hollow ache, she had learned to live with. She opened her eyes and looked straight into Ben's. He was not even a foot in front of her, ears forward, eyes steady on hers. Her face twisted and tears flooded – she never, ever denied grief when it came.

"She would have loved you, Ben, even though you're not a beautiful white Arabian. It should be her here, getting to know you. Not me."

"And there's the crux of it." Ignacio's hand curled over the cap of her shoulder, warm with compassion and comfort. "I felt her in you from the start, but I didn't want to intrude. Your daughter?"

Naomi nodded, staring at the ground and swiping at the tears. "Macy." It was both relief and torment to speak her name. "She loved horses more than anything."

"And it's not fair that she can't be here with you and Ben." Naomi nodded again, and Ignacio went on. "You've got to be okay with that – Ben can handle all the grief you or I have to dish out, it's the conflict that confuses him. All of us that are still here have to get over 'not fair.'"

Naomi sniffed and shot him a sideways look. "That is so much easier said than done."

"The hardest stuff always is. Now, let's shift gears. We'll just hang out with Ben here, get used to his sounds and movements, figure out where he likes to be scratched while you start to get your mind around that."

Naomi nodded and took a step closer to the horse, hesitated, reminded herself to not hesitate, then laughed. "Stop thinking," she muttered, and ran her hand down the warm, strong curve of Ben's neck. A few strokes, and his head swung towards her. He blew a soft breath through his nostrils, watching her with one large, dark eye. Reaching out with his nose, he nudged her gently in the center of her chest. Her heart wanted to speed up, but she kept her breathing even and her shoulders relaxed. Acting on instinct, she cupped his silky nose with her palm and gently but firmly pushed back.

"Good, good," Ignacio repeated, his approval wrapping around her like a warm blanket. "That's exactly right, Naomi. He's not being pushy. He just wants you to love on him, but he still needs to know where the lines are."

By the time Martin returned half an hour later, sweaty and no less irritable, Naomi was working her way around Ben with a soft brush, learning his idiosyncrasies while Ignacio taught her generalities. "Horses are prey animals, but more importantly, they're herd animals. In a herd, there can only be leaders and followers. You must be the leader. While you're brushing him, stop occasionally and press with your hand. Ask him to shift his weight, to take a step away from you. Ask with your hand and with your intent."

Naomi did as Ignacio instructed, trying not to feel Martin's critical watchfulness. When Ben didn't move, she pressed harder, and Ignacio shook his head.

"No, keep your pressure light. He's too big for you to use brute force. Be calm and firm and *intend* him to move."

Naomi darted a glance at Martin, who was watching with obvious disapproval, his lips a tight, straight line. She wished Ignacio would send him on another errand, but sooner or later, she would have to get over her discomfort around him. If they were going to travel cross-country together for weeks on end, she couldn't poker up whenever he was around. It would help a lot if he would try to keep his lack of respect to himself.

She hadn't realized how relaxed she had gotten until the muscles in her shoulders and neck knotted up again. Beside her, Ben shifted, restless with her nerves, then shook his head and blew. *Confusion. Anxiety.* The strength and clarity of his emotions startled, then delighted her. The connection was strong, so strong, almost as intimate as her bond with Hades.

She took a deep breath and closed her eyes, leaning against Ben's side and shutting out everything else. She turned her head so her ear was pressed to the powerful thump of his heart and breathed in his scent, delicious, dusty, musky horse. Draping an arm over his back, she let her heart warm with admiration and affection, *feeling* back at him. Ben nickered softly, giving voice to the *contentment* she felt radiating from his big, beautiful heart.

Naomi opened her eyes, and brushed a few more strokes down Ben's side. Then, she placed her hand on his shoulder and pressed gently. Calm, firm *intent*. Ben took an immediate step away from her pressure, then turned his head to her, their eyes meeting in perfect understanding. She grinned, her heart giving a happy little skip. This was going to work.

Ignacio laughed softly. "It's a love affair startin' up, you see that, Martin?"

"Yeah. Very sweet. How long until love becomes riding? We should be taking our practice run in a month and getting ready to leave in six or seven weeks. She's got to be able to handle him, even if the going gets rough." He grimaced. "When the going gets rough. Is she going to be ready?"

Naomi took a step back from Ben and narrowed her eyes at Martin. Outside the corral, Hades lifted his head, adding his stare to hers. "'She' is standing right here, Martin, and I'll be ready. I'm as anxious to go as you are."

Martin's skepticism couldn't have been more clear if he'd declared it. "You can't let fear cripple you, Naomi. You've got to be able to act, even when you're afraid. We could be facing situations that are a lot more frightening than a really big horse."

"I've been in those situations." Memory flashed — armed men surrounding the truck, the steadiness of her handgun while the rest of her body shook, the screams of the man she had run over. A frantic little dog, suddenly lifeless under her hands. A teenage boy between the sights of her shotgun, flexing his bat as he eyed her dogs, her finger cool and ready on the trigger. "I can act when I have to."

Their gazes locked and held. In the months since their first meeting, the social niceties had gradually worn thin until they'd finally shredded. He didn't like her. She didn't like him. But they had a common goal, and they had to work together to achieve it.

Martin dropped his gaze first, shaking his head. "I hope we don't have to find out you're wrong about that." He focused on Ignacio. "You said you had some things for us to take back to town?"

"Yes. Some winter clothes and boots. They're in bags on the kitchen table."

Martin nodded and headed towards the house without looking at Naomi again. She could feel Ignacio's eyes on her, and turned to meet his patient gaze.

"So now that Ben and I are such good friends, what's the command for 'Trample Martin?'?"

Ignacio chuckled, but his eyes were serious. "Be careful what you ask for. If you and Ben connect the way I think you will, he would do that for you, no hesitation. It's one of the great responsibilities of horsemanship. If he accepts you as the leader of his herd, he'll blow his heart out for you. All you would have to do is ask it."

Naomi stroked her palm down Ben's nose, gazing into his warm, soft eyes. She could get lost in this, in him, and she laughed softly. "It is like falling in love," she murmured. "Magical. Like there's no one else in the world but us. "

Then, she looked at Ignacio and answered the question he was too polite to ask. "I don't know what the problem is between Martin and me. We got along fine at first. But over time..." She brushed a few more strokes along Ben's side, thinking, then spoke again. "We started to grate on each other, I guess, and it's hard to hide that now. It's too easy to *feel* what others feel towards you. It's awkward. And it hurts."

Ignacio nodded. "Have you talked to him about it?"

Naomi snorted out a laugh. "Not hardly. He's just like Jack. He doesn't want to talk about the *feeling* stuff unless there's some kind of tactical advantage to be discussed, or he's cornered."

"Maybe you ought to corner him." Ignacio turned his gaze towards Pikes Peak, where the wind was whipping snow in curves and curls off the mountaintop. He didn't seem to be seeing the mountain, though. "If you don't trust each other, understand each other now, how can you hope to on your journey?"

"I don't need to know more about what he's feeling, Ignacio. I'm getting it loud and clear." She leaned on Ben and shut her eyes. "He thinks I'm too soft. A coward. He regrets ever agreeing to go on this trip together, and he wishes he had just taken off to look for his kids on his own. But now he feels responsible, because he knows I'll go looking for Piper alone. He doesn't think I would make it, and that would be on him. He resents the burden. Resents me."

Ignacio nodded thoughtfully. "There may be some of that going on. I'm picking up something different, but I'm on the outside looking in, so what I'm getting doesn't matter. Just ask yourself this, Naomi: What's he picking up from you?"

Well, that made her blink. She considered for a moment, then huffed out a laugh. "I haven't the faintest idea. I never even thought about it before."

"You might want to. And while you're at it, you might want to stop telling yourself you know what he's thinking. Only way to know for sure is to ask him."

Martin came out of Ignacio's house carrying a couple of garbage bags and looked up at the sky. He strode towards the corral, purpose in his swift steps. "We need to go, Naomi. That weather's moving in faster than I thought it would."

Naomi gave Ben's neck a final hug, then climbed through the bars of the corral. On impulse, she hugged Ignacio, too. "Thank you. I'll think about what you said."

He hugged her back. "Good. I'll see you back here when the weather clears, and we'll start with the basics." He leaned back and patted her shoulder, face serious, eyes mischievous. "Shouldn't take more than a couple weeks to master that 'trample' command you were asking about."

Martin shot a sharp look at Ignacio, then skewered her with his eyes. "Trample command?"

Naomi felt her face heat, but didn't look away. "Never know when you might need such a thing. Could come in handy in a tight spot."

"Sure." He held up the garbage bags. "Thanks, Ignacio. We'll see you in a day or two." Then he headed for the ATV they'd ridden here, clearly expecting Naomi to follow.

Naomi sighed and followed. It wore her out, being around him. She could hardly wait to get home, where the only thoughts she had to contend with were her own.

Hades and Persephone were already waiting by the 4-wheeler, which had a small trailer attached to the back. Martin loaded the bags, then held them aside so Hades could jump in and settle safely on the bottom of the trailer. Persephone, however, had jumped up to the seat of the ATV, and the moment Martin straightened, she launched herself into the air. Martin didn't miss a beat, catching her, sliding her into the front of his jacket and zipping it in the same motion. Naomi stifled another sigh as she bent to tuck a blanket around Hades against the gusting, icy wind. Talk about a love affair. She was pretty sure Persephone would choose to never leave Martin's side, if only Naomi could bring herself to let the little dog go.

Martin straddled the ATV and started it, and Naomi climbed on behind him. She flipped the hood of her parka up and tightened it while Martin slid on a stocking cap and wrapped his face with a scarf. He glanced over his shoulder to check that Hades was still settled safely in the trailer, then looked at her, only his dark eyes showing between his cap and scarf. His voice was muffled. "Ready?" She nodded, and leaned forward to put her arms around him, sliding her hands under Persephone's little butt to stabilize her inside Martin's jacket. She tightened her arms as they took off, and pressed her face between his shoulder blades to protect it from the wind.

As always, she wondered if touching another person would ever feel normal again. She could go weeks now without seeing or speaking to another human, much less being touched by one, and it felt strange, too close. But gas was now a precious commodity; full-sized cars or trucks were used only in the direst of emergencies. Salvaging what fuel had been left in abandoned vehicles was an ongoing job in the community, and they'd had enough to run generators through the worst of the winter, but their supply was finite, and no one ever forgot it.

People mostly walked where they needed to go, or rode horses if they had them. If it was too far, or if they needed the trailer for supplies, they used ATVs, snowmobiles, or small dirt bikes, which consumed less gas. The first time Naomi had ridden with Martin, she'd been so busy trying to touch him as little as possible, she had just about tipped them over. The memory could still warm her cheeks with embarrassment.

"Look," he had said, "This is never going to work if you stiffen up like some prissy virgin. I've got no plans to jump you. If you're going to ride with me, you have to move with me. There's no other way." He had kept his tone even, but his derision was there for her to *feel*, with painful clarity.

Mortifying, that being close to her meant nothing to him, when it roused such painful, conflicting feelings in her. She wasn't inclined to share with Martin that she had been a "prissy virgin" when she'd married her husband, and in the twenty-three years since, she hadn't so much as glanced at another man. Desire, lust, sexuality – all those feelings began with Scott and ended with his death. And given the way the world had changed, the idea of meeting someone new and falling in love seemed as far-fetched and irrelevant as a trip to Mars.

But it felt good, being close to Martin's warmth, his strength. His scent was familiar now, and that brought comfort, too. When they rode like this, she felt safe, something she took for granted in the time before, and which was now the most luxurious of feelings. It confused her, feeling such things for someone who didn't even pretend to like her.

She lifted her head to check how far they'd come, squinting against the snow that had started to come down in big, fluffy flakes. Ignacio's ranch lay to the southwest of Woodland Park, in the wide-open country that rose steadily towards the Great Divide. They were approaching the center of town already, zooming past deserted homes and businesses. Here and there, a thin trail of smoke marked someone's home, but the majority of survivors had moved, at Jack's request, to cluster around his old church, which had become the center of their social and working world.

Formerly a youth minister, Jack was now the leader of their small community. He had tried repeatedly to talk Ignacio and his daughter into joining them, but

Ignacio continued to politely decline. Naomi, too, refused to leave her cabin on Carrol Lakes. Like the animals they had such rapport with, both Naomi and Ignacio were adept at listening to instinct rather than being swayed by human persuasion, even with someone as supernaturally persuasive as Jack.

In the way Ignacio and Naomi understood animals, Jack understood people: specifically, how to get them to do what he wanted them to do. Naomi hated to use the word "manipulative," but there it was. Jack knew how to push buttons and pull strings, and though she believed he did so with the good of the community at heart, she didn't trust him. He was too good at justification, and she didn't think he stopped often enough to differentiate between his needs and the needs of the group.

Martin was an unexpected ally against Jack's tactics as well. He had more reason than most to resent their young leader's abilities; Jack had pressured Martin into staying with the community rather than going in search of his kids when the worst of the plague had burned out. Naomi doubted Martin would ever forgive Jack, either for the manipulation or for the delay. The two men maintained a working relationship, but it was strained at best.

The snow was falling fast and thick as they zoomed up to park under the portico at the front of the church, which now served as both a social center and a place of worship, as well as a place where supplies were collected, stored, and distributed to those in need. In the rapidly deepening twilight, most of the windows were dark. No doubt the weather was keeping people hunkered down in their homes. Martin waited, motor idling, as Naomi climbed down, went to uncover Hades, and grabbed the bags Ignacio had given them. The big Rottweiler leaped out of the trailer and followed as she lugged the bags towards the front door. It opened when she was a few feet away, and Layla hurried out to help her.

"We were starting to get worried," she said, as she took one of the bags from Naomi. "The storm came in so fast."

The two women hurried inside as Martin drove the ATV around to the covered parking structure that had been built last fall. Naomi set her bag down as soon as the door shut behind them, and brushed the heavy, wet snow off Hades. He gave a mighty shake when she was finished, then trotted towards the church library, no doubt headed for a spot by the wood-burning stove that had been installed. Naomi picked her bag up again, and followed Layla down the hallway to what used to be a row of classrooms, areas now being used for storage.

Layla turned as she walked, smiling at Naomi. "Did you enjoy your time with the horses? How is Ignacio?"

"He's well – his family, too." Naomi laughed a little. "And I would like horses a lot more if they were dog-sized. The closer I got, the bigger Ben got. I'd have sworn he was a mastodon by the time I stepped in the corral with him. It took a while, but I finally relaxed enough to touch and brush him."

"That is so interesting. I wonder if your rapport with certain animals and not others is controlled wholly by experience or if it's an in-born tendency? Did you experience anything like your connection with Hades and Persephone?"

Other than Ignacio, Layla was the only person Naomi knew who was completely comfortable with the intuitive evolution so many had undergone. A high school teacher before the plague, she still served the community's children, though she taught all ages now in a make-shift, one-room school downstairs near the church gymnasium. She was also a practicing Witch and read Tarot cards for those that asked – a fact that certainly didn't go over big with their Christian leader.

"I did, actually," Naomi answered. "It'll take some time to get to know him as well as I know the dogs, but the connection was strong." She set the bag down in front of one of the classrooms. "Do you want me to help you sort these?"

"No, they can wait until morning, when we have daylight. We're trying to conserve lamp oil." She set her bag down as well. "I know you were planning to stay for the evening meal, but will you think about staying the night? It's really coming down."

Naomi was shaking her head before Layla finished speaking. She never spent the night away from her cabin, not if she could help it. "Thanks, but I should get going. I'll ask Martin about taking one of the snowmobiles."

"I wish you'd reconsider." Jack's voice floated out of the dark at the far end of the hallway. Startled, both Naomi and Layla turned as he stepped out of a room, shutting the door behind him. He walked towards them, a handsome young man with eyes far, far older than his thirty-some years. "It would be safer for your animals to just stay the night here."

Naomi bit back a smile; he never stopped trying. And he knew her well enough to appeal to her concern for the dogs rather than her own welfare. "As always, I appreciate the offer, but we'll get home just fine."

The three of them walked back towards the library, the air around them now humming with the tension that twisted like a living, breathing creature, constantly, between Layla and Jack. For a time, Naomi had thought they would make a match, as so many people were starting to do. It was human nature, after all, for people to seek a partner, the comfort of a lover, someone to share the work and the long, lonely nights with. But now that she knew both of them better, she doubted it. There was caring between them, sure enough, but so many other things – fear, disdain, lust, respect, disrespect, longing, pain. Being around them made her dizzy.

The door opened just as they reached the lobby, and Martin blew in with the snow. He had Persephone cradled in his arms like a baby. He nodded to Jack and Layla, then honed in on Naomi. "I brought the snowmobile around, with the sled for Hades."

And wouldn't it be easier to figure this man out if he would just stop doing things like that? "Thank you," she said. She sent a mental summons to Hades, and heard him grumble as he heaved to his feet in the library.

Martin slid his hands under Persephone's front legs and held her up to his face, nose to nose. "You be a good girl," he murmured, and was rewarded with a delicate lick on his chin. He passed the little dog to Naomi, heading for the library and giving Hades a stroke down his spine as the two of them passed. "Send word by radio when you're home."

"I will." Naomi zipped Persephone into her jacket like Martin had done, and the three of them turned to the door. Weather permitting, they walked the distance between the town and her cabin, which was just under four miles. Tonight, though, she was grateful for the ride.

"Are you still planning to be here tomorrow to teach your class?" Jack opened the door for her, shuddering and hunching his shoulders at the bitter swirl of wind and snow. "Ugh, on second thought, let's just say the day after. Give this time to break."

"Sounds good. I'll see you all soon."

Naomi stepped out quickly, and hurried to the snowmobile, settling Hades into the sled attached behind – Martin had remembered the blanket from the trailer – then climbed on, started the machine, and headed towards home.

Other than the buzz of her snowmobile, the world was absolutely silent as she wound up Rampart Range Road. Tall pines and boulders marked the boundaries of the snow-covered road, and she kept the snowmobile right in the center. That she knew of, she was the only person that still lived out this way, so watching for traffic wasn't a concern.

She left the forest and entered a high mountain meadow. The noise of her snowmobile startled a large herd of mule deer, which had been grazing where the sun had melted the snow off the winter-dry grass. She felt Hades' keen interest as they paused to watch the animals bound towards the sheltering pines.

"Soon, boy. With this fresh snow, maybe tomorrow will be a good day for a hunt."

Hades had yet to bring down something as large as a mule deer, but he kept trying. Of the two dogs, Persephone was still the superior hunter, consistently bringing in rabbits and game birds to share with her big, clumsy companion. Hades got lucky every once in a while, but his kind had been bred for centuries to herd and protect. Power was his strength, not stealth. He was getting better each time they went out, but when he got too excited, he moved through the forest with all the subtlety of an enthusiastic tank.

The last of the deer disappeared, and Naomi started them on their way again. Night was falling rapidly around her, but she had walked this route, from her cabin to town and back again, over and over in the last year. She knew the way with an intimacy she could never have imagined in the time before when she had traveled this same ground inside a buffering vehicle.

Snow swirled and danced in the bright beam of her headlight as she pulled up to the cabin, tucking the snowmobile into the lean-to she had built by the front door for just this purpose. Her engineer husband would have winced at her cobbled-together creation – it had fallen down under the weight of the first heavy snow – but now it was as sturdy as it was ugly. In the spring, she mused, she'd see about pulling it down and starting over, putting what she'd learned to use to improve the appearance.

Either that or find a pretty vine to scramble over it as camouflage…

She remembered, then, that she wouldn't be here in the spring, and possibly not for most of the summer. A part of her brain kept denying that reality, even as she planned and prepared.

The outline of the journey had already been decided. From here, she and Martin would travel to Colorado Springs, stopping at Naomi's home to gather the weapons and ammunition she had left behind. Then, on to Limon, to look for Martin's son Benji and his daughter Grace. What they found in Limon would determine the next steps; if Benji and Grace were gone, Naomi and Martin would travel on to Greeley, a hundred miles to the north, to look for Piper. If Benji and Grace had survived, the plan was to bring the kids straight back to the safety of the Woodland Park community. When the kids were settled, she and Martin would leave once again, in search of Piper.

Naomi had nodded and agreed while these plans were discussed, all the while knowing she would not return to Woodland Park again, not without her daughter. She would go on alone if she had to. The thought made her laugh softly and shake her head in wonder. For a woman that wouldn't even go out to eat by herself in the time before, planning to ride cross-country alone should have been unthinkable. Yet here she was, thinking it.

"Needs must," she muttered, unlocking the padlock she had installed on the cabin's exterior door. "When the devil drives."

She stepped into the cool darkness, taking a moment to *feel*, as she always did, that all was as it should be. Beside her, Hades paused as well, sniffing and sensing. Naomi dropped her hand to his head, and for a moment, her senses linked with his. Layers of scent were now available to her nose – the lingering smell of the breakfast they had eaten here hours ago, the stink of Ares the cat, Hades' mortal enemy, and beneath that, the faint aroma of death, of slow, dry decay.

All was well.

Naomi shut and bolted the cabin door, then unzipped her jacket and set Persephone on the floor. She moved to light a hurricane lamp and then to revive the coals she had left banked in the fireplace. Hades and Persephone went to stand by the pantry cupboard; with no time to hunt today, they were both hungry. There was a small amount of dry kibble left from her original stores, and she fed them out of it, grimacing. She had planned to save some of the food for the journey, but at the rate they were consuming it, it wouldn't last.

She would just have to draw from the community stores. She calculated she had racked up enough points to her credit so the withdrawal wouldn't hurt the power balance between her and Jack. At his request, she had been giving members of the community instructions on firearms – how to handle them safely, clean them, and shoot. Some of them had become quite good, though none of them – not even Martin – could match her for consistency and accuracy. And therein, she knew, lay the root of the tension between her and Martin.

Naomi sighed as she continued to move around the cabin, doing what needed to be done to settle them in for the night. Martin couldn't care less that she was a better shot than him. What angered him was that she refused to hunt.

"Help me understand." His voice had been edged with incredulity. "You eat meat. Your dogs eat meat. But you won't supply any of that meat."

"I share what my dogs take when they take more than we need."

"Naomi, for Christ's sake! You're the best shot I've ever seen!" She remembered how he had taken a few breaths then, trying to settle himself. His tone had been calmer when he continued, but she had *felt* the boil of his emotions. "I know you've got this thing with animals, but we're talking about survival here. You've got to get over it and do your part."

Oh, her temper had spiked in response to that. "I am doing my part – the part I choose! I get to decide what I'm willing to give, not you or anybody else!"

She hadn't given him a chance to reply, storming away from the confrontation, and it hadn't been revisited. Their relationship had deteriorated steadily ever since, but Naomi wasn't willing to give him what he wanted. Nor was she willing to tell him why.

She had gone hunting. Once. Early the previous fall, after the first snowfall, she had gone out in the pre-dawn hours. Her long hikes and forays had made the task simple. She knew where the mule deer were likely to be found at any time between dawn and dusk. She had left Hades and Persephone behind, the former being too loud, the latter being too little to navigate the drifts of snow. From the time she left the cabin to the moment she found herself standing over a mortally wounded doe had been less than 20 minutes.

Naomi's shot had struck the deer right behind her shoulder, piercing her lungs. On a bed of crimson snow, she had gasped the last breath of her life, a breath that rattled in, then sighed out on a groan. That groan was carried on a puff of crystallized air right through Naomi's chest; she had felt the spirit of the deer, lovely and wild, lift out of its body. In the wake of that passage, Naomi felt again the tearing-free of all that had been Macy, experienced again the first moments of the gaping, raw hollowness that was the absence of her daughter's living presence.

Had she screamed? Fainted? She didn't know. When she returned to herself, the dogs had found her. The three of them were curled against the stiffening corpse of the deer in the bloody snow. Hades had been pressed against her back, whining low and constant, and Persephone had been so dangerously cold, she had just stared at Naomi. The three of them had staggered home, and though Naomi had returned for the deer the next day, she knew she would never hunt again. Could never.

Martin didn't know. No one did. In this new world, you didn't speak of your pain, your loss. There was just too much to go around.

The dogs finished eating, and Naomi shooed them into the night to "get busy." Some things were ever the same. From one of his hidey-holes, Ares emerged, sleepy and demanding affection. She leaned down so he could butt his head to hers, then went to check on Macy while the dogs were out.

The small bedroom was cold. Naomi carried the hurricane lamp in and set it on the bedside table, then sat down beside the small lump under the covers, reaching to carefully straighten and smooth what was left of her daughter's bright, strawberry-blonde hair.

"Hi, sweetie. I met a horse today. His name's Big Ben, and he's *huge*. Scared me half to death, but I'll bet you wouldn't have even blinked..."

She talked through the highlights of the day, leaving out the parts that were inappropriate for a ten-year-old, of course. Then she reached for the book she had left on the bedside table. They had finished the Harry Potter series and were half-way through *The Lightning Thief*, the first in the *Percy Jackson and the Olympians* series. Macy had read them all on her own, but it never hurt to hear a story again. Naomi heard the dogs come back in as she read, but they didn't enter the bedroom. None of the animals crossed the threshold into this room anymore.

Animal emotions weren't the same as human ones, but *disapproval* was the closest description for what they radiated when she entered this room. To animals, corpses weren't something to be afraid of. They were natural. Death was natural to them, though she knew animals could grieve. Reading to a corpse, though, or braiding its hair – these things were not natural, and somehow her animals knew it.

Naomi knew it, too. She just didn't care.

She finished the chapter they were reading and leaned to give her daughter's fragile mummy a careful stroke. "Goodnight, my love, my baby. I'll see you in the morning."

As soon as the door shut behind her, the dogs were there, rubbing against her legs and wagging their tails as if they hadn't seen her for days, weeks, years. She laughed, and headed for the couch she had dragged in front of the fireplace. She slept here when it was cold. A fireplace was an inefficient way to heat the whole cabin, and she intended to find a wood-burning stove to install as soon as she could. Before next winter, for certain.

Maybe Piper would be here to help with that task. Naomi shook her head slightly, settling in the middle of the couch so the dogs could cuddle on either side of her. No maybes - Piper would be here. She was alive, Naomi was certain of it. And Naomi would find her.

She closed her eyes and leaned her head back, drowsing as the heat of the fire and the warmth of the dogs relaxed her tired muscles. Ares jumped up on the back of the couch and curled up against the side of her head, purring.

When Piper was here, and safe, they would settle together into this new world, and make the best of it. Just as she experienced Macy's absence, she could feel Piper's life inside her own chest, a flame that had flared and surged continuously as the months passed. Just finding Piper again, just holding her living warmth in her arms, would be enough joy to sustain Naomi for a lifetime.

Things had been difficult between the two of them before the plague, but surely they would put that all behind them once they were together again. They would understand each other better, appreciate each other's differences as they hadn't before. Naomi was so grateful now for her daughter's indomitable spirit, the warrior's heart that must have helped keep her alive.

And surely Piper would have learned and changed as well. Maybe now, she could understand and appreciate the nurturing ways that were at the core of her mother's life. Maybe, Naomi thought, as she drifted into cozy sleep, maybe she had even learned to be nurturing herself…

TWO
Piper: Walden, CO

In the soft grey silence of early dawn, Piper stood by the bed, watching Brody sleep and rubbing the pad of her thumb back and forth across the edge of the knife in her hand.

"So easy," she murmured. Under his chin at an angle, up into his brain. He'd shown her the technique himself. Or rather, she'd learned it while watching him instruct the members of their group who were non-combatants. Amazing, what you could learn when people underestimated you.

She knew it was underestimation, rather than trust, that allowed her to rise from their bed and move around the cabin without waking him these days. Standing over him like this, knowing he was helpless, knowing she could remove him from existence whenever she wanted, had become the greatest pleasure in her life.

Actually killing him, though, would be the height of stupidity. That was another thing he'd taught her: Tactical advantage must be planned for and preserved at any cost. Piper was nothing if not an apt pupil, no matter what she turned her mind to. So Brody took his next breath, and his next, because keeping him alive worked to her advantage.

His eyes opened, staring straight into hers.

Piper tucked the knife behind her palm and forearm and let her "kinda dumb" mask drop into place. "It's too quiet. No birds. Pretty sure there's someone close by."

Brody rolled out of bed without a word, brushing by her as he headed for the clothes he always had laid out, ready to go. While his back was turned, Piper slid the knife back into its sheath on her belt. She watched him dress dispassionately, noting that he still hadn't put back on the weight he'd lost when an intestinal 'flu swept through the camp a month ago. Normally bulky with muscle, he was far leaner now, the weight loss hollowing out his stomach and cheeks. His face was sharp and cold as a blade when he looked up at her.

"Who's on watch?"

"Josh."

Brody made a disgusted sound. "He's still not back to full strength. Probably fell asleep."

"I wanted to leave him out of the rotation for another week. He wouldn't hear of it, though – he insisted he was okay." She layered a little more "dumb" into her voice. "I guess he was tired of missing out on the alcohol rations. He hates going without."

Brody frowned, and she smiled inside. Nothing set Brody off more than actions that endangered the group. Suggesting Josh would resume guard duty when he was unfit, just to score his ration of booze, was pushing it, but she judged the time to be right. She'd been subtly undermining Josh for months.

It was nothing personal. Just part of the plan.

Piper shrugged into her jacket as Brody finished tying his boots. They left the cabin in silence, both armed with military-issue AR15 rifles, and slid quickly into the cover of the trees to pause, listen, *feel* for strangers. Everyone in the group had trained for this before the intrusions even started. Brody predicted they would come, and as always, he had been right. Their cabin was the farthest outlying to the east, so more often than not, it fell to Piper and Brody to deal with the people who had started to stumble into their compound last fall, drawn by the smoke from their fires.

They made a good team. Piper could acknowledge that fact and store it away for possible future use, even though it stirred the secret rage deep in her gut. Brody could pinpoint intruders with supernatural accuracy. He never spoke of experiencing heightened senses as the others did, but Piper was sure he did. Once they were located, her own skills came into play.

The silence in the forest was heavy, thick with watchfulness. Brody took the lead, and the two of them moved through the trees with hardly a rustle, their footsteps further muffled by the snow that had fallen the night before. Piper's ability to move quietly was one of the few things that had earned her Brody's approval. They both heard the intruders long before they spotted them, and Brody altered their path to intercept. When they were close enough to hear the murmur of voices, he looked over his shoulder at Piper, gesturing to a pair of trees on the edge of a clearing. Piper nodded, and they both moved to stand behind a tree.

They moved into Piper's line of sight first, two men and a woman. Piper made eye contact with Brody and communicated what she could see using the hand signals he had taught her for close range engagement: A thumb and two fingers – three people. Two fingers, and a pumping motion – both men were carrying shotguns. Three fingers again, and her hand in the shape of a gun – all three armed with pistols in holsters on their belts.

Brody made an OK sign with his fingers, then lowered his hand towards the ground, telling her to crouch down and stay hidden. Piper did as he instructed, and Brody stepped into the clearing, rifle at the ready on his shoulder.

"That's far enough," he said calmly. "Do not raise your weapons, or I'll shoot all of you."

In spite of the warning, one of the men made an abortive move to bring his shotgun up; his companion slapped it down, and the three of them stood rigidly, staring at Brody, waiting. Not one of them glanced around, nor did they move to guard each other's backs. No training, Piper thought with contempt, and no discipline. Not even any common sense. Sooner or later, they were meat.

Without lowering his weapon, Brody started asking questions, the kinds of questions that would seem normal under the circumstances, but that were designed to give Piper the information she needed.

"Where are you from?"

"Brent and I are from Aurora. I'm James." The man who had pushed down his companion's weapon did the talking. "We picked up Elise —" A nod towards the woman, "- just outside of Golden on our way through."

"What's the situation in the Denver area?"

"Terrible. Rival gangs of looters taking everything, controlling the water supply, killing people that try to stand up to them. Fires burning out of control for days on end. Downtown is totally gone, and whole neighborhoods have burned to the ground. Disease. People starving to death. There are rats everywhere, and packs of feral dogs. We were going to wait 'til spring to get out, but it just got too dangerous. We didn't even dare light a fire to stay warm – couldn't risk drawing people to the light and smoke."

As they talked, Piper let her perceptions open, broaden, expand. Her eyes stayed trained on the trio, but went unfocused as she concentrated on *seeing* what they weren't saying. Faintly at first, then stronger, she began to see what she was looking for: The color-bond- lines of connection between the three, conveying information about the social dynamics at work.

The men were either brothers or very old friends, the lines that pulsed between them strong, established, the blue-green of love and communication. The woman was connected to them both sexually, but not emotionally – red lines, faint and flickering, from her to them, stronger orange lines from the men to her. She was probably bartering herself for safety or...no. To protect her children. At least two, Piper decided, though she was surprised. From what little information they had gathered, the plague appeared to have hit the young hard, and not many kids had made it this long. But sure enough, there they were:

Two distinct, brightly-colored bond-lines emanating from the woman to some spot back behind the trio, predominantly the green and pink of love, with flickers of violet. She loved those kids, and made decisions with their benefit in mind.

Brody shifted into a new line of questioning, this time directing his inquiries at the woman, Elise. "Do you have military or medical training?"

"Me?" The woman glanced at the two men, and Piper saw the exact moment she started to consider a new allegiance. Her eyes flickered over Brody from head to toe, and her body shifted subtly, conveying both question and invitation. "No, but I can cook. And I can...do other things."

"How old are you?"

The woman hesitated. "Thirty."

Piper barely resisted a snort – she was close to forty, easy – and Brody grunted. Piper knew without looking at him that the woman had already been dismissed. He returned his attention to the men.

"What about you two? Military or medical training?"

The men exchanged a glance, and James spoke for them both again. "No. But we're strong and willing to work. We're looking for a place to settle, somewhere safe. We'd do our part."

"How many others are with you?"

Elise spoke before James could. "None," she said quickly. "It's just us."

This time, Piper did snort. Brody's eyes shifted to hers, and he gave her a short nod. She rose, and stepped into the clearing, rifle at her shoulder.

"I understand lying about your kids," she said, speaking directly to Elise. "But why lie about your age? That's just dumb." She shifted her attention to the men, noted the similar bone structure, the same brown eyes. She spoke to Brody without taking her eyes off them. "The men are brothers, with really strong bonds. No other lines of allegiance, either to the woman or to the two kids she's trying to hide. They're somewhere off to the south-east, fairly close by."

The last piece of information was irrelevant to Brody, she knew, but she wanted to see the looks on their faces. Sure enough: shock, incredulity and more than a little fear. She allowed herself a tiny smirk. That was always fun.

The other man spoke for the first time. "How did you —"

Brody didn't let him finish. "You all can go back the way you came. There's a road due south of here that'll take you farther on to the west. There's a small group of survivors in Walden. You may find what you're looking for there."

The men capitulated immediately, both of them stepping back, but the woman wasn't going to give up so easily. She took several steps towards Brody, saw something in his face that made her reconsider, then turned pleading eyes on Piper.

"Please. There's nothing I wouldn't do to protect my kids. Their names are Sam and Becca. They're both eleven, fraternal twins. They can work, too." She raised her wringing hands to her chest. "Please. We've got to get off the road. It's too dangerous."

Eleven. Macy would be eleven this spring, Piper thought, and emotion twisted and fought for freedom in her chest. She battered it down, keeping her face locked and impassive. "Sorry. You don't have any skills we can use, and your kids are too young. Too many mouths to feed."

"Please!" Elise repeated, and this time, she dropped to her knees. She darted a glance over her shoulder at the two men, and whatever was in her face made both of them take another step back. "I can't go on with them. My daughter's only eleven, but she's mature, physically. I heard them, when they thought I was sleeping – they're talking about –" Her face contorted, and a desperate sob heaved out of her. "They're talking about selling her. She's a virgin, and they want to sell her for –" She couldn't finish, her face twitching.

The spit of weapons-fire made Piper flinch violently, and the woman scream and hit the ground. Two sets of three quick bursts, and both men dropped where they'd been standing. One of them never moved again; the other moaned once, convulsed, then was still.

Brody spoke to Piper as he walked over to the corpses and knelt to start stripping them of their gear. "Take her to get her kids, then wait there. Ethan will have heard the shots. When he gets here, I'll send him after you and he can take them on to Walden."

Piper was too surprised to obey right away. Just when she thought she had Brody figured out. Why had he shot the men? Why was he helping this woman and her children get to Walden? He never did anything without a reason. She narrowed her eyes, scrutinizing him, brain clicking through possibilities. There was valuable information here; she just wasn't sure what it was yet.

Brody looked up sharply. "I told you to move."

Piper bent to take the now-sobbing woman's arm and help her to her feet. "Come on. Your kids will be scared. Let's go."

"Oh my God! Oh my God !" Elise was in serious danger of hyperventilating. "He shot them! He shot them, just like that! Why did he do that?"

To Piper's amazement, Brody answered the woman's question. "There are rules. A code." His voice was as clipped and brusque as usual, but underneath, Piper heard rage. She squinted at him, and saw that his hands were actually trembling. He looked up at them both, and his arctic-blue eyes were white-hot. "What happens between grown men and women is not my concern. But any man that would rape a child is lower than an animal and needs to be put down. No exceptions."

"Thank you, thank you so much. I wish there was some way I could repay you."

Brody didn't even acknowledge Elise's sobbing gratitude. Piper took her elbow, and this time, the woman allowed herself to be led away. They worked their way through the still-silent woods, following the trio's obvious backtrail, Elise stumbling over and over as she tried to overcome her shock. Part of Piper's mind stayed focused on the task at hand, monitoring the surrounding forest for signs of trouble or additional intruders, while the other part whirred and processed.

She knew that Brody could kill in cold blood. Her friend Noah's death had branded that knowledge into the deepest part of her being. And she'd seen him kill since then, when he judged intruders too dangerous to be allowed to go on their way. What she hadn't known before today was that Brody could actually feel. Those buffoons hadn't posed any kind of threat. Brody had acted on emotion, and that emotion had been triggered by a threat to a child, specifically the rape of a child.

Piper felt her face stir in an unfamiliar way, and realized she was smiling, actually grinning, as they walked along. Brody had just handed her a weapon of enormous power. Now all she had to do was plan how to use it.

By the time they approached another small clearing, Elise had started to pull herself together. She paused before they stepped into the open, wiped both hands over her cheeks, and took several deep breaths. The remains of a campfire smoldered in a shallow fire-pit, and five backpacks were stacked in a heap nearby, though there were no children to be seen.

Elise called out. "Sam! Becca! It's safe to come out! King Tutankhamun!" She glanced at Piper, and gave her a watery smile. "Our code words for safety. If I were being coerced, I'd use 'pumpernickel.'"

Maybe this woman wasn't quite as dumb as Piper originally thought. A few moments later, two children emerged from the underbrush, both of them looking at Piper curiously. The girl was slightly taller than the boy, with long, coltish legs and a way of moving that hinted at the physical maturity her mother had spoken of. The two shared the same sandy hair and hazel eyes, and they moved like a unit, turning slightly as they walked so that their backs were protected. The bonds between them were brilliant rainbows of color, the strongest Piper had ever seen. Both of them scanned the entire clearing before they walked into their mother's arms, three becoming one as she bent her head and began murmuring to them.

Now these two had instincts, Piper thought. For a moment, she thought about trying to convince Brody to change his mind. There was amazing potential here. These two could be trained in no time –

Trained to do what, Piper?

Her mother's voice sounded in her ear, as clearly as if she was standing beside her, and Piper winced.

There wasn't much left of the moral structure Naomi had worked to instill in her daughter, though Piper could still hear the words. *Do unto others as you would have done unto you. Two wrongs don't make a right. Love thine enemy and drive them nuts!* Piper remembered the twinkle in her mother's eyes as she'd said that last, and the memory left her breathless with longing.

Piper's moral code was much simpler now: Do whatever was necessary to survive. She didn't permit herself to feel remorse or guilt. There were only necessities and decisions, and so far, she hadn't found any means she couldn't justify. Occasionally, though, she stepped too close to a line, and her mother's voice would murmur in her head.

Piper didn't know if it was a form of insanity or if Naomi had actually found a way to monitor her behavior remotely, but when that voice spoke to her, Piper obeyed. She did so, because to disobey meant becoming less-than human, a predator without conscience or soul. Like Brody. If she stepped off that edge and allowed herself to be remade in his image, the rape of her being would be complete.

So recruiting eleven-year-olds as co-conspirators was out. Her mother said so.

Elise and her children separated, and the kids' faces had hardened; whatever their mother had told them, there'd been something of the truth in it. The boy glanced at Piper with gratitude, and she was left to wonder what the two of them had been forced to watch their mother endure. The three of them began to sort through the backpacks and redistribute their supplies.

Piper glanced around the clearing, wondering how long it would take Ethan to arrive. A chance like this was too rare to pass up; never before had she been left alone with someone from the outside. She stepped closer to Elise. "What else can you tell me about what's going on? Is there any news from other parts of the country, or the world? Any official response to the plague from the government?"

"The government. Right." Elise rose to her feet, and shook her head in disgust. "Seemed to me they were the first ones out of Dodge. Rumor was that the state's bigwigs were all holed up down at Cheyenne Mountain in Colorado Springs, but that could just be speculation. People make things up when they don't have information. In the Denver area, things went to hell fast. People were looting and rioting in the streets, and they didn't even try to control it – no police, no national guard, nothing. It was pretty much the same all over the world, or so the media was reporting, until all the stations quit broadcasting. It's like the dark ages out there now. No one knows anything. We're all just trying to survive."

Piper's hopes sank. "So martial law isn't even in effect."

"There's no law at all, not where we've been, anyway. I don't know about other places."

Piper was quiet for a moment, thinking, then asked, "Is that how you came to be traveling with those men?"

Elise looked down and swallowed hard. She angled her body so that her back was to her kids and spoke low. "A woman alone out there is dead, even if you know how to handle a gun. And if you're trying to protect kids, well." She swallowed again. "That's just one more way for them to make you do what they want. Sam and Becca were gathering firewood when those assholes walked into our camp. I agreed to cooperate if they promised to not touch Becca."

Her eyes swung back up to Piper's, brimming now with angry tears. "I can't give my kids back their childhoods, either one of them, but I've got to protect my daughter from that. The world is so screwed up now, and I know I can't keep her safe forever, but her first time shouldn't be rape. I can't stand the thought."

Rage surged out of Piper's gut, and before she knew what she was doing, she had stepped forward and slapped Elise full across the face, snapping her head violently to the side. A heartbeat later, she was looking down the barrels of two pistols, both of them rock-steady. She ignored them, ignored the stone-faced children holding them, and let her gaze drill into Elise's shocked eyes.

"You want to protect your daughter?" she hissed. "Then stop being a victim! Stop crying! Learn to watch your backtrail for fuck's sake! Your kids are more aware of their surroundings than you are!" She shifted her gaze to Becca's hard eyes. "Cut your hair and wear boy's clothes. Learn to move like your brother. Don't talk to other people, especially men, but don't look down. Don't cower. You get me?"

Becca eyed her a moment longer, then nodded. In unison, she and her brother lowered their pistols. Elise was still staring at her in shock, cradling her cheek with her palm, when a low whistle announced Ethan's approach. Piper stepped away from the trio, and turned to watch him step from the trees.

Ethan's sharp eyes locked immediately on the unholstered pistols in the kids' hands, then zeroed in on the bright red handprint on Elise's face. He didn't bring his rifle to the ready, but he stopped walking and looked sharply at Piper. "What's the story here?"

She turned first to the kids. "Put your weapons away." When they had done so, she turned back to Ethan. "Just giving the kids a lesson or two in wilderness survival."

He didn't buy her story for a minute, but he trusted her not to endanger him. Regardless of the alliances, grudges, friendships, likes or dislikes in their group, they all knew their backs were covered. Piper had been the last one allowed inside that network of bonds, but she was in.

Piper turned to Elise. "This is Ethan. He'll take you to Walden and introduce you to the group there."

Elise looked up to meet Ethan's gaze, and Piper heard a soft, hissing, crackle – like a naked electrical wire going live. A line of pure white light arced between Ethan and Elise for the space of three heart-beats, then went out as quickly as it had zapped into existence. Piper's eyes darted between the two of them, but neither one seemed to have noticed anything out of the ordinary. They nodded at each other politely, leaving Piper to wonder if she'd imagined the whole thing. The bond-lines were one thing; that had been something altogether different.

Piper shook her head slightly, and turned to Elise. She found the other woman watching her with the strangest mixture of anger and hero-worship. Elise took a deep, shaky breath, and tried one last time. "If we could just stay with you. We're all hard workers, I promise –"

"No." Piper didn't try to soften the harsh bark of her voice, and Elise and her children all jumped. She glared at Elise – God, could she be this thick? Was she going to make her spell it out? "That situation you're so worried about? It's everywhere. Everywhere. Tell me you understand."

If she had seen pity in the other woman's eyes, she would have slapped her again. Instead, she saw comprehension. And a grim sisterhood. "I understand," she murmured. She bent to shoulder her backpack, her kids following suit, then squeezed Piper's arm on her way past. "Thank you."

Ethan spoke over his shoulder as he led the trio back into the forest, towards the road to Walden. "Brody's waiting for you. Said to tell you to meet him at your cabin."

Piper's stomach clenched. A return to the cabin could mean only one thing. She squared her shoulders, and headed back through the woods, using the rhythm of her steps and her breathing to drop to a place of still silence.

The old Piper could never have endured this life. She would have raged against the injustice, would have shouted about laws, and rights, and the barbarism of "might makes right." The new Piper had learned to lock her throat around words that could not be said, to turn that silence into a fortress. In silence she survived, and she planned.

She was deep in that quiet refuge when she opened the cabin door. Brody waited until she'd removed her rifle, then he was all over her. She obeyed his hoarse instructions, moved when he told her to, how he told her to; long since, she'd learned to cooperate, so he'd hurt her less. This time, though, he was out-of-control with a strange desperation. He didn't climax until he wrung a cry of agony from her. Then he left her immediately to shut himself in the bathroom. Piper stared at the ceiling through tears of pain, listening to the sounds of water splashing behind the closed door, and all the pieces clicked together.

Shooting the men. Trembling hands. The brutal sex. For the second time that day, her face lifted in a smile. He'd been abused as a child. It was obvious. And she'd find a way to use that to her advantage before this war was finished.

She was dressed and seated at the tiny kitchen table when he emerged from the bathroom, watching her birds. She didn't need the escape these days, but their flitting movements still captivated and soothed her. When he had finished dressing once more, she followed him in silence to the mess hall. Her mind touched on Elise and her children as she walked, and she wondered if they'd listen, if they'd learn to be smarter. Safer. Fifty-fifty, she decided. It made her so grateful that Macy had both a mother and a father to protect her; she missed her mother desperately, longed for her, but no way could Naomi alone keep Macy safe. No possible way.

Naomi was the embodiment of kindness, of nurturing motherhood. Before the plague, those qualities had driven Piper nuts; she had seen them as weaknesses, as a lack of intelligence and ambition. How her perspective had changed. Now, she could see the value in Naomi's choices, and the courage it had taken for her mother to choose a path society did not necessarily respect or value. Naomi had chosen to raise her daughters with thoughtfulness, attention, security, and above all, love. And her father had valued the same qualities. They made a beautiful team, Piper thought. Her father provided safety and security for her mother, who provided it for her daughters. World without end.

"Amen," she murmured, earning her a sharp backwards glance from Brody.

"What did you say?"

"I said 'amen.'" The truth, when possible, was always safest. "I just said a little prayer for Elise and her children. I hope they find safety."

Brody stopped walking and turned fully to face her. Under the hard features she had come to know and hate so well, a younger, more vulnerable face flickered. He lifted his hand to trace a bruise on her cheekbone, one he'd put there himself. "Do you think that works? Praying for children in danger?"

Oh, this was treacherous ground. He had never before asked for her opinion or her thoughts. She didn't want him to think of her even having thoughts. She gazed at him, willing her expression to cow-like dumbness, and really did pray this time – that she'd give the right answer. "Well, sure. God protects little children, doesn't He? I'm pretty sure it says so in the Bible."

Brody's disappointment was a beautiful thing. It drove the young face away, and made him press his fingertips, hard, against the bruise he had been caressing so tenderly. "He protects fools, too. How's that working for you, Piper?"

He turned away in disgust, leaving Piper to mentally pat herself on the back. "Just dandy," she answered, though this time she was wise enough to speak the words inside, into the silence, rather than out loud.

They arrived at the mess hall, and as always, their entrance was greeted by a moment of silence. Unlike before, though, it was followed by calls of greeting to both of them. She and Brody both nodded in acknowledgment, then moved through the chow line together and took their usual places to eat, Brody with Levi and Adam, Piper with Ruth and whoever she was sitting with that day. Today, it happened to be Max, which suited Piper just fine. They were old friends, and it was interesting, watching the kaleidoscope of colors play between them.

The bond-lines had started to become visible to Piper late the summer before. If others hadn't already been talking about experiencing changed perceptions, she would have been convinced she was hallucinating. Even then, she had hesitated to share what she could see, not sure which path offered the greatest tactical advantage. Some members of their group weren't experiencing any change at all, and it took some time for a group attitude to emerge and solidify. People who had changed were believed and accepted, and experienced greater respect and social standing. When she was sure that attitude was held by the majority, most particularly their leaders, she revealed what she was learning to see: The bonds between people, and information about the social dynamics that existed between them.

When the whole group was together, it was like a living tapestry, with lines that ebbed and surged in intensity and color, always changing, depending on who a person was interacting with. She had watched the group for hours, observing, learning, and analyzing. Over time, she had begun to associate the colors with certain emotional states and bonds. The green-pink of love between Jenny and her son Caden; the green-pink-orange of love with a sexual element between Jenny and her husband Aaron; and strong lines of survival-security red between every person in this room and Brody. Similar, though lesser, lines connected most of the group to Levi. They saw him as second-in-command, which was the group dynamic that troubled Piper the most. Levi hated her. The fact that the group looked to him for leadership was a constant detriment to her status.

The bond-lines also told her things she didn't have any business knowing. Though the bonds of love were steady between Jenny and Aaron, the blue of communication was an occasional flicker at best. The death of two of their children at the outset of the plague had clearly damaged their ability to talk to each other. And then there was the yellow-orange of sexual desire between Tyler and Adam; either they were doing an award-winning job of hiding their relationship, or neither one had acknowledged their feelings yet. The group as a whole accepted Ruth's homosexuality – except for Josh, who was an asshole no matter what he turned his attention to – but that acceptance could very well be conditional. Ruth was a woman, and older. Her sexuality was basically irrelevant to the much younger men of the group. Piper wasn't sure what would happen to the group dynamic if Tyler and Adam ever decided to act on the attraction between them; so much would be decided by the reactions of Brody and Levi, and she couldn't venture a guess as to what those reactions would be.

"Penny for 'em." Ruth smiled at her as she rose. "You haven't said a word this morning. Watching the color show?"

Piper smiled back. "I was." She stood, then held out her hand for Ruth's breakfast tray; she never missed a chance to make herself useful. "I'll take yours, then join you in the clinic, okay?"

Ruth smiled her gratitude. She, too, had been hit hard by the 'flu. The weight loss had aged her a decade, and her skin still had a grayish-yellow cast that hinted at liver stress. "I appreciate you saving me the steps. See you in a bit."

Piper walked towards the kitchen, carrying both their trays. Out of the corner of her eye, she saw Brody talking to Josh, who had just come in from his watch shift. She slowed her steps, watching their gestures, noting how they supported what the bond-lines were telling her: No lines from Brody to Josh, and what looked like a vibrating spider-web of desperate red emanating from Josh towards his leader. She couldn't hear Brody's voice at all, but Josh got louder and louder, until he was nearly shouting.

"I tell you, I wasn't drinking! I don't know how they got by me, but I wasn't sleeping either!"

Another low comment from Brody, and Josh's face flushed as red as the lines he was clinging to Brody with. "You got no right to take away my privileges for one mistake! Other people have gotten through. It ain't right, and I –"

Brody's command was brief and harsh, and Josh shut up, some of the florid color leaching out of his face. He listened as Brody spoke, face locked in stillness, then nodded. He turned away to leave and saw Piper watching. For a few seconds, Piper considered bringing this part of her plan to its conclusion right here and now.

Josh had been lusting after her since the day she set foot in this camp, and her position as Brody's woman had just egged that lust on. He saw Brody as a father figure, and it had been pathetically easy to feed his little Oedipus complex thing for her. Combine that with the subtle suggestions she'd been feeding the group about

Josh's incompetence, and she had created a lovely powder keg. Piper dropped her eyes in coy submission – Josh's favorite female expression – while she weighed the pros and cons. He was so primed, a single word could set him off. Another chance like this might not come along.

No. The timing just wasn't right. Piper turned away, continuing on to the kitchen without making eye contact with Josh again. He would try to convince himself she hadn't seen his humiliation, but a part of him would wonder. It was perfect, really. When she finally pulled his trigger, he'd blow so high, there would be no turning back. Besides, she needed more time. There were a few other people she wanted caught up in that explosion.

It was hard to keep a satisfied smile off her lips as she sorted her dishes into bins to be washed. All in all, it had been a very productive morning. News from the outside. Discovering a major chink in Brody's armor. And the situation with Josh, which couldn't be stacking up to play out better if she'd planned it. She hadn't, not this time – not like the intestinal "'flu" she had created via spicy chili and Sulfur Tuft mushrooms.

Ethan had pointed out the poisonous mushrooms last fall, when she had gone with him on a perimeter patrol. It hadn't been easy, slipping away to collect them, finding a secure place to dry and powder them, then experimenting on herself to get the dosage right. But the results had been worth the effort.

The crisis had given Piper a chance to vastly increase her social standing in the group. A few days before the others, she'd faked a milder version of the illness on herself and two other members of the group –

Tyler and Caden. In Tyler's case, the move had been strategic. It would look strange if every member of the group came down with an illness simultaneously. She knew Tyler didn't have any medical training, nor any patience with illness, and would likely be worthless when the rest of them were sick. She wanted the group dependent on her, beholden to her.

As for Caden, well, there was enough humanity left in her to not risk the boy's well-being. He was small for his age, his parents' only surviving child, and she wanted to spare him the wringer she put the others through.

For four days, she had kept them all as miserable as she could make them. She dosed them with tea and chicken broth laced with more of the mushroom powder, then worked tirelessly wiping their faces, cleaning up their vomit, and emptying their bedpans when most of them got too weak to stand. Tyler helped her convert the mess hall into a sick bay – there were too many ill to use Ruth's quarantine cabin – then cleared out and kept his distance. He claimed just the sound of vomiting would make him follow suit, and volunteered to keep tabs on Caden instead. Having his sharp eyes out of the mess hall suited Piper just fine.

The line she walked was a precarious one, and she drew heavily on the medical training Ruth had been giving her to judge when to back off. Both Jenny and Max got so dangerously dehydrated, she had to start saline IV's for them. And on the fourth day, Levi suffered a seizure.

She'd been on the far end of the mess hall when it started, and by the time she got to him, he had already vomited, then aspirated some of it into his lungs. It took all of her strength to get him onto his side and hold him there while his big body shook with violent convulsions. And it had taken an even greater effort to keep her face set in lines of concern, when all she wanted to do was laugh.

Served him right, sanctimonious bastard. He had never forgiven her for his brother's death, had continued to turn a blind eye to Brody's treatment of her. All of them had turned away. Not one of them cared enough to really look, to *see* what was happening to her. Only Ruth had tried to help, but even she deserved this suffering. She should have used her good standing with the others to make them see what Brody was. As Levi's seizure gradually subsided into slower and slower convulsions, she pondered how much mushroom powder it might take to push Brody into a seizure, or Josh, for being a Bible-thumping hypocrite whose eyes ran over her like hands, or Aaron, whose unrelenting, dazed grief for his lost children irritated her no end...

How could you, Piper? Naomi's voice. *I know you've been hurt, but it's wrong. None of this is going to make things right, or make you feel better in the long run.*

Piper had looked down at Levi's slack face, at his blue-tinted lips, slick with blood where he'd bitten the inside of his cheek, and had respectfully disagreed with her mother. But Naomi had spoken, and Piper had set about bringing her little drama to a close.

Now, four weeks later, they were all on the mend. Levi did not seem to have suffered any long-term damage from his seizure, though he had a lingering cough and his skin, like Ruth's, was sometimes tinged with the yellow of liver stress. The rest of them were in varying stages of recovery, and Piper was their hero. She could see it, in the new, vibrant green lines of trust and esteem connecting her to the people she'd poisoned, then nursed back to health. The bond-lines were the key to implementing her plans. They told her where she stood with the rest of the group, and showed her what still needed to be done.

Piper had a single, crystalline goal: Join her family at their cabin on Carrol Lakes. Before the intruders had started bringing them news of the outside world, she had intended to cut Brody's throat and take off in one of the compound's vehicles. With that in mind, she had started to squirrel away supplies, targeting early summer to execute her plan, when chances were better the weather wouldn't complicate the 200-mile journey through the heart of the Rocky Mountains.

Then, information started coming in via the refugees who stumbled into the compound. Thanks to them, Piper now knew it wouldn't be practical to steal a vehicle; even if the roads were open, and many of them weren't, the sound of a motor would draw people from miles around. In times like these, people were trouble. Therefore, she'd be walking the distance, but she wouldn't be doing it alone.

The bond-lines had helped her decide who her companions would be, and who would get left behind. With a carefully chosen escort in mind, Piper had been manipulating the group every which way she could manage. She undermined bonds here, strengthened them there, tugged, hinted, twisted words and lied. When the time came, if she had prepared properly, the people she didn't want would be severed from the group.

And only one of them would have to die.

THREE
Jack: Woodland Park, CO

Jack slowed as he approached the classroom where Layla was teaching. Was he early? He hadn't checked the time before heading downstairs, had left his office without really thinking about it. Even though it had been nearly a year since there had been phone service of any kind, he reached into his pocket for his cell, with half-formed thoughts of sending a text. The simple gesture stopped him in his tracks. He squeezed his eyes shut, feeling too many emotions to process; so, as he did so often these days, Jack shoved what he didn't want to deal with down deep, stuffed it, sealed it off. The resulting numbness kept him operational. His steps resumed.

He was early – Layla was still teaching. Jack stopped just outside the open classroom door, listening as she instructed the older kids to trade the essays they had been working on and to begin peer edits, then pulled the younger kids together for a science project involving plant growth. Practical, that, as these children would likely spend their lives growing most of their own food. Still out of sight, Jack sank to the floor and made himself comfortable, leaning against the wall and closing his eyes, listening to the comforting, familiar sounds of kids in a classroom, kids learning, kids being kids.

He dozed a little as he waited, letting his mind rest in the luxury of blankness he was so seldom able to achieve these days. In the time before, it was his habit to wake long before his alarm, to blink awake slowly, to allow thought and inspiration to rise from the uncluttered nothingness. He would pray during those early morning hours as well, ask God to direct his thoughts and actions for the day, ask to be made an instrument of His peace. In prayer, he would examine his life, analyze his progress as a human, and humbly thank God for making him worthy of the respect and leadership he had been gifted with. Pretty easy, in those days, to like himself.

Now, he didn't even know who he was. Self-examination was a black pit he avoided at all costs. And he hadn't found the time to pray in a long, long time. So much for resting his mind. Jack sighed, opened his eyes, and didn't manage to completely stifle a startled yelp.

Verity was sitting cross-legged in front of him, her knees almost touching his, grinning with delight at his discomfort. He resisted asking how she'd snuck up on him so silently; Verity was not capable of answering even a mundane question seriously. He made a move to rise, but she held her hands out, forestalling him.

"Wait!" Her delicate hands bloomed like a flower between them, an appealing gesture. "We so seldom get a chance to talk, just the two of us. One could almost think," she sparkled an innocent smile at him, "That you actively avoid me."

Jack contemplated and discarded several replies, and finally settled on a non-committal grunt. Generally, the less he said around Verity, the better. He never knew what was going to come out of her mouth, but he could usually count on it making him feel either stupid, ridiculous or uncomfortable. Often, all three.

And yet, he couldn't deny her gift or refute her claim that she could communicate with the dead. Verity knew things she shouldn't. Couldn't. She had been able to offer closure and comfort to some of the members of their small community. She'd also cheerfully traumatized some of them, a fact she seemed wholly oblivious to. Layla was good at buffering her; otherwise, Jack suspected she would have been run out of town long before now. At times, he was tempted to lead that charge.

Verity leaned forward, her face dangerously earnest. "I have a question, and some information for you. Which do you want first?"

Jack's heart sped up just a touch. Nothing good could come of this. "Verity, if you don't mind, I'd rather not...uh...participate."

"Ha!" Verity poked him in the center of his chest with her finger. "I told Zadkiel you'd say that! He said no, that people can't resist either questions or information, but I was sure. He just about never leaves you these days, by the way – says you need all the mercy and compassion towards yourself he can muster. Anyhow, guess he'll have to pay up! Ha!"

Only Verity would make a bet with an Archangel. What in the world had the stakes been? And what did it mean that Jack wasn't in the least surprised?

She persevered. "So. Information or question?"

Good Lord. Jack glanced at Layla's classroom, wishing they'd finish and provide him with his escape. "Question, I guess."

"Okay." Verity cocked her head to the side. "You never ask for information about your loved ones. Your parents, siblings, friends. Everyone else, even Layla, has asked. Why not you?"

Jack narrowed his eyes at her. Was this a trap? Did she already know the answer? Her expression was all open, golden, cherubic innocence, but he knew better than to buy that for an instant. Finally, he cleared his throat. "My folks were elderly, and my dad was in poor health. I don't think…"

He paused, and decided he didn't have anything to lose. "I can't feel them. Here." He touched the center of his chest. "They're gone. I'm sure of it."

Verity beamed her approval. "You're right – they are! And you actually said it! I'm so proud of you!" Her face darkened briefly. "Guess that makes Zadkiel and I even – he said you'd say that, too, but I figured you'd prevaricate, like usual."

Jack decided to give it a try, as long as he was already embroiled: "You know, Verity, generally when someone shares with you their certainty that their parents are dead, it's appropriate to express sorrow, or sympathy. Maybe you could try for just a moment of respectful silence?"

She blinked at him. "Huh. I hadn't considered that." Then, she wiggled side-to-side, scooting closer, a look of intense curiosity on her mobile face. "Your parents are with the One, part of the Divine. That fits with Christian beliefs. Why, then, does it make people so sad?"

Could she really not understand this? What in the world had this woman's life been? "Because even though we believe they live on eternally in Christ, and we'll be reunited with them one day, we're sad that our time with them here on Earth is over. We miss them, their personalities, maybe their advice, their company. Their love." Jack paused, letting that sink in, then asked his own question. "Haven't you ever lost someone you loved, Verity?"

She recoiled. For the first time, ever, Jack saw something on her face that wasn't impish or mischievous, and the light around her, the light he could never explain or dismiss, guttered and dimmed. Her hands fluttered to her heart, rubbed, then crossed to squeeze her own shoulders. She closed her eyes, and even though she wasn't touching him, Jack saw the angels. Layer after layer of ethereal wings wrapped around her, cradling her in glowing tenderness, until she heaved a deep hitching breath and opened eyes that once more shone with glory and humor. She shook her finger at him.

"Snuck past my guard. Shame on you. I don't visit the Ghostlands, Jack. The only person who used to be there for me moved on, long ago." Again, the inquisitive cock of her head. "What about your sister? Aren't you curious about her?"

It was Jack's turn to recoil. Damn it, he should have seen that coming. He concentrated for a moment, stuffed all the feelings her question had roused down with the others and sealed them off. Then, he returned her gesture, shaking a finger at her. He was proud, so very proud, of the light tone he achieved. "One question, you said. You asked it."

"Well, well, well. So you've learned to shield yourself from your own feelings, as well as the feelings of others." Verity shook her head at him. "Jack. You know better. How long do you think you can keep that stuffing business up without exploding?"

He smiled tightly. Of course she knew. Layla probably did, too, but he doubted she would ever bring it up. "As long as I have to, I guess."

"Why?" She looked genuinely concerned.

"To function. To survive." His own words surprised him. He shifted, and rose stiffly to his feet. This had gone on long enough. "As always, Verity, it has been an experience talking to you –"

"The answer to your question is, 'Yes.'"

He stared at her. "Excuse me?"

"The information I promised you. Raziel asked me to tell you."

No, oh no, it couldn't be. "Which question?" he rasped, though he knew. Of course he knew. There was only one question that burned in his heart and mind these days, one question he couldn't bear to know the answer to, and couldn't go on without answering: Whether or not the Rapture had occurred. Whether or not he had been passed over as unworthy.

Verity tilted her head as if listening for a moment, then answered. "You wonder if you were left behind for a reason. Raziel says yes, you were."

Jack's knees went watery. He braced a palm against the wall as the hallway started to do a slow revolve around him. Dimly, he heard Verity speaking.

"Oh, all right! Sometimes, you Archangels can be so exacting." She rose, and her hand landed on his shoulder, as light as a wild bird. "He says to take a deep breath, that it's not what you think." She huffed. "All right! It's not what *I* made it sound like. You were not denied the Rapture – that's not what this is about."

Slowly, the hall stopped spinning. Jack drew in a deep breath, then another. When his head felt like it was attached to his shoulders again, he glared sideways at Verity. "You are a menace."

In answer, she started singing in a high, crystalline soprano. "Jesus loves you, this I know, for the Bible tells you so –" She paused, listened, then sighed. "Raziel has informed me that your assessment is correct. He is *so* serious," she whispered confidentially, then continued on in a normal tone. "You survived, Jack, because you're being issued an invitation. The Divine has a Gift for you, and it would be best for all involved if you accepted it in this incarnation."

Jack shook his head. "You do know that no one but Layla understands you when you talk like this, right?"

"Fine. *Fine.*" She rolled her eyes. "Raziel agrees with you. *Again.*" Her voice dropped to a petulant mutter. "I am *not* being a smart-ass! Well, of course I can tell it to him straight, but what fun is that?"

"Verity." Jack had endured all he was going to. "Just tell me: Did the Rapture occur or not? That's all I need to know."

"Ugh, you Christians. So yes-no, black-white, good-bad. It's not that straightforward. Your question is based on your belief that the book of Revelation is a literal description of Earth's end times – a book of slippery language and vague suggestions if there ever was one – and that we're in those end times." Verity reached out and touched Jack's forearm, and the expression on her face was one Jack seldom saw: Earnest concern. "I know about the charts, the lists, the hours and hours you've spent studying, trying to fit everything into prophecy. Raziel told me. I know how hard you've been looking for answers."

Jack's head fell forward. He felt like a baited bear nearing the end of his strength. "People ask me, all the time: Why? Why did this happen? Why am I still here, when my loved ones are gone? Like I have some kind of insight they don't. Like I should know. And I should have something to tell them, some comfort to offer, some kind of guidance. But I..." He shook his head, lifted his helpless hands, and let them fall. "I don't. I have nothing to give them. No answers."

"Huh." Verity tapped her chin with her forefinger. "So, when you told everyone that the ways of the Lord were mysterious, and none of you could hope to comprehend the scope of His plan, and you all needed to keep faith and trust, and continue on – that was all just a lot of blah blah?"

Jack squeezed his eyes shut. "No. Of course not. But..." Oh, she was going to bust him on this, he was sure of it. The trap yawned before him, just waiting for her to snap it shut. After several moments of loaded silence, he cracked an eye open and gazed at her.

She gazed back. "Bust yourself," she said softly. "You don't need me to."

She turned and seemed to float down the hallway instead of walking. Jack watched her go, biting back all the questions she had left in her wake, but she heard them anyway. She pirouetted, dancing backwards as she answered.

"That would be neither a 'Yes' nor a 'No' on the Rapture thing. And if you don't accept the Gift the Divine has for you in this lifetime, it will be offered again in the next." She held up a cautionary finger. "You'll want to avoid that, if you can – lessons that get repeated tend to be more, hmm, strenuous, let's say." She shuddered. "Hubris. Oh, that one was awful..."

She disappeared around the corner, thank God and all the angels of heaven. Jack sucked in a huge breath of air, blew it out, and stepped into the doorway of the classroom. Early or not, he was desperate for the distraction. A few kids looked up at his entry and smiled; he returned their smiles, but gestured for them to re-focus on their tasks. Time spent in this classroom was essential, and he supported it however he could. The kids were thriving on the return to routine and expectations, and it gave their whole community a hopeful lift to rally around the fifteen children that had survived.

Layla was bent over the desk of her youngest student, little Rose, a five-year-old who currently refused to answer to anything but "Rainbow Dash," a character of My Little Pony fame. It was a coping mechanism – all the kids had them to some degree – and he and Layla had talked about it at length, deciding how to handle the little girl's need for fantasy, coming up with a strategy and a plan. They spent hours discussing the kids in the evening now, a huge improvement over the strained silence that had characterized their relationship before Layla started teaching again.

Layla looked up, her eyes met Jack's, and Verity's words seemed to echo in his head: A Gift from the Divine. He felt a flush start at his hairline and sweep down across his face, his neck, his chest. Layla frowned and stood, weaving towards him through the desks.

"Are you okay? You look feverish."

She hadn't regained the weight she had lost from the time before, but thin as she was, she still managed to radiate a lush voluptuousness that could go to his head like wine, if his guard was down. Apparently it was, because he was experiencing a distinct dizziness.

"I'm fine," he muttered, "Just stood up too fast. I was sitting in the hallway. Don't let me interrupt – I'll just sit back here and wait."

He took a seat in one of the back desks while she helped the kids wrap up the projects they were working on. He had been dropping in at the end of the school day for the last couple of weeks to take the kids to the gym for exercise and play. What had started as an invitation to the teens to shoot a few hoops had turned into a daily phys-ed session with all the kids. Jack had resisted at first – he had twenty five things to do with every minute these days – but it didn't take long for him to make it priority one. Of all the things he missed most from the time before, it was time spent with kids. For the first time since he'd opened his eyes under Layla's riotously-colored bed canopy, one of the rare survivors of the plague, there was something in his life that made him remember who he was.

"Okay, kids, let's end with 'Take it or Leave it,' then ya'll can go school Pastor Jack on the basketball court." The older kids shot him grins, and the little ones giggled. They loved it when Layla teased Jack, and didn't seem to notice that he never responded in kind.

Layla moved to the far side of the room, where the kids were keeping running lists on a pair of white boards, one labeled "Take it Forward," the other titled, "Leave it Behind." She picked up a dry erase marker and surveyed the room. "Let's start with 'Leave it.' Who has a suggestion?"

"Valentine's Day!" Karleigh, their oldest student at sixteen, had clung to the Goth look she'd favored in the time before, though black hair dye was harder to come by now. As a result, her natural red formed five inch roots before joining the faded black that hung to her shoulders. "It's lame and fakey. I say we get rid of it."

Jack bit the inside of his cheek against a smile, his eyes flickering to the pink, lacey hearts that still hung in scallops across the top of the white board. They had just celebrated the holiday in question; he wondered how Karleigh would feel when he suggested they abolish Halloween.

"The candy sucks, too." Viola was two years younger than Karleigh, and followed her lead in all things. She blushed when Layla raised a single eyebrow and re-phrased her comment. "I mean, the candy is less than delicious. Or it was, like, when there was candy.

Remember those gross sugar hearts with the weird sayings?"

"Thank you, girls. Any other input?" Layla looked around the room. "Anyone want to speak in support of keeping Valentine's Day?"

Charlotte's hand went up. At nine, she was their tomboy in a tutu, into sports and anything sparkly, and blissfully unconcerned with the opinions of the older girls. "I like the colors. The red and the pink. And the hearts." Her freckled nose wrinkled. "The 'love' stuff was lame, though. Like Karleigh said. 'Fakey.'"

"Shall we put it to a vote? All in favor of keeping Valentine's Day, raise your hands." Layla waited patiently while Charlotte's hand went up, then down, then up again to stay. She smiled, and raised her own hand. "Two votes in favor of keeping Valentine's Day. Those in favor of letting it stay in the past?"

The rest of the kids raised their hands, making the vote 14-2, and in this small corner of the surviving world, Valentine's Day went the way of the Dodo.

Jack went ahead and let his grin break free. He thought this activity was brilliant. Every day, Layla and the kids talked about what they missed, what they would like to bring back, and what they thought should forever be left in the past. Jack loved everything about the concept – it helped the kids understand their power to shape the future, using their knowledge of the past. The things they came up with never failed to astonish him. They had voted to include the internet, Disney movies and state parks in their futures; artificial sweeteners, reality TV and nuclear war would be left behind. Social media remained in hotly-debated no-man's land.

Layla called for another "Leave It," and Viola's hand went up again. She had just begun to discover social activism when the plague hit, and she had been working her way down a list for this activity. Jack was sure of it. "Puppy mills. Those should never come back!"

Agreement was swift and unanimous. Layla called for one more, and Jack couldn't resist chiming in. "Infomercials."

Layla laughed, and the older kids grinned. She wrote "Infomercials" on the "Leave It" list. "No more hyper salesmen pitching steak knives and fitness programs! Do we need to vote? No? All right, then – anyone else?"

James, one of the teens, leaned to whisper in his buddy's ear, and both of them started snickering. Layla zeroed in. "James? Have something to share?"

James forced his face to seriousness. "No Miss Layla. I was just joking around. I apologize."

Before Layla could go on, little Rose's voice piped into the quiet room. "What's 'Viagra?'"

James dropped his now-flaming-red face into his hands, the older kids collapsed into choked giggles, and the younger ones shot disapproving stares at Rose. She gazed around the room with wide, curious eyes for a moment; then those eyes filled with tears as she recognized her transgression.

Without a single exception, all of the children were demonstrating intuitive abilities. In many cases, their gifts were far stronger than what the adults were experiencing, which made guiding them even more difficult. Jack, Layla and Rowan had spent hours discussing the situation, trying to come up with a plan for going forward with the new social reality. How did you interact with someone when you *knew*, with absolute certainty, they were lying about something? What should you act on – what was said, or what was *sensed*? What to do, when you *knew* what someone wanted to say but was choosing not to?

The older kids were still awed enough to err on the side of caution, though Jack was sure – and Layla concurred – that it wouldn't be long before some of them tried their hands at manipulation. The little ones, though, had already forgotten that the world hadn't always been this way; one thing that certainly hadn't changed was the honesty of youth. Rose, being the youngest and also exceptionally gifted, suffered terribly when she accidentally crossed the line.

Layla and Jack's eyes met. She glanced at Rose, lifted her chin subtly at the door, then raised her eyebrows. Jack nodded; he didn't need to be a mind-reader to know what she wanted. While Layla called the room to order and asked for a "Take It," he rose from his desk and went to crouch beside Rose. She was now staring at the top of her desk, eyes brilliant with tears she refused to shed, lower lip plumped out and quivering. Her misery was so powerful, it overwhelmed his shields. It was all he could do not to pucker up himself. Instead, he leaned to speak just to her.

"Hey, Rainbow Dash. How about helping me get the gym ready for the rest of the kids? I didn't do it before I came down."

She shot him a suspicious look – the same sensitivity that had allowed her to pick up on James' unspoken joke was now directed at him, and she was detecting, at least faintly, his sorrow for her struggle. To a child, these kids despised pity. Jack reinforced his shields and resisted her probing. She frowned, and redoubled her efforts. To Jack, it felt like a battering ram. He gave her a look of mild reproof, and reached out to tap the end of her little nose.

"Remember what we talked about? We don't push past someone else's defenses. Can you feel where my wall is?"

Rose concentrated for a moment, then nodded, and Jack *felt* her back off. She gazed at him, chagrined, and fresh tears broke through and spilled over. "I'm sorry."

He stood and held out his hand to her, calling on his own intuition to infuse his voice with just the right amounts of *levity* and *love*. "It's okay. Let's go, and you can tell me how things are going in the land of Equestria these days."

Rose gave a gigantic sniff, then stood, tucking her soft little hand into his. He nodded at Layla as they headed for the door. She nodded back, and he *felt* her "thank you" as a brief warmth in the center of his chest.

They walked down the hall towards the gym in companionable silence; another difference these days. Folks were either more or less comfortable with silence, depending on the circumstances. Often, words weren't necessary. Other times, words were withheld, so they wouldn't give lie to the *feelings* that couldn't be concealed. Jack wished, sometimes, that he could be on the outside looking in. From a sociological perspective, what was happening to them was fascinating. It would be interesting to study, to theorize, to distance himself and just observe the shifting mores and changing social rituals. Instead, he was right in the thick of it. He looked down at Rose's small, thoughtful face and smiled. Sometimes, that wasn't as hard as others.

Rose slid a glance up at him. "So what *is* 'Viagra?'"

Jack did not smile, though he knew she could feel his amusement. "It's a medicine men take. Used to take," he amended. Rowan was still dealing daily with people suffering from drug-withdrawals, and lack of Viagra was the very least of their problems. "It helped their bodies function under certain circumstances."

Rose took another few silent steps, then again with the sideways glance. "But why was that funny?" Then, in a tiny, shaky voice, "Why did they laugh?"

And why was it so easy to meet her eyes, squeeze her warm little hand, and answer this embarrassing question? Jack wished he could spend all his time with the kids. Things got so clear when he was with them. "Because it had to do with man-woman, lovey-dovey stuff. James is interested in that right now, so he makes jokes about it." Rose made a disgusted face, and Jack did smile this time. "When you're older, and you're interested in that stuff, it'll make more sense."

"Boys are gross," Rose muttered, just as a five-year-old girl should, changed world or not. They arrived at the gym, and Jack set the little girl to work, spacing jump ropes and scooter boards around the room. They'd start with some good old-fashioned relay races, then break into free play and three-on-three basketball. Layla and the other kids arrived before they finished setting up, and Layla set them to helping.

Jack paused, watching them for a moment. So few children to carry on – only thirteen from their community, plus Dylan and Evie, the children Naomi had found almost a year ago in Cascade. Their futures were so uncertain, but chances were good they would spend their lives here in what was left of this town, doing their part to rebuild this corner of a shattered world. There had been no word from the outside since Naomi's arrival, but Jack suspected circumstances in Woodland Park were about as good as it got. He didn't speak of it, but he dreamed: Awful, portentous nightmares he *knew* were warnings of terrible possibilities forming and moving in the world beyond the blocked pass.

"Hey, Pastor Jack!" James again, hollering across the echoing gym.

Jack hadn't preached a sermon in over a year, but old habits and all. He hollered back. "Hey what, James?"

"Are we still the state of Colorado?"

Jack blinked and looked at Layla. She shrugged. He turned back to James. "Do you want to be?"

James considered, then nodded. "Yeah. Colorado was a pretty cool place to live." Before either Jack or Layla could say anything, he looked around, hollering again. "Any opposed?"

Rose's hand shot up. "I say we become 'Equestria!'"

Soft groans sounded around the room, but again, the kids acted without adult intervention. Ten-year-old Ella dropped a hand on Rose's head and gave it a soft rub.

Like both Jack and Layla, she could read the emotions of others, and her response was invariably tender and true. "How about if we stay Colorado for people on the outside, but we know that we're really 'Equestria.' Just us here, in this room. Like a special secret."

Rose's small face lit with delight, and Jack felt his chest clutch with love and terror. These kids. They had become his heart. He couldn't bear the thought of anything happening to any of them. He glanced at Layla and saw her blinking hard at the ceiling, not quite able to conceal the tears that brightened her beautiful dark eyes.

Jack clapped his hands together. "Okay, everybody!" He had to clear the roughness from his voice before he could continue. "Here's how we're going to do this..."

They raced and played, argued and made-up, competed, pouted and gloated for the better part of an hour. Layla had gone back to the classroom to prepare for the next day's lessons, and Jack kept the kids moving until Martin showed up in the door to the gym. Most of the kids walked to nearby homes in groups, but a couple of them lived farther out, and Martin ran them home on the snowmobile when the weather called for it. After snow the night before, the day had been bright with sun but clouds were building again in the west; it looked like they were in for another wave. Jack shooed the kids on their way back to the classroom for coats and boots, then trailed them with Martin. He glanced at the older man as they walked. As usual, Martin's feelings were locked down tight, unreadable.

"How's Naomi doing with the horses?"

"Fair." Martin shrugged. "Maybe a little better than that. She's got a touch, when she forgets she's afraid." He walked a few steps in silence, then spoke again, low, so the children wouldn't hear. "I wish you would talk her out of going."

Jack huffed a humorless laugh. "What makes you think I can talk her into or out of anything?"

Martin glanced sideways at him, eyes sharp, and the memory of their old disagreement simmered between them. Martin didn't trust Jack, or his ability to persuade people to do what he wanted. He'd been on the receiving end of Jack's "gift," and he would never forget it.

"Layla, then. Somebody has to talk sense into her. She has no business out there."

Jack frowned. "Why do you think that? She came to us from out there, and it wasn't an easy journey. I think she's tougher than you're giving her credit for."

It was Martin's turn for a humorless laugh. "Tough. Naomi. Right." Martin stopped walking and turned to face Jack. "She's fragile as glass. The only thing keeping her going is Piper. If we don't find her, or worse, find out she's dead, Naomi will shatter. All that's left of her is mother-instinct."

Martin's honesty had opened the door a crack, and Jack *sensed* the other man's feelings: frustration, towering admiration, and fear. Lots and lots of fear. He frowned, trying to sort out the why of it...then it all clicked. He looked down, hiding his realization, respecting Martin's right to figure this one out on his own. "If you don't take her, she'll go without you. If I knew of anything that could stop her, I'd do it or say it, believe me. I don't want either of you to go, but it's something you both have to do." He made eye contact now. "Even if you get her to stay here, there's no guarantee she'll be safe."

Martin frowned. "I know that. There is no 'safe.' Not anymore." His eyes focused on a distance Jack couldn't see, far-away and troubled. "I was in combat in the middle east before the plague. I saw what happens when a society breaks down, what people are capable of doing to each other in the name of survival. She shouldn't see that."

"She already has."

Martin shot him a look filled with disdain. "She hasn't seen anything. Some hungry kids. Amateurs with baseball bats and guns they probably didn't know how to use."

Jack found he couldn't rebut the other man's statement. The dreams. There was so much worse out there. He *knew* it. He started walking again, and Martin fell in beside him. Neither man spoke until they reached the classroom, where the kids were bustling around, preparing to leave. They waited in the hallway, avoiding the chaos.

"I'll ask Layla to speak to her," Jack said quietly. "I think if Piper's alive, she'll make her way here. It doesn't make sense for Naomi to go out looking for her, but I doubt she'll change her mind. You're right about one thing, she's not exactly mentally healthy. She's broken, and hardly cobbled back together."

Martin's glance this time was filled with a pain so deep, Jack felt it in his own bones. "Who isn't?"

The kids flooded by them in an exuberant rush, and for a moment, Jack closed his eyes, letting their joy fill him and drive out the shadows. Martin lifted a hand in farewell as he left with Ella and her little brother Alexander, and gradually, the room emptied. Jack waved the last group of kids off before he stepped inside, mind buzzing with all the things he wanted to go over with Layla – not the least of which was Martin's request – then stopped short. Layla wasn't alone.

Owen Weber had worked in the logging industry in the time before. He was a quiet giant of a man, and if he was experiencing any heightened intuition, he didn't talk about it. He had lost his wife and three children in the plague, and was one of the most tireless workers their community had. Without fuss or fanfare, he was always there, always helping, and he took on some of the hardest jobs – specifically, collection and burial of the dead – without complaint. Right now, he was sitting on the corner of Layla's desk, leaning towards her, radiating an emotion Jack couldn't mistake.

And Layla was radiating it right back. Her midnight eyes were sparkling, mouth curved and lush as she smiled at something Owen had said. The warmth of what she was feeling for the other man spilled over and stirred heat into Jack's blood. He coughed, and they both looked up.

Owen nodded in greeting, but Layla dropped her eyes, locking down behind her wall of ice. A little too late for that, Jack thought grimly, but he locked down behind his own wall and put on the mask of a smile. "Hey there,

Owen, good to see you." Then, to Layla. "Shall I plan on the same time tomorrow?"

She nodded. "That would be great. Is there anything I need to know about your talk with Rose?"

Jack shrugged. "Not really." Look at them chatting away, as if they were casual. As if they were just friends, with nothing else stirring under the surface. He resisted the urge to glance at Owen, to see if the other man sensed the undercurrents. "She's just going to have to keep figuring it out, like we all are." He stood. "Do you need a ride home, or..." He let his voice trail off.

Layla cleared her throat and looked down again. "No, I've got some things to finish up here, then Owen said he'll run me there. I won't be long."

"All right. I'll see you later, then." He nodded at Owen. "Have a good night."

Jack walked out, still maintaining rigid control over his emotions and thoughts. Not until he was well away from the classroom did he let his mind freely respond, and the first thing that occurred to him was to wonder why this hadn't happened sooner.

All over their community, the survivors were pairing up. Alder, Rowan's brother, was now living with a woman, Sophie, and her surviving daughter just across the street from Layla's cottage. They were expecting a baby of their own, soon now. Rowan claimed she was too busy for romance, but Jack didn't miss the interested eyes that followed her at community functions. Even Verity had her admirers, though Jack honestly couldn't see the appeal, in spite of her physical beauty. How could you ever relax around her? If you kissed her, would the Archangels intervene? The corners of his mouth twitched at the thought, though humor was the last thing he was feeling.

It was natural, to seek a mate. People needed to love and be loved, needed connection, needed hope for the future. Layla was a leader in their community, known and loved by all, and he knew most people assumed they would eventually become a couple. They'd been the subject of some not-so-subtle matchmaking, which they had both ignored or politely deflected. Since that day so long ago when she'd revealed her feelings for him, Jack hadn't caught so much as a flicker of emotion from her.

Had her feelings died? Had she begun working to change them that very day, when his response to her had been so complicated? She must have been disappointed, must have hoped for something different. He had avoided sorting through the morass of his feelings for her, just as assiduously as he avoided self-examination. Day-to-day, he kept it simple and surface. He admired her as a teacher and community leader. He appreciated her intelligence and her contribution to the greater good. He despised her spiritual beliefs and ignored her ridiculous references to "casting" and spells – what she called "prayers made physical." Not so different from the time before. Not different at all, as a matter of fact.

But when he dropped his guard, lust for her warmed his skin and tightened his whole body with a gnawing, restless hunger. He had a thousand images of her stored in his brain, all so lovely he ached. He knew her scent, and the shape of her, but never, not ever, would he let the heat he felt meld with the respect and admiration. She was not for him, not in that way, not with her beliefs.

God intended a helpmate for him, a woman that shared his faith and would share the journey. He was sure of it. Layla did not fit into the empty place by his side, in his heart. He wouldn't let her.

Jack pulled on his outdoor clothes, then headed out into the fading light. Martin had gassed up one of the ATV's for him, and the black leather seat still held some warmth from the sun. The church was only a couple of miles from Layla's cottage. Normally, such a distance wouldn't warrant a vehicle, but Jack's position in the community sometimes required a quick response, as did Layla's. They shared one of the emergency radios and had gotten into the habit of riding together wherever they went. Looked like all of that would be changing.

They couldn't share the same house any longer, Jack realized, as he started the ATV and headed down the silent, still street. Even if the situation with Owen didn't blossom into a relationship, it was no longer appropriate. He stuffed down the pang of loss he felt, and focused on thinking through his options. People didn't indulge in the luxury of living alone these days; they had sufficient generators, but the gas that powered them was finite. He had stayed with Layla to conserve resources, but he'd have to find a spot elsewhere.

Maybe he'd just stay at the church, have Alder help him come up with a way to heat the space he needed for the night. The more he thought about it, the more he liked the idea. It would save time, and after everyone left for the day, it would be nice to be alone. He spent all day, every day, surrounded by people. He was never completely free of the pressure of their emotions, their feelings.

Why, then, had he never felt so alone in his life?

FOUR
Grace and Quinn: Rock Ledge Ranch, Colorado Springs, CO

Grace looked up when the outside door burst open, bringing with it a swirl of snow and Quinn. Wind gusted through the room, and she spread her hands out on the papers she was working on to keep them in place. Quinn didn't greet her, shutting the door swiftly behind him and making sure the heavy drapes they had hung to keep out cold and keep in light settled properly in place. Grace frowned, watching him move swiftly around the room to snap all the drapes shut tight.

"What's wrong?"

Quinn stepped to the table and blew out the hurricane lamp she'd been using to augment the weak, grey daylight coming in the windows. "I saw people. From up on the ridge. Two people in the neighborhood south of here, moving this way." He didn't wait for her to reply, but went to the sliding doors that partitioned the dining area from the parlors and hallway and cracked them open, slipping through.

Grace's heart started to pound. She heaved out of the chair she'd been sitting in and had to wait for a minute, getting her balance before she lumbered after Quinn. He was standing at the bay window on the southeast corner of the house. This window was covered with horizontal blinds, and he'd lifted one of the slats to peer out intently. Grace started to do the same on the opposite side of the window, but her belly hit the wall first. She huffed in frustration, shifted to the side, then leaned to peek out at the gathering dusk and thickening snow. Her stomach nudged Quinn in the side, and his hand came up automatically to steady her, cupping her elbow and holding it firmly.

"What did they look like? Were they carrying guns? Did they move like they had military training? Are you sure there were just two of them?" Grace barked the questions out one right after another. Then, she closed her eyes and pressed her lips together, pulling a deep breath of air in through her nostrils. She winced at the sudden flurry of agitated kicks in her abdomen – it always happened when she got tense or upset – and looked back up at Quinn.

"I'm sorry. Just tell me what you saw."

"I was too far away to get details, but it looked like one was carrying a rifle or shotgun, and the other one had a club of some kind, maybe a baseball bat. The dog pack was trailing them, but back a ways, like they had a reason to be wary."

As he spoke, his palm came to rest on her stomach, right over the invisible, drumming feet. Immediately, the kicks eased in intensity, then stopped altogether. Grace felt a great roll and a shift, as if the burden she carried was snuggling into Quinn's palm. Happened every time. She didn't know whose distress Quinn was picking up on, and it didn't really matter. She was just grateful he could make it stop.

"Those don't sound like military-issue weapons. Chances are they're not from the gang, then." Grace squinted up at the sky. "The snow's really starting to come down. Maybe they'll head back to wherever they came from."

"I just hope they're not looking for someplace new," Quinn said grimly. He let the blind drop back into place, and took her elbow once more, steering her back to the table. He shut the partition doors, then joined her. The only light in the room now glowed through the grill of the fireplace in the corner. They sat across from each other, on opposite sides of an old argument that rose between them more and more often these days.

Grace was always the first to start. "If we go right after the weather clears -"

Quinn cut her off with a groan and dropped his head back, scrubbing his hands over his face. "Please don't start. Please. It's not safe, especially not now."

"It's not safe to stay here. If you had listened to me last summer, we wouldn't still be having this argument."

"Graaace..." Face still buried in his hands, Quinn dragged her name out over three disgusted syllables. He dropped his hands to glare at her. "We said we would stop with the 'I told you so' stuff. We agreed. It doesn't do any good."

"I don't know what else to say! We should have been out of here months ago! Now, here we are with armed men..."

Without warning, her world shrank to a pinpoint of light and her face was suddenly greasy with sweat. Through the heavy buzzing in her ears, she heard Quinn say, "Oh, Gracie."

Then, nothing.

She blinked her eyes open, and had just enough time to recognize the familiar ceiling of the bedroom before she rolled over to vomit her lunch into the bowl Quinn had waiting. When she was finished, she rolled back and draped her arm over her eyes, taking deep breaths to bring the remaining nausea under control. Quinn left her to take care of the bowl, returning a moment later with a warm, damp washcloth. He wiped her palms and dried them – for some reason, the sweaty palms bothered her more than anything else – then lifted her arm away from her face and smoothed the washcloth over her forehead and across her mouth.

Grace opened her eyes. He was sitting on the floor beside the bed, just gazing at her patiently. They'd been through this too many times to count. "Don't say it. Please don't say it."

He leaned forward, suddenly intense, until his nose was about three inches away from hers. "I. Told. You. So."

Tears flooded her eyes, which made her angrier still. She had no control over anything – her body, her emotions, nothing. "Just go away," she choked. She sounded like a grumpy toddler, but recognizing that didn't help her get herself under control. She heaved over onto her side, pressing her face into the pillows, curling up as much as her huge belly would allow. "Just leave me alone."

He didn't listen. He never did. Instead, he covered her with the soft afghan from the foot of the bed and sat beside her, rubbing her back until the nausea receded and she drifted on the edge of sleep, aware only of the patient circling of his hand on her aching back. She must have slept, then, because when she next opened her eyes it was full dark and she was alone.

She sat up cautiously. A dim light from the kitchen and the muted clanking of the stove told her where Quinn was. She sat for a few moments, listening to the wind wail around the house. After a few days of warm sunshine, winter was back with a vengeance, and she knew the worst snows were likely ahead of them. By their count, it was mid-February, though they were not sure of the exact day, and Colorado's snowiest month was March. It had been a fairly mild winter so far, but that could change in a hurry on the front range of the Rockies.

Grace stood, waited a minute or two to be sure she wouldn't pass out again, then wrapped the afghan around her shoulders and shuffled towards the kitchen. Quinn looked up when she appeared in the doorway, his eyes probing her face. Whatever he saw satisfied him that she wasn't about to do a header, and he turned back to the pot he was stirring.

"I left your papers on the table. If you want to put them away, we can eat."

Grace shuffled back to the dining room and double-checked the curtains. Then she re-lit the hurricane lamp she'd been using earlier and started methodically stacking papers. She had a numbering system, but it was easier to just keep everything in order. Phrases she'd written jumped out at her as she cross-stacked in organized piles: "Haven't seen a patrol leave Fort Carson for three days." "Desperate people are disobedient." "I recommend we look for another site, something with greater tactical advantage."

She had been working on this project since the summer before, and she was nearly finished. Writing down everything she had heard while she'd been held captive, word for word, had been both horrific and cathartic. But if this information could be used against the gang of men who currently controlled most of the city, maybe she could find meaning in what she had endured. She needed to get it all down, all of it, so she could identify patterns, look for themes, analyze for weaknesses. She could sense all those things starting to coalesce, could catch glimpses of the big picture that was clicking together piece by piece in her mind, and in the process, she came as close to peace as she got these days.

Quinn would be relieved when she was finished; her project was one of the two major sources of disagreement between them. The other was Quinn's refusal to leave their cozy little sanctuary at Rock Ledge Ranch.

Grace had continued to suffer frequent fainting spells throughout her pregnancy. Without much more than a few seconds of warning, she could be covered in sweat and headed for the floor, rousing a few minutes later only to vomit whatever she'd eaten last. In the early days, Quinn had gone on a rampage, looking for information on what was happening to her. He had walked all the way to the library branches in Old Colorado City and in the

Rockrimmon neighborhood and had cleaned out the shelves on pregnancy-related topics, lugging home hundreds of pounds of books.

When Grace had refused to read them, he'd struggled through the books himself, finally coming up with a name, if not a treatment, for what was happening to her: Vasovagal syncope, which was just a fancy way of saying stress-related fainting, in Grace's opinion. According to Quinn's books, it wasn't uncommon for this to happen during pregnancy, and it could be triggered by any number of things – an unpleasant smell, standing or sitting too long, lack of sleep, or any kind of stress. Hence Quinn's disapproval of her writing project, and his refusal to leave the ranch. And since their arguments often led to Grace's eyes rolling back into her skull, Quinn wouldn't even discuss it anymore. He had put his foot down the previous fall.

"Grace, it is not going to happen and I'm done talking about it. I don't care what you say, or how many ways you try to twist me up with your arguments. You can't ride a horse out of here when you could pass out at any minute. Stop and think! If we got in trouble and had to ride hard, how is that going to work? You can't stay conscious through a whole argument with me – how are you going to..."

And that had been all she'd heard. As soon as she got angry or upset, things started to go dim around the edges. Quinn was very good by now at reading the signs; sometimes, he could stop it before she lost consciousness by rubbing her back and murmuring to her, in the same way she'd heard him comfort fractious animals. Mostly, though, he just refused to engage in any kind of discussion that might upset her.

But the appearance of strangers on their doorstep wasn't something they could ignore in the hopes it would go away. Quinn set a bowl of steaming stew in front of her, then returned to the stove to pull a pan of fluffy biscuits out of the warming oven. It had taken months, but both of them had finally gotten the hang of cooking and baking with the wood-burning stove. Quinn juggled the hot biscuits to a plate, slid them enticingly close to Grace, then sat down with his own bowl of stew and a jar of honey. He didn't take a bite until Grace was eating steadily.

"After you fell asleep, I went upstairs and watched for a while. I didn't see any sign of those people, and the dog pack didn't head over here to bother the stock. I think they must have headed back the way they came, for now."

Grace nodded. "Makes sense, what with the storm." She took another bite of stew, chewed, then went on. "But we've been lucky. Really lucky. We have to talk about what to do, Quinn. If the gang finds us, we're dead."

Quinn frowned. "I know. And I think I have an idea."

Grace waited as he broke open a steaming biscuit, drizzled it with honey, then set it in front of her. Quinn would not be rushed when he had thoughts to share. Once again, he waited until she was chewing on her second bite of sweet, soft biscuit before he prepared one for himself. Finally, he started talking.

"You're right – we have been lucky so far. We haven't seen anyone nearby, not in all the time we've been here. After today, though, I don't think we have a choice. We need to relocate."

At last! Grace leaned forward, filled with equal parts relief and triumph. "I know it'll be fine – maybe we can come up with some way to tie me to Kava – you know, like they do with disabled riders? Straps, or ropes, or something? She's sure-footed, and she's steady; I don't think she'll spook, even if I pass out. It's not that far to Woodland Park, and when the weather breaks…"

She trailed off. Quinn was shaking his head. "No. That's not what I meant." He hesitated, clearly reluctant to upset her again. His eyes dropped to the enormous mound of her belly, then lifted back up to her face. "Grace, we don't talk about it. We haven't talked about it, not once this whole time. But have you done the math? Do you realize how close you are?"

Grace stared at him. Then, she dropped her eyes, staring without seeing at the wooden table-top. Just like that, she couldn't breathe. Chills of panic started racing up and down her arms and legs, making them tremble randomly. This was a precipice she was not brave enough to look over. "It doesn't matter. It's not…I can't…please, don't. I don't want to talk about it."

"I know you don't." Quinn's voice was so tender. "But Gracie, we're out of time. We have to talk about it." He slid out of his chair to kneel beside her, lifting her chin with one hand, the other rubbing her arm and shoulder with long, firm, steadying strokes, just exactly like he calmed a spooked horse. "We have to talk about the baby."

Grace flinched. She avoided reference to her pregnancy whenever possible, and never, not ever, thought of what was growing in her as "the baby." It was a burden, a temporary problem. When she was free of it, when the fainting stopped, they could be on their way to safety, to Woodland Park, to her father and his family. Her step-mom and little baby half-brother. After this was over.

Quinn was gazing at her with sorrow and knowledge in his eyes. "You haven't thought about the baby at all, have you."

Grace stared back, and couldn't think of a single thing to say. The stew she'd eaten rolled around in her stomach and she swallowed hard to keep it in place. Sweat sheened her forehead, and Quinn read the signs instantly. He tucked her suddenly numb face in the crook of his neck and rubbed her back, his voice a low murmur.

"Just keep breathing, Gracie. Just think about your heartbeat staying steady and even. Think about all your muscles relaxing..."

Grace closed her eyes and did as he instructed, breathing in the comfort of his scent. Quinn had never again spoken of his feelings for her, of wanting their relationship to be more, not since the day they discovered she was pregnant. But it was there, every single day, in the way he cared for her, in the tenderness of his touch and the thoughtfulness of his care. She knew what he hoped for, and knew with equal certainty that it could never be.

In spite of all they'd been through, in spite of the horrors she knew he had seen, there was something about Quinn that remained so pure, so innocent. To Grace, he was of the Earth, a part of nature, like the plants and animals he communed so effortlessly with. Strong and beautiful and natural. Clean. Next to him, she felt wrecked and dirtied. Like an oozing hulk, bloated with poison and anger, swollen to bursting with pain and plans for vengeance she would never allow him to be a part of.

Quinn shifted so he could look at her face, supporting her head in the crook of his elbow. For long moments, he just gazed at her, a troubled frown wrinkling his forehead. Then he heaved a hitching sigh. "I'd usually just stop talking about whatever upsets you, but we've done that too much." He paused, and Grace could hear the determination in his tone when he continued. "We can't do that this time. You've got maybe a couple weeks left. We need to go to ground and get ready for the birth." He paused again, then said deliberately, "We need to get ready for the baby."

"Don't call it a baby!" The words were out before she knew she was going to speak them. She pulled away and pushed at Quinn's shoulder at the same time, suddenly unable to stand his closeness. "It's just a...a thing! Just something I have to get over with – something I have to get out of me. I want it out, Quinn. I just want it out, so I can..." Her voice dropped to a miserable whisper. "So I can be *me* again. It's like a tumor. Like a rotten growth that takes everything from me."

Quinn's frown deepened. "That's not right. I know you know that. It's a little boy or a little girl, and it's not the baby's fault– "

"Don't you dare!"

Grace breathed, breathed deep, willing her body to obey her for once. Quinn was right about one thing – they had let too many hard conversations go unfinished, cut short by the damn fainting spells. But she would make herself understood on this point, if she had to regain consciousness and come back to it a hundred times. She went on in a voice she had forced to be level and calm. "Don't tell me how to feel about this, Quinn. It's my body, and you're not going to tell me what I should feel. I don't want this thing, and I will never want it. Once it's out of me, I'm not going to have anything to do with it."

It took a moment for her words to sink in. When they did, Quinn stood suddenly, and took a step back. In the wake of his physical withdrawal, she felt his emotional distance, as a chill in her chest and stomach. She couldn't stand the way he was staring at her, like she was a stranger. He started to say something, stopped, swallowed, then managed to get the words out. "What are you saying, Grace? What...what are you...planning?"

"I don't know!" She yelled the words at him, what little control she had achieved gone. Then she looked down and repeated them in a halting whisper. "I don't know. I haven't thought about it. I...can't. Maybe it...won't survive. Please," she whispered, not to him, but to God, the Universe, the Fates – whatever had set her on this path, "Let it not survive."

Silence settled around them, absolute and cold. Quinn seemed frozen, and Grace did not have the courage to look at his face. She couldn't bear to see what her honesty had wrought in him. Minutes passed, and finally, Quinn stirred.

He cleared away his dishes without saying a word, leaving her to stare at her congealing stew. Grace could hear him moving around in the kitchen, putting things away and washing dishes, and still she stared. She sensed his return to the doorway, his hesitation, then he cleared away her dishes as well. When he appeared in the doorway again, he spoke in a voice that was so stiff, he sounded like a stranger.

"I think we need to move, down to the little cabin. It's a lot more hidden, and the trees will help break up the smoke from our chimney. We're too exposed here, too easy to see, and the cabin is smaller. It'll be easier to keep it heated."

Grace blinked, then nodded slowly. The Galloway homestead cabin was just a few hundred yards to the north, but it was tucked in a copse of trees on the edge of the creek. If you didn't know it was there, it was tough to find, and it wouldn't be an obvious target for scavengers. It didn't get them out of the gang's range, but they'd be better concealed. She looked up at Quinn's face, but he was avoiding her eyes. Her hand lifted in a fleeting, beseeching gesture, then fell back to her lap.

"Whatever you think, Quinn."

Another long silence, interrupted only by the whistling rise and fall of the wind outside, fell between them. When Quinn finally moved, his burst of sudden, determined energy startled her.

"I'm going to start taking supplies down tonight. If the storm keeps up, it will cover my tracks. The less sign we leave that we've been here, the better."

"Okay." Grace heaved herself to her feet and lumbered towards the kitchen. "I'll start packing up what we'll need, then I can move stuff back where it belongs –"

"No!" Grace jumped at Quinn's sudden bark, and he softened his tone, though he still hadn't looked at her. "No. I can do it. You should rest."

"But I can help, really —"

"I don't want your help." His soft words slid gently between her ribs and sliced at her heart. He was looking at her now, and the disappointment in his eyes opened another slicing cut. "I want to do it alone. I just...want some time alone."

"All right. Okay." She couldn't seem to catch her breath. "I'll just go on to bed then..."

But she was talking to thin air. Quinn was no longer standing in the doorway. Grace heard the outside door open, then close quietly. She stood by the table, lungs hitching as she tried to breathe around the hurt. Quinn had been upset with her before, he had been frustrated, angry, and irritated, but he had never looked at her like that. Like he didn't know her, and didn't want to. Like he wanted nothing more to do with her. A sob surprised her as it broke free. She had literally never considered, not once, what would happen if Quinn left her.

Grace picked up the hurricane lamp and headed for the bedroom before she could take another step down that mental path. It didn't bear contemplating. By the time she finished hauling Quinn's pallet out from under the bed and straightening the covers, she was gasping for air. She paused, pressing down on the tight upper curve of her belly, so high under her ribs they ached constantly. An answering thump on her palm made her yank her hand away.

With the wind pressing and rattling around the corner of the house, the room was rapidly growing bitter with cold. Grace set the lamp on the table beside the bed, but rather than undressing, she layered on another big sweatshirt and pulled a stocking cap onto her head. Her shoes came off and she awkwardly wrestled a pair of wool socks over the ones she already wore.

This had become a task Quinn helped her with every night, just as he always stoked the warming stove in the corner of the bedroom with a pan of coals. Tears flooded her eyes again, and she gave herself up to them, sobbing without restraint. She wasn't crying about Quinn, and on some level, she knew it. But it wasn't safe to open that deeper well, the well with no bottom. So she cried out her hurt over Quinn, cried because of the way he'd looked at her, cried because the stove in the corner was cold and her socks were on crooked, cried until the sobs subsided into halting breaths and some of the terrible pressure inside her had eased. She swiped at her face with her sleeve, blew out the lamp and slid between the icy sheets, moving her arms and legs around to break up the chill before she curled up on her side.

In the dark, in the stillness, she missed the familiar sound of Quinn's breathing so deeply it made her bones ache. She bit her lip, holding back fresh sobs. He would never leave her. She knew him, better than she knew herself these days, and he would die before he would leave her. He would do the right thing, no matter his feelings. It was the most miserable realization she'd ever come to. Being a burden was awful enough. She could not bear becoming a duty to him. She simply could not live with it.

She drifted in and out of fitful sleep as the night wore on, sometimes hearing Quinn moving around in the kitchen or dining area, waking fully when he settled on the pallet beside the bed in what had to be the wee hours of the morning. Words crowded into her throat, words she wanted to say to him in the safe darkness: I'm sorry. Thank you. You're a jerk. Don't leave me. I'm sorry. She swallowed them all back down, because she didn't understand any of it. Instead, she listened to his breathing and finally fell fully, deeply asleep.

When she opened her eyes, bright white light was leaking around the edges of the heavy curtains, and Quinn was gone again. Grace slid reluctantly from her warm cocoon of blankets, driven first to use the bucket Quinn had rigged up as a mini port-a-john, complete with a toilet seat and a curtain for privacy. During the warmer months, they had used the outhouse in the yard, but colder weather and Grace's advancing pregnancy had necessitated the change. She'd been humiliated at first, sharing such private bodily functions with him. She remembered plugging her ears, cheeks roasting with embarrassed heat, the first time Quinn had used the bucket. Now, it was just a part of daily life.

Sometimes, she wondered if they would ever again enjoy luxuries like warm, clean bathrooms and flushing toilets, but she didn't allow herself to dwell on such thoughts for long. Thinking about how things used to be, worrying about what the future held – she couldn't do either. There was just today, with its tasks and problems to solve. It was the only way she knew how to keep going. She just kept taking the next step.

When she was finished dressing, Grace moved to the window and peered out. Snow was still coming down in huge, fluffy flakes, so thick she couldn't even see the barn. Faintly, she could see where Quinn had been trekking back and forth, either between the house and the barn, or between the house and the cabin, but the trail was filling in even as she watched. Moving during the storm was a good idea, and today, he was going to get her help whether he wanted it or not.

She started by gathering and folding all their clothes and stacking them on the bed. With that finished, she scooted outside to empty the port-a-john, leaving the bucket by the door so it could be moved to the cabin. She paused then to eat some cold stew and drink some water. It still shocked her, how fast hunger could sneak up and debilitate her, and she was determined to be useful today, determined to pull her weight. Quinn still hadn't returned by the time she finished, so she shuffled awkwardly up the steep stairs that led from the kitchen to the storage space above.

Before the weather had turned cold, they had both continued to use the upstairs bedroom, Quinn on his pallet, Grace in the bed. Views of the surrounding area were better, and there was often a cool breeze to lift the curtains in the north windows. The colder months, though, had driven them into the downstairs bedroom. They used the partition doors to close the parlors and upstairs off, living in the kitchen, dining area and downstairs bedroom to conserve heat. Quinn had moved all of their supplies into the storage area above the kitchen as well, in case they needed to get out in a hurry. Grace nudged at the piles, wondering what they might need and what should just be left here.

The saddlebags – they should keep those at the ready. She picked them up, eyed the steep stairs, then tossed them down. She misjudged the drop, though, and one of them caught the stairs, bumping and tumbling through the air to land right against the stove. Grace huffed in annoyance, and started shuffling back down. The last thing they needed was a fire. She was halfway down the stairs when the outside door was snatched open and Quinn's frantic face appeared.

His gaze flew back and forth between the saddlebags and her face, his forehead creased with confusion and...was it fear? His chest was heaving, and to Grace's consternation, his eyes filled with tears. What in the world?

She made it to the bottom of the stairs, pulled the saddlebag to safety, then laid a hand on his forearm. "Sorry about that – it seemed safer to drop them than to carry them down. Did you think I fell?"

He stepped back and swiped at his face. "No, I thought... I was on the porch, and I heard this thump... I didn't know... I didn't know what you'd done."

Grace frowned. "Didn't know what I'd done?" Click, click, click – like puzzle pieces, she understood. "You thought I threw myself down the stairs. On purpose. To hurt this." She pointed at her stomach.

He just swallowed and stared at the floor. After a moment, he bent and gathered up the saddlebags. "I'll take these down to the cabin."

"Quinn." She followed him towards the door, but he didn't turn. "Quinn! Please look at me."

He turned, but his eyes still wouldn't rise. "I don't want to talk," he mumbled. "Just forget it. The storm's starting to ease up, and I want to make these last trips before –"

"I would never do that. Hurt myself, I mean." She ducked down, trying to get him to look into her eyes, to see her truth, feeling more desperate by the minute. "Don't you know that about me by now? Don't you know *me*?"

He did look up then, and one of these days, she would learn: When Quinn was avoiding eye contact, it was because he didn't want to hurt her. "I don't know you, Gracie. And I don't know how to help you. The way you're thinking... I'm in over my head. I don't know how you or anyone else could blame an innocent baby for what those men did to you. I can't get my head around it. So, no, I don't trust you not to try to hurt yourself or the baby."

He turned to gaze out the window at the falling snow. "I don't want to talk. I'm afraid of what you'll say. I'm afraid of what you feel. Most of all, I'm afraid of what will happen after the baby comes."

Those eyes, sad and honest, swung to touch hers again, and she flinched. She opened her mouth to answer, to reassure, to defend herself, but not a word rose. Anything she could think to say, anything he would want to hear, would be a lie. And it was as if he read her mind. His eyes dropped again, but she saw the shine of fresh tears first. Without a word, he opened the door and stepped out into the storm, saddlebags thrown over both shoulders.

Anger came first. How dare he? How could he? On that surge of energy, Grace moved from room to room, thoughts boiling as she straightened and gathered, returning things to rights. He saw! He saw everything that had been done to her! And he presumed to judge?

Her rage dissipated as quickly as it had come. In its wake, she felt weak and nauseated, sick with misery. She sank down to rest on the bed, and focused on keeping her breath steady, her muscles relaxed. Enough with the fainting. She could do this, at least – learn to stop the spells when they started, without relying on Quinn to do it. She relied on him for far too much.

She wasn't sure when the balance had shifted, but at some time in the past months, Quinn had become the strong one. He made decisions. He kept them safe. He took care of her when she couldn't care for herself. He was as trapped by her helplessness as she was, but the time for that to end was rapidly approaching.

Grace looked down at her belly, really looked, for the very first time. As if in response to her gaze, the thing inside her rolled, shifted, pressed. Grace watched the bizarre contortions, felt the alien movement, and knew she could never do what Quinn wanted her to do. She could not feel love for this...being. It had taken over her body, endangered her and Quinn, and would never stop reminding her of what she had suffered.

But Quinn would never forgive her if she tried to harm it. All life was precious to him. She couldn't change that about him, and wouldn't, even if she was able. It was what made Quinn, Quinn. Life seemed to surge around and through him, a force she could almost see, especially when he was in his garden or working with the animals. Living things leaned into him, pressed close, in a give and take of energy that was as natural as sun and rain. This being she carried would be no different. He would care for it, nurture it, because he couldn't do otherwise.

Grace made herself think it through, bent her logical mind to the task she had avoided all these long, waiting months. She couldn't relieve him of this burden. If it survived, he would lift it to his strong shoulders, without hesitation or regret. If she survived, he would continue to carry her as well.

Therein lay the only thing she still had the power of choice over.

By the time Quinn returned, Grace was ready to go, bundled in a scavenged winter coat that still smelled faintly of a dead woman's perfume. The fires were out, the house restored as much as possible to the condition they'd found it in. Grace had collected a small bag of things she wanted: her writing project, the book they'd been reading together, a few items that brought her comfort or had meaning to her. When Quinn reached to take it from her, she calmly, gently refused. Step one to reclaiming her strength and independence: Help herself, whenever possible.

She took her walking stick from its place by the door and stepped out onto the porch. Then, in spite of it all, in spite of the fear and anger, the bitter heartache, the distance from Quinn that made her feel breathless and lost, she smiled. Fluffy snow covered the small valley like winter fairy dust, transforming the world into a clean, bright, pure place. Around the now-frozen pond, a small herd of mule deer foraged under the towering evergreens and bare-branched trees, where the snow wasn't so deep. She loved their elegant silence, their grace. It took her outside herself, for just a heartbeat, and the tiny respite strengthened her further.

Quinn stepped out beside her and shut the door, and still without speaking, took her arm. Grace allowed him to steady her as she crept down the icy walkway, then gently pulled her arm away and headed towards the cabin, Quinn trailing a step or two behind. They trudged past the barn, then past the open paddock, which didn't see much use anymore. Late the previous fall, a pack of dogs had started to bother the animals, eventually killing one of their goats. The dogs had probably all been pets at one time – some still wore collars – but even Quinn wouldn't try to approach them. They made him sad, he said. He wasn't as in-tune with dogs as he was with horses, but he said most of them were disconnected from humans now, their minds focused on the pack, the hunt. Neither he nor Grace went outside these days without stout walking sticks, and Quinn always had some rocks for throwing in his pocket.

They walked along the trail that curved around the north end of the paddock, the only sounds the soft shuffle of their boots in the snow and the increasing huff of Grace's breath. She stopped to rest where the trail swung back to the north, and turned to look up at the soaring red rocks of Garden of the Gods, the top of Kissing Camels just visible over the ridge. Once, millions of people had come from all over the world to visit this park, these towering, timeless monoliths. Before that, the Ute Indians had wintered here. Now, it felt as if she and Quinn were the only ones left alive who remembered its existence.

These rocks had stood for millennia and would stand long after she and Quinn were gone, whether there were tourists to admire them or not. Grace turned and started walking again, trying not to feel small and meaningless. They entered the clearing where the old Galloway cabin stood, and Quinn hurried ahead of her, stomping his boots on the spot he'd cleared in front of the door before he opened it for her. Grace stepped inside, and when he pulled the door shut behind them, the darkness was almost total.

The tiny log cabin had been built in the late 1800's, according to information they'd found in the Chambers house. Two tiny windows were currently covered by wooden shutters, and the only light glowed from the coals Quinn had left banked in the fireplace. A tiny, rickety table and some chairs with seats of woven rags were situated near the hearth, and Grace could see where he had made an effort to clear away some of the unnecessary historical artifacts, which were stacked in the corner farthest from the warmth of the fireplace. Quinn lit a hurricane lamp that was sitting on the table before he bent to stoke the fire into life. When he was finished, he stood.

"I know it's dark, but it's snug and it'll be easier to keep warm." In his gestures, Grace could see his uncertainty. "There's water here by the fireplace in this bucket, and I set the port-a-john up in the corner over there. At night, I figure we can just move the table out of the way and drag our pallets in front of the fire." He paused. "Is it okay? Are you all right with this?"

Grace made a show of looking around so he wouldn't see the sudden tears in her eyes. It was a hovel. A dark, dirty little shack. No antiques with fine lines here; everything was hand-made and crude. What had Quinn said? They needed to go to ground, to prepare for the birth? Well, it certainly seemed they'd done just that. The cabin felt like a den for animals.

Grace lifted her spine into straight strength and set aside her longing for the bright, drafty, old-fashioned charm of the Chambers house. If he knew how she felt, Quinn would move them back again before the day was out. She met his eyes, smiling through the first of many lies she needed to start telling him.

"It's just fine."

FIVE
Naomi: The Cabin on Carrol Lakes, CO

Sun sparkled through the cabin windows and fell across the scraps of shiny green paper on Naomi's kitchen table. The dogs were outside exploring the thick fall of fresh snow, and Ares was taking advantage of Hades' absence to wallow in Naomi's attentions. He wound around and around her ankles, purr rising and falling like a cantankerous motor. When that failed, he jumped up on the table and flopped right in the middle of her craft project, gazing at her with slitted eyes, a rajah demanding adulation. Naomi chuckled and tickled his nose with a scrap of paper. He batted at it lazily, then offered his soft tummy for rubbing, which she obliged.

"I'd call you spoiled, but your life isn't exactly Fancy Feast and silk cushions these days, is it?"

Ares just stretched and purred louder. Naomi figured she had about 20 more seconds before he decided that was more than enough affection and closed his claws around her wrist – such was the way of cats – so she relaxed into the moment, enjoyed the warm bond of connection with him, the way the sun glinted off the metallic green paper strips she was looping into a chain, and the smell of the fresh pine boughs she'd brought in to soften the mantel. In small moments of joy, she had learned, sanity was found.

Their time was cut short when Hades bounded through the dog door, whining with a combination of excitement and anxiety. Naomi swung around to look at him, and frowned when Persephone didn't immediately follow. She reached for his perceptions with her mind, but didn't have time to complete the link before the door opened. Martin stepped in, stomping off snow, Persephone tucked in the crook of his arm. In his hand dangled a dead rabbit, but his attention was fixed on the little dog.

"She's hurt." He didn't greet Naomi, didn't even look up when he spoke. "There's something wrong with her back right leg." His tone was calm, but *frantic worry* radiated off him. He stepped up to the table, shoved aside the decorations she had been making, and set Persephone down.

Naomi's brain went in five directions at once. What was he doing here? Her eyes flew to Macy's open door. Should she go shut it? Could he see in from where he was standing? She sucked in a deep breath and forced herself to prioritize. First things first.

She stepped to take the rabbit from Martin's hand and gave it to Hades along with a silent command to take it outside. Hades obeyed, bounding back through the dog door with greedy glee; whatever was going on with Persephone, he didn't seem too concerned. Naomi ran her hands over the little dog, looking for the source of her distress. "I don't understand – how did you find her? What happened?"

"I was on my way here," Martin said, eyes fixed on Naomi's hands. "You didn't answer your radio, and I wanted to check on you, talk through some things. I was almost here when…" His voice trailed off for a moment. He took a step back, and ran his hands up over the top of his head, peeling his ski cap off with the motion. Under the cap, his short, dark hair glinted with strands of silver in the sun. He ran his hands over his head again, and Naomi frowned. She had never seen him so agitated.

"When what? What's the matter?"

He made eye contact then, for the first time, and in his dark eyes, wonder shone. His gaze dropped to Persephone again. "She connected with me. At least I think she did. All of a sudden, it was like the world wobbled, and I could *see* and *feel* what she was feeling. I could *feel* that she was hurt, and where."

Naomi's hands stilled, and a stab of jealousy rendered her breathless for a moment. She was proud of her even tone when she spoke. "Well, that's not a huge surprise, I guess. She's very attached to you." But why hadn't she linked with Naomi? She looked down at Persephone, who was panting and whining softly, eyes glued to Martin. Her hands started moving again, and she found the source of Persephone's pain: Her hip was dislocated. She had probably taken a bad kick from the dying rabbit.

"We need to get her to a vet." She grimaced. "Scratch that. We need to see if Rowan can help. If not Rowan, maybe Ignacio knows how to –"

"Let me see." Martin stepped close and his hands nudged hers aside. A frown of concentration creased his forehead, and his eyes went unfocused, though Naomi could *feel* the intensity of his focus on Persephone. Naomi watched his hands travel carefully over the dog's back leg, probing gently when he reached the injury. Persephone yelped softly, but her eyes stayed fixed on Martin in complete trust.

"Be careful, injured dogs can bite." Namoi turned away, hurrying to collect the things they would need for the trip into town. "Let me get a blanket for her, and we can –"

Another sharp yelp from Persephone made her spin back around. Martin shushed the little dog, soothing her with gentle strokes from head to tail. He took a step back from the table, and Persephone rose. She seemed to test her back leg for a moment, then trotted the length of the table, following Martin's retreat. When she reached the end of the table, he scooped her up before she could jump into his arms.

"I think that took care of it."

Naomi stepped to take Persephone from him, cradling her to her chest and closing her eyes in relief when the little dog finally connected with her. She basked for a moment in the *love, love, love,* then opened her eyes to gaze at Martin. "How did you know to do that? Were you a medic?"

"The Marines don't have medics – the Navy takes care of that. But I've had some basic medical training." He looked down at Persephone. "Mostly, I just let her body tell me what to do." His eyes rose, again filled with awe. "I just connected with her and she knew what was wrong. She knows her body, and could tell me by *feeling* when my hands did the right thing. I could tell the bone wasn't broken and how to move the joint."

Naomi dredged up a smile. "If we could get people to do that, for themselves and each other, it would take a lot of pressure off Rowan. We need to tell her about this."

"True." Now that the crisis was past, their usual awkwardness settled in. Martin cleared his throat and looked down at the floor. "I'm sorry I barged in like that – I was so worried about her. I tracked snow all over your floor."

"It's fine. The dogs do it all the time." She glanced at Macy's open door, wondering how she could walk by him casually to close it. At least his back was to it. "Did you come on a snowmobile? I didn't hear one."

"No, I rode Ben. He's tethered outside. Ignacio wanted to see how he'd handle the deeper snow drifts, and he said Ben was missing you." Martin almost smiled – a corner of his mouth actually twitched up. "I, ah, think I get that a little better now."

Naomi's eyes flickered to Macy's door again. It would be too strange, draw too much attention, to walk all the way across the room to shut it. From the depths, the old Naomi rose to offer hospitality. "Can I get you a cup of tea or something to eat?"

"You have tea? Black tea? With caffeine?"

Naomi shook her head regretfully. "Not anymore. I went through it when the coffee ran out. Just herbal." She walked over and handed Persephone to him. "Have a seat and I'll get it. Peach or cinnamon apple?"

"Peach, please," he answered. He sat at the table, and focused on the scraps of paper, the bright chain she'd been making, the shamrocks she'd already cut. His eyes lifted to scan the room, taking in the pine boughs on the mantle, then fixed on her and narrowed. "What's all this?"

"Oh, you know." She couldn't stand it any longer. Moving with what she hoped was nonchalance, she walked to shut Macy's door, allowing herself a quiet sigh of relief when it was done. She turned back, not meeting his gaze, and set about getting his tea. "Just cheering the place up for St. Patrick's day. You said peach, right?"

Martin didn't answer. Naomi looked up, and he was staring at Macy's door speculatively. Her heart rate kicked up a notch. "Would you like a muffin, too? I just made them yesterday – I'm almost out of flour, so I used some canned pinto beans to augment, and I think they came out good, even if they're not a very pretty color…" Her voice was too high-pitched and she was talking too fast. She took another deep breath and took it down a notch. "You said you wanted to talk about some things? What's on your mind?"

Martin looked away from Macy's door, but Naomi's relief was short-lived.

"You know I can tell when someone is lying or hiding something."

Not a question. "Yes." She felt her mind start to scrabble. Could he be fooled? She'd read once that some people could fool a polygraph machine. If she could make herself *believe* that she had nothing to hide, would that throw him off the scent? "Did you say you wanted a muffin?"

He just gazed at her, and she could *feel* his probing. Her temper kicked in, then, and she was just about to call him on it when he backed off. "Sure. A bean muffin sounds interesting."

Relief again. What a roller coaster. Naomi set about making tea and getting him a muffin, feeling suddenly exhausted. She didn't try to fill the silence with polite small talk, as the old Naomi would have. Honestly, she didn't think she had any of those old social skills left in her. Not now, maybe not ever again.

And she'd bet some serious money that Martin had never had so much as a drop of "polite" in him. He said what he thought, bluntly, without trying to soften it out of consideration for the other person's feelings. On the flip side of that, though, he never embellished or exaggerated. You always knew where you stood with Martin, which was frequently painful and reassuring at the very same time.

Scott hadn't been one to play passive-aggressive games or be dishonest, but Naomi knew he had often maintained his silence rather than upset her. At the time she had appreciated his tender care of her feelings. She had trusted his judgment, trusted him to share with her what she needed to know. But those times were not these times. She couldn't afford to be crippled by her sensitivity, any more than she could rely on Martin to shield her from the ugliness in the world, the way Scott had.

She set a mug of tea down in front of him, then brought him a muffin on a little tin plate with a cloth napkin tucked beside it. He snorted softly. "Very fancy. Still so civilized."

Her temper, which hadn't really subsided, rumbled again. "It's not about being 'civilized.' It's just..." How in the world to explain this to him? Should she even bother? Could he understand? "There's no reason to not make it nice. It pleases my eye. It makes me feel better. Cozy." She plunked a mug down for herself, harder than she needed to, and sat down. She glared at the steam rising from her tea, rather than look up to see the disdain on his face. "Just forget it."

"As you wish."

Naomi gritted her teeth at the mockery in his tone and took a scalding sip of tea. "What did you need to talk about?"

"I came to ask you, one last time, to reconsider this plan."

Well, there it was. Out there and blunt. So Martin. Well, she could be blunt, too. "No."

Martin acted as if he hadn't heard her. "I'm going to run through this one last time. If Piper is alive – and I do believe that you can feel that – she will head here. You're sure of that. It makes no sense for you to go looking for her. It's an unnecessary risk, and this community needs you."

"Well, that was admirably calm and persuasive. Have you been getting coaching from Jack?" She heard Piper's voice, cutting and sarcastic, come out of her own mouth. "I understand the logic of the arguments as both you and Jack have presented them. I even agree on some points. But here's the point you both seem to have trouble grasping –"

She leaned forward, and hit him with the full force of her *will*, her *desire*, her *need*. God, it was gratifying to see him start back, to see his eyes widen. "I have to go. I have to. If I sit here and wait, I will either lose my sanity or

–" Unexpectedly, grief rolled over her head like a tsunami, choking her, making her gasp for air. She fought for control, but couldn't stop her voice from shaking. "Or I will die. I'm sorry for the melodrama, but I don't know how else to say it."

Martin remained leaning back, and though he no longer looked surprised, there was something different in his eyes, something that almost looked like admiration. "That is some punch you pack, lady. Where have you been hiding that?"

Naomi sipped her tea again, hiding her embarrassment behind the genteel gesture. "I apologize. I know we're teaching the kids not to do that."

"See, there's the problem." Martin leaned forward, and she felt the power of *his* will. "You worry about stuff like that. Apologies. What you're 'supposed' to do. You claim you're not worried about being 'civilized,' but Naomi, you are civilized to the bone. I know you saw some hard things on your way here, and I know you handled yourself. But you have no idea. What we've got going on here in Woodland Park is incredible, but I guarantee it's the exception, not the rule. The ugliness that we would see–" He took a deep breath and shook his head. "I would spare you that. I'm asking you to spare *yourself* that."

"And all this time, I thought you were worried about the chubby housewife physically making the trip. How ironic." Her lips twitched, though not in amusement. "Which is it that you don't think is strong enough? My heart or my mind?"

"Neither."

They stared at each other across that abyss for long moments. Naomi refused to indulge the hurt indignation she was feeling by responding with a Piper-sharp retort, though she couldn't stop herself from rubbing the center of her chest to soothe her heart. His honesty hurt. But she had asked. Finally, she folded her hands around her mug of tea and groped her way forward.

"My pride is not going to let me sit here and try to convince you. I still have some of that left." She paused again, thinking, and decided she had nothing to lose by laying it all out. "I can't promise you anything. I can't guarantee I won't see or experience something that I can't handle. But here's the thing: If I'm not a wife and mother, I have no idea who I am. A mother does whatever she needs to, whatever it takes. When Macy died," she swallowed down the tightness that rose from her chest to her throat. "I took the next breath for Piper. It's not that I want to go. It's that I can't do anything else."

He didn't speak for the longest time. They sat in silence, but this time, the silence was a thoughtful one, rather than uncomfortable. The fire rustled softly, and Hades came in from outside, making a beeline for Naomi. He pressed against her, smelling of the cold and the fresh, raw meat of the rabbit he had consumed. Naomi slid her hands over his head, returning the *pure love* he always, always greeted her with. Her generous boy.

Martin's resignation and acceptance preceded his words. "I had decided that if I couldn't get you to agree, I would just sneak away and leave you behind. I kept trying to tell myself it would be for the best, that you wouldn't be crazy enough to go on your own." He sighed. "But you've convinced me of one thing: You are most certainly crazy enough."

Naomi's lips twitched again, but this time, it was in amusement. "I am. Thanks for noticing."

"Yep." He picked up his muffin and took a bite, then made a sound of surprise. "These did turn out good. Beans, you said?"

"Yep." She mimicked. For the first time in the longest time, she felt easy around him, as if they'd reached an agreement. Then, his eyes turned to Macy's door. He nodded towards it.

"What's in there?"

When his eyes returned to her, she felt the sharp edge of his scrutiny. He was *feeling* for her honesty. Well, she'd be damned if she'd give him another reason to think she was nuts, not after they'd made some progress here. She thought about the food, the dried goods and cans she'd been slowly gathering from the surrounding, abandoned cabins, which she'd been stacking along the wall of the cool bedroom. She smiled sweetly.

"Storage."

To her surprise, he grinned. "Atta girl. Don't let anyone bully you, least of all me." He rose. "I need to get going. Do you want to come out and see Ben before I leave?"

"I do." As she slid into her coat and boots, she watched Persephone dance around Martin's feet. "She's moving well, but I'll keep an eye on her. Unfortunately, once that hip has been dislocated, it's more likely to happen again. My husband's dog, Zeus, dislocated his three times. He was a black lab. They're prone to hip problems."

"Hmm." Martin scooped Persephone up, and ran his hand over her tiny haunch. "What happened to Zeus? Why isn't he with you, too?"

Naomi remembered cold, silky ears, and a stiffly curled corpse. She swallowed. "He died. When Scott did. I always felt like he chose to go with him."

Martin's eyes lifted to hers. "Your husband's name was Scott?"

"Yes."

Martin gazed at her, then took a deep breath. "My wife was named Isabella." He swallowed, too. "My son was called Michael, for my wife's grandfather."

Naomi nodded and dropped her gaze, feeling her face warm. So this was intimacy, in this new age: Naming your dead. "Thank you for telling me."

They stepped outside, and Ben immediately nickered a greeting. Naomi went to him, stepping to his left side, the way she had learned he preferred to be approached. She ran her hand down the curve of his neck, and leaned against his shoulder. In response, he curled his head around her, blowing softly. Naomi closed her eyes and felt her heart open and expand with love for him. "I missed you too, big guy. It's so good to see you."

"There's one more thing I need to say, Naomi."

Naomi opened her eyes but didn't move, watching Martin from the warm curve of Ben's body. He returned her gaze steadily, absently rubbing a gloved finger around Persephone's ears, and once again, she *felt* his resignation.

Naomi sighed. "Why am I certain I don't really want to hear this?"

As he had before, he ignored her words, pressing forward with his own agenda. "I won't ask you again to stay behind, but I will ask you to prepare mentally, before we go. In the Marines, we ran through mental dress rehearsals, talked through some of the scenarios we were likely to face. Our job was to think through these scenarios and rehearse what we would do, in our heads. My CO used to say, 'Win in the mind first.' I want you to do that."

Naomi absorbed comfort from Ben's body, and nodded. "That seems reasonable."

"All right." His voice took on a teaching cant. "First, you need to be able to handle it if something happens to one of the animals. They could die or be so badly injured we'd have to leave them behind. We might not be able to take the time to put them down, and they could suffer. You need to be able to break the link, if that happens, or it will cripple you."

Just the thought made her heart clutch and stutter, but she kept her gaze steady on his. "I'll think that through. What else?"

"We've been lucky here. People started working together right from the start, and we had enough resources to get our people through the first winter. We haven't experienced either deprivation or desperation – not yet, anyway. I guarantee there are places where they aren't doing as well as we are." He turned his head, and his eyes focused on something far away. "I can't predict exactly what we'll find, but there are a few common features of any society that has broken down: people killing each other over basic resources; senseless crimes, looting, vandalism; rape, of both women and children." His eyes returned to hers. "We are likely to see these things. And we're not going to be able to help. Not if we want to find our kids. You need to be able to walk away. Can you do that?"

Naomi remembered waking in the night, so long ago, the sensation of being choked, the certainty that Piper was in trouble, terrible trouble. She frowned, and replied honestly, though she was sure these weren't the words he wanted to hear. "Piper... I woke one night, and I could tell she was..." She swallowed, "Probably being attacked. Raped." She gazed into Martin's eyes. "I could be wrong, of course. It could have just been a bad dream. But it raises an important question. What if someone could have helped her, and didn't? What if they told themselves to walk away? We're both looking for our daughters, praying they're alive and okay, praying they have someone to look out for them. What if we see someone else's daughter who needs help? How can we walk away from that?"

Martin took a deep breath, and looked up at the sky for a moment. Naomi was sure she heard him mutter, "Son of a bitch," under his breath, but his eyes, when he returned them to hers, were patient. "I'm not saying it won't be hard. That's why I want you to think all of this through. We need to execute a very specific objective: Find our children and bring them back to safety. If we let other objectives get in the way of that, even if they're altruistic and humane, we will fail."

It was Naomi's turn to gaze at the sky. She pondered for a few minutes in silence, then sighed. "I may need to be reminded of that one. But I agree. Anything else?"

"One more thing." He paused. "If we get into trouble, run into the wrong people, you could end up facing that scenario. Rape. They might use coercion, threaten violence to one of the animals or me, or just use brute force. If that happens, you need to submit, especially if we're outnumbered. Play dead, go limp, try not to cry or fight."

Naomi's face colored. "Is that the Marine version of, 'Lie back and think of England?' Or should I plan what color to paint the ceiling?"

Martin snorted out a laugh that surprised them both. "Jesus, Naomi. Just when I think you wouldn't say 'shit' if you had a mouthful." He shook his head, and returned to his topic. "The important thing is that you can't disassociate. If you do, you lose control over what you think and do. You have to stay with the program enough to see opportunities for escape. If I'm dead or unable to help you for whatever reason, you'll need to get yourself out. I meant it, when I said this community needs you."

"No more than they need you." Ben knocked her in the shoulder with his nose and shifted restlessly. She pushed his head back firmly, and reminded him via a mental *nudge* where the lines were. He chuffed, apologetic and impatient at the same time. "I think this big guy has had about enough chit-chat. And you've given me plenty to think about."

"All right. You've got a couple of weeks to ponder. When we hit mid-March, if the weather holds clear and Jose's knee gives us the go-ahead, we'll head out for

Divide, then Cripple Creek. We'll check for survivors, see if we can scavenge anything, and make sure we've got our gear all settled in."

It was all suddenly so real, and she was suddenly breathless. Then she remembered walking into the wilderness with Macy with only what she could carry on her back, the terror of that first step. By contrast, riding out with Martin for a trial run camping trip/scouting expedition felt like a weekend excursion.

"Jose's knee hasn't failed us yet. I swear, he's more accurate than the forecasters used to be." She untied Ben's reins from the post he'd been hitched to, and walked him towards Martin. "I'll be ready."

"Good. Answer your radio next time." He deposited Persephone into her arms and took Ben's reins from her, mounting the horse with a smoothness she still hadn't achieved. "And thanks for the muffin."

Naomi shaded her eyes and looked up at him. "You're welcome. Thank you for bringing Persephone in. She would have hurt herself worse, trying to get home."

Martin just nodded and swung Ben's head around. He trotted towards the edge of the clearing around Naomi's cabin, then turned suddenly, making Ben dance a little. "One more thing: For the record, you are not a chubby housewife."

This was said so flatly and matter-of-factly, it took a minute for the blush of self-consciousness to flood Naomi's face. "Oh. Okay. Right." For Pete's sake, she thought. "Ah, I'm not sure why that matters, but thank you just the same."

"It matters because you need to see yourself clearly and understand your capabilities. You were fat and out of shape when I first met you. You still see yourself that way."

Her face torched into crimson, equal parts irritation and embarrassment. "Well, thanks so much for that observation, Martin, I sure do appreciate it."

"Christ on a crutch." He muttered the words, but she heard them anyway. "I'm not trying to insult you or make you uncomfortable. You're stronger and more fit now, that's just a fact. It's all part of understanding yourself, your strengths and weaknesses. You still see yourself as weak, and you're not. You've hiked all over this area. Hell, you could probably walk me into the ground. So you can stuff the sarcasm – I'm just telling it like it is, not trying to flatter my way into your pants."

So much for the truce they had achieved. "Martin, right now, I am marveling that you *ever* talked a woman out of her clothes," Did she really just say that? "Much less got two of them to marry you." She turned back to the cabin, sending him on his way with a disgusted wave. "I'll see you in a few days."

She heard the retreating crunch of Ben's hooves on the snow as they headed into the woods, and resisted the urge to turn and watch, muttering her litany of complaints to the attentive, sympathetic dogs. "Jerk. Idiot. Moron." Those didn't satisfy. "Numbskull. Dolt." Better, but, "Jackass!" There it was.

She made it half an hour, by her estimation, before she stomped into her bedroom, made sure the curtains were shut, stripped down to her underwear – baggy granny panties and a tattered, greying tank top – and was momentarily overcome by a desperate longing for a huge glass of wine. She took a deep breath and ditched the underwear as well, then stood in front of the mirror, grimacing at what she saw.

The soft, ample curves she'd always hated and Scott had always loved were gone. Time and life had not been kind to this poor old body, she thought, eyeing the sags, the stretch marks, the tired skin. She took another step closer to the mirror, and saw muscles flex in her legs. She lifted her arms and tightened them experimentally. Loose skin hung from her triceps where plump mama-arms used to be, but Martin was right about one thing: She was stronger, underneath the droop. Almost scrawny, more than a little scary, but definitely stronger.

It made her unspeakably sad, right down to her very bones. Since Piper's birth, she had battled her weight. She was always either on a diet or planning to go on a diet. Scott had ridden that roller-coaster the way Scott did everything, with good-natured tolerance. He had eaten cabbage soup and lean, dry chicken breasts without complaint, obliged her without a word of judgment when a Sunday-afternoon craving led them to Culver's frozen custard, and every possible variation in between. The only constant through those years had been his unwavering love for her, no matter what she weighed. Under the warm slide of his hands, her body became beautiful, always, every time. She felt like she had lost the last vestiges of his touch, the last traces of his lovemaking on her skin, along with her curves. She ran her hands over her much-smaller breasts and unfamiliar hips, and swallowed hard. Would he even recognize her now?

She lifted her eyes to her face and really looked, for the first time since Macy's death. The loss of her baby was there, written in lines around her eyes and mouth. Skin that had once been pampered with weekly facials had weathered to an uneven, wind-reddened brown. Her hair was longer, and almost completely silver at the roots, just a few gold strands mixed in with the grey now. She was 43 years old, and she looked like a crone. Would Piper even know her own mother when they were reunited?

"Bah!" She dashed the tears off her cheeks angrily. "Quite the pity party you've got going on here."

But she couldn't deny the anger she was feeling. Sags and all, she would have relished showing off a slimmer version of herself to Scott. She felt cheated, like she'd lost an opportunity she could never regain. She grumped her way back into her saggy underwear and too-big jeans, then crossed her arms over her bare breasts and scurried for Macy's room, where Piper's cabin clothes were still stored.

"Hi, honey." She never entered this room without greeting her daughter's corpse. "I just want to try something. This could be a waste of time, but..."

They fit. The underwear and the jeans. Naomi honestly couldn't decide how to feel, elated or enraged. Her mind, as ever, decided on the practical set. It would be nice to not have to deal with the discomfort of shifty underwear and jeans cinched up with a belt. The chill in the room seeped into her skin, and she rummaged for a sweatshirt. The faintest trace of Piper's perfume still clung to the fabric, and she pressed it to her face, closing her eyes and breathing deep.

She left Macy's room and moved around the cabin for a while doing chores, half her focus on feeding the dogs and bringing in more wood, the other half on settling into her new skin. Piper's clothes felt good, streamlined and efficient. Maybe, in wearing them, she would absorb some of her daughter's warrior spirit. The thought made her smile.

She hesitated when faced with the craft project she'd begun, which was still spread out on the table. She had intended the cheerful chain and shamrocks for Macy's room. Just yesterday, she had taken down the garland made of pink and red paper hearts she'd draped over the window for Valentine's Day. Naomi fingered the shiny green chain. She'd been so excited to unearth this paper in a forgotten drawer, but now she had to wonder if this activity was really the healthiest thing she could be doing with her time.

"You know what?" She plopped down and snipped a new strip for the chain, waving it at Ares, who was giving her a bored stare from across the room. "We're going to go with, 'Who gives a rip?' on this one."

By God, if there wasn't room for beauty and lovingly hung decorations in the future, she didn't want any part of it. No, she corrected herself, as she placed a precise drop of glue on the end of her paper strip and looped it through its neighbor. She'd *make* room for the things that mattered to her. The monotony of the craft soothed her, as did the simple achievement of watching the chain grow. When she had used up the last of the paper, she had a six-foot-long chain, and the cabin was growing dark. She left the chain to dry and slid into her coat, stepping outside into the twilight.

The day had been warm, and the air was soft and moist with melted snow. Naomi headed for the ridge at the edge of the clearing, her favorite spot for watching the sunset. The dogs had followed her out – they always did – and ranged around her now, endlessly sniffing. She reached out for Hades' perceptions, and marveled at how rich the twilight became when she connected with him. The clearing brightened, but the colors flattened out; layers of sound and scent bloomed like flowers, and a parade of the animals who'd been through their clearing that day started to flicker like a slideshow: fox, deer, magpie, more deer, and, oh, a coyote. That was new.

Winter sunsets in the Rockies could be spectacular, but this one was understated and soft – faded golds bleeding out to rosy purples and soft blues on the edges. Naomi reached the top of the ridge and folded her arms around herself, hugging her coat close against the rising wind. She tilted her face up, letting the colors soak into her eyes and brush over her skin. In her center, the place that spun and whirled with tasks and worries slowly wound down into peaceful stillness. She took a deep, deep breath of air and let it out slowly.

Just over her left shoulder, a low croak made her smile and turn. "You again. I thought maybe you'd deserted us."

On one of the lower branches of a towering pine, a huge raven cocked his head, watching her with his bright black eyes. He croaked again, as if in reply, and side-stepped a little closer. Naomi had learned to not reach out to any wild animal, especially ones that'd had extensive contact with humans; they just startled and fled. This fellow, though, was different. She couldn't initiate a link, as she did with Hades, but if she was patient...

And there he was, his curiosity probing along the edges of her awareness. As always, she was struck by his intelligence – he was easily as smart as the dogs – but his mind felt completely different. He was young, a juvenile, still fascinated by anything new, a conclusion she'd reached by comparing him to some of the other ravens she'd encountered on her rambles as well as a strong, sure *knowing* – he just felt young. In spite of his youth, there was a canniness about him, a cagey, opportunistic edge to his mind. He'd brushed her awareness too many times to count in just this way, and she'd learned to relax and let him poke around. If she reached out or tried to strengthen the connection, he took offense and flew off, croaking his indignation.

She smiled again, let her heart warm the tentative connection between them, then turned back to watch the sunset. Without warning, the sky exploded into brilliant color, the myriad hues of the sunset fracturing into thousands of shades she had never seen before. She gasped, hardly able to comprehend what she was seeing, struggling for words to label the experience. Psychedelic came the closest. She glanced at the raven, who was regarding her intently. He had initiated a full connection between them, and to her amazement, he wasn't fleeing the contact. She swung her eyes back to the sunset, and felt emotion roll up from her chest into her throat. She had never seen such beauty. The tears that filled her eyes faceted too many colors to count.

Another blink and it was over. Naomi sniffled and wiped at her eyes, then looked back up at the raven. He side-stepped a few feet away, but didn't fly off. Not indignant this time, just even more curious. She smiled at him and again let her heart warm the tentative link they still shared.

"Well, pal, I have to say that was one spectacular gift. That clinches it. You need a name."

He cocked his head and clicked his beak at her. Naomi sorted through her knowledge of ravens and Greek gods, but only came up with an association with Apollo. Maybe it was time to branch off into new territory. "Well, let's see. Odin, if I'm not mistaken, was often depicted with ravens on either shoulder. 'Odin' might be a good name – or 'Loki,' because I get the feeling you are definitely a trickster." That was it, she was sure of it. "'Loki' it is. Welcome to the family."

The newly-christened Loki croaked again, then launched into the deepening night, his wings making an almost musical creaking sound in the still forest. Naomi watched him go, then looked down at the dogs. Hades had curled up in the snow with Persephone tucked in the curve of his body, and both were dozing. "C'mon, you two. Time to call it a day."

She thought about Loki through her evening chores, wondered what else she'd learn about him as the days went on – what she wouldn't give for the chance to Google ravens – and wondered as well what his contact had been with humans, that he seemed so interested in her and willing to interact. She went in and wished Macy a goodnight, promising to put up the decorations she'd made in the morning, then curled up in bed with the dogs and Ares snuggled around her in their customary positions. Finally, as always, she called Piper.

Or at least, that was how she thought of it. Eyes closed, she breathed deeply, feeling her heart open and expand, seeking the connection that kept her going day after day. It was there, strong and steady tonight, her own personal ley line pointing straight at her daughter. Due north. Every time. Naomi concentrated, and with every bit of focus she possessed, sent love and encouragement through the connection, imagining her mother-love cloaking her girl in white light and protection. She smiled in the darkness. Layla's new-agey ways had definitely rubbed off on her a bit. After a few minutes, she relaxed the connection, though she never let it go altogether. Never.

"Soon," she whispered, as sleep took her into its deepening spiral. "Soon, Piper. I promise."

SIX
Piper: Walden, CO

"Soon," Piper murmured. "G'night, mom."

She tipped her head back and gazed up at the night sky, whispering the names of the constellations she'd been teaching herself. Star-gazing, she had learned, was best done on a moonless night, a minimum of 15 to 20 minutes after being around any light source, even a candle. That was the reason she gave Brody, anyway, for the long stretches of time she spent outside after the sun went down. It wasn't like she could tell him she came out here the better to visit with her mother.

In spite of the weirdness they'd all experienced, it still seemed impossible, but Piper was sure of what she was feeling, and of what she saw. Always, always, a green-pink-purple bond-line connected her to her mother, who was somewhere straight south of here. The cabin. Piper was sure. And almost daily now, she heard her mother's voice and felt her presence, usually late in the day after the sun had gone down. At those times, the line between them became so substantial, Piper had tried to reach out and touch it.

The possibility existed, of course, that she was nuts. But she'd rather embrace insanity than give up the comfort of her mother's daily presence. And what defined "sanity" anymore, anyway? It's not like any of them were stable. Not really. People adapted in twisted ways, performed whatever mental gymnastics they had to in order to keep on keepin' on.

The cabin door cracked open suddenly, polluting the night with light. Piper snapped her eyes shut, but not fast enough. Brody's low voice rumbled out. "It's time to come inside."

Piper opened her eyes. Sure enough, her vision had been compromised by just that brief flash. The constellations above her seemed dimmer, the Milky Way muted. She sighed softly and rose from her chair to walk inside, silent and obedient. Leave it to Brody to stifle the night sky, just like he stifled everything else.

He held the door for her, then swung it shut when she'd entered. They moved through the nighttime rituals with the silent efficiency of long habit, opening the blackout curtains when the hurricane lamps had all been extinguished, banking the fire for the night, double-checking that their clothes and weapons were at the ready, in case the night brought the unexpected.

Once in bed, Piper turned her head when Brody's hands slid under and around her, pulling her underneath him. She named the stars and constellations she could see through the window while his body moved against and inside hers: Orion, the hunter, with his two hunting dogs; Canis Major and Canis Minor; Sirius, the Dog Star; Gemini; and Pleiades, the Seven Sisters.

Brody's use of her finished, and she rolled on her side away from him, tucking into a ball and ignoring the sticky discomfort between her legs. Her eyes drooped immediately, and she had mere moments to marvel at how tuned she – a former, die-hard night owl – had become to the natural rhythms of night and day before sleep took her.

She woke in the gray pre-dawn to Brody's once-more-insistent hands, kept her eyes closed until he was finished, then rose to wash and dress. When she was ready for the day, she sat at the small table by the window and watched her birds, their movements a flickering oasis of joy to her. Her mother visited at night, but it was in these early-morning moments that she most missed her father. Her memories of him teaching her the names of the birds they both loved were worn as smooth as worry-stones, she took them out so often.

"Cedar Waxwing," she whispered. "Downy Woodpecker. Chickadee-dee-dee." God, Dad, I miss you so much.

"Time to go." They were the first words Brody had spoken to her since the night before, and his gravelly voice made her jump. She stood, accepted the daypack he handed her, and followed him out the door.

After breakfast, she took her turn at KP then headed for the clinic, where she spent her days with Ruth, continuing her lessons and gradually taking on more and more of the health-care duties of their group. The older woman just wasn't rallying like the others; she remained too thin, and the cough Piper's 'flu had left her with lingered on and on. Piper knew she should feel guilty about the harm she'd done to her only ally, but, well, she didn't. The place inside her that used to feel guilt seemed to no longer exist.

Ruth was dozing on one of the cots when Piper arrived, but she roused when Piper started rummaging around and setting out supplies, prepping the clinic for the day. The older woman yawned and stretched, then scrubbed her hands over her face. "Man, I just can't get caught up. Doesn't matter how long I sleep, I just feel wrung out."

Piper patted her shoulder sympathetically on her way to the supply cupboard. "Nothing big's going on. Maybe you should go back to your cabin, try to get some rest. You can teach me sutures another time."

"No, I'll be fine. It's not every day we have fresh pig's feet to work with."

"True," Piper agreed, but she had heard the longing in Ruth's voice. She would get her to at least lie down for an afternoon nap. "Before we start, though, how about a haircut?"

Ruth rose from the cot, darting a glance at the door. "Brody's out on patrol?"

"All day. I'll get the clippers."

They didn't discuss the circumstances; they never had. With the efficiency of long practice, Ruth ran the clippers swiftly over Piper's head. Tiny pieces of blonde hair fell to the floor and clung to the plastic Piper had wrapped around her shoulders, dusting her with gold. They performed this task an average of once a week, keeping Piper's hair less than an inch long, and no one – not even Brody – ever questioned why Piper's hair never grew. Piper didn't know if it was disinterest or male cluelessness, but either way she was grateful.

When Ruth finished, Piper carefully removed the plastic drape, then swept up every piece of hair and washed her face. Ruth had the clippers cleaned and put away by the time she was done; the whole ritual took less than ten minutes, and when it was over, Brody had one less weapon to use against her. A solid start to the day, Piper thought, as she collected suture supplies from the cupboard.

Tyler and Adam had returned from patrol the day before, hauling a pig carcass between them. The sow had apparently been someone's pet in the time before, because Tyler had walked right up to her and killed her. Neither he nor Adam volunteered any details on the actual kill; both of them had been covered with blood and their eyes had been a little wild. Piper knew only that they hadn't shot her – Brody had strict rules about discharging weapons: Only in defense of the camp, or if you were in mortal peril and needed help. In the latter case, he had drilled into them, you'd better be bleeding out or hanging from a cliff. Otherwise, you were expected to help yourself rather than call others into a dangerous situation.

So for a few days, they were enjoying fresh pork. Max had plans to smoke the belly for bacon, and Ruth had asked for the lower legs and feet so she could teach Piper to suture. So far, their group had been lucky, and injuries had been few. Other than the occasional abrasion and Piper's 'flu, only Jenny had suffered even a moderate injury, spraining her ankle. Piper had been disappointed when Ruth determined the bone wasn't broken. Learning to treat such an injury would have been interesting and useful.

Ruth lined up the pig's legs on the plastic-covered treatment table and began to create a series of wounds with various sharp implements: a scalpel, a serrated knife, the sharp edge of a tin can, and an arrowhead. Piper reached out and fingered the reddish mud still stuck to the animal's cloven hoof and had to swallow hard. Her mother's work with animal rescue groups had brought her into contact with a few potbelly pigs that were no longer tiny and cute enough for their owners; she could hear her mom's voice, talking about the misconceptions people had about pigs, about their intelligence and loyalty. Had this pig been frightened and lonely? Had she been relieved to find people, only to die in terror, wallowing in mud created by her own blood? Piper swallowed again, tasted tears, and looked up to find Ruth gazing at her.

"You gonna go all animal-rights-activist on me?"

"No." Piper blinked at the ceiling, fighting for control. What the hell was this, getting all teary over a pig? She had deliberately harmed the kind woman standing right in front of her and would do so again if it served her tactical plans. But mud on a pet pig's hooves made her weep? God, she was really not okay. "I don't know what my deal is. Just ignore me."

"Happily. Now, let's start on this simple laceration. Hand me the hemostats and I'll show you a few stitches. First, you should always start in the middle..."

Within the hour, Piper had mastered the process and was working on the more difficult lacerations Ruth had created: flaps of skin, wounds where chunks of flesh were missing, and puncture wounds. Ruth puttered around as Piper worked, muttering her way through an inventory list. In spite of their injury-free status, they were starting to run low on some basic supplies, and Ruth had been talking about sending the patrols into surrounding towns to scavenge for necessities. She set the clipboard down beside Piper, then went to get a stepladder, and Piper glanced at it curiously.

Acetaminophen and ibuprofen. She'd dispensed those like candy during her 'flu, so that made sense. Sterile saline in IV bags and any form of electrolyte replacement drink, whether for children or adults. Clearly, Ruth wanted to be prepared in the event of another illness. Piper squinted at the list, then blinked. Could she be reading that next word right?

Condoms? Really?

Piper straightened, her hands going still as she stared into space and processed all the implications of that single word. How could they be running low on condoms? Who was using them? Okay, probably Jenny and Aaron, though the thought made her cringe. She couldn't imagine Aaron doing anything but moping. Scratch that. She didn't want to imagine it. But who else?

She glanced up at Ruth, who was now rummaging in the top of their supply cupboard, still muttering to herself. Swiping her hands on the apron she wore and leaving a smear of pig's blood behind, she reached out to pull the clipboard a little closer, lifting the top paper to peek beneath. Ruth's neat handwriting marched down the page, listing the date, the supplies dispensed, and the person she'd dispensed them to. The ledger began just after they'd arrived here. Starting late last summer, there were regular notations of condoms being dispensed to Aaron. Ew.

Piper lifted the next page, and the next, scanning. She wasn't allowed to give out supplies, so this was a revelation. Almost all of the men had been in here asking for condoms at one point or another, and the pattern of those requests was fascinating. Aaron was the only regular; the other men were more sporadic. Josh, Ethan, Tyler, Adam and Levi had all made requests within days of each other early this past fall – what to make of that? Had they found a willing woman nearby, maybe in Walden? She flipped another page. With the exceptions of Josh and Levi, the requests hadn't been repeated. Then, just last week, Ethan had been in. Interesting.

She scanned the list over again, and frowned. There were only two men whose names didn't appear: Max, and Brody.

Brody.

It hit her then, like a kick in the chest, that condoms weren't just used to protect against STD's and AIDS.

Ruth cleared her throat, and Piper looked up to see the older woman glaring down at her from the top of her stepladder. "That's not exactly your business."

Piper found she couldn't reply. She returned the papers to their proper position and slid the clipboard back where it had been, but she didn't start stitching again. She could barely admit, even to herself, that until this very moment it had not occurred to her that Brody could get her pregnant. How could she not have considered this?

She was suddenly chilled. Was there something wrong with her, with her mind? Maybe she really was crazy.

Ruth climbed down and came to stand by her. "What is it?"

Piper looked up, reminded of the first day they'd worked together, when she'd had to decide to trust. Without speaking, she pointed at the word "condoms" on Ruth's list. She looked back up at Ruth, and her lips parted, but again, she couldn't speak.

Ruth's eyes narrowed. "You need some? I figured Brody had his own supply."

Piper shook her head and just gazed at her in wordless misery. How could she explain? She wasn't totally inexperienced and hadn't been a virgin when Brody raped her. She was humiliated to the core that something as basic as pregnancy had never even crossed her mind. She cleared her throat. "He doesn't... I mean, we don't use..."

Ruth's eyes widened. "Are you shitting me? You haven't been using any protection at all? If that isn't the dumbest thing I've ever heard, I don't know what." She stalked to the supply cupboard and returned with a plastic-sealed box, slapping it down beside Piper. "From what I heard, Brody was real clear on this. No pregnancies, no more mouths to feed, not until our situation stabilizes. I'd like to know what the story is. Does he think the rules don't apply to him?"

She gazed at Piper, clearly expecting an answer. Piper looked down at the box of condoms and whispered the honest truth. "I have no idea what he thinks."

She looked up at Ruth, and struggled to explain. "Ruth, I never even thought about it. I can't explain it. I..." She was gasping out the words, and suddenly found herself sitting in a chair Ruth had shoved under her knees. With brisk practicality, the older woman took the hemostats out of Piper's hand and set them on the treatment table. Then she knelt in front of Piper, every inch the experienced medic.

"Take a deep breath with me. Good. Another." Ruth's fingers wrapped around Piper's wrist, monitoring her pulse while her eyes probed. "You're pale and your skin is clammy. Your pulse is racing, your breathing is shallow, and you're having trouble forming words. What are these symptoms of?"

They had played this game for hours on end. Piper responded to the barked question automatically. "Emotional shock or acute stress response."

"Good. Treatment?"

Piper's head was clearing, and she was having trouble making eye contact with Ruth. Shame was closing over her head at both her naïveté and her dramatic response to it. "Hot cup of tea and a warm blanket." A sob hiccupped out of her. "And a smack upside the head for being an idiot."

Ruth's warm, strong hand coasted down the side of her face and landed on her shoulder to deliver a firm squeeze. "There's my sassy girl," she said softly. "Let me get those first two. Then you can tell me why you need the third."

Piper just sat and stared while Ruth wrapped a soft blanket around her shoulders, then left, presumably headed for the kitchen. She returned a few minutes later with a mug and put it in Piper's hands, wrapping the younger woman's hands around the warmth herself. Then she slid another chair to face Piper's and seated herself with a soft groan.

"Getting old sucks. I know you can't imagine it now, but one day, every bone you've got will ache, and you'll remember me saying that." Piper lifted her eyes, and Ruth smiled wryly. "Maybe you can imagine. Now. Tell me, and don't you look down. Unless you murdered Mother Teresa with your own two hands and ate her brain with fava beans and a nice chianti, you've got nothing to be ashamed of. I did admire that woman."

Piper's lips twitched. "I'm pretty sure it was the liver. The quote. Hannibal Lecter." Words were coming now, though they weren't necessarily making sense, even to her. "Ruth, I don't think I can talk about this."

"Spit it out and we'll move on. I don't want whatever it is to blindside you again. Besides, there's the matter of birth control to discuss. Let's start with this — are you pregnant right now?"

"No." She had just finished her cycle. Now that she was thinking about all of this, how the hell had the sanitary supplies gotten into their cabin bathroom? She should have had to request them, but never had. They were just there when she needed them. Nor did Brody attempt to have intercourse with her when she was menstruating. The realization of how closely he still watched her made her shudder and clutch the blanket around her shoulders. "Holy shit, Ruth, I can't believe how stupid I've been."

"Stupid, maybe. Lucky, for sure." She paused, then glanced over her shoulder and lowered her voice. "The situation between you and Brody. I assumed it had become consensual. That things had changed, and you'd reached an understanding. Is that right?"

"No." The word grated out of her. "Not consensual."

Ruth's lips tightened. She stared at Piper for long moments, then heaved a sigh that seemed to come from her toes. "I won't insult your intelligence by asking why. If there was a way out, you'd have found it, brilliant as you are."

Piper's breath caught. "You could help me," she whispered. "All of you. If all of you helped me, we could make him leave, or at least make him leave me alone." Her words started picking up speed and her voice rose on a current of soaring hope. "They'd believe me, if you backed me up. It wouldn't just be my word against his. We could tell them what he has been doing to me, and they would help, I'm just sure of it. Please," she begged, and didn't care that she was. "Help me tell them. Please."

It was a moment she would remember for the rest of her life. The desperate, wild, winging hope. The way Ruth's eyes dropped, the troubled frown that wrinkled her forehead. Piper would come to think of it as the moment she lost her grip on the last vestige of what was innately good in her being, the best of herself, a state of grace she would struggle all her remaining days to recover.

Ruth stood up and turned away, moving things around only to replace them the way they'd been. She turned back to Piper, tried to meet her eyes, and failed. For long moments, she stared at the floor between them. Then, she spoke two words: "They know."

Oh. The room swam and spun around her. "All of them? Everything? How?"

Still, Ruth couldn't look at her. "Brody spoke to the group, not long after the beginning of your arrangement. That's what he called it: an arrangement. He said you didn't bring any valuable skills to the group, that he'd chosen a way for you to earn your keep. He said you were having trouble accepting it, but if any of us interfered, we'd be out of the group." Her eyes flickered up, a brief flash of guilt before they dropped again. "The only person who could have stood up to him was Levi. And, well. You know."

She did know. Levi's hatred had been the final nail in her coffin. Brody had planned this, from the first moment he decided he wanted her to this very moment, and his execution of that plan had been flawless. She closed her eyes, and would never be able to speak of what happened inside her heart at that moment: a shattering. A solidification. A path chosen.

She looked up at Ruth through eyes that burned. How she hated them, all of them, from this kind and cantankerous woman standing in front of her, right down to sweet, young Caden. She stood so abruptly she knocked the chair over and dropped the mug on the floor. It shattered, spraying hot tea over her lower legs, which she barely felt. Stepping over the shards, she headed for the door.

"I need some time." She paused, then whirled back and grabbed the box of condoms Ruth had left on the treatment table. "I don't know when I'll be back."

"Piper. Hon." Ruth's voice was layered with emotions: regret, apology, and sorrow. "Please don't do anything stupid. Just take some time to calm down. Watch your birds. Do whatever you need to do, but get a grip. You're a valuable member of this group, and people care about you."

"Really?" Piper spun and hissed the word from the door. Her skin felt incandescent, her eyes like orbs of fire. "You're going to try to feed me that? Well, you know what, Ruth?" She smiled a terrible smile. "Fuck you. Fuck all of you."

She left the clinic, blind and deaf to anything but the thoughts shrieking like harpies inside her head. Slamming through an outside door, the cold brought her up short. She stood for a moment, panting, and forced herself to think. If there was one thing she'd learned at great cost during this past year, it was to always, *always*, think before she spoke or acted. Pure reaction was a luxury she could never afford.

She needed outdoor gear. She needed a safe place, and some time. She needed to get her thoughts ordered and her emotions under control. Ruth had been right about that, at least.

Still clutching the box of condoms, she jogged to the cabin she shared with Brody. Her heavy winter coat was still at the clinic, but she could layer on a sweatshirt and a lighter coat. She did so, and after long consideration, she stuffed the box of condoms into her coat pocket. If she left it here, she was certain it would disappear as mysteriously as her feminine supplies had showed up, without a word of discussion. She paused, considering, then slipped out.

She hadn't been inside the cabin she and Noah had shared since his death. The door was unlocked, and she slipped inside, inhaling cold, stale air. All of his things were still here, just as he'd left them so many months ago, though they were dust-free. His body had been buried beside his father's, but this place had been preserved as a shrine.

By Jenny, no doubt. The loss of her brother, so soon after two of her children and her father, had left the woman a fragile wisp. She drifted around the edges of the group, clutching at her only living child and shadowed by her ever-despondent husband, insubstantial as a ghost, worthless in the day-to-day workings of their group. But did she get accused of being dead weight, of lacking "valuable skills?" Piper's jaw clenched, and the harpies started up again.

She sat down at the table and took one deep breath after another. All this time, a part of her had clung to the belief that eventually, when she'd gained enough status, she would be able to speak up and free herself. She had used her knowledge of people and social dynamics to plot her course; when she had gained enough social value, her voice would be set free. She could reveal the injustice she was suffering, and she would be heard. Heard and helped. With that always in mind, she had carefully nurtured relationships and had worked her ass off without a single word of complaint.

To find out that every member of the group had known, all along, that she was being held against her will and repeatedly raped was like having the keys to her prison ripped right out of her hand. She dropped her head onto her crossed arms. She had been the most pathetic of fools. How many times had her mind whispered that they knew, they must know? How many times had she convinced herself otherwise, because to believe it was not bearable?

Well. It was bearable. She had just found that out, hadn't she?

Methodically, she thought about every member of the group, reconciling herself to the truth: Adam knew. Tyler knew. Max knew. All of them, and not a word in her defense, not a single offer of help, not one. When she was finished, her last hopes lay shriveled behind her, but the path ahead was clear and uncluttered by any sort of obligation.

It was time for some changes.

She stayed in the cabin until lunchtime, watching her birds and getting her center still and quiet. She'd been playing a calculated role all along, but she needed to step it up a notch. That required control, and she couldn't be in control when she was angry, frightened, or hurt. By the time the bell sounded for the noon meal, she was ready.

She sought out Ruth first, murmuring a soft apology for her outburst, accepting the older woman's brisk hug. Ruth didn't return the request for pardon, but why would she? In her mind, Piper's situation was justified. In all their minds. Piper swallowed hard, pictured her birds, and felt her heartbeat slow once more.

Except for Brody and Josh, who were out on patrol, all of the men were in the mess hall for lunch. Piper pretended to eat, pushing her food around and watching, until Ethan rose with his tray and headed for the kitchen. She followed him, hoping no one else would follow, grateful when no one did. In the kitchen, she waited quietly while he took care of his dishes, then spoke just as he was turning to leave.

"Ethan, wait. I wonder, do you ever see Elise?" There – the startled jerk of his head, the way his eyes darted to hers and narrowed, and most telling of all, the flaring arc of a bright white bond-line, pointing to the southwest. Only between Ethan and Elise had she ever seen a line like it. She widened her own eyes slightly, innocent and guileless. "It's just that I worry about them, and wonder how they're doing, her and the kids. Sam and Becca. They made me think of my little sister." Not true – those two young predators couldn't be more different than her sweet Macy –but none of this was true. "I know you guys patrol in Walden. I just wondered if you'd seen her."

"I, ah..." Bright flags of color flew on Ethan's cheekbones. He looked down, scuffed his boot on the floor, and cleared his throat. God, he couldn't possibly be more obvious. "I've seen her. She's good. Fine, I mean. Her and the kids."

"I wish they could have stayed here." Wistful, with just a touch of longing. "It would be good for Jenny and Caden, I bet. Another woman, some kids." She bit her lip to hide an inappropriate grin; that last had been a stroke of genius. Tender-hearted Ethan, like Max, fretted over

Jenny, Aaron and their son. "Anyway. If you see them, please tell them I said 'hello.'"

"Will do."

Piper took care of her own dishes while he left the kitchen. She needed genuine allies. Step one towards that goal had been taken.

She spent the afternoon working on her suturing techniques under Ruth's watchful eyes. Then, while Ruth took a nap on one of the cots, she memorized the list of requests for supplies, speculating as to what those requests might imply and making mental notes for future reference. Just as she had guessed, Brody made regular requests for feminine sanitary supplies. Jenny and Aaron were both on anti-depressants, which didn't surprise her; so were Tyler and Adam, which did. Max took painkillers – for his back, she guessed, which he had injured in Afghanistan. And lookee there. Ethan had come in while she'd been out this morning, asking for more condoms. Looked like he was seeing Elise even more frequently than Piper had guessed. When she finished, she flipped through the confidential medical files, memorizing allergies and drug intolerances, anything that might be of use someday.

Piper let Ruth sleep until the dinner bell sounded, then shook her awake and headed to the mess hall alone, leaving the older woman to stretch and groan. As she approached the doors, her heart sped up; what she was about to attempt could backfire, ruining the months of work she'd done to gain a sympathetic position in the group. It could also tip her hand to Brody. Either possibility sent chills of fear dancing down her spine and arms. She paused just outside to take deep, calming breaths and remind herself that she'd been performing without a net all along – the only difference was she knew it now.

However, it was still in her best interests to keep Brody in the dark. She took one last steadying breath, opened the mess hall door, and stepped onto the tightrope. Except for Ruth, everyone had already gathered. She felt Brody's eyes on her and turned, meeting his gaze and nodding, just as she always did. Habits and patterns. She'd been using them for months now, to stay safe.

"No net," she murmured to herself, and abandoned both.

She stepped into the mess line, close behind Josh. It was something she never would have done before today, and he glanced back at her, startled by her proximity. She murmured an apology, letting her eyes linger just a little too long. As the line crept forward, she crowded his personal space over and over, always apologetic, always letting her eyes lift and hold his, stroking him with interest, admiration, and just a hint of desire. Not too fast, she admonished herself. This was just step one. No need to rush things.

Josh, however, had other ideas. They reached the end of the line, and instead of moving to take a seat, he deliberately stepped right in front of her. His bold move caught her off guard, and she stumbled, almost dumping her tray. Josh's hand closed around her upper arm, but instead of steadying her, he pulled her even closer. Piper looked up, not needing to pretend to be startled. He smiled down at her, the expression so obviously intimate, Piper felt her face flush. My god. He was either fearless or stupid.

"Watch yourself," he murmured. His eyes flicked down her body before returning to her face. "I certainly am."

Okay. He was both.

He let her go and headed for a seat. Piper could feel Brody's eyes drilling into the back of her head like nails. This was escalating much faster than she'd planned, but she could adapt. She turned towards Brody but kept her eyes down, rubbing her arm and letting the tiniest, pained grimace touch her features. There. That ought to do it.

Ruth was at the end of the line, and rather than taking a seat, Piper joined her, chatting as she moved through the line a second time. Behind Brody's back, she snuck repeated glances at Josh and found him watching her every time. If she sensed the eyes of others, she let hers drop immediately. If she didn't, she resumed the lingering admiration. By the end of the meal, Josh's face was flushed, and his jaw was slack. What an over-sexed baboon. This was too easy.

It was customary for people to linger after dinner, playing cards or board games in small groups. Sometimes, Levi brought out his guitar and sang, accompanied by his sister. Their voices were beautiful, but their eyes were sad; sometimes, you could hear where a third voice should have completed the harmony. Noah had often spoken of singing with his siblings. Good memories, he always said. Wherever he was, Piper hoped he couldn't see what she was about to do.

She walked to where Brody was already playing poker with several other men, including Josh. "I've got a headache," she murmured, loud enough for all of them to hear. "I'm going to head to the cabin. Is that okay?"

When she looked up, her heart stuttered. His eyes were sharp, too sharp, and there was something in them she couldn't identify. It took him forever to nod. "That's fine."

"Thank you."

She turned and left without looking at anyone else, though she could feel Josh's eyes running over her like hands. She paused to say good night to Ruth and Max, who were playing Parcheesi with Caden, and dawdled into her coat, giving the situation time to ripen. Finally, she judged the time was right to leave.

The night was brittle with cold when she stepped outside, tightening her lungs and making her cough. Piper flipped her hood up and dug her hands deep into her pockets, though she didn't zip her coat. She moved to stand just inside the tree line and started counting, murmuring the numbers on soft puffs of frozen air. If Josh didn't show in two minutes, she really would head to the cabin. She could always pick the gambit up again tomorrow. He was proving surprisingly susceptible to her tactics.

At a minute and a half, the mess hall door opened, then closed, and she heard Josh cough. Her heart picked up speed. This was where it got tricky. She had to play this just right.

Piper stepped into the open. "Who's there? Brody, is that you?"

Josh strode towards her, light from the half-moon revealing a face that was tight with lust. "You know it's not." He had her pinned to a tree before she could reply, and his wet mouth crunched down on hers. Piper tasted blood, and managed to turn her head to the side. She let his mouth slide down her throat, opening her coat to his hands while he groaned against her skin. "You been coming on to me all night. I knew you'd be waiting for me."

Piper let her body reply, moving against him suggestively, making soft, whimpering sounds. It took an amazingly short time to work him into a frantic lather, his body grinding against hers, his groans getting louder and louder. When she had him on the very knife's edge, she brought her hands up between them and shoved as hard as she could. "No!"

The force of her movement sent her sprawling in the snow. Josh stared at her, slack-faced for a moment, then reached down to haul her to her feet, banding his arms around her again. "The fuck you say, Piper. This isn't high school." He hunched over her, bending her backwards painfully. "Brody won't find out. Just relax."

She squirmed against him strategically, whimpering, and he groaned again. He released her, only to reach up and fist his hands in the front of her shirt, parting it with several hard jerks. Perfect – she'd been about to do that herself. Just one more item on the to-do list, and she could take this to the next stage.

Again, she let him grope and grind and pant himself into desperation. Then, she shoved again. This time, though, she stayed on her feet. She lifted her chin, and made no attempt to cover her proud, naked breasts against the cold. As he had done with her, she let her eyes feel their way down his body, lingering on his crotch. She cocked her head to the side, considering, then she laughed with soft disdain and shook her head.

"Know what, Josh? I've just decided it's not worth it." It took forever for what she was saying to sink through his lust. She waited until his face finally went stiff with shock. Rage and arousal blended on his features, rendering him truly ugly. She took a step back, bracing her weight, preparing. "So, thanks but no thanks. I'll see you aroun –"

She didn't get to finish the word before he caught her with a full-arm-swinging, open-handed blow. Her lip split and her nose crunched, but she kept her wits – she had Brody to thank for that skill – and used the momentum to spin away. He advanced on her, spraying spit and obscenities in his rage.

"You god-damned cock tease, you sure as fuck are not going to pull this shit. You been begging for it, and you are fucking going to get it."

Piper danced backwards, deflected a second and third slap, and kept him drooling with careless flashes of bare breasts and taunting words. "C'mon, Josh, you've been turned down before. Oh, that's right. *I've* turned you down before. Guess it just goes to show you should always stick with your first impulse."

She could not allow him to start thinking, couldn't let him sidestep the trap she was just about to close around him. He grabbed at her wrist and she barely broke free. Christ, he was fast. She spun again, found her back against the mess hall door, and paused just long enough to flash him a grin with bloody teeth. "Show time, asshole."

She shoved the door open and let herself sprawl on the floor. Josh stumbled in after her, and she couldn't avoid the kick he aimed at her midsection, barely managing to turn so she took the blow on her hip. She scrambled backwards as fast as she could, no longer faking her fear – he could seriously injure her before anyone intervened – and let the barriers she'd been maintaining around her emotions, month after month, drop. Opening this well was a risk – she might never get the cover back on – but her performance had to convince every person in this room, especially those with heightened intuition. Most especially, Brody.

Piper thought about all of these men and women looking the other way while she was forced to endure abuse and rape. She thought of Noah, of a sweet and intelligent young man snuffed out by the calculations of a monster. She thought of her mother and father, of little Macy, the longing for them that made her very bones ache. Were they okay? Did they think she was dead? Finally, she thought of red mud on a pig's hooves, about a pet that had been killed not by Tyler's knife, but by trust, and the kindness shown to her by humans in a softer time. The cry that broke out of her chest was more wounded animal than human, as the emotions she'd conjured ripped free of her control. The sound brought every person in the mess hall to their feet.

She kept crawling, and let it all surge out of her: the pain for the people she'd lost, the hurt that was equal parts emotional and physical, the agony of betrayal by people she worked and lived with. Sobbing, she scrambled to avoid another kick from Josh. "Help me," she gasped. "Please, help me, make him stop, help me help me…"

Sound and motion erupted around her, cacophony and kaleidoscope. Ruth's arms were the first thing she separated from the morass; strong and warm, they closed around her, protecting and anchoring her. Piper burrowed as close as she could get, shuddering. She fisted her hands in the front of Ruth's sweatshirt and let grief roll out of her in wave after wave.

She was vaguely aware of Josh bellowing, but she knew he wouldn't be believed. Even if she hadn't stacked this deck perfectly, his reputation as an arrogant, self-important blowhard would have cast doubt on his claims of innocence. Piper could huddle here in Ruth's sheltering arms, luxuriating in her grief storm, and know that the situation would resolve to her satisfaction. Josh had put his hands on Brody's woman, and she had made sure everyone in the group knew it. If Brody wanted to maintain his status, there was only one course he could take.

It surprised her when Ruth's arms parted and other hands grasped her elbows. Brody lifted her to her feet before she had a chance to wipe her face clean of tears, blood and snot. She heard Ruth huffing indignantly as she struggled to her feet beside them. The older woman shoved Brody's hands to the side, and turned Piper by the shoulders to face her. Briskly, she pulled the edges of Piper's shirt together, then zipped her coat for her.

"Christ on a crutch, at least keep her from catching her death," she muttered. She snapped her fingers to the side, and Max put a dish towel in her hand. With gentle, slow strokes, she cleaned Piper's face, examining her injuries. "Your pretty nose is bruised, but I don't think it's broken." She touched Piper's mangled lower lip, winced in sympathy, then commanded. "Open your mouth. Good. Any teeth loose? No?"

Brody stepped close, angling his body between Piper and Ruth. "That's enough. She's fine."

Piper barely stifled a hysterical giggle at that. Sure, she was fine, and he ought to know. He'd dished out much, much worse, and she had recovered. She gazed up at him, allowing the tears to continue welling and overflowing – oh, the relief of tears, the sheer relief of them – and gave him the words she knew he was expecting: "I'm sorry."

Sharp, sharp eyes, again with that something she couldn't identify. He stayed like that for what felt like an eternity, gazing into her eyes while he held her upper arms – not ungently – in his big hands. To the others, it must have looked like he was offering comfort in his cool, reserved way. Piper, however, knew when she was being measured. She closed her eyes and let herself remember, let herself *feel* the shock of that first rape, the rage, the horror, the disbelief. When she opened her eyes to his again, it was there for him to see, all of it. Just as long as he thought those feelings were attached to Josh, she was home free.

Finally, he released her, and she looked around. Adam and Tyler were holding Josh over by the door, rough hands twisting the struggling man's arms cruelly. Ethan stood close by, ready to help. All three of them were bristling with outraged aggression, and their eyes dropped respectfully when hers touched theirs. Max was beside Ruth, both of them wearing identical expressions of angry concern. Jenny, Aaron and Caden were gone. No doubt, the parents had decided their son had seen enough drama and bare breasts for one evening. Piper stifled another giggle and curled her hands into fists, digging her nails into her palms. Okay, it was time to get a grip now.

Levi stood alone, his expression neutral. When Piper's eyes met his, he kept his face still, hiding whatever he might be feeling behind an impassive façade, though he clearly wasn't overcome by concern for her. Piper let her eyes coast right on by, and returned her eyes to Brody.

"Please. Make him leave." Her voice hitched pitifully as she made her request, but she made sure every person there heard it. "Make him leave and never come back. Please?"

Brody's face tightened. He looked over at Adam and Tyler, and jerked his chin at the door. They obeyed, hauling Josh between them with Ethan close behind. Piper felt a flood of relief – she'd done it, she'd actually pulled this off – but it was short-lived.

Brody took Piper's arm and steered her towards the door. Max and Ruth fell into step behind them, with Levi bringing up the rear. She didn't understand the expressions on any of their faces: grim resignation, dread, anger. What was happening? She didn't need to be a part of escorting Josh from the compound. Bond-lines were flaring and fading all around her, so fast she couldn't understand what she was seeing.

Outside, Adam and Tyler were holding Josh on his knees. The captive man renewed his struggles when they emerged, and started talking in a fast, high-pitched voice that didn't sound anything like him. "Please, Brody, no. I'll go. I swear to God I won't come back – don't do this! I swear she started it! She set me up, I swear it on the Bible, man, please!" He was sobbing now. "Please! Don't!"

Without explanation or ceremony, Brody drew a pistol and walked straight up to Josh, pressing the barrel of it against his head. Josh screamed, his words dissolving into incoherent sobs interspersed with the occasional "Please." The sudden sharp stink of urine filled the air, and the front of his camouflage pants started to steam in the frigid cold.

Piper sagged against Ruth, struggling to overcome her shock. She had not anticipated this. They were brothers-in-arms. Josh's exile had been her goal, making room for Elise and her children while simultaneously relieving her of his odious presence. She had gloated over the prospect of him being cut loose with nothing but the clothes on his back. But this...this was execution. Her eyes darted around, and her shock deepened. Every person here was accepting this.

Then, the unthinkable happened.

Brody turned and looked straight at her. He lowered the pistol, then held it out to her butt first, his eyes locked on hers. "This is Piper's kill."

Piper's knees wobbled, and she clutched at Ruth's supporting arms. Max stepped up to help, wrapping an arm around her waist, and her eyes locked on his kind face. He met her gaze with calm implacability. "He's a danger to the group. It has to be done." His warm eyes were cold as they held hers. "And Brody is right. It's your kill, and you should take it."

Her eyes snapped to Ruth, but she found the same cold practicality there. The speed with which this was happening had her reeling. She couldn't think.

Piper. Her mother's voice. *No. This is wrong. Undo it.*

Then, she looked at the man she had condemned, at his piteous face.

"Piper," he gasped, "Piper, please, tell them the truth – it was just a misunderstanding! I'm sorry I hurt you, I never should have touched you – please don't let them kill me! You know what happened!" His face contorted and he changed tactics. "You fucking bitch! You tell them the god-damned truth! You tell them how you were waiting for me, how you rubbed all over me! Tell them, or I will hunt you down and make you beg to die, you worthless piece of –"

Piper's spine straightened. She strode to where Brody stood, took the pistol from him, and without hesitation, shot Josh between the eyes.

"Sorry, Mom," she whispered. But she wasn't.

SEVEN
Jack: Woodland Park, CO

"Jack, this is Martin, come in."

Jack's pen skittered across the piece of paper he'd been working on – a list of urgent "Rowan Requests" – and he turned to glare at the offending two-way radio. How he missed the pop-music ringtones he'd programmed his cell phone with. He'd take vintage Michael Jackson over that squawking, popping, hissing radio any day. He set his list aside, picked up the radio and braced himself for the trouble that always came with such a summons.

"Martin, this is Jack, go ahead."

"Jack, I'm at location India, and we have a situation here that requires your expertise. Over."

Jack frowned, and swung to look at the map pinned to his office wall. Though Martin didn't insist on the use of call-signs on the two-way, he had strict rules when it came to identifying locations by name on the open air. The last thing they needed, he said, was for other people to know where there was trouble. Jack agreed with the precaution, so they all carried maps of the area with locations of common or strategic interest identified in military alphabet code. Codes for the most often-used locales were rotated. This week, the church was location November.

Jack squinted at the map. The library? He keyed his radio. "Martin, say again. Over."

"Jack, you're needed at location India." There was a loud booming noise, a pause, and when Martin's voice returned, there was an edge to it that made the hair on Jack's neck rise. "Sooner rather than later, preacher man. Out."

Jack pulled his coat on as he jogged down the hallway, stuffing his radio in his pocket and retrieving the keys to the ATV that was waiting outside. It was unusual for Martin to call him in – when he needed finesse, he usually called Layla. Jack started the ATV and zoomed away from the church, only vaguely aware of the beauty of a rare, unseasonably warm February day around him. Martin's use of the words "preacher man" hadn't been lost on him, either – an epithet Martin only used when he was under duress. Whatever this was, it was serious. Jack's heart rate accelerated steadily as he approached the library's location.

A cluster of people were huddled together behind the old Grandmother's Kitchen restaurant. Recognizing Martin among them, Jack pulled up and shut off the engine. Martin approached, his face equal parts grim and exasperated.

"Well, I hardly know where to start. It looks like we have another refugee from Colorado Springs, but I'm pretty sure she's looney-tunes."

Martin lifted his hand towards a man and a woman who were both holding rifles, waving them over.

Jack frowned when he recognized them – Andrea and Paul – and his brain clicked through the duty roster. "Who's at the sentry post if they're here?"

"I left Thomas there, and we'll send these two back as soon as they've told you what they heard. This woman didn't make much sense, so I wanted both of them to report." Martin nodded at Andrea. "Tell him what she said, everything you can remember. Maybe it will mean something to him."

Andrea looked up, concentrating, remembering. "Well, she came roaring up to the roadblock on her motorcycle –"

"Dirt bike," Paul interrupted. "Honda CRF 230." He returned Andrea's glare. "What?"

Andrea gave an irritated huff before she went on. "She came roaring up on her *dirt bike*, and I didn't think she was going to stop. I was off to the side. She saw Paul first, and I thought she was going to run him down. I stepped in beside him, and she slowed down, then stopped. She didn't shut the bike off, though – she sat on it and talked to us."

"She was armed." Paul broke in again. "Combat shotgun. A Benelli M1014. I'm sure of it."

"What does it matter what kind of gun it was Paul? Do you want to tell this?"

Martin answered Andrea's question before Paul could bluster up. "It matters because that's a top-of-the-line military issue weapon. Marines or special forces."

Jack spoke, directing his soothing tones to Andrea, who was so jumped up on adrenalin she was about to swat

Paul, if he was reading the situation accurately. "Did she identify herself as military?"

"No. That's the thing." Andrea's forehead wrinkled. "She said she was from Tara, and that her name was Scarlett. She spoke in this syrupy southern accent, and kept saying –" She glanced at Paul. "What was it?"

Paul's face warmed to a rosy pink. "Fiddle-dee-dee."

"Yeah, that was it. She said she'd made it past the damn Yankees, and then she shook her fist in the air and yelled, 'As God is my witness, I'll never go hungry again!'"

Jack and Martin exchanged a glance, and Martin's mouth turned down. "It gets worse. Please go on, Andrea."

"Well, she said she needed to get to the library. The accent came and went; sometimes she sounded British. She said she needed information from the 'restricted section,' that the chamber had been opened, and she thought she knew what to do about it." Andrea looked down and swallowed hard. "My daughter used to love Harry Potter. What she said – it sounded just like something the Hermione Granger character would say. We told her we had to clear all newcomers with Martin, and called him"

"That was when it got really weird." Paul couldn't hold back any longer. He glanced sideways at Andrea, who made an exaggerated gesture, inviting him to continue. Paul paused long enough to sneer at her – honestly, were they siblings? They acted like squabbling children – before he went on. "This whole time, she mostly ignored me. She'd glance over every now and then, but she would look at my rifle, not at my face. She didn't like it. She was afraid of it, and of me. I could *feel* that."

Jack nodded. Like him, Paul picked up on the emotions of others. "Go on."

"Well, when Martin arrived, she took one look at him and she...changed. It was like I *felt* her become a different person. I'd been trying to get a handle on her since she rode up – some people are harder to read than others – but this was so drastic. What she *believed* changed." Paul shook his head. "It's really hard to explain. But when she saw Martin, her face got really hard and mean. She yelled something about him being a 'Big Bad' and gunned her bike past us. We followed her, but when we got here, she'd already booted everybody out of the library. Judy – what did she say?"

Judy, an older woman who had been standing off to the side, stepped up. She had been an accountant in the time before and was now doing her best to keep the library organized. "She said her name was Buffy Summers and she wanted to know if her Scooby Gang had arrived yet. When we asked what she was talking about, she started shouting for us all to leave. I hustled the kids out as fast as I could."

"She thinks she's Buffy. You know – the Vampire Slayer?" Karleigh stepped into the growing circle, flanked by James and Ben, with Viola bringing up the rear. "It was, like, my favorite show. She thinks Martin is a vampire, or a demon or something."

Jack frowned. "What are you all doing here?"

"Miss Layla asked us to work in the library today. We're helping Judy with a card catalog, for the books. She had something going on, I guess. The littles are working in the greenhouse with Carla."

Jack looked at Martin. "Has anyone tried to reach her? So far, we've got two literary characters and a pop-culture icon. This is right up Layla's alley."

Martin's eyes evaded his. "We've tried. She's not answering."

Jack's eyes narrowed, and his stomach went tight; whatever was going on with Layla, Martin knew about it, but he didn't want to tell Jack. He shoved it to the side – time enough to deal with whatever it was when he didn't have an obviously imbalanced stranger on his hands. "Where is this woman now?"

"Barricaded inside the library. She took three shots at me before she made it inside, but she aimed high, and I don't think she wants to use her weapon in there. Judy said she saw me through the glass, and she raised her weapon, but then looked around and lowered it again."

Jack looked at the library, a beautiful building, with its wood and stone façade and soaring glass windows. "She knew right where to go. Bet she was a librarian before, either in the Springs or somewhere else nearby. She wouldn't want to damage the building or the books." He looked around at the circle of faces. "She didn't shoot at or threaten anybody but Martin?"

Heads shook all around, and Jack decided there was no time like the present. "All right. Judy, you and the kids go home – this could take a while. And if it doesn't sound too ridiculous to say, I'd appreciate it if you'd cover me, Martin."

Without waiting for agreement or discussion, he stepped into the open. He spread his arms wide, and started walking slowly towards the front doors. "Hello? I'm not armed. I just want to talk to you."

He doubted the woman could hear him through the glass, but he was more interested in projecting his intent than in the actual words. If this woman, too, had changed, she might be able to *feel* his sincerity. He made it to the front doors without getting shot, and turned to look back at Grandmother's Kitchen. Martin's rifle was trained, rock-steady, on the front door. Jack gave him a thumbs-up, and walked through the doors.

"Hello?" His voice echoed in the soaring foyer. "My name is Jack. I'm one of the leaders here. I used to be a youth pastor, before." He didn't know if that would make her more or less hostile, but it felt right to say. "Can I help you with something? Are you a librarian? If you are, we could sure use your help. It's pretty hard to find things without computers these days."

"I used to be a librarian." A voice floated up from behind the circulation desk. As Jack watched, short silver hair appeared, then a pair of bright-blue eyes that were narrowed in suspicion. "Now I'm whoever I need to be. Boudica. Scout. Beatrice."

She rose to her feet, revealing a face that matched the eyes, set in lines of distrust. Her gaze flickered to the glass front of the building and her face hardened, just as Paul had described. Jack looked over his shoulder and saw that Martin was now standing in plain view, rifle held across his chest. He didn't have his weapon aimed at the building, but Jack knew how fast that could change.

"'O God, that I were a man. I would eat his heart in the market-place.'" Her hands were white on the shotgun, but she didn't point it at either Jack or the inexplicably hateful Martin.

"Uhm. Is that Shakespeare?" Her eyes flicked back to him, and she nodded, once. He gave her his best charming smile; boyish self-deprecation was usually effective with older women. "Well, that was a lucky guess. Literature wasn't my best subject."

Eyes that had seen much lasered in on him. "You can cut the schmooze. Religious men aren't my type, and even if they were, I wouldn't be interested in a puppy like you." Her gaze returned to Martin, and this time, she brought her shotgun up. "If that asshat doesn't stand down in ten seconds, I'm sending him back to hell."

"Hold on! Just hang on a second!" Jack stepped into her line of sight, hands up. "He's my friend, and he's a good man. I'll ask him to put down his weapon and step back, but he won't leave. We don't leave each other alone in tough situations. Not here."

It was as if he hadn't spoken. The woman stepped to the side and once more sighted in on Martin. "One. Two..."

Jack took a deep breath and threw his shields down, letting everything she was feeling buffet him. He needed to understand her, understand what was driving her hostility. He pressed his fingers to his temple and blinked hard and fast. Criminy, what a mess. It felt like he was in a room with ten overwrought people. But overriding the chaos was something that helped him understand –

pure hatred for what she believed Martin represented: The military.

Again, he stepped between her and Martin. "You had a bad experience with a military group in the Springs, is that right?" Her eyes returned to him, and he nodded encouragingly. "I don't know what you saw, but I can tell you that Martin isn't like them."

"He's a vampire," she hissed. "Oh, I'm sorry. Was that an offensive term? Should I say undead American?"

Where was Karleigh when he needed her? "Ma'am, I'm not sure I understand what you're saying, but I'm pretty clear on what you're *feeling*." He paused, watching her eyes narrow as she processed what he had said. "You *know* Martin used to be a Marine, and I *know* how that makes you feel. How about you put your shotgun down and we talk about that for a minute?"

Slowly, she did as he asked. "People here are psychic, too?"

Jack wished he could put his shields back up; keeping all of her emotional personas sorted out was exhausting. First things first, though. "We call it 'intuitive,' and yes. Not everyone, but a lot of people, some stronger than others, and in different ways. Our children, especially." He judged the moment to be right, and stepped to the side, gesturing to the still watchful Martin. "Martin can tell when people are lying. He helps us stay safe by letting us know whether people are trustworthy or not."

"Hmph." She sounded skeptical, but her shotgun stayed down, and her face no longer held a killing edge. "And how do you know *he's* on the up and up?"

Jack worked up a hearty chuckle, then let it drop when she eyeballed him. If his suspicions were correct... "Why don't you tell me? I have a feeling you're pretty good at reading people. That's the second time you've caught me being insincere, if I'm not mistaken."

Her lips twitched at the corners. "I was a public school librarian for 30 years. I've heard every version of 'The dog ate my library book!' there is, and then some." She shifted her gaze to Martin once more, and her eyes went unfocused. After a few moments, she blinked and set her shotgun down on the circulation desk. "Well. I see what you mean. He's not going to leave you in here alone much longer, so why don't you go tell him everything's peachy? He may not be a vampire, but jury's out on whether or not he's an asshat."

Jack's chuckle this time was genuine. He turned and walked to the door, stepping outside. "Martin, you're making her really tense. She's picked up on your military 'vibe' and I'm pretty sure she's seen something bad that she associates you with. How about you clear out of here for a while and leave someone else here to back me up?"

Martin frowned. "I don't like it. Will she let us search and disarm her?"

"Ah, here's the thing – I'm not even going to ask her. Not a chance." Jack lifted his hand to his eyes on the guise of shading them from the bright, mid-day sun. "Has anyone reached Layla yet? I could sure use her literary background. I think we've got about ten characters rotating around in here."

Again, Martin's eyes evaded. "She's on her way. Fifteen minutes or so." He looked at Jack, but kept his eyes unreadable. "Owen's bringing her in."

He should have known. Should have known right from the start, and still, it was a kick to the gut that left him without wind for a minute. Layla had taken the day off, which no one had seen fit to share with him, and she was spending that day with Owen.

"Good. That's fine. Good to know." What a steady tone he produced. Jack was inordinately proud of it. "When they get here, why don't you send Layla in and see if Owen will stand watch. In the meantime, it would help a lot if you would just step out of sight."

Martin nodded. "I'll be behind the restaurant."

Jack turned, but before he went back inside, he took a moment. A deep breath, another, some mental gymnastics, and he had his shields up and solid, as well as his feelings about Layla's blossoming love life shoved into the deepest crevice he could find.

The woman was sitting in a chair behind the circulation desk now, head resting in her hands. She looked up as Jack approached, and she looked so tired, so done-in, that Jack's heart twisted in empathy in spite of his shields. Without speaking, he dragged a chair up and sat down across from her, offering his hand in silence. She stared at his palm for a moment, then laid her hand in his, a surprisingly delicate hand that was hard with calluses and hidden strength. She pillowed her head on the crook of her other arm, clung to his hand, and wept.

He went to a still place, a peaceful place, and honored her grief with his silence and his presence. He didn't try to shush her or ease her pain. By the time the door behind him opened, her sobs had diminished to slow, hitching breaths. Layla pulled a chair up beside him and sat down. His nostrils flared, and before he could lock it down, violent jealousy sank long claws into his chest. Owen, on her skin, all over her skin, thick as over-done perfume.

Jack felt Layla's startled glance – yeah, she had to have picked up that emotional spike – and ignored it. That milk was spilled. He took a deep breath and concentrated on keeping the woman's hand cradled gently in his. "Ma'am, I'd like you to meet Layla. She's our teacher, and also a leader here."

The woman shifted her head to gaze at Layla, but didn't sit up. "There's a book of Revelation in everyone's life," she whispered. "And I've read mine this bitter night. I've kept vigil through storm and darkness."

Layla leaned across the table to gather the woman's other hand between her own. "So have we all. 'Weeping may endure for a night but joy cometh in the morning.'" She smiled. "Shall I call you 'Anne?'"

The woman sniffled and nodded. "Anne spelt with an 'e.'" She sat up. "When we've become kindred spirits, you may call me 'Cordelia.'"

"I'll look forward to it. It's good to meet another literature lover. I used to teach English and drama at the high school." She smiled wryly. "Now I teach all ages, everything."

The woman surprised them with a gritty chuckle. "At least you won't have to worry about the standardized tests this year. There is that."

"True." She glanced at Jack, silently asking his permission to take the lead. He nodded, and her eyes returned to "Anne." "Martin says you've come to us from Colorado Springs? Is that right?"

"It is." Her gaze turned to the soaring windows, but she wasn't seeing the spectacular view, Jack was sure. Her brilliant blue eyes dimmed, and her shoulders hunched.

When she didn't volunteer more, Layla gave her hand a soft stroke. "I can feel that it's hard to talk about, but can you tell us about the situation there? We've only had one other person make it here from the Springs, and that was last summer. We have no idea what's going on."

"Anne" nodded, but had to swallow several times before she could start talking. "It's bad," she finally said. "I started out in the refugee camp on Fort Carson with my...with my..." Tears flooded, and she turned her head to glare at Jack. "Why did God let me live through this? Do you have an answer for that, mister youth pastor?"

"I don't. I've asked myself the same question. All of us have."

"Huh. Well, at least you're honest." She closed her eyes and firmed her mouth, then spoke in a rush. "I was in the camp with my son and grandson. My daughter-in-law died of the plague, but the three of us survived. We stayed, even when the food ran so low they were only feeding us once a day. There were riots. My son – he died –" The word cracked out of her, a whip of pain. "He died trying to protect my little grandson. People rushed the food wagon, and they were crushed." She looked down at her hands. "I buried them where they fell. So many dead, and no one would help. So I put my grandson in my son's arms, and I wrapped them both in a blanket, and I held them one last time before I gave them back to the Earth."

"Anne" rocked as she spoke, arms clamped around herself, clutching at the meager comfort of her own embrace. Layla went around behind the desk and slid an arm around her shoulders. The woman shifted to grip Layla's forearm with her small, graceful, strong hands. "I left after that. Most people did. There was no reason to stay – they were out of food. Some of us had heard about a group that started out camped in Memorial Park, then moved to take over the Colorado College campus and part of the Old North End. You know, those mansions up on Wood Avenue, along Monument Creek. When we got there, it was worse than Fort Carson. A lot worse."

She shuddered. "There was more food to eat, but the things they did. The men in charge were monsters, there's no other word for them. Vampires." Her angry hiss made the hair on the back of Jack's neck rise. "They used fear to keep people in line. Raped women and young girls, every night, where everyone could see. Killed people – publically executed them – if they spoke out or protested. When I got there, people were just keeping their heads down and their mouths shut."

Jack stood and silently scooted a chair under Layla's legs. She murmured her thanks, not taking her eyes off "Anne." "What made you leave?"

The woman's spine straightened and lifted, and a queen appeared suddenly before them. "I may have regrets," she said, and though her voice was quiet, it thrummed with power. "I may have wished for death, but when I finally meet Hippolyta in the afterlife, when I can beg her forgiveness for the hunting accident that took her life, I must be able to tell her I died honorably, in battle." Pride made her face beautiful. "I couldn't take their food and enjoy their protection, not while others paid the price. I decided I would rather starve with honor than live like that."

Layla smiled. "We welcome you, Penthesilea. Your sister will welcome and forgive you, I'm sure of it. In the meantime, your strength and your wisdom are much needed here."

Jack was getting dizzy, but he managed a warm smile. "I don't suppose you have a name us non-literary folks can pronounce?"

The woman glanced at him disdainfully, then looked at Layla. "Again with the smarm. Is he always like this?"

Layla snorted out a laugh before she caught herself. "Yep. He keeps forgetting that people can see through him now." She darted twinkling eyes at Jack. "Some of us always could."

Nothing for it but to ignore his smarting pride and play along. "Sitting right here, ladies. Hearing every disrespectful word." He achieved the light tone, but his head had started a steady pound. "Are you hungry? Can we take you to get food, or medical attention, if you need it?"

The woman looked around wistfully. "I am hungry, but could I stay here? The books, they're so...orderly. They make sense. They don't change. It's so good to be with books again."

Layla raised her eyebrows at Jack, though she directed her words at "Anne." "Of course you can stay. Jack can get someone to bring us some lunch, and I'll bet we can track down Rowan, too. She's our healer, though she hates when we call her that. Later, if you're comfortable, maybe you could meet Martin and talk to him. He'll be very interested in what you observed in the Springs. He's pretty impressed by your fancy shotgun, and he's hoping you'll share how you got it..."

Jack left her chatting easily to "Anne," telling her about their small community, settling and soothing as only Layla could. Stepping through the front doors, he came face-to-face with Owen, and just like that, his words left him.

God, he was so tired of pretending.

Apparently, so was Owen. Without greeting, or preamble, he said, "I waited. I waited for her while she waited for you."

Jack gave him a tight smile. "Do you ever wish for the days when we could just nod civilly at each other and not have this conversation?"

"Layla says the changes are hard for you. That you've still got one foot in the past."

Humiliation heated Jack's face. "Seems like you two would have better things to do than talk about me behind my back."

"Oh, we do." Owen looked down, but not before Jack saw the very male, very private smile that touched his lips.

Jack shut his eyes. Merciful Lord, he prayed, his most heart-felt prayer in almost a year. Please seal my lips.

Please bind my hands, before I attack this much larger, much stronger man. Please get me out of this before it gets any more awful than it already is. Jack opened his eyes to find Owen watching him.

"I'm not as smart as you, Jack. I'm not near smart enough for Layla, and I'm not ashamed to admit that. You two might have had something, but now it's too late." He gazed at Jack steadily for the space of three heartbeats, letting his resolve be seen and *felt*. "I just want us to be clear on that."

"We're clear." Jack snapped the words out behind another tight smile. "Crystal clear." Then, before he could say any one of the hundreds of things Satan was goading him to say – he believed completely in Ultimate Evil in that moment – he took refuge in doing, as he always did these days, world without end, amen. "I'm going to go get our visitor some food. I'd appreciate it if you'd step inside, just in case Layla needs help."

He didn't wait for Owen's agreement, just headed for his ATV. Throughout the long afternoon, while he was zooming to and fro with food, and then ferrying Rowan, while he sat in on Martin's meeting with the woman they were now calling "Anne," he kept it stuffed down. Layla and Owen. Owen and Layla. Every time it bubbled up, every time his brain taunted him with imaginings that made him want to roar, he crammed it back down into the crevice.

By the time he, Martin and Layla met to debrief over a late supper, he was pretty sure it was locked down for good. He could sit across the table from her and not wonder if her pretty skin would turn rosy pink with whisker burn. Not wonder if her lush mouth would be soft or firm on a man's skin. Not wonder if her night-black eyes would spark with light or go sleepy when she was aroused. Nope. Not wonder at all.

She looked up at him just as the thoughts scrolled through his mind and pinned him with narrowed eyes. Angry eyes. Before he could analyze that, she turned her attention to Martin. "You're worried."

"Very." Martin stopped pretending to eat and leaned back. "What 'Anne' described – it's a scenario we saw a lot of in other countries, where law and order had broken down. The powerful hoarding resources, using violence and fear to control a population. I warned Naomi about this, just the other day. We're likely to see these situations, or worse, when we leave here. It's probably happening all over the world, to varying degrees."

Jack tilted his head to the side, "But it's not happening here. And it's actively worrying you. Forgive me for my honesty, but it's not like you to trouble yourself with the problems of people you don't know."

"No forgiveness needed. I don't. Trouble myself, that is." He sighed. "I just don't think we're going to have the luxury of not knowing them forever."

"You think they'll come here?" Layla asked. "Why?"

"I know what I would do, in the same situation. Eventually, they'll need to get out of the city, to establish a more defensible position. They'll also need resources the city can no longer provide. Right now, they're probably still able to live quite well by scavenging what was left behind. So many died, so fast, there were a lot of resources left. We just made it through our first winter pretty easily by collecting and distributing canned and dried goods, and they've got a much bigger city to scavenge from."

Martin shook his head, his eyes far-away, fixed on a difficult future. "We're in a time of transition, though. We've been able to use generators for at least minimal electricity. We've got gas from all the abandoned vehicles, and it hasn't started to degrade yet. Batteries, laundry soap, pre-made clothing – you name it, we've still got it. But this time will end, for us and for them. We'll all have to find a new way. When their resources are exhausted, they'll probably look to move to high ground. They'll either come to us or through us; either way, they'll take everything we've got and leave a wasteland behind."

Jack's scalp prickled with the remembered terror of his nightmares. "They will," he said hoarsely. For the moment, the drama with Layla, the confusion and misery in his heart, were the last things on his mind. He looked at both Martin and Layla, and said simply, "I've dreamed it. Like I dreamed of the plague. No information about 'when' – I just know it'll happen."

"What can we do? Surely we're not going to just sit here and wait for them to destroy everything we've built?" Layla's anger crackled around all three of them, power and outrage and protectiveness in equal parts. "We have to mount a defense. Stop them."

Martin eyed her warily. "Are you going to change me into a toad if I ask you how? I'm the only person with a military background. Some of us know how to handle weapons well enough to hunt, and more are learning, but our only other marksperson won't shoot at anything with a heartbeat."

When Layla just gazed at him in tight-lipped silence, he leaned forward, bracing his elbows on his knees and lacing his fingers together. "I don't disagree. We can't just sit here, but we need to be realistic about what we're up against. Before the plague, Colorado Springs was having a lot of problems with what law enforcement called 'Super Gangs' – men and women with military training that got out of the service and returned to their gang roots. We can't know if one of those gangs formed the basis of the group 'Anne' described, but we can be fairly certain that many of them have combat or other specialized training that we just don't. We can't outfight them. We'll have to come up with another way."

"Are you talking about relocating?" Jack asked.

"Yes. Though no matter where or how far we go, we'll have to deal with them eventually." Martin rubbed his forehead wearily. "I know a lot of people have moved in closer, but we're still wide open. There's no way to secure the town – we just don't have enough people. Our checkpoints will only stop the folks who aren't interested in sneaking in. Otherwise, a fairly sizeable group could slide right into the town square before we even knew they were here. But before we make that decision and ask people to move, we need more information."

"Maybe 'Anne' can tell us more, when she's had time to settle in and calm down." Layla turned a troubled frown in Jack's direction. "She can't remember her own name. When I pressed her on it, 'Penthesilea' came back. She was a queen among the Amazons, according to Greek myth, and fought at Troy. She's very regal and intimidating, and certainly doesn't answer questions she doesn't want to."

"What does Rowan say about it?" Jack directed the question to a point beyond Layla's right shoulder. Not looking at her helped him stay focused. "And where is Rowan, by the way?"

"I hope she's home sleeping. With all the hullabaloo, I forgot to tell you; our numbers have grown by one." She grinned. "Sophie and Alder had their baby this morning, just before dawn – a little boy they've named Oliver. Rowan was with them all night long. She's thrilled to be an aunt, but she was wiped out. When I asked her about 'Anne,' she said something snarky about psychology not being her specialty. I'll ask her again when she's had some rest."

One of the items on the "Rowan Requests" list had been birth control of any kind – little Oliver was just the first of what she was calling the "post-apocalyptic baby boom." At last count, eleven women were pregnant in their small community – well, ten, as of this morning. As ever and always, survival led to sex, but in a society that had grown accustomed to reliable, readily-available birth control, it was also leading to a lot of unplanned babies. Against his will, Jack's eyes slid to Layla. No. No, he would not permit himself to go there. Before his mind could create that awful what-if, he grimly re-focused his attention on the conversation, which had gone on without him.

Layla was smiling wryly at Martin. "At least Buffy didn't show up again when you met with 'Anne.' I'm pretty sure she reserves that character for people she perceives as extremely dangerous, so maybe you should be flattered. I don't know what all the psychobabble would be to describe it, but I think she 'becomes' these characters to handle what she doesn't think she can handle as herself. And I don't think we've scratched the surface of what she saw and experienced in the Springs."

"Neither do I." Jack's sigh came all the way from his soul. He didn't want to know about the awful things people were doing to each other. "All we can do is reassure her that's she's safe and wait, I guess. Martin, does this information change your plans? Is it a good idea to leave, in light of this?"

Martin's defensiveness preceded his words. "My kids remain my priority. That's non-negotiable. Weather permitting, we'll leave in a couple weeks. We plan to be gone at least four or five days, possibly more, depending on what we find." He made an obvious effort to throttle back his emotions. "I don't think the threat is imminent, Jack. A group that size isn't easy to move, especially not with the pass blocked. They'd be fools to try it before late spring, in any case. We'll watch for scouts or for activity on Highway 24, and we need to send people to find out what condition Rampart Range Road and Old Stage Road are in. We don't want them sneaking in the back door."

"I'll help coordinate all that." Jack reined in the desire to argue, convince, manipulate. Martin had made it clear that he wouldn't tolerate such machinations, not ever again. "Tomorrow's soon enough, I think."

Martin nodded and rose, murmuring a good night. Layla rose as well, but Jack held out a hand, forestalling her. "If you could wait just a minute, I need to talk to you."

Layla's eyebrows rose; typically, Jack turned back flips to avoid being alone with her. She folded her arms over her chest and propped a hip on the table, watching him with narrowed eyes. By unspoken agreement, they waited until they both heard the faint sound of Martin's ATV start up outside. Then Jack rose to his feet as well.

"For future reference," he said as levelly as he could manage, surprised by the amount of rage that was still surging in him, "I would appreciate it if you'd let me know next time you're taking a day off. None of us have the luxury of sneaking off for a day of –"

Of what, Jack? He should have thought this through better. The pause got more and more suggestive, the longer he held it. Finally, he burst out with, "You're welcome to sleep with whoever you want, whenever you want. Just let us know where you are in case you're needed." He slogged on, even though he could hear what a pompous jackass he was being. "All of us have responsibilities that supersede our sex lives. I hope you recognize that."

Oh, holy Father. The look in her eyes. Jack felt vulnerable parts of his anatomy tighten close to his body for protection, and his scalp prickled, echoing the alarm. She straightened slowly, and let her arms drop to her sides. Why did it always look like her hair writhed to life when she was angry?

"Sneaking around? Is that your perception?" Her voice was a dangerous hiss. "An interesting distortion of what I would call common courtesy and privacy. My sex life is none of your business – it never was, and it certainly never will be – but thanks so much for your permission for me to carry on, whenever and with *whomever* I want." She tapped her chin thoughtfully, while Jack fought to buffer the pure rage she made no effort to hide from him. "Would you mind if Owen and I made use of the sanctuary, next time we have a sunny day? Those stained glass windows are so pretty, and the way the light falls on the pulpit, I think the effect would be quite artistic..."

Jack's hold on his own rage slipped, hard. "There's no need to be obscene."

"*I'm* being obscene? *I* am?" Layla took a step towards him, then another, chest rising and falling swiftly. "Did you think I couldn't *feel* what you were thinking earlier? You were all over me, and you had me all over you!" She shook her head at him in disgust. "Goddess grant me patience. You had your chance, Jack. I made that plain enough, to my ever-lasting humiliation. And now that I've moved on, *now* you want to play the jealous lover? I don't need these childish games."

"I'm not a child," he said roughly. Then he, who had never laid a violent hand on another person in his life; he, who counseled gentleness and respect for women at all times and in all situations; he, who prided himself on mastering the needs of his body through prayer and self-control; he snapped.

Two steps brought him nose-to-nose with Layla, who, of course, stood her ground. He didn't put his hands on another man's woman, though. Oh, no. What he did was far worse.

Jack ducked his head, bringing his mouth so close to Layla's, he inhaled her startled exhalation. Her eyes were startled, too, those exotic, dark eyes that promised such exotic, dark things. Things he could make her do. He locked his gaze on hers, and dropped his shields completely, letting her *feel* what she did to him, what she had always done to him. Her eyes went wide.

He could feel her shields trembling as she fought to keep them up, and he bent every bit of his will and purpose on getting her to drop them. Persuasion, coercion, manipulation – everything he'd learned of these things and the often blurred lines between them, he brought to bear on her faltering defenses. He needed to be inside her in this way, desperately needed the connection, more intimate than any sexual contact he'd ever experienced.

"Let me in." He breathed the words onto her lips, watched them part, and felt lust slide, molten hot, down his spine. He shared that with her too, and was gratified when she shuddered. "Let me in, Layla. It would be so good. We would be so good together."

"I want you to stop." Power vibrated in her command. He *felt* the hesitation permeate his body. Muscles, blood, heart and mind wanted to obey her. She so rarely used this thing she could do, he forgot about it at times. It was wrong, she had said, she who was so hesitant to label things as "right" or "wrong," "good" or "bad." Wrong, to force another to obey your desire, to override their will and conscience, even if your intent was benevolent.

She's lying. His own will slid the words into his mind. *She wants this. Wants you.* Jack smiled, and shook off her imperative as easily as he would shrug off a light jacket. "Kiss me, Layla. Put your mouth on mine."

Just like that, her shields shattered around her. The avalanche of emotions staggered him – confusion, desire, anger, fear, lust, tenderness, exasperation, disappointment. He zeroed in on those that would serve his purpose and stroked them, amplified them. A low growl rumbled in his chest when one of his questions was answered: Sleepy. Her eyes went sleepy when she was aroused.

Her eyes. Her mindless, blank eyes. Eyes without Layla in them.

Jack took a step back. Then another.

She came back to herself as he watched, shaking her head slightly, as if she'd been in a trance. It began to sink in, then, what he had done, the vulnerability he'd inflicted on her like an attack. He had used what he knew of her, what he *sensed* from her, to control her. To take her will away, and insert his in its place. Worst of all, he realized, her trust in him had given him that power.

Jack thought he might vomit.

There they stood, both of them more than naked, completely exposed. Jack stared at her, as she lifted a hand to shield the mouth he had tried to force her to give. She stared back, eyes now filled with angry tears. Before she could speak the words of censure he *felt* rising in her, he held up his hand.

"I'm sorry. Layla, I'm so sorry."

She left without saying a word. Left him, to sit alone in the growing darkness and marvel at the horrifying thing he had just learned he could do.

EIGHT
Grace and Quinn: The Galloway Cabin, Colorado Springs, CO

Their days became mostly silent, a monotonous cycle of sleep, prepare food, eat, rest, prepare food, eat, rest, and on and on and on. Grace kept track of the passing days in a spiral-bound notebook, on a page entitled: Time Spent in Captivity. The attempt at humor was feeble, but it was the best she could produce under the circumstances.

She couldn't shake the sensation of being an animal in its den, venturing outside only to use the outhouse, then scurrying – or lumbering, rather – back inside to hunker by the stingy fire Quinn allowed them during the day. The shutters over the tiny windows were kept closed at all times. Unlike before, they didn't play games or read together. To speak was to unleash truths that neither one of them were prepared to deal with, truths that would strand them on opposite sides of an unbridgeable chasm.

Quinn came and went, adding to the ever-growing pile of supplies in the corner farthest from the fire. Grace tried not to see but found her eyes drawn over and over to the diapers, the cans of formula, the bassinet, the cute little black-and-white animals on a wind-up mobile. Where was he finding this stuff? Were these the leavings of dead babies? That was as much as she allowed herself to wonder before she turned her eyes away. All of it seemed abstract, unconnected to her in any way.

She had finished her account of her time with the gang and was strangely sorry she had. She was left with nothing to occupy her mind or her time, and though Quinn had brought her hundreds of books, she couldn't seem to bend her mind around any of them. Hour after hour, day after day, she stared at the fire, her mind flitting around and touching an image here, a fragment there, none of it connected or purposeful. Waiting. Always waiting.

Only once during the long days had they attempted to talk. They had been sitting in their usual positions by the fire, Grace staring while Quinn paged through a book on the flora and fauna of the Pikes Peak region, which he'd found in the general store. He read all the time these days, lips moving silently as he plowed determinedly through the words. If he wasn't reading, he was tinkering with a farm implement or repairing something. Stillness was not in Quinn's repertoire. So it had startled Grace to glance up one afternoon – or had it been evening? Did it matter? – to find him staring at the fire, a troubled frown on his face.

"What are you thinking?" She had blurted the question without thinking.

Quinn's eyes swung in her direction, but he didn't really focus on her for long moments. Then, he sighed. "I was just wishing we had never come in off the plains. That we'd stayed out at Ramah. Or back at our ranch."

Grace frowned. She tried not to think of their ride into Colorado Springs, of the time they'd spent at the wildlife refuge, of waking in the mornings to sunshine and birdsong. Of Buttons, cropping grass nearby, the morning sun gleaming on her glossy neck. That had been a different world. A different Grace. She couldn't return to either. "I guess I don't really get that. Why not just wish the plague never happened?"

"I wasn't warned about the plague," he replied, sudden sharpness and heat. "Not like I was warned about the city. About what happened."

They stared at each other for a few moments, the rustling and hissing of the fire the only sound. Grace pondered his answer, then decided it couldn't hurt to ask the next logical question. "Have you had any other dreams like that? Warnings?"

"Yes."

He didn't hesitate, nor did he elaborate. He just gazed at her steadily, telling her without words that once again, the warning had been about her. Did she want to know? Was it bad? Of course it was bad; warnings always were. Grace turned her eyes back to the fire. If she asked, he would lie to her. So she wouldn't ask. Nor would she speculate. What good would it do?

That seemed to be her criteria for making all kinds of decisions these days: Should she learn how to sew by hand, so she could repair their clothes? Should she teach herself how to crochet? Study one of Quinn's flora and fauna books to learn more about foraging for food in the surrounding environment? Why should she do any of those things? There was no guarantee she'd be here to put those skills to use. No guarantee that she'd wake up tomorrow. What good would any of that effort do?

So she did nothing. Nothing but stare, and drift, and wait.

After a while, Quinn got up and left the cabin without so much as a murmur of goodbye. They hadn't spoken since, beyond the occasional word of necessity. She forgot he was there for long stretches of time as she drifted on an internal sea of nothingness, only vaguely aware that her body was resting, changing, preparing.

And then, one night, she dreamed. She was back with the gang, on the day she escaped, hiding under the semi trailer. She was naked, and so cold, still filthy and sticky from the rapes of the night before. She could hear the men shouting to each other as they searched for her, but this time, they didn't move away. Around and around they circled, their voices getting closer and closer, until she couldn't silence her gasps of terror. She had to urinate so badly, the pain and pressure so intense, she doubted she could stand up straight. Finally, to her horror, she couldn't hold back any longer. Water gushed from her, water that became blood, flooding out from under the semi trailer, giving her position away. Hands reached into her hiding place, hands she tried to slap away, hands that dragged her through the mud her blood and urine had created, into the cold, cold light.

"Grace! Wake up! Gracie, you need to wake up!"

Grace heaved out of the dream with a guttural scream, a horrible, tortured-animal sound. She blinked and blinked, lost. Quinn's worried face above her, the soft murmuring, shushing sounds he was making, his strong hands propping her up and stroking her back were her only anchors. It took forever, to come back to the where and when: They were at the cabin. She had been sleeping on her pallet by the fire. But that was where things stopped making sense. She was soaking wet, freezing, shivering.

Quinn eased her back down. "Your water broke. I'll get you some dry clothes and bedding, and we'll get ready."

There was an excitement about him, an air of anticipation she did not understand. She didn't understand any of this. She watched in silence as he bustled about, feeling her heart rate slow and her breathing calm. She was not grasping something major here. She knew that. What had he said? Had she wet the bed from the terror of the nightmare? That had happened to her a few times when she was little, she suddenly remembered. She had a flash of her mother's silhouette in the door of her bedroom, her soft, exasperated voice saying, "Oh, honey. Here, it's okay, let's get you cleaned up." But before she could puzzle it all out, the first contraction hit.

Grace wheezed and arched her back, trying to relieve the sudden, red-hot agony. Her back hurt all the time these days, a constant dull ache, but this was different. It felt like a giant was trying to break her spine over his knee. Then, as quickly as it had come, it eased. Quinn was back beside her, and she clutched at him wildly. "Quinn! Something's wrong! My back!"

He smoothed her hair back from her forehead in long, soothing strokes, frowning down at her. "What do you mean wrong?" When she just stared at him blankly, his frown deepened. "Gracie, you're in labor. The baby is coming."

Labor. Baby. That's what he'd said – that her water had broken. Grace's head swam, and she heaved over onto her side, breathing until the dizziness retreated. Quinn stayed beside her, stroking her hair, her arm, massaging her shoulders with firm gentleness. She closed her eyes, lulled and comforted in spite of the chill of her wet clothes. He hadn't touched her since they'd moved to the cabin. She hadn't realized it until this moment, hadn't realized how much he had touched her before: a strong hand cupping her elbow when she stood, a calming palm placed on her contorting belly. It was so good to be touched again, so good to be close to his warmth and scent. She nearly drifted into a doze; then the second contraction hit.

Quinn was ready this time. When she arched, he held her shoulders firmly and put his face right next to hers. "Gracie, look at me. Look at me!"

Her eyes snapped to his and clung. She couldn't breathe, couldn't think. All she could do was try to twist away from the red hot pain. She tried to say his name, but the agony took her breath. This couldn't be right. She was going to die. When it finally eased, she started to sob. Quinn lay down beside her, right on her soggy pallet, and held her. He pressed his forehead to hers and gazed into her eyes.

"You're going to be okay, shh, I've got you. Tell me what's happening, what it feels like, so I know how to help you."

"My back." Grace struggled to speak without sobbing. "My back feels like it's going to break." She started sobbing again, and though she had known true terror, had survived horrors she couldn't have imagined, she had never been so scared in her life as she was at that moment. "Quinn, I'm afraid I'm going to die. What if I die? I want my mom – please – I just want my mom!"

"You're not going to die." But he closed his eyes. He kept his forehead pressed to hers, swallowed hard several times, then seemed to shake himself. He opened his eyes again. "I read about this. I think you're in back labor. Let me get the book so I can see what they say helps..."

Too late, too late. Twisting, grinding pain. The bones of her spine were grating together, they had to be. This time, the pain locked around her middle like a vice, her stomach tightening into a rock-hard mound between them. She heard a roaring sound, then Quinn's voice cut through it.

"Breathe with me! Gracie, you've got to breathe through it – I'll breathe with you!"

He pressed his face to hers and forced her breath into rhythm with his, his eyes burning into hers. When she gasped along with him, his face broke into a relieved smile. "That's it. Just keep breathing with me. We'll make it."

Again, it eased, and she could breathe on her own. She lay on her side in a stunned stupor, vaguely aware of Quinn bustling around her, pulling off her wet clothes, shifting her, naked, to a fresh pallet that crinkled when she moved. It didn't even occur to her to cover herself. Quinn slid a big, soft sweatshirt over her head but left her lower half bare, covering her with a light blanket. When the pain came again, he was already lying on his side next to her, face pressed to hers, forcing her to breathe with him while she writhed and twisted.

Each contraction brought back memories she never wanted to revisit, awful flashes of casual, brutal slaps, of flinching away from teeth on her skin, of humiliating, tearing, private pain on public display, over and over. But this was worse, so much worse, the pain enormous, bone-grinding, like nothing she could have imagined. Her body was not hers to control. Worse, neither was her mind. She struggled to listen to Quinn – she knew that he was trying to help her – but it was no use. Grace went away, as she had never permitted herself to do during the rapes.

Between the escalating contractions, she drifted in a bizarre half-doze. Nothing seemed real, foggy and insubstantial, as if she'd become a ghost. She heard herself moaning, then screaming, but couldn't connect the sound with any kind of meaning. Quinn's face shimmered in and out of her vision, and his lips moved, but she couldn't hear him.

Time passed, and passed, but she couldn't keep track of it. Hours? Days? She had been in this agony-punctuated drift forever, and would be in it until she was at last allowed to die.

She would have died, had Quinn not hauled her off the pallet and onto her feet.

"Grace, god damn it to hell! Look at me!" He roared the words in her face, spit flying, and she was startled into awareness. My god, he looked awful – white as a sheet, black circles of exhaustion ringing his wild eyes. He held her up by her shoulders and though his voice was softer, it was no less forceful. "If you don't push, now, you are going to die. Grace, you are going to die! Can you hear me?"

He lowered her to a squatting position, and when the next wave hit, he roared at her again: "Push! Push now, as hard as you can!"

What could she do but obey? Grace pushed, feebly at first, then stronger, as her body took over. Something ancient rose up, something that went deeper than knowledge or experience, an instinct that knew what was necessary to preserve her life. The contraction ended, and she panted along with Quinn, staring into his eyes, suddenly hyper-focused. It was like being possessed. He didn't need to tell her what to do the next time, or the next.

Grace felt a huge, tearing pressure, and swore she heard the bones of her hips crack, the sound transmitted through her body to her ears. She sucked in huge breaths of air, knowing, somehow, that this was it. On the next contraction, she bore down with all the strength she had left, and felt a sudden rush, a give, a parting.

Quinn eased her back hurriedly, and reached down to cradle a tiny, scrunched face emerging from her body. Propped on her elbows, Grace stared, shocked, while Quinn muttered hoarsely to himself. "Let the baby come naturally. Don't pull. Make sure the chord isn't around its neck. Don't pull..."

Another contraction, another stinging pain as the shoulders slid free, and his hands were suddenly filled with a slug-white, blood-covered baby.

The look on his face. She would never forget it. Stunned awe. Sudden joy, so incandescent, it should have burned her eyes. He lifted the baby from between her legs, cradling it to his chest, gore and all. Grace heard a tiny cough, a whimper, and then a shockingly loud wail. Quinn's face split into the biggest smile she'd ever seen, and he laughed, laughed with pure delight. His eyes lifted from the baby's face, bright with tears. "She's here. She's here, Gracie, and she's okay."

Grace eased from her elbows to her back, staring at the rough ceiling above her, and waited to feel something. Anything. Her eyes drifted to Quinn; it was if all feeling, all emotion, everything had been expelled with the squirming, screeching baby in his hands. The adrenalin from the birth seeped out of her body, leaving her limp, with involuntary tremors vibrating through her arms and legs. She closed her eyes, and must have slept, because when she opened them again, everything was different.

She was dressed in a soft, clean sweatsuit. When she shifted her weight gingerly, she could feel something, a towel maybe, pressed against the sore ache between her legs. Her pallet was clean and fresh, and her hair had been brushed and secured into a soft braid. She turned her head.

Quinn was lying on a pallet beside her, a bundle tucked against his chest. He looked as exhausted as she'd ever seen him, but in spite of that, he opened his eyes when her gaze touched his face.

"Hey. You're awake." At the sound of his voice, the bundle stirred and a tiny fist shot free. The baby's skin had warmed to a dusky rose. Quinn patted the baby, soothing her. "Do you want to see her?"

Grace returned her gaze to the ceiling, still waiting for any feeling at all to pierce the numbness that had enfolded her like a thick, rubber coating. She thought about what would happen if she recognized the eyes of a rapist in that newborn face, but still, felt nothing. No rage. No resentment. No curiosity, or tenderness. Nothing.

When she didn't answer, Quinn cleared his throat and started talking, obviously just filling silence. "Ah, well, you're okay, too. You were out-of-it when you delivered the afterbirth, but I'm pretty sure you've stopped bleeding. You tore a little bit, but just a little…"

Grace didn't want any of this information. Besides being gross, it just seemed so…irrelevant. It was over, and she was alive. That was all she needed to know. She closed her eyes and turned her face away, and Quinn stopped talking. She must have slept again, because when she woke, she was hungry and needed to use the outhouse.

Quinn and the baby were still sleeping on the pallet beside her. He had shifted to his back with the baby on his chest, a little bottle filled with formula on the floor next to his hip. Neither one of them stirred when she eased into a sitting position, then slowly stood up. The room swung a little, and she moved to brace her palm against the rough log wall until it stilled. She was sore in strange ways she didn't want to explore, and her legs felt shaky, but when she breathed in, the lack of restriction was a welcome surprise. She took an experimental step towards the door, then another, and before she knew it, she was standing outside.

The sun was so bright, she had to squint for several minutes until her eyes adjusted. The warmth soaked into her skin like a healing balm, and she lifted her face to the winter blue sky, sucking in breath after breath of the fresh, soft air. The last time she'd been outside, it had been bitter cold and snowing. Now, it felt like springtime. Her dad always said, "If you don't like the weather in Colorado, wait five minutes. It'll change." At the thought of her father, she felt a stirring in her chest, but it never connected with an emotion she could name.

Grace picked her way across the muddy clearing to the outhouse, trying to adjust to her newly restored center of gravity. The fluting call of a meadowlark, Quinn's favorite, sounded nearby, and Grace paused to listen. It hit her, then, that she was alone. Truly alone. For the first time in ever so long. Once again, she felt a lift in her chest and would have called it happiness, if she weren't still so curiously numb.

Once in the outhouse, she blanched at the amount of blood on the towel between her legs, then hissed in pain when she finally worked up the nerve to sit down to go. Her appreciation of the beautiful day flagged in the face of physical realities she didn't want to deal with, leaving her wrung out and shaking again. She opened the outhouse door, intent on getting back to her pallet for more sleep, and found Quinn standing in the door of the cabin with the strangest expression on his face. When he saw her, he sagged against the doorway, shutting his eyes in obvious relief.

She started towards him, waving him off when he would have helped her. "I can do it."

He obeyed her wish but watched her progress with worried eyes. Under the numb, irritation stirred. She was so sick of him looking at her like that. By the time she reached the cabin door, though, she didn't care how he looked at her anymore. She was so tired, all she could think about was lying down. Quinn shadowed her movements until she was settled on her pallet.

"Are you hungry? I've got some soup I can heat up quick."

"Yes, hungry," Grace mumbled, her eyes rolling as she tried to keep them open. "So sleepy."

"Sleep." His hand stroked over her heavy eyes, closing them. "I'll wake you when it's ready."

He was true to his word. Through the rest of the afternoon, she slept and woke, and he was always there with a cup of soup, a granola bar, a drink of water. Increasingly, she woke to the sound of the baby crying and Quinn's worried murmurs as he tried to soothe her.

She sensed it was the middle of the night when next she woke, once again in need of the outhouse. As before, Quinn was sleeping on his pallet with the baby next to him, but this time, there were four different bottles filled with formula surrounding their still forms. Even in his sleep, his face was creased and old with worry. Grace felt a brush of curiosity, but no more, and turned her eyes away.

When she shifted to rise, she gasped in shock; her breasts were swollen, rock-hard and hot. She gazed down at them, baffled, then recoiled when two wet circles appeared on the front of her sweatshirt. Oh. That. Moving as quietly as she could, she rummaged through her clothes until she found a fresh shirt. Then, she took two small towels from their supply and opened the outside door.

Sure enough. Full dark. She sighed and stood there, looking out at the moonless night.

Grace hated using the bucket, but they had agreed it wasn't safe to go outside at night. Not only was there the pack of dogs to consider, but other wildlife as well. Quinn had seen coyotes, and the tracks of mountain lions, and last fall, Grace had come face-to-face with a foraging black bear, roly-poly and mellow with winter fat. He had been as surprised as she, and after a moment of stare-down, he had waddled off into the scrub oak, leaving Grace with a pounding heart and a crazy grin on her face.

She had still been hiking the trails in Garden of the Gods then, the growing burden in her womb hardly slowing her down. After a long, wet season, some of the trails were eroded and overgrown, but she loved those best of all, loved the solitude and the sensation of being hidden, safe. Quinn hadn't really approved, but she never once suffered a fainting spell while on one of her hikes, so he couldn't put his foot down.

She could feel the pull of those trails now, a longing that swelled in her chest, the first feeling she could readily identify. Solitude and safety. Her long ordeal was over. She could go, just walk away from this dark, dirty cabin and...and...never come back.

A soft gasp left her, a breath that lifted and froze, obscuring her view of the black night sky. *Why not?* It seemed like someone else whispered the words in her mind. She waited for an answer to that question, waited for a sense of responsibility, or loyalty to Quinn, or any kind of obligation at all to rise in her, but nothing volunteered.

The damp front of her shirt clung to her skin, making her shudder with chill. Reluctantly, she shut the door and turned around. Quinn was standing by the fire, and again, there was a look on his face she couldn't define. She didn't say anything, just looked down and went to the corner of the cabin to use the bucket, slipping behind the sheet he'd hung for privacy. While behind the screen, she changed her shirt, pressing the towels to her aching breasts to absorb what was leaking out of them. She didn't want to come out; somehow, she was sure, he knew what she'd been thinking. She waited until she heard him settle back down, then hurried to her pallet.

She hesitated a moment, then dragged her pallet from its spot in front of the fire, settling the bedding against the wall to the side. She just wanted more room. Some distance and space. She glanced at Quinn and found him watching her. She gestured at the pallet but found that she didn't really have anything to say. Instead, she lay down facing the wall, huddling under her blankets while she tried to ignore her painful breasts and the disgusting dampness of the towels. The baby started to cry, and she wrapped her head in her pillow, dropping swiftly into sleep in spite of the wails.

Her inner sense told her it was morning when she woke again, sensing movement nearby. Quinn was pacing in front of the fire, the baby in his arms. As Grace watched, the baby twitched, and started crying suddenly, the sound both frantic and weak. The cries gradually whimpered into silence while Quinn paced and shushed, paced and shushed. The pattern was repeated three more times; then, Quinn stalked to stand over her.

"I need help!" He blurted.

Grace gazed up at him, and knew that she should feel bad. She should. He was so tired he was staggering, and his eyes were wild with despair. Why couldn't she feel bad for him? "Excuse me?"

"I need help," he repeated hoarsely. "I can't get her to drink the formula. I've tried four different kinds, but she just spits it up and cries. She's getting so weak, Gracie, I don't know what else to do!"

Grace's heart started to pound, and feeling stirred. What, she wasn't certain, but it wasn't good. "What are you asking me for?"

Quinn's jaw clenched. He was blinking rapidly. "I can't feed her, and she's suffering. I can't stand it, Gracie. I just can't stand it. I'll do everything else for her, if you'll just feed her."

Grace sat up, leaning against the wall behind her, staring at them both. She was hyper-aware of her heavy, hot, leaking breasts. "I don't –" Her voice came out as a rough croak. She didn't know exactly what she wanted to say. *I don't want to? I don't want to touch it?* What came out of Grace's mouth was, "I don't know how."

Quinn dropped down beside her so fast, she started back. "My mom nursed my little brothers," he said in a rush, "If you just lift up your shirt, I can –" He broke off, dull red blooming on his face. "I can, ah, just hold her to your –" He gestured with the baby to her breast, unable to meet her eyes.

She was definitely feeling now: An almost overwhelming urge to get out of this cabin, away from this situation. Quinn waited, not looking at her, and she tried to think of a single good reason – other than the fact that she desperately didn't want to – to deny him his request. He had saved her life; she knew that for certain. Probably several times over. He never asked her for anything.

Grace swallowed hard and shut her eyes. Without giving herself any more time to think about it, she yanked up her shirt, exposing her swollen breast to the cool air. She kept her eyes shut while Quinn maneuvered the baby into position, felt his hands brush her body and couldn't stop the jump and twitch of her flesh as she fought not to yank away. Then she felt a small wet mouth clamp onto her nipple so hard it stung. Her eyes flew open, and she glared accusingly at Quinn.

"That hurts!" She hunched her shoulders against the pain, refusing to look down. She wished she was still numb, but feelings, awful feelings, roiled around inside her. This was gross, disgusting, this was not happening to her body. She slammed her eyes shut again, feeling her whole face tighten as she fought the urge to scramble to her feet and get away.

The baby's squirming increased, her small mouth chomping harder and harder, her angry whimpers finally ratcheting into an enraged scream. Grace looked down reflexively, and caught the first glimpse of her daughter's face, glowing red and scrunched tight with rage.

"What does she want? Why is she screaming?" Grace covered her ears with her hands. "Take her away, Quinn! She doesn't want me any more than I want her!"

Quinn's head dropped for a moment, and he shook it slowly. Then he straightened his shoulders, and repositioned the baby again. His voice stayed level, but it was shaking. "Listen to me," he said over the baby's shrieks. "You have to relax, so your milk lets down. My mom used to talk about it. Said she couldn't nurse the babies if she was stressed out. So just...calm down."

"Just calm down?" Grace repeated, her voice rising. "How am I supposed to calm down with a screaming –"

"Shut up, Grace!" Quinn's voice was a lash, his face set in hard, unfamiliar lines. "Just shut the hell up! You can either do what I tell you, or you can live the rest of your life knowing you let this baby die! What's it going to be?"

Grace stared at this harsh stranger, barking commands at her, telling her to shut up, looking at her with hot, angry eyes. The disapproval she saw there made her own eyes fill with tears. God, she couldn't stand this. She swallowed. Again. "I'll try," she said finally.

"Okay," he said gruffly. "Just – close your eyes again. And think of something far away. Think of your best memories when you were a little girl, or whatever, just something that makes you feel calm and peaceful..."

Grace obeyed, and his voice murmured on, soothing all of them. It was magical, what he could do with his voice; he was an animal-whisperer, a Grace-whisperer, too. The thought made an actual smile touch her mouth. Behind her closed eyelids, she conjured visions of holidays on the ranch, the 4th of July picnics with family and friends bringing potluck dishes wrapped in newspaper and towels to keep them warm; Easter, with the eggs she had loved to color even as a teenager, and then hold snuggled in the palm of her hand; and best of all, Christmas, all warm scents and twinkling lights. And all the while, she listened to his instructions to lower her shoulders, to take a deep breath, to roll her head on her neck.

"Holy shit!" Her eyes flew open, and once again, she looked down reflexively. The baby had clamped onto her nipple, and she felt a tingling, pulling sensation spread throughout her breast. The baby was gulping audibly, her tiny body curving with fierce intentness towards her source of food. Something huge stirred in the center of Grace's chest, and she looked away, terrified.

Quinn kept his calming murmur going for the next half hour, stopping partway through to shift the baby to her other breast. Grace kept her eyes closed, concentrating on keeping her body relaxed, her hands lying loose at her sides. The baby fell asleep between one drawing pull and the next, her body going abruptly limp. Quinn lifted the baby away, set her against his shoulder, then stood, swaying and bouncing while he alternately rubbed and patted her back.

Grace pulled her shirt down, and slid back down to curl up on her side. In spite of herself, she watched through slitted eyes. Quinn kept up the bouncing and swaying until the baby let loose with a wet-sounding burp. Then he shifted the baby in his hands to look at her face. He stayed that way for a moment, eyes worried and intent. Then, his chest lifted in a huge sigh, and his eyes once again filled with tears. His face contorted, and he buried it against the baby, who slept on in spite of the sobs ripping out of him.

He slid down the wall beside Grace, still clutching the baby to hide his face. "I miss my mom," he choked. "I miss my baby brothers, so much. I was so scared she would die – I don't want any more people to die, Gracie, I just can't – just can't –"

His broken voice dissolved into quieter sobs, and he lay down beside her, a lost and heart-broken boy. His misery sliced into her heart, and she wished, truly, that she could go back to numb.

As he had done for her, she stroked and soothed and murmured, tucking his face into the curve of her neck. It felt good to be the strong one again. For too long, she had been so utterly dependent. The baby was tucked between them, but she did her best to ignore it, keeping her face turned away as she evened the scales, giving back some of the comfort he'd given to her. Gradually, his sobs subsided into hitching breaths, then into the deep rhythms of sleep.

Grace eased free and stood, looking down at the two of them. The baby was on the pallet, Quinn half off, but she didn't want to disturb him, even to roll him off the cold floor. She pulled a blanket over them both, tucked another under Quinn as best she could, then grabbed her coat and dragged one of the rickety wooden chairs towards the door.

The sun was up, but just barely, and the sky held thousands of shades of orange, peach, rose, and pink. It was cold, but not bitter. She would bet they were in for another unseasonably warm day. Her legs were stronger, she noted, as she trekked to the outhouse and back, and it hurt less to go. The release of pressure in her breasts was a relief, too, but she didn't linger on that. Instead, she eased down onto the chair and absorbed the outdoors, drawing in breath after breath after free breath. She stayed there until her coat couldn't hold the chill at bay any longer, and she was shivering convulsively.

When she stepped back inside, Quinn was still sleeping, though he had rolled onto his back. The motion had pulled the blanket off the baby, and though she wasn't crying, she was awake. Grace watched the squirming, softly squeaking bundle warily, out of the corner of her eye. She knew Quinn would wake if the baby started crying in earnest, and he needed more rest so badly. She fidgeted, reluctant to go closer. Maybe she could just cover her up, and she would go back to sleep.

She sidled over to the pallet and knelt, pulling the blanket from under Quinn's hip. She leaned to drape the blanket over the baby, glancing down to be sure she wasn't covering its face, and froze.

Those eyes. She knew those eyes.

Grace fell heavily onto her hip, staring. Her daughter stared back, from dark eyes only slightly hazed with newborn blue. Memory slammed into her, her arms heavy with the warm, blanket-wrapped weight of her new baby brother, baby Benji, her mother's voice tickling the curve of her ear as they both looked down at his sweet, scrunched-up face.

"Look at the way he looks at you. He knows his big sister, doesn't he? His eyes are going to be dark, like yours, and your father's. I'm so glad – I love your beautiful dark eyes."

The same face, the same eyes, here in an awful cabin – how was this possible? Was she seeing a ghost? Had Benji come back, somehow, to inhabit the tiny body of his...niece? My god, he would be this baby's uncle, if he were alive. Her mom would be a grandma, her dad a grandpa? She could hardly conceive of it, couldn't connect her Marine-tough father with her own twinkly-eyed grandpas. And that would make Grace...

She scrambled backwards, panting, and the world shrank to a single goal: She had to get out of here. She stood up and quivered, wanting to dart in four directions at once. She needed supplies. She needed clothes, and some food, though she wouldn't take much. She couldn't leave Quinn low on food. Her brain clicked into gear, and she was able to move with purpose, grabbing her saddlebags and filling them with swift silence.

She changed her clothes for the warmest she had, then layered on all her outdoor gear in spite of the warm day. She could always shed down as she went. In her mind was a vague plan: She would stop at the Chambers house, see if there was anything she could use, and then she would...go. Just go. Over the ridge and into the Garden of the Gods, through the familiar, silent monoliths on secret, solitary trails.

She grabbed her walking stick, and paused with her hand on the door. Under the singular, pure purpose that filled her roiled the kind of chaos she hated. She would never be able to make sense of it, put it in a logical order. She couldn't delve into it without losing her mind, so she clung to her purpose. This was the only thing she could do. This was the only thing that made any kind of sense. And then, in spite of herself, she turned to take one last look.

Quinn was watching her. His eyes. Oh, his eyes. He opened his mouth and spoke a single word. "Go."

Grace whirled away and fumbled with the door. When it was finally open, she stepped through, shutting it behind her. Her boots crunched in counter-point with her walking stick as she headed south, following the path that curved around the barn to the Chambers house.

Quinn's eyes came back to her, the way they had glittered – hard, angry, jagged. Already betrayed. Her stride faltered then. He knew. He knew what she was just recognizing.

She wasn't coming back.

NINE
Naomi and Martin: Cripple Creek, CO

"Oh, for the love of Mike!" Naomi gave up trying to work her shovel into the hard-as-concrete earth in any kind of controlled manner. Instead, she stood the small spade upright, then crouched to jump, intent on hammering it into the ground with her weight.

"I wouldn't, if I were you." Martin's drawl slid lazily out from behind her. "You'll break your ankle. Or wreck your boot. Either one could be fatal out here."

Naomi turned to glare at him, feeling sweat cool on her forehead in the rising, late-afternoon wind. He was sprawled against a log, resting on top of his sleeping bag, his hat tipped over his eyes. How the heck had he even known what she was about to do?

"You're predictable," he answered. "That's how I knew."

Naomi hefted the spade in her hand, suddenly energized, and indulged in a richly detailed fantasy of bringing it down on the top of his head. Martin tipped his hat back and his eyes locked onto hers.

"I wouldn't do that, either."

"Martin," her voice shook, and she clamped down on it, hard. By thee gods, she would not cry. "If you read my mind one more time, I will ask Hades to rip your kneecaps off." She smiled with syrupy sweetness when Martin blinked in surprise, and threw the spade down beside him. "How's that for predictable? Dig your own damn fire pit."

She stalked away from their camp and headed for the stream, Hades on her heels. Three days. Three days of listening to him boss, and condescend, and criticize. Nothing she did was good enough. She was too slow, too loud, too careless, too hesitant, too careful, too wrong. All the time.

This morning, he had announced that they would swap tasks for the day – he would do the cooking and cleaning up, while she performed the heavier jobs he had been handling. She needed to know how to be on her own, he'd informed her. Pompously. If something should happen to him, she'd need to carry her own water, gather her own firewood, dig her own fire pit. Naomi stopped at the edge of the stream and looked down when Hades pressed against her leg.

"Something *is* going to happen to him, you can bet your sweet bippy on that." She stroked Hades' silky ears, letting his ever-present love soothe her. "I'm going to poison him. That's the plan."

She blew out a huge breath of air and tipped her head back, gazing at the far-away line of snow-capped mountain. The Sawatch range, if she remembered the map right. Or was it the northern part of the Sangre de Cristos? She'd lived in Colorado all her life, and it had never occurred to her to learn the different ranges and their names. So much about this life had never occurred to her before.

This was not going to work. She thought she and Martin had reached an agreement, an understanding, but she must have been wrong. He didn't trust her. He never would. And if she had to spend one more day listening to him harp about her inadequacies in the guise of teaching, she would make an exception to her rule about shooting living things.

Naomi's attention returned abruptly to the here-and-now when part of the stream bank shifted under her feet. She stepped back quickly, startled, then narrowed her eyes. Of course.

Ten minutes later, she was digging again, in soil she'd moistened with water from the stream. She completed the first half of the Dakota fire hole, returned to the stream for more water, and finished the task in under an hour. Martin didn't budge from his cushy sleeping-bag sprawl or say a word to her until she had a small, hot, nearly smokeless fire blazing. Then, he rose, clapped her on the shoulder, and sealed his doom with two words.

"About time."

Naomi looked at Hades. "Don't eat the eggs tomorrow morning."

Martin assembled the supplies he needed to cook dinner with damnable efficiency and produced a delicious meal of fried potatoes and ham in half the time it had taken her to dig the fire pit. He cleaned up just as efficiently, and the two of them were left with nothing to do but sit in silence with the softly crackling fire and their own thoughts. So far, the trip had given them both plenty to think about.

They'd reached Divide easily the first day, making the less-than 10 mile trip in just a few hours. They had spent the rest of that day and most of the next systematically searching for survivors and supplies. The evidence suggested that at least one or two people had survived the plague itself – many of the homes they searched had already been cleaned out – but whoever they had been, they were long gone.

They had left Divide early that morning, and had begun working their way up Highway 67, headed towards Cripple Creek. Via the road, they had only traveled about 8 miles, but they had made so many side-trips, they had easily doubled that number. They had yet to find anyone living in any of the remote houses they searched. Some had been left open to the elements, and several had been infiltrated by bears. They found some medical supplies Rowan would be glad to see – baby aspirin and rubbing alcohol, which Verity used to produce herbal tinctures – and a couple of generators that were still in working order. But little else.

Little else, that is, except for bodies.

Most of the dead, it appeared, had succumbed to the plague. Naomi was becoming numb to those – they had all seen so many corpses, had all helped bury countless remains. She wouldn't allow herself to not care, though she didn't judge those that handled it that way. Rather, she regarded the bodies, the once men, women and children, as the natural, discarded husks of people, like a snake skin or an outgrown sea shell. They seemed peaceful to her when she thought of them that way, nothing to be afraid of. It was the obvious suicides that got to her, and left her with an uneasy prickle on her skin. Not that she judged such a choice, either – who knows what she might have done, without Piper in her heart, pulling her forward – but the violence to self, that final despair, seemed to linger in the air long after.

They'd found a pair in the last group of houses they had searched, a cluster of homes near the Rainbow Valley Ranch. Martin had entered the house first with Naomi bringing up the rear. They alternated the lead on these searches, one of them clearing the home before the other entered. When twice the allotted time had passed and Martin still hadn't called the all-clear, Naomi had linked with Persephone, who rarely left Martin's side these days. She'd picked up distress, but not a threat, and had gone inside to find Martin standing, frozen by the tableau in front of him.

A pair of withered corpses hung from the second story balcony of a soaring great room. They were holding hands. They must have jumped together, Naomi realized, squinting as she took in the details, as if squinting would make it more bearable. She looked closer, and shivered. They had bound their hands together with rope, as carefully as they had knotted the nooses they hung by.

"Could you do this?"

Naomi had turned her head to find Martin gazing at her with bloodshot eyes. "Could you?" he repeated hoarsely. "Could you check out like this when you still had someone to love? They still had each other. Why did they do this?"

Naomi looked back and answered the only part of his question she could. "No. I couldn't do this. Not while I had someone left to live for. Let's go."

They hadn't discussed it since, nor did Naomi expect to. Martin was as ever-practical as he was ever-critical. If he bent his mind to philosophy, to thoughts of life, death and the meaning of it all, he kept those thoughts to himself.

Naomi sighed and settled back against the log she'd commandeered while Martin was fixing dinner. Now that her stomach was full of food she hadn't had to cook, and the dishes were done without a finger lifted on her part, she was feeling markedly less irritable. It helped that the biscuits Martin had attempted were currently smoking on the edge of their campsite, black and rock-like. Hers, in the morning, would be extra soft and fluffy. She'd make sure of it.

She sighed again, tired but not exhausted, enjoying the ache of the new muscles she'd used, knowing that ache would be strength tomorrow. Her feet were delightfully warm, kept that way by her efficient little fire, burning in the efficient little fire pit she'd dug. It was possible Martin had a point. It felt good, knowing she could do for herself.

"You did a good job on the fire pit."

Naomi looked up sharply. "Okay, that is just the last straw. Can you actually read my mind?"

"No." Martin hunched his shoulders around his ears. "Not really."

His discomfort was a surprise. Naomi teetered between irritation and amusement, not sure which way she'd end up tipping. "Why don't you clarify that?" She refrained from repeating her threat to his kneecaps, but only just.

Martin picked up a stick and poked at the fire. "I can pick up on the direction of your thoughts. It's like the truth/lie thing, but more specific. I've always been able to do it, even in the time before." He looked chagrined. "It drove my ex-wife nuts. I just kept my mouth shut with wife number two."

"Huh." This, she had not expected. "So, you've always known you were intuitive? This isn't a new thing to you?"

"I never thought of myself as intuitive. I still don't. I just trust my instincts because they're almost always right. When I've spent time with someone, gotten to know them," he paused and shot a look at her she couldn't quite read, "I can just tell. By what you're looking at, the sounds you make, the look on your face. It's kind of a thousand little clues that just come together, like the pieces of a puzzle."

It made her uncomfortable, thinking of being scrutinized so closely all the time. No wonder his ex-wife had protested. And as long as he had brought it up... "How long were you married? Both times?"

"Thirteen years, with my first wife. We had Grace right away, but Benjamin – Benji, we called him – didn't come along until five years later. I was active duty most of that time, deployed more than I was home. It took us a while, after things settled down, to figure out it just wasn't working." Again, he poked at the fire with his stick. "Isabella and I had only been married two years. She was a lot younger, the polar opposite of my first wife." He grimaced. "High maintenance. I figured she'd mature when Michael was born, but –" He shrugged. "Never got the chance to find out. Anyway. What about you? How long were you married?"

She had just learned more about Martin in two minutes than she'd learned in the last nine months. She'd rather keep him talking – who knew how long his chatty mood would last – but tit for tat, she supposed. At least they weren't bickering. "It would have been twenty-four years, this year. I wasn't yet twenty – younger than Piper is now. She was born a couple of years after we were married, but I miscarried several times afterwards. We thought she'd be our only." Naomi smiled, remembering, and rubbed her heart, warming the memory against the chill of the sorrow she carried with her always. "Macy was a surprise tag-a-long. We were all so excited."

"That's admirable. It takes grit, to stay married that long."

"We were lucky. Well-suited. And we were just kids. We grew up together, I always said." She shifted the subject, uncomfortable talking about her happy marriage when both of his sounded less than ideal. "Do you think your kids have changed? Macy had, for sure. She was a lot like Verity." Martin shot her a sideways glance that made both of them chuckle. "Yeah. That would have just gotten more interesting as time went on, I'm sure. And of course I can't know for sure with Piper, but I sense...something."

It was her turn to grab a stick and poke at the fire. What was it about poking a fire, staring at it, that made it easier to talk? "It's not good, what I sense. There has always been a tough edge to Piper, and that's what I feel coming from her. She was studying sociology in college, and I never felt comfortable with that. It didn't seem like she wanted to understand people so much as she wanted to manipulate them. It's difficult for her to show love or tenderness. It always was, until Macy came along. I dread telling her." She didn't want to continue down this path. "So, what do you think, about your kids?"

"I can't feel them like you do. I'm not sure if I wish I could or not. When I was deployed, I learned to keep my family out of my head when I needed to. I couldn't afford to be distracted – I would have ended up dead." He was silent for a few minutes, thinking about her question. "I would bet they've both changed. Kids are more likely to, as we've seen. My Grace, she's a lot like me – she sees patterns, and gets the big picture before other people do. But she's a lot more book-smart than I ever was. Benji, he's a little computer genius, like his Mama." He grinned, and shook his head. "My little techno-geek. If anybody's going to be able to get the internet back up and running, it'll be him."

Silence fell between them again, an easy one this time, disturbed only by the soft crackle of the fire and an occasional, whuffing breath from one of the horses. All three were tied to a tree line close by: the brown and white Appaloosa named Shakti that Martin was riding; Pasha, another Appaloosa that was serving as their pack animal; and Naomi's Ben. Every once in a while, Naomi reached out to brush Ben's awareness with her own – Ignacio swore horses were better than guard dogs when it came to sounding the alarm. If trouble approached, he had promised, the horses would be sure to let them know.

Martin had grown so sure of their perceptions, he didn't insist on setting a night watch.

Ben was alert but relaxed. He nickered softly when he *felt* her touch, and she smiled. "Ben says it's dark o'clock and all's well."

"You talk about her more easily now. Macy. You say her name, and it doesn't sound like it's being ripped out of you."

Naomi gazed into the fire, and after a moment, shrugged. "It helps to say her name. It keeps her close." She frowned; she had been trying not to think of Macy, unprotected at the cabin. She didn't like the idea of her there, alone, in the dark. It would be cold – obviously, she hadn't been able to leave the fire burning – and Ares was there, but he was no guard dog...

She looked up sharply, remembering Martin's particular ability, and found him watching her with a quizzical look on his face. Rather than let him ask a question she wouldn't answer, she blurted the first thing that came to mind. "The weather certainly has been nice, hasn't it?"

Martin's lips curled into a slow smile. "The weather? Really? Is that the best you can do?"

Naomi looked at Hades, who was curled against her hip, head resting on her thigh. "Remember what I told you about the eggs. We're still on with that," she whispered.

"Rest easy. I'm not going to bug you about whatever it was that drove you to the weather. But yes. It has been very nice, and we've been very lucky."

The plan had been to stay in deserted houses if the weather proved too inclement, but as Martin said, they'd been lucky. Naomi was glad. She vastly preferred the outdoors, near the horses, where she could hear and see what was going on around her. Never could she have guessed she'd rather sleep in a mummy bag with nothing but a tent between her and the winter sky, than in a dead stranger's house, with its unfamiliar creaks and strange scents...although when she thought of it that way, it didn't seem strange at all. They had an abundance of top-of-the-line cold-weather gear with them. Folks in Colorado had loved their extreme sports, and many had hiked and camped year-round. It hadn't been difficult at all to outfit themselves with more than they needed. But that was part of the purpose of this trip – to figure out what was necessary to carry, and what wasn't.

The other was to scout out Cripple Creek as a potential site to re-locate. The arrival of the woman they all called "Anne" – well, Martin called her "that flaky librarian from the Springs" – had altered the trajectory of their plans. Naomi had resisted being in what she thought of as the "inner circle of command" – Jack, Layla, Rowan and Martin – but when Martin wasn't correcting this or that petty little nuance of her behavior, he had talked about what the woman had told them, and the implications. And that reminded her – while she was thinking about it –

"I want to thank you."

Martin looked like he'd been half-asleep. He blinked at her, and frowned. "Thank me for what?"

"For not telling me what a rotten trail-partner I am for at least the last hour." She had meant the comment to amuse him, to solidify the camaraderie they were enjoying, but his frown deepened.

"I haven't told you any such thing. When did I say anything like that?"

Was he serious? She asked him. "Are you serious? Only every ten minutes for the last three days."

"Naomi, I don't know what you're talking about. I haven't said anything of the kind."

"Let me recap." She started ticking points off on her fingers. "I'm too slow, too loud, too careless, too hesitant, too careful – let me know if I miss something – and when I finally finished the fire pit, you said, and I quote, 'About time.' Meaning that you could have done it better and faster than my inept self."

"Of course I could have. That wasn't the point, though." He shook his head, and the long-suffering-male look on his face made her want to skewer him with her fire-poker. "You are all those things. But you're learning – *that's* the point. And you're starting to figure things out on your own. Using the water to soften the ground – that was a good idea. If you want to twist stuff around and make shit up about what you think I'm thinking, that's your problem, not mine."

"My problem? *Mine?* You're a critical, condescending jackass!" God, it felt so good, yelling that word at him. "And I'm the one with the problem?"

"Yeah. The way I see it, you are."

Camaraderie time was over. Naomi shot to her feet and stomped around the campsite, picking things up and setting them down at random, looking for some task – any task – to distract her. Her agitation made all three horses toss their heads and Ben nicker anxiously, so she stopped stomping and just stood, arms crossed over her heaving chest, and got it all clear in her head before she turned around and blasted him with it.

"You know what? I'm done. I'm through. I'm not going to spend one more minute trying to prove myself to you. So what, if I haven't spent much time camping and roughing it? So what, if none of this stuff comes naturally to me? I've made it this far, haven't I? I'll figure it out, and I don't need you telling me how bad I am at it every time you exhale, thank you very much!" She tilted her chin up and looked down her nose at him. "I'll accept your apology, whenever you're ready to give it."

He laughed. He actually laughed. "Don't hold your breath." He rose, stretched, then shook his head at her. "Maybe I'm not a very good teacher. I don't praise you every time you tie your shoes without my help or when you manage to walk and chew gum. That's not how I was raised, and it sure as hell isn't how it's done in the Marines. You're inexperienced. You're slow, and loud, too cautious sometimes and too careless others. But you never make the same mistake twice, and you try so damn hard." He gestured at her fire pit. "I told you you did a good job on the fire pit – did I not?"

She had been so sure she was in the right...until he started talking. This always happened with him. She'd never met someone more difficult to communicate with. "I'm going to bed."

She made it halfway to the tent before his voice sounded behind her, quiet and firm. "No, you're not."

She turned around, incredulous. Had he really just said that to her? "Pardon me?"

"You haven't finished your chores for the night. You need to put the fire out and re-fill the water buckets before you turn in." He brushed by her on his way to the tent. "I'll leave the lantern on until you come in."

Her mouth worked, but nothing came out. She tried to remember if she'd ever been so angry, so frustrated, but nothing came to mind. Just when she was sure a blood vessel was going to burst in her brain, Martin spoke over his shoulder.

"Before you spend half the night plotting how you're going to sneak something awful into my eggs – yeah, I heard what you said to Hades – you might ask yourself one question." He turned and looked at her. "Which of us are you really trying to prove yourself to? Because it sure as hell's not me."

Well. That didn't take the wind out of her sails; it shredded them. Her shoulders slumped. Wrong again. Just like that. Martin disappeared inside the tent with Persephone trotting at his heels, leaving Naomi to her chores and her uncomfortable thoughts. Shadowed by Hades, she reduced the fire to stone-cold soggy ashes, filled buckets, and double-checked the horses' timber line. The curve of Ben's shoulder was a good place to lean and think, and, if she was honest, avoid joining Martin in the tent.

She'd never struggled so hard to stay on her feet with someone, not like this. Piper had tested her temper to the limit, and of course she and Scott had disagreed upon occasion, but she'd never worked so hard and failed so thoroughly at keeping her balance with another person. She hated the way Martin thought of her. She grimaced the moment the thought crossed her mind. She hated what she *guessed* Martin thought of her. Maybe she'd been all wrong about that. One thing was certain; there was no way she was going to ask.

Exhaustion wanted to pull her body to the ground, right where she stood. She gave Ben a final hug, stroked the other horses for fairness, and headed to the tent. Martin was already asleep when she crawled inside, Persephone curled on his chest. She was as quick and quiet as she could manage, pulling her outer clothes and boots off and sliding into her cold mummy bag. Hades curled up between her and Martin, snuggled against her side. Between his warmth and the low shush of Martin's breathing, Naomi dropped into sleep like a stone.

She started awake hours later, instantly alert. Before she could wonder what had woken her, it came again – a hard, mental *nudge* from Ben. He and the other horses were shifting, restless, uneasy. She could hear them outside the tent as well as *feel* Ben's anxiety. Naomi took a steadying breath and opened her mind to his awareness; what she learned made fear streak cold down her spine.

Men. At least two – no, it was three. Sneaking up on their campsite. Ben could see one of them as plainly as if it was mid-day – the moon was nearly full and the night was clear. He could hear the other two. They had the camp surrounded and were closing in on the tent with slow stealth.

Naomi reached out in the darkness and grasped Martin's arm. His body stiffened as he woke, but he didn't jerk or make a sound. He put his hand over hers and squeezed; then she heard the barest whisper.

"What is it?"

"Three men. Ben sees them." Her whisper trembled. "To the north, east and south."

Martin leaned over Hades and put his mouth right by her ear. "Slide your boots on and get your rifle. I'm going to unzip the tent, then we're going to step out, quickly, and stand back-to-back. Rifle at the ready. After that, be prepared to do whatever I tell you to. Do you understand?"

Her legs were shaking so badly, she wasn't sure she could stand. She had to work up spit to creak an answer out to him. "Yes."

"Good. Boots, now."

She was going to wet her pants. She slid her feet into her boots, then crouched, ready to stand when he said to. Hades was awake now, as was Persephone. She sent both of them a silent command to *stay*. She didn't want them in the middle of a firefight, and they might come in handy as an element of surprise if things didn't go as Martin planned. She had to chomp down on a hysterical giggle at that thought. She was pretty sure there was no *plan* per se. This was as seat-of-the-pants as it got.

Martin reached for the zipper. She was still partially linked with the dogs, and she could see his face clearly, even in the dark tent. How could he look so calm? His chest rose and fell slowly, steadily, and his eyes were cool and intent. He met her gaze and smiled, and that was when she saw the adrenalin running through him, in that ferocious smile.

"I'll unzip, then we go." He didn't give her time to ask questions. "Now."

Naomi forced her legs to straighten. She staggered an extra step and had to lock her watery knees against falling, but she made it, her back pressed to Martin's, her rifle at her shoulder. Movement off to her left caught her attention; she tucked her cheek in close and sighted in on a man who froze when he saw her. The moon was so bright, she could make out the Seattle Seahawks logo on his baseball cap. He was holding a shotgun at his hip, and his eyes darted, giving away his companion, less visible in the heavy cover near the horses. Ben tossed his head and whinnied an alarm, and the darker shadow in the shadows stopped moving.

Naomi didn't see any need to whisper. "I see two of the three." She kept her rifle trained on the man she had the clearest shot on, though the proximity of the other man to the horses was making her skin twitch. "To the north and east." Ben shrilled again, and Naomi shuddered in response, struggling to disconnect from his anxiety. Shakti and Pasha both snorted and tossed their heads. "East is awfully close to the horses."

"I can hear that. I've got the third – he ducked behind that stand of scrub oak when we stood up and he's still there." Martin's shoulders pivoted against hers briefly as he turned to mark the locations of the men Naomi was covering. "Keep your rifle on the guy to the north." Then, he raised his voice so the men could hear him, his tone flat and calm. "We can see all three of you, and we're armed. We'd rather not shoot the first living people we've seen, but we will."

After a moment of silence, the man to the south called out. "We don't want trouble, either. But we'll be taking your horses, and whatever other gear we need. We've got you surrounded and outnumbered."

"Naomi, honey?" Martin's voice carried clearly in the still, cold night air. "Could you remove that gentleman's hat for him, please?"

Her rifle cracked the stillness open; the man's baseball hat flipped to the ground, and she saw his eyes, wide and white, before he dropped to flatten himself on the ground. Naomi shifted to target the shadow in the shadows, linking with Ben to better pinpoint his location. From inside the tent, Hades whuffed, and she sent all the animals waves of reassurance, though her teeth were chattering.

"Christ, Nick! She about took my head off!"

Martin's voice was warm with approval. "Thank you, sweetheart, I appreciate it. You got that other fellow in your sights?"

She swallowed, again and again, but couldn't un-stick her tongue from the roof of her mouth. Finally, she just nodded against his back, and he spoke for her.

"Good job, honey, you just keep him there." He spoke again to the man hidden in the scrub oak. "If she had wanted to take his head off, she would have. Nick, was it? She's a pretty good shot – taught her everything I know. Now, how about you reconsider your plans?"

In the heavy silence that followed Martin's words, Hades overrode Naomi's stay command, his big head emerging from the tent. He locked his eyes on her, and she *felt* the whine vibrate through him, though he didn't make a sound. Closing her eyes, she visualized what she wanted him to do, then released him with a whispered, "Go!" He shot into the underbrush in typical tank fashion, and she heard startled exclamations from all three men. When he reached the stand of scrub oak concealing Nick, he bellied low to the ground and let loose with a growl so resonant and threatening, it made the hair on even Naomi's nape rise.

"Call off your dog or I'll shoot it!"

And if that didn't bring Naomi's voice roaring back. "Call off your men, or I'll let the other one go! You won't know she's there until she's taken a chunk out of you!"

She reinforced her directive for Hades to stay low, then linked with Ben. The man in the shadows was out of his reach, but not Shakti's. She took a deep breath and extended her mind as gently as she could. She wasn't unfamiliar to Shakti, and that helped. The big Appaloosa snorted, and the link was tenuous, but it was enough. Shakti lunged on her lead, snapping at the man and driving him out of the shadows. Naomi sighted in, aiming right between his startled eyes.

Behind her, Martin chuckled, and the "good old boy" was thick in his voice when he spoke. "Well, I'm feeling mighty superfluous, I don't mind saying. Nick, you've gone and pissed this lady off, and let me tell you, that is not a good thing. You think her dog is scary?" He snorted out a laugh, belying the tension she could feel vibrating through his body. "Now, if you want to come back in the daylight, maybe get something to eat and talk like civilized people, we might have some supplies we can spare. Otherwise, you're welcome to try mounting one of her horses. The dogs'll take care of anything that's left after the attempt."

Again, thick silence fell. Then, Nick spoke. "Teddy. Liam. Let's go."

All three of them backed away via the directions they had come. Naomi's knees wobbled, and Martin pushed her down into a crouch before they gave out altogether. "Call Hades in and stay low," he said. "Don't move, no matter what you hear. I'll call Persephone with my mind when I come back in."

Naomi nodded and he was gone, ghosting through the underbrush. She summoned Hades, who plowed back to her, panting and delighted by the fun game they were playing. She looped an arm around his neck and pulled him close, sucking in breath after breath and wondering when she would be permitted to break down and blubber. Persephone slipped out of the tent, and Naomi scooped her up, burying her nose in the little dog's familiar scent.

She endured the wait by monitoring the horses. They settled fairly quickly; Pasha fell into a doze, while Ben and Shakti remained alert but relaxed. After what felt like both an eternity and just a few heartbeats, Ben snorted and Persephone struggled to be free, darting into the darkness as soon as Naomi set her down. Martin stepped out of the shadows less than a minute later with Persephone tucked in the crook of his arm.

Naomi slumped in relief. "Are they gone?"

"I followed them back to their camp, listened in on their plans. They're staying put for the night." He strode towards her. "Stand up."

Naomi struggled to her feet, stumbling on legs that had gone numb. Her head swam from standing up too fast. "What's wrong? Are we breaking camp? I...oh..."

She knew what that look on his face meant. Any woman who had hormones and even ten minutes of experience with men knew what that look meant. He stopped when his chest brushed hers.

"Pretty sure I'm going to kiss you, Naomi."

The swimming sensation increased. Images of Scott flashed across her mind, his smile in all its variations, his hands, the sound of his laugh, and a thousand, thousand kisses. She got out, "I, uh, well –" before the black closed over her head.

Sun was shining through the wall of the tent the next time she opened her eyes. She frowned and turned her head to find herself nose-to-nose with Hades. He whined low in his throat, then licked her from chin to forehead with one slobbery swipe.

"Gah!" She sat up, sputtering. "Thanks, buddy."

The tent zipped open, and Martin's face appeared. "You're alive."

Memory was returning. "Did I pass out?"

"Yep." He smiled tightly. "First time announcing my intention to kiss a woman has ever made her keel over."

Naomi dropped her face into her hands. "Martin..."

"Don't hurt yourself." He stood, and moved away from the tent, his brisk voice floating back to her. "Chalk it up to after-battle lust and move on. So if you'd like to get up anytime soon, we can get going. We're wasting daylight."

Naomi hurried into her boots and outdoor gear, then disappeared into the underbrush to relieve a bladder that was perilously close to bursting. A quick stop by the stream to splash water on her face and she was heading back to camp, the smell of eggs and bacon warming the air. She didn't let herself pause, or feel uncomfortable, or any other such nonsense, as she stepped into the clearing surrounding their campfire.

"Can I do anything?"

Martin looked up from the frying pan he was tending. "How long would it take you to throw some biscuits together?"

By way of answer, she started assembling what she needed. "I'll make extra for lunch."

"Good idea."

They worked in companionable silence until Naomi's biscuits were tucked in the coals in a cast iron skillet and Martin had finished their breakfast. He handed her a blue tin plate heaped with eggs and bacon, then sat down next to her on the log she was occupying.

"We'll break camp then head into Cripple Creek. Our friends from last night must have decided not to join us for breakfast. They're squatting in one of the old Rainbow Valley Ranch guest cabins not far downstream. I snuck over this morning while you were sleeping and checked out their set-up in the daylight. Looks like they've been there a while. We'll want to watch out for them on the way back through."

Naomi looked down at her plate, remembered fear cramping her stomach. "I'm not cut out for this," she muttered. "Do you think everyone we meet will be like them?"

"Hard to say. Depends on so many things, but right down at the base of it is fear. Fearful people can justify anything, including theft and murder." He paused, and she looked up to find him watching her with his no-nonsense eyes. "And don't sell yourself short. You handled yourself last night. I was proud of you."

It took a moment for the compliment to sink in. Naomi's skin warmed, and she looked down again, pushing the eggs around on her plate. "Yeah, well, I was certainly fearful. If one of them had hurt Hades or one of the horses, I'd have –" She broke off and grimaced. "Big talk. I have no idea what I would have done."

"I have a pretty good idea, but let's hope you never have to find out." Martin stood up, but instead of clapping her on the shoulder as he sometimes did, he rested his hand there in what was almost a caress. "Maybe one of these days I'll make your list, along with your animals." This time, he did clap her, hard enough to make her yelp. "Finish your breakfast, and we'll eat those biscuits on the go. The sun's shining, but the wind's up. Something's blowing in, I'm sure of it."

They were underway in less than an hour, walking the horses at a steady pace up the middle of the road. The sun had melted the snow off the blacktop in most places, leaving them with ice and snow to traverse only occasionally. From where they'd camped, the road rose and twisted steadily, with fewer houses and steeper drop-offs. Where Country Road 81 diverged toward Victor, they saw smoke rising from a cluster of homes set well off the road, but Martin decided not to investigate.

"We'll check it out on the way back through," he said. He turned in the saddle to check their back trail, something he'd been doing all morning. "We're only about five miles from Cripple Creek," he murmured, then scrutinized the group of homes again. "Makes me wonder..." Then he scanned the horizon. "I don't like the look of those clouds. I think our luck is about to break, weather-wise. We need to pick up the pace."

Sure enough, by the time they were traveling up the switch-backs that would drop them down into Cripple Creek from the north east, a light snow had begun to fall. Naomi hunched her shoulders against the gusting wind, looking up when Martin dropped back to ride beside her. He was scanning the ridges above, frowning. "We're being watched."

Alarm zipped down her spine. "How do you know?"

"I can feel it. Don't freak out on me. I'd post watchers here, too. Either they're unarmed – which is pretty unlikely – or they're not interested in shooting us. Yet, anyway." He drew his rifle and let it rest across his lap, and Naomi followed suit. He checked their back trail, the ridges again, then looked at her and smiled, the same ferocious smile she'd seen last night. Reaching into the front of his coat, he scooped Persephone out, handing her over to Naomi. "I'm going to ride ahead. Just around this curve, you can see most of Cripple Creek. If it's not safe to go on, I'll head back and we'll clear out of here. If I'm not back in ten minutes and you haven't heard any gunfire, come on ahead."

A whole fleet of protests rose, but the only one she dared verbalize was, "I don't have a watch – how am I supposed to know when ten minutes have passed?"

Martin grinned and kicked his heels into Shakti's sides. "One-one-thousand, two-one-thousand, three-one-thousand…"

Naomi huffed in irritation and watched him canter ahead. Risky situations sure brought out his playful side, and how strange was that? Like she was going to count off – good Lord, how many seconds was ten minutes, anyway? He disappeared around the corner, and both dogs whined her anxiety. The sun had become only a slightly brighter spot in the sky, hidden behind clouds with bulging grey bellies. Naomi fidgeted, squirmed and jiggled her legs nervously until Ben tossed his head and nickered his annoyance.

"Well, that's about all the waiting I'm going to do." She urged Ben forward, Pasha following behind, all her senses open. The horses were alert but not nervous, which was reassuring. She rounded the bend in the road, got her first glimpse of Cripple Creek, and felt her heart plummet.

The city, with its cute little Victorian homes, its casinos, restaurants, museums and souvenir shops, was a blackened ruin. Up and down the main drag, brick walls still stood, but she'd bet they were burned-out shells only. Martin had stopped near the visitor's center, which appeared to be undamaged. He turned as Naomi rode up, his face cut with lines of sadness she'd never seen before.

"I used to come up here with my buddies, whenever we needed to get away from the wives," he said, his eyes swinging back to what had once been a thriving mountain community. "We'd gamble a little, drink a little, then head home. I proposed to my wife over breakfast at Maggie's. We honeymooned up here, at the Cherub House."

She didn't think about it; she just sent a pulse of comfort from her heart to his. He started, but didn't look at her. After a moment, he held his hand out and she took it, again without thinking. They sat like that for a few minutes, holding hands in simple comfort as the wind rose and the snow swirled around them. Finally, Martin heaved a deep breath and let go of her hand.

"Wonder if we'll ever get over counting up everything we've lost," he said quietly. "Just when you think you've dealt with it, something kicks you in the teeth."

Naomi hunched her shoulders against the stinging wind. "What's the plan now? Do you want to go down and check it out?"

Martin looked away from the ruins of his memories, scanned the skies, then reined Shakti around and started back the way they had come. "No reason to, not with this weather moving in. Let's head for home."

TEN
Piper: Walden, CO

"No regrets." Piper leaned close to the mirror in the dimly lit bathroom, and hissed the words she began each day with. She gazed into her own eyes, eyes that crackled and sparked with the rage that never left her these days. She touched her reflection self tenderly on the forehead, the cheek, the lips, and the rage lit her from within, an inferno under her skin. "None."

Then, she sat down on the closed toilet lid and carefully sliced the inside of her left bicep open with a scalpel she'd taken from the clinic. Sting, then burn, then blood sliding free. Piper took a deep, shuddering breath. With the blood flowed rage, terror, frustration, horror. Another deep breath, and sweet calm, sweet relief, flowed in its wake.

The first time she'd done this had been the night Josh died. The second, a few days later. And every day since. How she had despised the kids who cut in high school and college – attention-getting behavior, she'd scoffed. Humbling, to know they had been right: The pain you could control was infinitely better than the pain you couldn't. Piper knew the mechanics of it, the rush of endorphins, the illusion of control and all that, and still was helpless to deny the need. She existed as two people these days – one who continued to watch and reason and scheme, and another who had to slice open her own body to keep the wailing berserker at bay.

She bandaged her arm with the ease of practice, discarded the bloody tissue she had used to stanch the flow, and returned the scalpel to its hiding place on top of the window frame. When she was finished, she once again met her own eyes in the mirror. "You'll be okay," she whispered. "You will. You can make it one more day."

Piper left the bathroom and sat at the table to watch her birds, waiting quietly while Brody finished his preparations for the day. She had kept her head down for the past three weeks, pretending to be subdued in the wake of Josh's death. It sounded almost benign when she said it to herself that way: "Josh's death." Not "Josh's murder," or "Josh's execution by my hand." But why should she eat guilt over it? They had all – Josh included – played the cards that had been dealt. It wasn't her fault that Josh's hand had been the loser.

As always when these thoughts crossed her mind, she listened for her mother's voice. Naomi despised nothing so much as people who didn't take responsibility for their decisions and actions. Piper could still remember the battle-fire that lit her mother's eyes when one of her daughters dared utter the forbidden words, "But mom, it's not my fault!"

As she'd gotten older, they had battled royal over Piper's refusal to own the consequences of her hurtful words. Piper's stance: She could think and say what she pleased. If her words hurt people, well, that was their problem. Naomi's stance: There was no such thing as carte blanche when it came to the feelings of others. Round and round they'd gone, and Piper regretted that now, regretted all the strife and conflict she'd stirred, just to stir it. What did it mean that she could feel remorse for every one of those long-ago arguments with her mother, but not for the death of a man she'd set up and then killed in cold blood?

She didn't know. And her mother wasn't talking.

She had been back over the day of Josh's death so many times, she could repeat parts of it verbatim, and it still struck her as a shock that they knew. All of them knew how it was with her and Brody, and they not only tolerated it, they looked the other way. She knew now that this same dynamic had sealed Josh's fate. In a survival situation, individuals were expendable. The survival of the group was paramount. She had been trying to make herself indispensable, to earn respect and status in order to free herself, but she had misread this situation and these people.

She knew the truth of it now: Only death could set her free. Whose, she was not yet certain.

Some instinct made her look away from her birds, and she turned her head to find Brody watching her, his expression...confusing. He looked down, fussing with his pack, and Piper frowned. If she didn't have reason to know better, she would say he had looked worried. Piper shrugged, and returned her attention to the flock of Cedar Waxwings that were squabbling over the scraps of bread she had collected for them. What did it matter what he was thinking?

When Brody had finished with both their packs, they left the cabin and headed for the mess hall. Piper followed him in silence. They rarely spoke these days. Brody had not hit her since the day of Josh's death, and she wasn't sure what to make of that. His use of her sexually had not changed, though, so she wasn't entertaining any delusions.

Her day went as too many of them were starting to go, without event or change. She ate, she worked, she had Ruth give her a haircut, she watched the people around her, and she hated them. As far as she could tell, no one was aware of her feelings, not even those whose intuitive skills had increased. She had never imagined she could be surrounded by people, all day, every day, and be so profoundly alone. The need to change things, to stir things up, was growing to volcanic urgency inside her.

With increasing frequency, she found herself entertaining bizarre thoughts: What if I stood up on one of the tables in the mess hall and sang, "Ninety-nine bottles of beer on the wall" until one of them shot me? What would getting shot feel like? Too bad she couldn't ask Josh – he would know – but she'd shot him! Ha! What if I took off all my clothes and walked into the woods? What would freezing to death feel like? Would the ravens eat me? What would they eat first? Maybe my eyes? Would she be able to see as ravens saw, then? She rather liked that idea...

She knew, of course, what all of these thoughts meant. Thank you, Psych 101. She knew her instinct to survive was wobbling, dangerously so, that the rage she struggled to control every minute of every day was destroying her from the inside out. What she didn't know was what to do about it.

And then, opportunity and inspiration showed up hand-in-hand.

She was sitting next to Ruth in the mess hall after supper, as she usually did, watching and analyzing bond-lines, as she always did, when Ethan walked in. He'd been absent more and more often at the communal meals lately, so his presence was a bit of a surprise, as was the total absence of bond-lines she detected between him and the group.

Piper blinked and squinted. Nope, not a one. There were, however, three vibrant bond-lines connecting him to people unseen, people to the southwest, including an arcing, bright white bond she'd watched crackle into life with her own eyes, months ago. Elise and her children. There was no amount of money she wouldn't bet on it. As she watched, Ethan wound his way through the tables, eyes locked on Brody, an expression of grim determination on his face. Instinct had her on her feet and moving in the same direction. She reached Brody at the same time Ethan did, though he didn't acknowledge or even appear to notice her.

Ethan cleared his throat. When Brody looked up, he said without preamble, "I'm leaving the group. Tonight."

Piper couldn't imagine what it would take to surprise Brody, and this certainly wasn't it. He regarded Ethan calmly, but before he could answer, Piper stirred the pot.

"Bring them here. Elise, and the kids." She looked around, found Levi watching her, as well as his sister and brother-in-law from the next table over. "Another woman, and kids about Caden's age." Bond-lines flared between Levi and his young nephew, between Jenny, Aaron, and their son, and Piper tugged harder. "It would be healthy for him, to have other kids around. A little bit of normal childhood."

She could feel Brody watching her, but she knew better than to look at him. A bird, after all, who looks into a snake's eyes can get so frightened she cannot move. Thank you, Riki-tiki-tavi. She turned to Ethan.

"They'd be safer here with us, and this group needs you." He flinched, and she saw how hard he'd been working to suppress the connections he felt to these people. She zeroed in on his closest bond and yanked on it without remorse. "I don't know what Max would do without you. He'd be lost. We're stronger, safer with you as a part of us. Elise and the kids might not have skills we need now, but they can learn. I did."

And then, there was nothing for her to do but wait to see if it had worked. She had thought to bring the pressure of the group to bear on Brody to save herself, but this was almost as good. For the first time since the night she had killed Josh she felt something she'd thought lost for good: Hope.

Brody was silent for so long, hope faltered. Then, "Bring them in. You can take cabin nine. In the morning, we'll work them into the duty roster."

Hope soared. Piper kept her eyes down, but couldn't control the smile that tugged the corners of her lips upwards, even when Brody rose and murmured a good night to the group. She knew what was expected and followed, donning her outdoor gear and trailing him through the silent dark to their cabin.

The door shut behind them, and the side of her face exploded into a fireworks display of bright lights and pain. The blow spun her around and off balance; she dropped to a crouch and shook her head, trying to clear it. Shit, shit, she had forgotten how much that hurt.

Brody stared down at her impassively. "If you ever force my hand like that again, I won't wait for privacy. I'll correct you right then and there."

He reached down to grasp her arm, and something in Piper broke and soared free. She slapped his hand away, shocking them both. Brody reached again, and again, she cuffed his hand away, springing to her feet to land in the fighter's stance she had watched him teach the others.

"No," she hissed. "Not again. Not ever again. Do you hear me?"

Brody stared at her with glittering eyes, his chest rising and falling swiftly. It aroused him when she fought back, which was why she hadn't in almost a year. This time, though, the instinct to protect herself would not be denied. He stepped in, close and fast, grasping her upper arms to yank her body against his; his lust was his undoing. She didn't think, just acted, slamming her forehead into his nose with a satisfying crunch. He grunted and took a staggering step backwards, letting her go, and Piper didn't waste her freedom.

She spun to put the table between them, remembering how she'd done this on that long-ago night, the night of that first rape, and remembering how easily he'd gone through the table to get to her. She was out of options, except for one. She didn't stop to think about whether she should or whether she could; she unsheathed her knife and held the sharp point pressed to the soft flesh under her own chin, pressed so hard, she felt blood trickle down her throat.

"I'm done." She said the words quietly, and repeated the one that really mattered: "Done."

And to her surprise, she meant it. What had gone before was finished. She felt a sweet, quiet calm settle over her, and knew with absolute surety that she could and would do this.

Brody swiped at the blood trickling from his bruised nose, and there was that look again. He *was* worried. About her. Piper felt laughter rise in her throat, tried to stifle it, then thought: What the hell? It burst free from her mouth, a wild cackle of freedom and desperation.

The skin around Brody's eyes tightened, and for the first time ever, she saw a bond-line flare, emanating from him. To her. So bright, it made her squint. She laughed again, then again, wild, sobbing whoops. "Well, what do you know?" she managed. "Advantage: Piper. It's about time."

He waited until she wound down into hiccupping breaths, until she'd wiped the tears off her face. She had managed to keep the knife steady at her chin through her sudden hysterics, and blood now soaked the neck of her sweatshirt, warm and sticky. They stared at each other from their new positions on the game table; then, Brody spoke.

"You've got one shot at this, Piper. If you ever try this again, I'll kill you myself. Negotiate well."

Her heart was pounding so hard she could hardly hear herself speak. "You will never hit me again. Never."

"Done."

She could not believe this was happening, struggled to think it all through. How she knew he would keep his word, she couldn't say, but she was sure of it. "Elise and the kids. They can come stay with us."

Impatience. "You're asking for something I've already given my permission for."

Shit! "I knew that. I'm not stupid." But she was acting stupid, wasn't she? Piper took deep breath after deep breath, calming and clearing her mind. "You won't change your mind and make them leave. Your word on it."

"Very well. Anything else?" He didn't say it, but she knew she had one request left. She stared at him, probing, prodding, trying to read him, but he had his barriers back up and then some. Well, what did she have to lose?

"No more sex." She lifted her chin, felt the berserker rage stir in her chest. "No more *rape*."

He didn't so much as flinch at her use of the word. A smile touched his mouth, and he slowly shook his head at her. "Try again."

Fuck. If she locked in on this, she'd lose everything. She was sure of it. He'd make Elise and the kids go, just to school her. He'd beat her bloody, to reinforce the lesson. She glared at him, then came to a decision. Still holding the knife at her chin, she reached into the pocket of the coat she still wore, dragging the now-battered box of condoms free. She slapped it onto the table between them.

"I will not bring a child into this."

A strange corona of light flared around him, but otherwise, he remained impassive, unreadable. Finally, he reached out and picked the box up. And nodded. "Done. Give me the knife."

Piper lowered the knife, but did not hand it to him. She returned it to the sheath on her arm, then stood still as he walked around the table. He didn't stop until his chest was pressed to her breasts, and she stared at his throat, resigned, reminding herself that while he used her, she could count the points she had won. To her surprise, though, he just stood there, chest pressed to hers, his chin barely touching her forehead. He didn't put his arms around her, nor did he speak.

Finally, he took a step back and reached for the left cuff of her sweatshirt, tugging her arm free. His movements were slow and gentle, as if he didn't want to frighten her. He lifted the sweatshirt to her shoulder, exposing her left arm and breast, then took her wrist and carefully turned it.

"I have a condition of my own." His fingers traced the bandage on the inside of her bicep, then moved to the myriad other partially-healed cuts, brushing them with a care he had never shown her skin before. "This stops."

She stared into the ice-blue of his eyes. "And if it doesn't?"

"Then all the rest of it is off," he answered. He touched the bridge of his nose, bruised and swollen. "If you need to let it out, you find another way."

He was inviting her to fight him? She narrowed her eyes, probing again. He was offering her another outlet for her rage. The question was, why? Brody lifted a hand, using a forefinger to trace the curve of her ear, another tender caress that made her shudder with unwanted sensation. He held his finger in front of her eyes, showing her the tiny, golden clippings of hair from the cut Ruth had given her just that afternoon.

"I've never thought you were stupid, Piper." His voice was a low rumble. "You're just not as smart as I am."

She dropped her eyes and stared at his throat again, feeling her pulse pound. He knew about the haircuts. What else did he know? Before she could think that through, he encircled her with his arms, his big hands spreading out on the bare skin of her back. She squeezed her eyes shut and swallowed hard. Oh, god. Not this. Not now.

"It could be so different between us, Piper." He leaned to breathe the words against her ear, his hands moving in warm, caressing circles on her back. One of them slid lower to splay at the base of her spine. His fingers pressed, and without warning, sensation shot up her spine and warmed her whole pelvis. "I could give you so much pleasure."

Piper took a step back and tilted her head to look at him. For the first time ever, she saw the mercy in him, that he had not forced a response from her. To capitulate would make her life easier. She didn't doubt that. It would also mean nothing less than the death of her soul. She let all her protective barriers drop, let him see right through her walls, for once not caring about tactical advantage. In this, he held all the cards.

"If you do that to me," she said quietly, "I will die. I won't need a knife."

She saw it again, the flare of the bond-line connecting him to her. He didn't snuff it this time, though he had to know she could see. He gazed down into her eyes, then lifted his hand to touch her forehead, her cheekbone, her lips. Still without speaking, he lifted her hand and pulled it back through the sleeve of her sweatshirt, settling the material warmly around her waist. Then, he took her shoulders and shifted her back. He used his foot to knock her feet shoulder-width apart, then lifted her hands and curled his around them, forming fists.

"When an opponent comes at you, don't fight their energy. Absorb it. Let it flow around you, like water around a rock." He lifted his own hands in front of him. "I'll show you."

She stared at him. The bond-line was still vibrating between them, totally one-sided, a prism of colors connecting his chest to hers. There was no way he should be letting her know this; it had to give him an advantage of some kind. This had to be a trap.

Brody smiled tightly, then reached out and pushed her in the center of the chest, a gentle nudge that nonetheless knocked her off balance. She frowned, but before she could analyze his inexplicable action, he did it again, this time in the center of her forehead. Her temper flared, and his smile widened. He flicked his fingers at her. Invitation. Provocation.

Piper erupted. She swung wildly, flailing with all her strength, panting, sobbing, then screaming. Adrenalin and strength poured through her, and she abandoned all pretense of control. She flew at him, driving him backwards with out-of-control punches and slaps, and when those failed to connect, kicks. He deflected everything, gliding smoothly backwards, letting her spend her strength. She ended up at the kitchen table again, bracing herself on shaking arms as she sucked in air and stared at him. He hadn't even broken a sweat.

Slowly, she straightened. She rolled her neck and felt the last of a terrible tension fall away from her shoulders. The next breath she took filled her all the way to her toes with beautiful oxygen, and she realized that she'd been breathing in the top third of her lungs for longer than she could remember. Cutting had been a controlled release, a steam valve. This had blown the top of the pot off. She would never look back.

Another deep breath, and strength surged through her. She raised her fists again, moved her feet into the fighting stance he'd shown her. "Show me."

The bond-line between them flared to incandescence. Brody bowed his head for a moment, and his hands dropped to fist on his thighs. Piper's eyes followed, and she felt her stomach clench. He wasn't even attempting to hide the fact that he was aroused. Just when she thought the agreements between them had meant nothing, he snuffed the bond-line and looked up at her with cool eyes.

"The first thing you need to understand is that defense is your best strategy. You can't learn to win against a far more experienced opponent, no matter how hard you train. You're seeking a stalemate. In defense, you must learn to recognize where the blow is coming from, so you can decide which way to move." He walked over to her, and Piper decided if he was going to ignore his obvious erection, she could, too. "Sometimes it's better to absorb a blow if getting out of the way will compromise your balance. Like this."

He moved in slow-motion, throwing a punch with one hand, showing her how and where to move with the other. Piper lost track of the time, completely absorbed, her mind kicking into hyper-drive, just like it had with Ruth. He taught it and she learned it, as fast as that. Simple blows, simple blocks, over and over, until her body was reacting before her mind could analyze. Every word he said, every concept he taught, became hers forever. When he finally called a halt hours later, she was both energized, and loose with the kind of relaxation she hadn't felt in over a year.

She vibrated with energy as they shifted into their night-time rituals, sure she wouldn't be able to sleep, astonished by the exhaustion that rolled over her when they were lying side-by-side in bed. Piper curled on her side away from him as she always did, and her eyelids slammed down, the drift towards sleep immediate. Just before she was sucked under, she felt his hand settle on her hip and tighten.

And so, she thought, here is the price to be paid. And pay she did.

ELEVEN
Jack: Woodland Park, CO

Just about the whole community had gathered to see Naomi and Martin off. Jack moved through the crowd, shaking hands, asking after the few who weren't present, solidifying bonds and reinforcing the goodwill he could *feel* radiating from virtually every person he interacted with. People loved him. They had in the time before, and they certainly did now. They loved him because they needed a leader. They needed someone to tell them what to do, how to act, what to think, what to believe. And Jack was just the guy for the job. He knew that now, with certainty.

The mantra whispered in his brain non-stop these days: "I could make you." He thought the words, as he clapped Alder on the back and admired his newborn son; as he nodded to Andrea and Paul, the siblings who never stopped squabbling and never left each other's sides; as he greeted Carla, their head gardener, and assured her that repair of her main greenhouse was the next project on the group work list. "I could make you. I could make you do whatever I want."

He would have loved to blame Satan for his current mental state, he surely would have. But he couldn't. No, this was all him. The things he conjured in the deep of night, the things he was imagining, right now, in the bright April sunshine... Deviant, twisted things. Didn't matter who, didn't matter the circumstances. In his day-to-day interactions, half his mind was engaged by the task at hand, while the other half manipulated and toyed with and tormented the people around him. He could make them do whatever he wanted, whenever he wanted. His imagination supplied endless variations on the theme.

There was one exception, one person he didn't dare feature in his dark fantasies, and he avoided her as if his life depended on it. His eyes swept the crowd as he moved towards Martin and Naomi, searching for golden curls and the almost-indiscernible glow of light that always surrounded them, but if Verity was here, she was keeping a low profile. Which, of course, meant she wasn't here. Verity was incapable of fading into any background. Jack's chest lifted and fell in a sigh of relief.

On some vague level, he was aware that his soul was poised on a knife's edge. Up until now, the abilities he'd found himself with in the wake of the plague had been nothing more than an irritation, something to be ignored whenever possible or used to his advantage when he judged it necessary. But the kind of power he now knew he had, power he could wield over anybody he chose... Jack had only been drunk once in his life, and had never tried drugs, but he couldn't imagine any high that could match the hectic euphoria he felt when he imagined what he could do.

Martin and Naomi were in front of the church, well-wishers and petitioners alike gathered around them. So many people had loved ones in Colorado Springs and other communities on the front range, and over the last several weeks, the requests had been pouring in: Could you check to see if my mother is alive? My kids were both at UCCS – will you look for them? My brother and his family, they're in Manitou, and you're going right through there...

Finally, Jack had put the word out: No more. The travelers had very specific objectives, one of the most important being reconnaissance. When they returned, if it was safe, more trips could be planned. In the meantime, Martin and Naomi were not to be deluged with any more requests. Jack had delivered this message with firmness and humor, just the right amounts of each, but the other half of his mind had been having a heyday. The pressure that could be brought to bear, the unlimited power to be found in people's desperation... The temptation was indescribable.

In spite of the directive, a few frantic souls were still trying. As Jack watched, Martin gently but firmly pressed a piece of paper back into an older woman's hands. He shook his head at her, lifted a hand to forestall the protest that burst from her, and Jack read the word that formed on his lips: "No." Martin turned away, and the woman stood for a moment, eyes brimming with tears and chin quivering, until a friend looped an arm around her shoulders and led her away.

Jack had met with Martin and Naomi early that morning, before the crowd had gathered; he had already said his goodbyes. Rather than jostle for a place near the travelers and add to the chaos, he stayed on the fringes, nodding at Thomas, Martin's second-in-command, and smiling at the kids, who were either hanging in groups of twos and threes trying to look cool or chasing each other through the crowd. Neither Layla nor Rowan had arrived yet, and Verity was still blessedly absent. Jack scanned the crowd again and was surprised to see Anne standing a few feet away, wringing her hands. She had managed to leave the library to see the travelers off, although she didn't look too happy about it.

Since her arrival over a month before, Anne hadn't so much as stepped outside to enjoy the increasing warmth of spring. Panic attacks kept her confined to the library, which was the only place she felt comfortable and secure, but it looked like her adoration of Martin had overridden her fear. Once she'd given up trying to kill the man, her attitude had swung in precisely the opposite direction. These days, she called him Angel, which never failed to make Martin cringe and Layla laugh, though they both did their best to hide their reactions from the fragile older woman. Anne was a rich source of knowledge; she had relived terrible memories in her efforts to supply Martin and Naomi with all the information she could as to the whereabouts and activities of the men currently in control of the city, as well as the remnants of the military in the Springs.

As he watched, Anne glanced over her shoulder, then looked up suddenly and flinched. The fear on her face was so real, it was hard not to look up as well. Jack stepped to her side, reinforcing his shields against the terror she barely had a grip on and skipping the preliminaries. "How can I help you?"

Anne hardly spared him a glance. "It's too bright out here." Her voice shook, and she patted her chest, her eyes darting around like a frenzied bird. "I can't catch my breath. There's no air."

Jack narrowed his eyes, wondering. Could he...? He let his shields drop enough to read her, really *read* her, and pitched his voice to slide right into her mind. "Look at me, Anne. Good. Now breathe with me to the count of ten." He kept his eyes locked on hers while he counted out the breaths, then continued. "Your heart rate is slowing, and your breath is coming easier. It's getting easier to think now, isn't it?"

Anne nodded. Jack could see reason returning to her eyes, and he kept talking, marveling at how easy this was – and how different from what he had done with Layla. That had been a descent into the dark, but this... He felt like he was lifting them both into the light. His voice vibrated with tones of respect and authority, as he pulled her free of the fear that had sunk its talons into her. "What you're feeling is frightening, but you're not in danger. Think about the words, Anne. Words have great power. You can use them to your advantage."

Anne nodded again, and again, her eyes flicked around. People were watching them curiously, and before the first tendrils of embarrassment could take root, Jack commanded her attention once more. "Don't worry for a single moment what they're thinking. And don't think you're not strong. Your cracks might show more than others', but everyone here has them. Every single one of us." He crouched, keeping her gaze when she would have dropped it. "I'm really proud of you, coming out to see Martin off. And I know he'll appreciate it, too."

Anne's face flushed with pleasure, and she reached out to clutch his hands with both of hers. She drew a deep, deep breath, and her eyes closed for a moment in relief. "Thank you," she whispered. "For helping me."

Before Jack could reply, Rowan stepped out of the crowd, eyes snapping sharply from Anne to Jack and back again; she always knew, when one of her flock was in jeopardy. "Hey. It's good to see you outside, Anne." Her gaze swung to Jack and her eyes narrowed. "How are we doing?"

"Why do doctors always say 'we?'" Anne's voice was only slightly breathless. "It's annoying, Rowan, and moreover, it's condescending." She looked at Jack and smirked, and he *felt* her natural vivacity rise to fill her. The lift it gave his own heart was a delightful surprise. "Words are powerful things, young lady. Now, if you'll excuse me, I'll wish our travelers 'Safe journey and safe return,' so I can get back to my duties at the library."

She gave Jack's hand a last squeeze. "Maybe you're not so smarmy after all, mister youth pastor." With that, she turned to make her way towards Martin.

Beside him, Rowan huffed in indignation. "'Young lady.' Whatever. And I'm not a doctor – why can't people remember that?"

"I think you'd better give that fight up, Rowan. You're the closest we've got. If it comforts people to call you 'doctor,' why not let them? What harm does it do?"

"That's an interesting question. Especially coming from you."

Jack turned to find himself pinned by eyes that saw too much. Rowan held the contact for a long moment, then returned her eyes to the crowd. "Have you seen Layla and Owen yet?"

"No." If she wasn't going to pursue that cryptic comment, he certainly wouldn't. Her eyes probed and skimmed the crowd, assessing the health of every person here as only she could; watching her, Jack felt a stab of genuine concern.

The needs of the community had aged Rowan unspeakably. She was not yet thirty, but her dark hair was mostly silver at the roots; lines of care and worry had gouged her face into premature middle-age. She didn't complain, ever, though she had no patience with stupidity. Her snapping reprimands were universally feared, and woe to the person who wasted her time with trivialities. As he watched, her eyes roved the crowd, pausing here and there. Sometimes, a frown would crease the skin between her eyes. Sometimes, she would nod, and her lips would lift into a brief, satisfied smile. Jack had been watching her do this for over a year, and it never failed to awe him.

"Have you had any luck training those assistants of yours?"

"Bah. Stefan is willing, but he faints dead away at anything deeper than a paper cut. Tara is lazy and not terribly bright. She says she used to be a receptionist in a doctor's office, but she didn't absorb a damn thing as near as I can tell. But both of them can *see* glimmers of what I can, so we'll keep working." Rowan's scanning eyes stopped, and the frown creased her forehead. "There's Layla. And Martin keeps looking at the sun. He's anxious to be off. C'mon, let's go send them on their way."

Together, they worked their way through the crowd. Jack kept his eyes off Layla until he was sure he had his shields at full strength, and reinforced at that. The last thing he needed was for her or anyone else to catch the drift of his thoughts whenever his eyes touched her. Of all the players in his twisted fantasies, she was his shining star.

She was hanging a pouch attached to a leather cord around Naomi's neck when he looked up. She moved on to adorn Martin with a similar pouch, and as Jack moved closer, he could hear her explaining the gifts. "Black tourmaline and fire agate. They'll turn away evil intent and return it to the sender. Bay leaves. Angelica root. Cinnamon." In unison, both Martin and Naomi lifted the small pouches to their noses, and Layla smiled. "To protect your spirits from despair and negativity." She closed her eyes and placed her palms over both charms. "Spirit of Divine Light; spirits of the elements earth, water and fire; spirits of the winds that will journey with them. Empower these symbols and watch over the travelers that carry them. As I will, so let it be."

Martin looked pained, but Naomi laid both her hands over Layla's. "What a lovely blessing. Thank you."

"You're welcome. Wear them against your skin, please."

The travelers lifted the pouches and obediently tucked them inside their shirt collars. Layla stepped back into the waiting circle of Owen's arms. Jack watched her hulking lover press a kiss to the top of her head and dropped his eyes, not trusting his shields to hold against the combined surge of outrage and jealousy.

The nerve of her, inflicting her pagan sacrilege on them without so much as a *by your leave*. He closed his eyes and took deep breaths until he was confident of his defenses once more. Looking up, he again found himself the object of Rowan's all-seeing eyes and smiled tightly at her. She turned away, taking her turn to give Martin a clap on the shoulder and Naomi a warm hug. She spoke to them both for a moment, made them grin at whatever she had said, then returned to Jack's side.

"I told them if they could bring me back a bag of Cadbury Mini Eggs, there was nothing I or my descendants for seven generations would not do for them," she said. "I know it's a long shot, but it's just not spring without egg-shaped chocolate."

Then she skewered him before he saw it coming. "Your blood pressure is dangerously high. And you experience a severe spike whenever you see Layla and Owen together. That was to be expected at the beginning, but you should have adapted by now. It's become a conditioned response." Her eyes drilled into his. "If you don't learn to control and re-train your physiological response, you are increasing your risk for stroke or heart attack. The genetic precursors are in you – I can *see* them."

Jack wanted to look away, but couldn't. "My granddad died of a massive stroke when he was in his fifties. And my dad had heart disease. It started when he was quite young."

Rowan nodded. "Obviously, medication isn't an option." She released him from the relentless pressure of her eyes, but didn't let up. "In technical, medical terms, you need to get a grip, Jack. Pray about it, meditate about it, whatever, but you need to accept their relationship emotionally, so your body can accept it physically." Her gaze returned, and he *felt* her genuine caring, though her voice remained brisk and no-nonsense. "You're making yourself sick. And I would rather see you walk away from this community and never look back than watch your heart explode."

Jack's mouth twisted bitterly. He didn't even try to make it look like a smile. "Right. Like that's an option."

"It is." When he didn't look at her, she grasped his arm in her strong hand, demanding his attention. "It *is.* Jack, I know leadership of this community isn't something you asked for and that you have mixed feelings about it. I don't have to read feelings to know that. But you need to remember that you have the option to leave it all behind. No one's holding a gun to your head. We would go on if you dropped dead tomorrow. Which you might, if you keep on as you have been." She shook her head, her expression wry. "How do you think I go on, day after day? I don't have to do this, and I tell myself that every damn morning. I choose to do this."

They stood in silence for a while, watching the crowd ebb and flow, and finally start to thin. People dispersed to their assigned or chosen tasks for the day, the party atmosphere giving way to the warmth of cooperation and camaraderie. These people, all of them, had survived horrific losses; they had chosen to go on, helping each other, learning to live again, forming new bonds that strengthened with each passing day. Rowan was right about one thing, Jack thought, watching them. This community would continue to grow and thrive with or without him.

Ignacio had been waiting on the fringes with the horses, and he led them to the travelers now. He stroked the animals' foreheads and gazed into their eyes as Naomi and Martin mounted, ran his crooked brown hands over the face and ears of the pack horse, and Jack could feel his sorrow at the parting from clear across the parking lot. As he watched, Layla rubbed the center of her chest, then moved to loop an arm through Ignacio's as the travelers rode away amidst calls of farewell and well-wishes.

He turned to Rowan, to find her watching Layla with an all-too familiar frown on her face. Three times, her eyes moved on, and three times, they returned. After the third frown, Jack couldn't deny the chill that twisted down his spine.

"What's wrong with her?"

Rowan's frown deepened. To her credit, she didn't pretend to not know what he was talking about. "I don't speak of possibilities, only certainties. Not to mention the fact that it's none of your business."

He grasped her elbow harder than he meant to, and forced himself to modulate his grasp. "It is very much my business," he said. His voice was pitched just right: calm, reasonable, quietly authoritative. Without thought or decision, he took what he knew of Rowan and used it. He took her admiration for rational, logical thought, her healer's instinct, took her love for every one of her patients, and used it to push his way in and *control*. "I may struggle with it sometimes, but I am one of the leaders of this community. So is Layla. If there's something I need to know, a burden that needs to be lifted from her —"

Rowan jerked her elbow free of his grasp and glared at him. "Just for the record, if you ever try that mind control shit on me again, I'll break your arm."

Jack stared at her, shocked, then turned unseeing eyes away and spoke through stiff lips. "Layla told you."

"No." She waited until he looked at her again. "You just did. And I could *see* what you were doing with Anne, earlier." She shook her head slowly, her eyes filled with worry. "I thought what Layla can do — that thing where she can make people obey a one-word command — was the most dangerous manifestation of this evolution, or whatever it is we've got going on. I was wrong." She paused, and he heard the incredulity in her voice when she went on. "You did that to Layla? And she let you live?"

"What? Did you think she'd turn me into a toad?" Jack snapped the reply at her, but kept his eyes averted. "That's none of *your* business. I'd prefer to drop it, if you don't mind."

"Sure, whatever. But Jack?" She would stand there until he looked at her, he could *feel* it, so he got it over with. The expression on her face conveyed both her interest and her trepidation. "This needs to be discussed, at length. Did I see what I thought I saw, before? You were in control of Anne's mind, weren't you? You controlled her physiological responses. You shut down her panic attack. Is that accurate?"

He couldn't think of a way to not answer, though it made him powerfully uncomfortable. "More or less. I didn't so much control her as influence her." The more he thought about it, the more he began to understand the difference between what had happened with Anne versus his experience with Layla. "I pulled her away from her fear and reinforced her own control. I don't really know how to describe it, or control it. It has only happened a couple of times. And it was different with Layla."

It was as close as he could force himself to an admission. Rowan nodded thoughtfully. "I don't need to know what happened. I can guess, and I don't think we need to discuss the specifics, especially not with everyone. I'd rather not sew your arms back on after Owen gets through with you. But we would be fools not to talk about how to use what both you and Layla can do, the possibilities for medical application, or for defense, if that gang Anne is so worried about heads this way."

He hadn't thought about either possibility, and he should have. No, he'd been too busy getting down and dirty in his fantasies. For the first time in a long time, Jack felt shame, which in turn enraged him. God, he was so sick of the push-pull inside of him, the lure of the dark in constant opposition to what he knew in the center of his soul was right. He was so tired of questioning, endlessly, the source of the *knowing*, of never being sure whether it was a window into his own, deepest desires, or inspiration from God. And for today at least, he was finished with hiding his feelings on the subject.

"Sure, Rowan, I'll rush right in and put that on my calendar: 'Discuss one more way to use Jack and his quite-possibly Satanic hocus-pocus abilities to serve this community.' Can't tell you how much I'm looking forward to it." Before she could rip a strip off him in reply, Jack bared his teeth at her in the facsimile of a smile. "Thank you for your medical advice. I'll be sure to think about it. Now please excuse me – I've got so many things to do, not one of which I volunteered for."

He walked away, and couldn't possibly have cared less that he was clearing a path with the angry energy that preceded him. People stared, startled, not used to seeing him out of control. Jack kept his head down until he reached the front door of the church, then stood there, seething, his hand on the door handle.

"Forget this," he muttered, and swung away, walking around to what used to be a remembrance garden and now was being prepped to grow vegetables and herbs. He dropped onto a bench, screened by a trellis from what was left of the crowd, and scrubbed his hands over his face. People strolled by, unaware of his presence, chatting, laughing, discussing, planning. Not for the first time, Jack felt removed, separated. He led this community, but he wasn't a part of it, not anymore. Not like he had been in the time before.

Through the trellis, he could see Layla and Owen talking with Ignacio and Thomas. Layla still had her arm looped through Ignacio's and every once in a while, she patted his hand, or stroked his arm. She was a toucher with everyone but Jack, always resting her hand on someone's forearm or shoulder as she spoke to them or reaching to hold a hand. He had seen her stroke the back of a child's head affectionately a thousand times. And a thousand more, he'd imagined her eager touch on his own skin, wondered what it would be like to be the recipient of her caresses.

Why was it so much more titillating to imagine coercing that touch? The outside world paled beside the rich detail of his fantasies, a thousand images of his beautiful Layla subjected to his will, to his smallest and greatest desires while Owen stood by helplessly. Jack closed his eyes, his breath shuddering in, then out. Layla's wall of ice was nothing to him now. He could breach it whenever he wanted, and his own defenses made it look like a child's flimsy snow fort. He opened his eyes, watching them from his place of concealment and let his mind have at the two of them.

"Wow."

The word was breathed near his right shoulder, and made him start violently. How he had dreaded hearing that voice. He turned, and somehow, some way, Verity was sitting right beside him on the bench. She was also shaking her head at him, an awed expression on her face.

"I have seen some dark stuff, you know. The dead, they always want to tell me how they died. Usually, they show me and let me tell you what –" She shuddered and closed her eyes for a moment. "I've seen awful things. Things that shouldn't have ever been dreamt of, Horatio."

She opened her eyes, and in them, Jack saw flashes of those awful things, shadows that writhed in misery and torment. And for just a moment, he saw her as he had never seen her before: An ancient soul, battered, beleaguered, sometimes to the limits of her endurance. Then, she blinked, and her cornflower blue eyes held only the innocent mischievousness that was the essence of Verity.

"Yep." She shook her head again. "I thought I had seen it all. But that thing you just had going on with Layla and that red —"

"Shut up." He didn't try for control; he was too shocked to even think of it. She could read his mind? Had she always been able to do this? With everybody?

"Pretty much," she answered. "It's not that big a deal, you know. Ask Martin. He's pretty good at it, too."

For maybe thirty seconds, he couldn't think of a single thing to say to her. Questions bombarded him so fast, he couldn't sort them out or prioritize them. The one that burned through all of them, over and over, was: Would she tell Layla?

"Nope. Not my place." She shook a stern finger at him. "But if you don't tone it down, I will drop some whopping hints. Get a grip. Or else." She glowered at him, then ruined it with a grin. "Dang it. One of these days I'll be able to 'Or else' someone and keep a straight face."

On any other day, he'd have made up some excuse and bolted. But not when he'd already heard "Get a grip." Not today. He glared at her, and even though he doubted it would do any good, he threw up every defensive wall he had. "Know what Verity? You don't get to tell me what I can and cannot do in the privacy of my own mind. I don't care how many archangels you think you've got backing you up. My thoughts are my own, and as long as I'm being honest here, I'm not interested in hearing yours. Ever. Again."

A sharp slap stung the back of his head. Jack whirled, but there was no one behind him. He swiveled back to Verity, who had both hands clamped over her mouth, blue eyes wide and a little scared. A nervous giggle exploded between her fingers, and she held both hands up, demonstrating her innocence. "It wasn't me! Dude, I've never seen Michael swat someone before! Yeesh!"

Jack dropped his head forward and shut his eyes. If only he could scoff. If only he could disbelieve. No such luxury, not where Verity was concerned. So he'd managed to tick off the head honcho of Archangels, had he? What a fabulous day this was turning out to be. "You win," he said wearily. "From here on out, my thoughts towards Layla will be pure as the driven snow. She's safe from me, in both thought and deed. Happy?"

In reply, Verity slid off the bench to kneel beside him. She reached to gather his hands in hers, her fingers tiny, child-like and warm. As always, her touch made him see things, beings he could not explain or deny. Like a wall of light, they were, tall and so beautiful they made him want to both laugh and cry. As Jack gazed down at Verity, he felt himself enfolded in wings of power and love, and he knew without asking: The Archangel Michael had forgiven him.

"Of course he has, you silly," Verity said fondly. "He loves you, without reservation or condition. But you've lost your way. What you focus on, what you allow your thoughts to dwell on – that becomes your Higher Power. Michael isn't worried about Layla. She can take care of herself. He's worried about you. You've lost your True North."

Jack lifted his gaze to Layla, watching her head tilt back as she laughed at something Owen said, knowing and loving how laughter made her eyes sparkle and flash, though he couldn't see it from this far away. "Is it her? Is she the Gift from God you spoke of?"

Verity followed the direction of his gaze. "Layla? Oh, no – at least not anymore. Maybe before the plague, or before Owen, but she's on another path now, one that leads where you can't follow." She blinked away a flash of sorrow before he could even be sure he'd seen it, then smirked up at him. "Your helpmate is on her way here, rest easy on that. I know you're lonely, and so does the Divine. Your prayers for a true companion have been heard."

Jack felt a blush burn his throat and cheeks. If God had indeed heard the prayers of his heart, He had been privy to the degradations of Jack's mind as well. How could he have forgotten that? How had he journeyed so far away from his own soul? Verity was certainly right about one thing: He had stopped listening to a higher call, had created and worshipped idols of lust and power.

He looked up at Layla and ran his eyes all over her, drinking in her dark allure, longing for the lovely mystery of her. He didn't want to give her up. Didn't want to stop sinning with her, even if it was just in his mind. Not just yet. But did one ignore a swat from an Archangel, Michael at that? One did not.

Jack shut his eyes, and forced his mind to Proverbs, to the kind of woman he should have been focused on all along. Christian. Pure of heart. Kind, giving, self-less. His eyes slipped open, and he was captured by the lush fall of Layla's dark hair, that rich, silky waterfall that had featured in so many of his fantasies... He slammed his eyes shut once more. Blonde. Please, Lord of All, let his helpmate be blonde. "Favor is deceitful, and beauty is vain: but a woman that feareth the Lord, she shall be praised."

Beside him, Verity snorted, and somehow made it sound delicate. Jack opened his eyes just in time to catch her rolling hers. "Yeah, that 'Rebecca of Sunnybrook Farm' thing you've got going on there – ain't gonna happen." She shook her head and rose to stand beside him, taking away her touch and his ability to see the heavenly host in the same motion. "You are such a *guy*. There's more to women than saint or sinner, pal. I'd suggest you leave the deets to the Divine – expect her to arrive but be open to the form."

She winced, then hunched her shoulders and rubbed the back of her head, speaking to the unseen. "What? I wasn't making fun of him! Well, okay, I was, but he pictured her in a *sunbonnet*, for pity's sake!" Verity turned to go, then whirled back as she always, always did. "I almost forgot! The woman who's on her way here? Yeah. She's not your Gift. Just thought you ought to know."

TWELVE
Grace: Colorado Springs, CO

"Hey! You!"

Grace turned. Loudmouth was headed straight towards her. Her stomach lurched, as it always did, but she held her ground and stared dully at a spot in the center of his chest. It was a trick she'd perfected in the past several weeks: Not quite making eye contact. Eyes were too recognizable, and she'd been far too close to his, too many times.

Loudmouth stopped in front of her and grabbed at the bottle clutched in her arms. "Whatcha got there, Stinky?"

Grace resisted for a moment, hanging on, then let him jerk the half-full bottle away. She sniffed loudly, and swiped at her perpetually streaming nose with a filthy forearm. "Whiskey. Found it in a doctor's office down on Circle. I was just gonna take it to –" Her mind blanked for a second, and all she could think was "Bean Counter" – the name she'd given the gang's clip-board-carrying accountant. "To Mr. Watts." She sniffed again, swiped again, then snuck a grimy forefinger up one nostril. "He said we could get double rations if we brought in alcohol."

Loudmouth curled his lip at her, then averted his eyes in disgust. "So, what – you thought you'd save this back 'til then? You been hoarding it?"

"Nuh-uh! Found it this morning, I swear! Give it back," she wheedled, her voice a nasal whine. She grabbed at the sloshing bottle. "I walked all day to get it here! I'm hungry!"

Loudmouth let her grasp the bottle, let her pull on it, then ripped it free of her hands and shoved her in the same motion. He cackled as she sprawled in the dirt and was already walking away when Grace sat up. Grace stared after him, mouth hanging open – but not far enough to reveal the cotton pads that disfigured her cheeks and lower lip – wearing an expression of dull anger.

"Not fair," she whined, for the benefit of anyone watching, and because she never, ever broke character. Under the act, though, she felt a rush of adrenalin that bordered on euphoria. It happened every time she interacted with that blowhard, paraded right under his nose, and left him none the wiser.

As far as these people were concerned, she was a scrawny prepubescent boy with a hack-job haircut, a boy whose nose ran constantly, whose eyes were always red and diseased-looking, and who smelled so awful, people gagged if they got too close. A not-too-bright boy who breathed noisily through loose lips and stained teeth, who scuttled around the fringes of things, always looking for a handout. Grace inhabited the character so completely, she sometimes forgot she had ever been someone else.

She struggled to her feet, rubbed her rump, then hurried away, shoulders slumped in dejection. A glance to the west decided her course; she only had a couple hours of daylight left. She didn't check over her shoulder – to do so would show too much street-savvy for her character – but she did throw all her senses open, *feeling* for eyes on her, skin prickling as her awareness expanded. When alarms didn't sound, she headed north, clinging to the cover of the trees that ran along the western edge of what used to be Monument Valley Park and was now part of the new gang stronghold.

It had only taken her a few days to find them, watching from a series of high vantage points at night, looking for the lights and the fires. Logic told her they would have moved by now, and she'd been right. They had taken over the Colorado College campus, as well as many of the mansions on Wood Avenue to the north. The dorms and nearby apartments were occupied by what she'd come to think of as the "dumb masses," with higher-ranking individuals occupying some of the beautiful old fraternity and sorority houses. She estimated there were at least a thousand people living inside the gang's territory.

Monument Creek supplied them with water, and the park, which ran for several miles along the river, had been haphazardly planted with gardens and small patches of crops. Some of the larger open spaces were now crudely fenced. She had seen horses and goats, but no cattle. Patrolled borders were maintained from the far north end of Monument Valley Park, south to Colorado Avenue, and to the east, ending at Nevada. I-25 formed the western border, and it was a busy one, between patrols and scavengers. Outside those borders, people were left alone, unless they had something the gang wanted.

The nightly keep-'em-in-line show was now staged at Washburn Field, with roaring generators powering the stadium lights. Grace had forced herself to be seen at a few of these events, but it tested her right out to the ragged edges of her play-acting abilities. They had expanded their entertainment options; the rapes were still going on, but death had now been added to the repertoire.

From what Grace had gleaned, people who broke the rules or displeased the leadership in some way were forced into the gladiator-style, kill-or-be-killed spectator events. On a beautiful spring evening ten days ago, she'd watched a pair of sobbing, terrified women hack at each other with machetes, alternately shrieking in rage and begging for mercy, until one of them finally inflicted a killing wound. Grace had been completely incapacitated for two days afterwards, unable to close her eyes without seeing them, unable to keep even a sip of water in a stomach that wouldn't un-cramp. Already dangerously thin, she knew she couldn't afford another episode like it. Greater than the physical toll was the mental one; her mind could only tolerate so much horror, so much fear. She was right at her outer limits on both. But she had a job to do.

When she had first started to observe the group, Grace couldn't figure out what made people stay. Why would these people subject themselves to this kind of fear and brutality, day in and day out? Her prior contact with the group had been limited to the leaders, and in spite of the terror of her circumstances, she'd wondered that even then. She had listened to the reports, listened to the men talk amongst themselves about the "sheeple" that kept them fed and supplied with luxuries and vices, and she hadn't been able to come up with a single incentive to stick around.

Now that she'd been studying them from a different perspective, though, she was beginning to understand. The people here were more frightened of being on their own than they were of arbitrary violence. Just over a year ago, they'd been citizens in a society with rights and protections, but they had let fear strip them of those ideals. Someone was in charge, and that was all that mattered. At first, it had disgusted her. Now, she just felt pity.

One simple truth had begun to emerge from the disparate puzzle pieces she'd been clicking together: Fear was the gang's only strength. They wielded it like a weapon, with full knowledge of its destructive power. That weapon, though, could cut both ways. She didn't have it all figured out yet, her ideas half-formed at best, but she knew her fingertips were brushing answers.

A faded scrap of red cloth wrapped around a rock marked today's crossing point. Still *feeling* for watchers, Grace stepped out of the cover of the trees, scurried across the railroad tracks, then hopped the barrier at the edge of the parking lot that was I-25. She crab-walked through the still, silent vehicles, keeping low, then stopped and counted to 50, *feeling, feeling* always. Then, a scrambling leap onto the hood and roof of a pick-up that had collided with the rosy-pink granite sound wall, creating a slim, broken gap for her to slip through. She dropped lightly to the ground on the other side, then ran for her first hidey-hole. From the attic of a nearby house, she watched her back trail through a cobwebby window until she had counted to 200.

She had seven crossing points, all of them with hidey-holes so she could watch and be sure she wasn't followed. She rotated among them daily, never using the same one twice in a row, varying her pattern and keeping track with innocuous objects like empty soda cans or rag-covered rocks. "Lucky seven," she murmured, as she always did, and headed on her way. There was a pedestrian cross-walk just south of here, and farther to the north, Uintah Street crossed under the interstate, but she couldn't imagine being stupid enough to try those routes. Predators were everywhere, packs of both humans and dogs, and they hunted the easy, obvious paths. Grace's paths weren't safe – nothing was safe – but she wouldn't get picked off for being foolish or lazy.

It took her a full two hours to travel four miles, hiding and checking her back trail repeatedly as she made her way. The sun was just touching the top of the mountains as she slid out of the neighborhood bordering Garden of the Gods and sprinted across the open space for the cover of the scrub oak that abounded in the park. She hid there for a fifty-count, then climbed the ridge, heart pounding more from anticipation than from exertion. When she reached the high point, she retrieved a pair of binoculars she'd wrapped in a garbage bag and hidden between two boulders. She climbed onto one of the boulders and crouched there, meticulously quartering the trail she'd just traveled until she had counted to 1,000. There was no way she would risk bringing danger to this place. Finally, finally, she turned and trained her binoculars on the tiny, barely-visible cabin.

A thin trail of smoke from the chimney simultaneously weakened her joints with relief and made her stomach clench with anxiety. They were still here. Why were they still here? Quinn knew the danger – why hadn't he left for Woodland Park as they'd discussed? She was afraid she knew the answer to that question, and it added another layer to the crushing load of guilt she already carried.

Shifting to a more comfortable position on the boulder, she scanned the whole area, checking for anything out of the ordinary, finding nothing. She returned her binoculars to the cabin and settled in to wait. She didn't always get to see them, which would bring her back the very next night in spite of the danger of routines. She only allowed herself to visit every third night, as long as she at least caught a glimpse of them.

Luck was with her tonight. There was still plenty of sunlight left for her to see easily when Quinn rounded the corner of the cabin, walking stick in one hand, the other resting on the baby sling across his chest. He strode down the trail towards the paddock and barns, no doubt headed for his evening chores. Then, he stopped. His head lifted, and Grace lowered the binoculars, hiding her face against her knees. He couldn't possibly see her, but she was sure he *felt* her. He almost always did. She closed her eyes and counted to 25, listening to the sounds of the gathering dusk around her – the rustle of a breeze in last year's dry leaves, the flitter of wings as birds found home, the occasional skritch and skitter of an animal in the underbrush. When she lifted her head, Quinn had resumed walking, though the binoculars showed her the watchful frown on his face. He walked with swift purpose to the barn, looked around once more, then ducked inside.

Grace lowered the binoculars again. It usually took him about thirty minutes to do what needed doing, and she used the time to repeat what she'd learned this day, reinforcing the information in her memory. She didn't dare commit anything to paper, not until she had learned all she needed to and was well away, ideally in Woodland Park with her father. She didn't permit her thoughts to dwell on her dad, on the safety and security he represented, lest she lose heart. The task she'd set for herself was one only she could complete, and complete it she would.

Grace knew the gang, probably better than any other person alive. She knew the leaders: the sounds of their voices, their individual cadences and word-preferences, the very smell of the breath that carried those words. During the time she'd spent as their captive, she'd begun to understand their psyches as well, both individually and as a group. She had recorded everything she had learned in the document Quinn had hated, had recorded facts, and augmented them with carefully labeled hypotheses and speculations. She had read and re-read that document right after she'd run away, desperate for the distraction, vaguely aware that she was punishing herself with it.

Those had been terrifying, fuzzy days. Weak from so recently giving birth, she ran an on-again-off-again fever and her breasts were so swollen and painful, she could hardly stand to move. But move she'd been forced to do; she had taken only enough food and water for a couple of days, and Quinn had been methodically raiding the nearby homes for supplies for months. She had trudged from house to house the first two days, disappointed over and over. Late on the third day, out of food and low on water, she'd lucked out in an office building in Old Colorado City. She'd been looking for a safe place to stay the night, and she'd found a break room that contained intact vending machines. Breaking into them had taken the rest of her strength, and she'd holed up there for over a week, eating junk food and drinking cans of soda, growing steadily stronger in spite of the abysmal nutrition.

During that time, she had studied what she had written and had recognized the document for what it was: A months-old record of reconnaissance that may or may not be accurate any more. She needed updated information. How many people still supported the gang? What of their plans to relocate? Were they still interested in Woodland Park? Had they sent spies there already? What about the routes – Highway 24, Rampart Range Road, Old Stage Road? Were they open? Did the gang control them? And finally, what of the men she'd been brutalized by, the leaders? In a violent regime, coups were common. Was the leadership structure still the same, or had it changed?

In the weeks that followed, she'd gathered an abundance of information, though she still had critical questions to answer. In her guise as a ragged, smelly boy, she'd learned that the refugee camp on Fort Carson no longer existed. She'd learned that the gang now controlled what was left of the mountain post, in particular the helicopters that had been part of the combat aviation brigade, though rumor was they didn't have someone who could pilot them.

She'd learned that someone had freed many of the animals from the Cheyenne Mountain Zoo; people still spoke of the giraffe that had been served up at a mid-winter feast, and on still nights, you could hear lions roaring to the south. She'd learned that the barter system she'd observed before was still in place. People could bring in scavenged items in exchange for food rations and the "protection" of the group, such as it was. The penalty for hoarding food, alcohol, drugs or other highly-valued commodities was a slow, horrifying death under the stadium lights, while the penalty for theft was a merciful, on-the-spot execution. All other crimes were ignored as irrelevant, up to and including rape and murder.

Outsiders, people unfortunate enough to stumble into the gang's territory or stupid enough to try living nearby, were either assimilated – if they were determined to have some kind of value – or given to the stadium games. Grace had slithered in on the fringes, bringing carefully chosen goods to barter – valuable, but not too valuable – and she was now tolerated as a stray dog might have been, regarded as harmless as long as she didn't get too close. And therein lay the problem: To answer her remaining questions, she needed to get close to the leaders, and she hadn't figured out how to do that yet.

She'd seen all of them but one – the man she had called Sleeper – but had only had contact with Loudmouth and Bean Counter. There had been eight men before – six leaders, and the two Trigger Fingers that never left The

Boss' side – but the group had expanded. There were fourteen of them altogether now, and she hadn't figured out how the new group functioned. Once, she'd snuck onto the roof of a nearby building with her binoculars, planning to watch and analyze during the nightly show. No more than ten seconds after she'd sighted in on the group, The Boss had looked up sharply, right into her eyes, she would have sworn it. Grace had lost control of her bladder on the spot. She had spent the whole night on the roof, too scared to move, too scared to watch, sure they were coming for her any minute. Finally, dawn and the end of their revels had released her, and she hadn't yet found the courage to try again.

Below her, the barn door opened, and Quinn stepped out. Grace snapped the binoculars to her eyes, drinking in the sight of him. A hundred times, she had decided to go back, and hundred and one, she'd talked herself out of it. Not until she had gathered all the information she needed. Not until she had something valuable enough to make up for what she'd done. He wouldn't see it that way – she knew that with absolute certainty – but it wasn't his conscience she was trying to appease.

He was smiling, and his lips moved as he talked to the baby snuggled in the sling across his chest. As Grace watched, a little arm encased in bright yellow burst out of the sling to wave and pat. Quinn laughed, and caught the tiny fist, bringing it to his lips for a kiss. Grace felt tears burn her always-red, always-irritated eyes. She couldn't even remember the last time she'd heard Quinn laugh. He looked so happy, not at all the haggard boy he'd been in the weeks before the birth.

She dropped the binoculars to her lap and wrapped her arms around her knees, rocking, rocking, trying to ease the awful hollowness in her chest. Maybe they were better off without her. They certainly didn't need her – that was obvious. She endangered them every time she came here. She should leave a note for Quinn in the barn, tell him not to wait for her, tell him to head for safety before he and the baby were discovered.

The gang's scavengers had been through this area already, but they patrolled everywhere. Where they would, they roamed, and she hadn't figured out the pattern yet. It was just a matter of time until this beautiful little haven caught their interest. She should leave the note, now, tonight, then go. Go, and never come back.

Just the thought made her feel like she was dying inside. She fumbled the binoculars back up to her eyes, clinging to the sight of Quinn's back until he rounded the cabin and disappeared. She waited, knowing she wouldn't see them again tonight, but watching until full dark dropped over her, just in case. When she finally re-wrapped the binoculars and stowed them back in their hiding place, she was stiff with cold and shaking with hunger, but a part of her had been filled and sated.

Guided only by the light of the rising moon, she ghosted along trails she now knew by heart, trails she loved in spite of what her life had become. The red monoliths rose above her, their silent majesty reminding her that they'd be here long after she was gone, long after the members of the gang were dust, long after the troubles of this age were memory and myth. Remembering that kept her sane.

The night was crystal-clear and cold with it, and she was glad tonight's den was close by. She traveled via the same easy, light-footed lope that had made her hopeful for a shot at state in the 3200 meter – sometimes, she remembered things like that, and it was as if she'd read about that girl, that Grace, in a book long ago. She slowed her pace when she hit the neighborhoods that bordered the park, flitting from shadow to shadow, every sense she had wide-open.

In minutes, she was as safe as she ever got, in the attic of a house inhabited only by the dead. They didn't smell anymore, the withered corpses that were everywhere, and only the little kids bothered her. There were none of those here – just a man who had died in his bed, and a woman who had collapsed on her way back from the bathroom, a dusty water glass still clutched in her desiccated hand.

Grace had become intimate with the attics and closets of many homes; she couldn't sleep unless she was hidden where no sane person would choose to sleep. Nor could she risk discovery of the tools of her disguise: the cotton pads that dried her mouth out but disfigured her features; the hair gel and bucket of dirt she used to keep her hair and exposed skin filthy; tea bags to stain her teeth; and finally, the can of black pepper, which she had always been mildly allergic to, and which kept her eyes and nose constantly streaming. People were far less clean these days, but bodily fluids still repulsed. Top it all off with the clothes she took off corpses and some garlic-enhanced mouth breathing, and people kept their distance.

In the beginning, she'd stripped down and washed each night, but she'd soon figured out she slept better if she just stayed in the disguise. "Stinky" had become her protector as well as her alter ego; his stupidity was her shield, his foulness her sword. After checking that her belongings were right where she'd left them, ready to be transported to tomorrow's location in the morning, Grace curled up on the pallet of blankets she'd tucked between neatly labeled boxes of taxes and school records, feeling exhaustion press her down like a heavy hand.

Nights were the worst. So quiet, without the sound of Quinn's breathing. She had never known before, that loneliness could make your bones ache. She knew it now.

This hadn't been her plan, when she'd walked away from the cabin over a month ago. She hadn't had a plan then, had just needed to get away. Then, as the reality of what she'd done had begun to sink in, the idea had taken root. Punishment. Atonement. A voluntary descent into Hell, to make up for the fact that she'd deserted her newborn daughter and the boy-become-man who had never, ever left her. She didn't know if she could ever balance the scales, but she had to try.

If she could get the information she needed, she would permit herself to go. She whispered the questions she still needed answered out loud to herself; it helped keep her mind organized, and the sound of her own voice comforted her. She knew what she needed to do, and the thought made her sick with dread. At least once, she needed to hear what she'd heard night after night after night last summer: The reports the men gave to The Boss. Those reports would contain the pieces to complete her puzzle, she was sure of it.

Then, if Quinn and the baby were still here, she would take them with her to Woodland Park, to her father, to safety. Not even in her darkest moments could she admit that there might not be safety even there, that her father might be dead. That way lay madness, and Grace lived too close to that state already, each and every day of her life.

Soon. She needed to finish this, before she ran out of strength, courage, sanity or luck. She whispered the word aloud to herself, to reinforce it. "Soon."

THIRTEEN
Naomi and Martin: Colorado Springs, CO

Naomi reached the end of her endurance when they rode into the parking lot of Gold Camp Elementary school. She reined Ben in, staring at the brick building where both her girls had attended, Macy just last year, Piper so long ago. From Manitou Springs, they'd ridden cross-lots to get here, through neighborhoods and across green spaces, in ways unfamiliar to her from the time before. She'd done a double-take, startled by recognition, and the past had risen up to drown her.

Shiny new first days and end-of-school award ceremonies. Parent-teacher conferences, and volunteering at holiday parties. School carnivals, music concerts, and so many years of waiting outside for her girls in the pick-up line. She couldn't see through her tears, through the flashing images of face paint and balloons, of art projects stiff and bright with tempura paint, of little girls flying towards her on skinny, churning legs, one blonde, one with hair the color of sunrise. The sob tore out of her and took all her strength with it.

Naomi slid out of the saddle, boneless and clumsy, clinging to Ben's neck to keep her legs under her. Ben curled his head around her, and she pressed into his shoulder. "I'm done. I can't. Please."

The words didn't matter; she didn't even know what she was saying. The pressure had been building in her chest for days, and if she didn't let it out, she couldn't keep breathing. She had grown accustomed to living without Macy at the cabin. Here, just a few miles from their home, on ground Macy's feet had run over, the loss was brand new and unendurable.

It had started on the trail two days ago. They had decided to travel back over the route Naomi and Macy had taken last spring rather than risk riding into unknown dangers in the narrow canyon that cradled and confined Highway 24. For Naomi, it was a surreal and horrifying trip back in time. There was the spot she'd confronted Dylan and Evie; here was where Macy had rested, waiting for her to come back with a vehicle; and here was where they'd camped, the very spot Naomi had held her living, breathing daughter in her arms on that last night. Here, right here: Macy's last sunrise.

When they had located her truck in Manitou Springs, it had taken every bit of grit she possessed to sort through the items she'd packed so long ago, to move aside a small purple sweatshirt and a backpack covered with brightly-colored owls to locate the items they would pick up on the return trip. She held her breath the whole time, terrified that Macy's scent might have lingered on her things, knowing that would be the end of her. She had not anticipated this. How could she have let herself be so completely blind-sided?

A large, warm hand landed on her shoulder, and Naomi turned, eyes streaming, to face Martin. "I can't do this. I do not have the strength, do you hear me? I can't see the places where she should be." Her voice, already shaking, broke on a wail that tore the wound wide-open. "She should be here, and she's not, she's not, she never will be again!"

Martin lifted his other hand so he was holding both her shoulders, squeezed, then gave her a little shake. He ducked until his dark eyes met hers. "Naomi, I'm sorry you're hurting, but this is where I say 'I told you so.'" His eyes were somehow tender and hard as flint at the same time. "If you decide to turn back, I'll ride with you to the trail head, but I've got to go on. I told you this would be hard, but you didn't want to listen. So, what's it going to be?"

Naomi gaped at him, literally stared with her mouth hanging open. Where was the comfort? Where was the gentle hug, the shushing, the reassurance? She slapped angrily at the tears tickling her cheeks.

"Your compassion is overwhelming." Her voice was still shaking, but the grief had retreated, burned off by the swift wild-fire of anger. "I'm not quitting that easily." She shoved his hands away, then stared at him with narrowed eyes. "Did you do that on purpose? Or are you just that heartless?"

Challenge flared in his eyes, but that was as far as it got. He shook his head at her, then headed back towards Shakti. "Think whatever you want." He remounted, then turned to face her, his eyes concealed by the brim of his hat. "Can we get going? I'd like to get there while we've still got plenty of daylight."

Naomi turned away and shut her eyes for a moment. Hades, who had been ranging and sniffing, came charging around the side of the school, called by her distress. He slowed to a trot as he approached Ben – they'd worked that out, thank goodness – and pressed against her for a hug and an ear-ruffle. Naomi obliged him, then mounted Ben. She took the time to scrub her hands over her face, tighten her pony tail and re-settle her hat, putting herself back together before she nudged Ben into motion. Without another word to Martin, she took the lead and rode out of the parking lot.

There was the mini-van she and Macy had seen in the middle of the road on Cresta, the man's body now just a pile of bones and rags. And here was her street. Naomi was gritting her teeth so hard her head ached, but she didn't allow herself to slow or falter. She would not say, not even in the privacy of her own mind, that Martin might have been right. That this was too hard. That she shouldn't have come.

She summoned Hades to her side with her mind, then *joined* with him, using his senses as well as her own to *feel* her way down the street. He was alert and watchful, and though nothing was actively alarming him, he was agitated. He recognized the area, Naomi realized, when she felt the *pull* inside him towards his old street, his old home, his dead people. She chirped at him softly, and when he looked up, she sent him a wave of love. "I know, boy. I know. It'll be okay, sweet boy."

Hades whined softly, and she felt the return wave, so generous. The clop of the horses' hooves on the pavement sounded so loud, here in the silent neighborhood. Martin nudged Shakti up until they were riding side by side.

"Seems deserted." He glanced at Hades. "What do you two think?"

Naomi frowned. "I'm not sure. It's quiet, but not...empty. I don't feel like we're being watched, but I don't feel like we're alone, either." She glanced at Hades, concentrating for a moment. "He's picking up recent scent, but nothing hot, nothing immediate. There've been people around, though. In the last couple of days, I think."

Martin pulled his rifle free of its scabbard and let it rest across his lap, then undid the snap on the pistol holstered at his waist. Naomi swallowed but followed suit, adding to her list of things she never could have dreamed she'd do: Riding a horse into her old neighborhood, armed and ready to shoot. Welcome to the wild, wild West. Surreal. When they reached her house, she rode up the driveway and dismounted. "This is it."

She turned to see Martin scrutinizing the exterior. He looked at her with raised eyebrows as he dismounted, lifting Persephone from her perch behind the cantle of his saddle and setting her down to stretch and sniff. "Damn, Naomi. What did you say your husband did? Nice place."

Naomi turned back to the house and tried to see it with his eyes. Through the piled-up trash and the dead, overgrown front lawn, it was still possible to see that it had been a cared-for home, a tended-to home. It was a nice place. Scott had made good money, and she'd poured her heart into this house, making it beautiful. For all the good it did either of them now.

Naomi took a deep breath. This, she had prepared for, and she was as ready as she'd ever get. She called both dogs to her, then put them on a stay in the front yard, reinforcing that with a mental command to *watch*. Then she headed for the front door, which was only half there. "Looks like someone has been inside."

Sure enough, the house had been looted. In her mind, she had walked through each and every room, had imagined just this kind of destruction, and she was able to let her eyes coast past shattered vases and gutted, broken furniture. Things. Just things. "The storeroom is downstairs. Let's see if they found it."

She started to pick her way through the wreckage, then realized Martin wasn't following her. He had moved to the fireplace and stood gazing up at their family portrait, taken the autumn before the plague. She joined him, and a smile lifted both her heart and her lips.

The shot had been taken at Helen Hunt Falls, and though the vivid fall foliage and waterfalls had been beautiful, they'd all frozen half to death. They had traipsed from spot to spot, wrapped in winter coats until the last possible second, then tossed their coats to the side just long enough to smile for the photographer. As always, her eyes touched the sliver of bright turquoise where Piper hadn't tossed her jacket quite far enough for this picture. The photographer had offered to Photoshop it out, but Naomi had declined. She loved that small imperfection.

"We went downtown to Rico's, afterwards," she murmured. "For some of their Aztec hot chocolate. Scott and Piper loved that stuff. Piper was home from college for the weekend. It was a good visit." She turned to find Martin watching her. "What?"

He shook his head. "You lose it in a school parking lot, but this doesn't faze you. Looking at this picture. Seeing your house wrecked. I'll never figure you out."

"I was ready for this." She looked back up at the picture. "It's what I don't see coming that I struggle with."

"You had a beautiful family. Piper looks just like you."

Naomi had been hearing that for years, and she responded automatically. "Sure, if you add 50 pounds and lotsa mileage." She blinked. "Well, the mileage for sure. Let's go."

Martin followed this time, trailing her through the gutted kitchen – oh, they had ruined her beautiful butcher-block island, why would someone do that? Naomi pressed grimly on, opening the basement door, but Martin put his hand out to stop her, taking the lead. He slung his rifle over his shoulder and un-holstered his pistol, stepping silently down the stairs ahead of her. The looters had been here, too, but they hadn't discovered the secret storage room. Martin watched while Naomi scooted boxes to the side, then whistled when she pulled open the hidden door. He whistled again, longer, when he stepped inside.

"You folks were prepared, that is for sure." His eyes swept the shelves. "Over-the-counter meds and medical supplies, Rowan'll dance a jig. Food, water, paper goods, an extra generator. We can't take it all back with us, but this is great. We'll come back with pack animals." He turned to where Naomi was fingering the rim of her grandmother's orange juice pitcher. "What's all that stuff?"

"Treasures." Naomi had to clear her throat. "Things we couldn't take with us but that I wanted to keep safe."

She ran her hand over the pile of photo albums, then noticed a bright beribboned and sequined little box she hadn't put there. It must be something Macy had added. Her hand hovered over the box then closed into a tight fist. "Grab anything you think we'll need. I...I've got to get out of here."

She waited just outside the door for him, looking around at the holiday décor and seasonal clothes that had been dumped out of boxes, strewn about and trampled underfoot. Honestly, what was the point of that? She folded her arms across her chest and tucked her hands in her arm pits, resisting the urge to tidy and straighten. She had prepared for this, she had, but it was hard not to feel violated.

A minute or two later, Martin stepped out with a bulging rucksack. He held it up. "The medical supplies. Everything else can wait."

He helped her close the door and re-stack the boxes in a deliberately haphazard fashion, so it looked like the rest of the basement. Then they headed upstairs, to see what was left of the weapons Naomi had left behind in the gun safe. This, too, she had prepared for, but it was a shock just the same, seeing the door to their bedroom hanging crookedly from one hinge. She hurried ahead, then gasped and rushed into the room.

The bed had been torn apart, the mattress sliced open and hauled to the side so the box springs could be similarly vandalized. Scott's corpse lay on the floor, half underneath the mattress, and she could see where some of the seals on her make-shift shroud had broken and fluids had leaked out. Zeus' body was nowhere to be seen. The disrespect for her husband's remains made a red haze drop over her vision. Rage gave her strength, and she reached down to haul the mattress back to its rightful place and off her husband's body.

"What the hell!" She looked up. Martin was standing in the doorway, staring not at the destruction, but at her. He jabbed his finger at her. "If you ever – *ever* – rush into a room that hasn't been cleared like that again, I will..." He clamped his mouth down tight and breathed through his nose, staring at her.

Naomi didn't even register his words. She straightened, and gestured at Scott's body with a shaking hand. "Do you see this? Why? Why couldn't they just leave him alone?" She bent again and grasped the plastic covering Scott's body, preparing to lift him back onto the bed. "Why would someone do this? It makes me sick!"

Martin was suddenly at her elbow, nudging her aside. "You take the other end. Okay, on three."

Together, they lifted Scott's body back where it belonged. Zeus' body had been under the mattress as well, but his plastic shroud had been torn open, strewing black fur and bones across the floor. With loving hands, she scraped the pile together as best she could and nestled her sweet old boy next to Scott. She stalked to the closet to get a clean quilt from the shelf, and suffered her second shock.

The safe had been cut open, apparently with some kind of torch, given the burn marks. It was empty. Scott's weapons all gone, Piper's too, along with the ammunition. She must have made a distressed sound because she felt Martin right behind her seconds later. She dug into her pocket for the key to the safe, holding it up. She had carried this damn key all the way to Woodland Park and back again, so proud that she'd kept track of it. "Guess we won't be needing this, then."

In a sudden rage, she threw the key as hard as she could at the empty safe. It pinged off the metal with a satisfying sound. Naomi grabbed an empty hanger – because, of course, they'd dumped all her clothes on the floor, too – and whacked and whacked at the safe, venting her fury. She kicked it for good measure, and the pain that zinged through her big toe calmed her a bit. She stood on one foot, eyes closed, and breathed hard. Then she looked up at Martin, who was just gazing at her.

"I'm fine," she snarled. Martin nodded slightly but didn't say a word, his expression guarded. Naomi bared her teeth at him, then bent to rummage around in the mess on the floor until she found a quilt. She pushed past Martin, and unfurled it over her husband, smoothing, patting, until it was just so, just the way she wanted it. Then she straightened the things on the bedside tables, setting the lamps back up, restoring the pictures to their proper places, making sure Scott's book, bookmark still in place, was just where he liked it. When she was finished, she stood, staring without seeing. Martin's hand on her shoulder made her jump.

"Take a minute, but then we've got to go."

Naomi nodded, heard him leave, then went to sit beside Scott on the bed. "Not doing too great, honey. Sure wish you were here to pick up my slack." Oh, it felt so good to talk to him again. She had missed him so, so much. She reached out to the place where Scott's hand would have been, and fisted a handful of quilt. "Our baby girl, I just couldn't keep her alive. She's with you, I know that, but I'm sorry. I'm so sorry." It surprised her, to feel tears on her cheeks, and she wiped them away absently. "Piper, well, I'm on my way to find her, but I kind of suck at this, honey. It should have been you, who survived. You were the one with the skills and the smarts to protect our girls. I wish you were here, instead of me. I wish I were braver."

A sound in the doorway made her look up. Martin had his pistol in one hand, Persephone in the other. The little dog was quivering with nerves, and it only took a moment for Naomi to ascertain why. She looked up at Martin, and they spoke in unison.

"Someone's here."

Naomi followed Martin down the stairs in swift silence, pistol in her hand, stomach jumping. At the doorway between the kitchen and the front room, they stopped, leaning to look out the big bay window to the front yard. They had left Ben and Shakti tethered right in front of the window. Beyond them, Hades bristled at full alert, staring at a group of four men. All of them had rifles or shotguns cradled in their arms.

One of them took off his baseball hat to wipe his forehead, smoothing back a brush of iron-grey hair in the same motion, and Naomi gasped. "Oh my god! I know him!"

She started forward, but Martin's hand flashed out to block her way. "I go first. Holster your pistol and use your rifle to cover me from the door. Do not let them know you're here, and do not come out unless I call for you." He curled a fist in the front of her shirt and thumped her chest sharply. "Tell me you understand every single word of my directions, and will follow them exactly. *Exactly*."

"I understand." He let her go. She rubbed at her chest, then crouched low and followed him into the front room. Martin un-slung his rifle and holstered his pistol, waiting until Naomi had done the same. Their eyes met and held. Then, he nodded, stood up and stepped out the front door, rifle held at his hip, Persephone slipping out behind him.

"I'd appreciate it if you fellows would take a few steps back from my dog. Strangers make him twitchy, and I'd hate for him to lose his temper."

Naomi recognized the "good old boy" tone from the middle-of-the-night confrontation with – what had their names been? Didn't matter. She slid along the wall, heart pounding, sighting in on the closest man. Their voices carried clearly through the broken front door.

"He's not a stranger to me." The man she had recognized did the talking. He and his wife had lived across the street and down a few houses. Their son had been just enough older than Piper that they hadn't been regular playmates, though they'd run in the same neighborhood pack. She'd waved at him a thousand times. He walked their dog, rain or shine, every single day, a lab/greyhound mix named Spencer. She could remember his dog's name; why couldn't she remember his?

"I know him, or at least I think I do." The man held out his hand, palm down. "Brutus. That's a good boy. Come see me, Brutus."

Naomi felt Hades' mind explode with conflict. He shifted, whining, ears going forward and back. He'd been told to stay, to *watch*, but that name...he knew that name... He looked over his shoulder, and though he couldn't see her in the shadows, his eyes locked onto Naomi.

She almost went to him; the need to reassure him was overwhelming. But for once, Martin's instructions rang in her head, and she stayed where she was. She sent the big Rottweiler all the love she could muster, wave after wave of soothing, calming love. She *felt* him relax, just as she heard Martin speak again.

"Who are you, and what can I do for you?"

"We're here to ask the same thing." Spencer's "dad" gestured to the house. "I knew the people that lived here. They're gone, but they were good people. We understand the need to gather supplies and necessities for the living, but we've already been through this area so you won't find much. And I'd ask you to keep the damage to a minimum. Out of respect."

For long moments, Martin gazed at the men. Naomi could *feel* his concentration, the intensity of his scrutiny as he listened for the lie or untruth. Finally, he called over his shoulder without looking away from the men. "It's all right to come out now."

Ed. His name came to her as she stepped out the front door. She moved to stand beside Martin. "Hello, Ed – I'm so glad to see you're alive."

His mouth dropped open. "Piper?" He squinted. "Holy shit! Naomi!"

The men flanking him shot him disapproving glares, and his face reddened. "Please forgive my profanity," he muttered. "Naomi, I just can't believe it. I thought you were all gone for good. I know you lost Scott." He nodded at the house. "But did your girls make it?"

Naomi *felt* Martin's tension ease a fraction, and realized he had deliberately not used her name. He had wanted to see if the man would recognize her. She tried to answer Ed's question, but her throat closed up. She looked down for a moment, swallowed, then looked up and spoke of what she could. "We're on our way through, looking for our kids. Martin's are in Limon," she clarified, "And Piper was at school, up at UNC." She snapped her fingers, and Hades rushed to her side, pressing close. "You said you know this dog?"

"I'm pretty sure. His owner and my son were friends. They lived just down the way, little family with a baby girl. They didn't make it." Ed paused for a moment, a heartbeat given to respect for the dead, then went on. "I'm pretty sure this is Brutus. We used to watch him when his owners went out of town for softball tournaments." At the name, Hades' ears shot forward again. "He and Spencer used to have a time, didn't you, boy?"

Naomi dropped her hand to stroke the big dog's blocky head. "I call him Hades now. We found each other." She sent a summons with her mind, and Persephone streaked out from under the juniper shrubs, leaping into her arms. "You remember Persephone?"

Ed nodded, and tears filled his eyes, tears he didn't try to hide. "I sure do – couldn't forget a pretty little lady like her. It does my heart good, seeing you all. My Julie didn't make it, nor our son." He wiped at his eyes, then gestured to the men he was with. "We were on a supply run when we saw your horses and I recognized Bru... Hades." He smiled, then nodded again at the house. "Did you find what you were looking for here?"

Naomi and Martin exchanged a glance. Martin answered. "More or less. We need to leave a message, in case Piper shows up here, then we'll be on our way." He paused, dark eyes sharp as he scrutinized the men. "What can you tell us about the city? Anything we should look out for?"

It was the men's turn to exchange glances. Naomi felt Martin tense again. Finally, Ed looked back at them. "You could say. If you don't have other plans, you're welcome to stay the night with our group. There's just over a hundred of us up around Bear Creek. We use the nature center as a community center, for gatherings and such."

"Excuse us for a moment, would you?" Martin grasped Naomi's arm, and turned her away from the group, though he kept his eyes on them. "My instincts say they're on the up and up. Yours?" When she nodded, he did, too. "Let's spend some time with them, then, find out what they know. Stay here. I'll be right back."

He jogged into the house, and Naomi turned back to Ed. "Do you know if anyone else from the neighborhood made it? By the time we left, it was deserted. I lost Scott in early April. Macy and I left after the army came through. She survived the plague, but..." She dug her nails into her palms, sick of being silenced by grief. Nestled in her arms, Persephone licked her chin in comfort and encouragement, and she went on even though her voice shook. "But she never really recovered, not completely. I lost her a few weeks later, in May."

"Septicemia." One of Ed's companions spoke. "The same thing happened to my wife. At least that's what Doc called it."

"You have a doctor?"

"A dentist." The man smiled. "And a whole bunch of medical textbooks. When Doc's not patching somebody up, he's reading."

"We have a similar situation where we're from." Instinct made her refrain from revealing specifics. She knew Ed only in passing and nothing about this group he was with. She smiled, hoping they wouldn't notice her omission and focused on Ed. "Why are you at Bear Creek, instead of here, at your home?"

Again, looks were exchanged. Finally, Ed answered. "Water, mostly."

He didn't add more, and a silence fell among them. Naomi felt an unmistakable pressure, the sensation of someone probing and pressing around her defenses. She looked up sharply, and the man on the far end smiled tightly. She stared him down, but it was Hades' rumbling growl that made him drop his eyes, as well as the subtle invasion.

So, Naomi thought. They've changed, too. She would wait and see if that was a subject that could be broached. In the meantime, she wasn't detecting a threat from these men, but they had secrets. She was sure of it.

Martin came back out the front door, carrying two cans of spray paint. He handed them to Naomi and took Persephone. "For the message to Piper. The garage door would work best, I think."

Naomi stared at him blankly for a moment, then remembered the messages they'd seen, spray-painted on the sides of houses, or as Martin was suggesting, on garage doors: "Max, go to Grandma's house," or "Marian, if you get this, we're with Lynn." She cringed at the thought of defacing her home like that, then rolled her eyes at herself and started shaking the cans.

"Piper," she spelled out in neon pink. Then, she hesitated, looking over her shoulder at Martin. He stepped closer and bent his head so she could speak quietly into his ear.

"Ed knew we had a cabin on Carrol Lakes, I think. Pretty much the whole neighborhood did," she said. "If I say, 'Go to the cabin,' he may know what that means. Are we okay with that?"

Martin glanced at the men again, then shook his head. "No. Not yet."

Naomi nodded, and went back to her task. "You know where to meet us," she spelled out. "I love you. Mom." She stepped back, cocked her head to the side, then shook the other can of paint. In under a minute, neon green vines and leaves swirled around her message, transforming the vandalism into a cheerful work of art. She met Martin's amused gaze and shrugged. "Now she'll know for sure it was me."

The men had been talking quietly among themselves but broke apart when Naomi and Martin approached, leading the horses. Ed gestured at his companions. "They're going on to finish the run. I'll take you back to our group."

"It was nice to meet you." The man who'd been prodding at them spoke. "Maybe we'll see you at the evening meal." The other two men nodded in parting, and the three of them headed deeper into the neighborhood.

Ed led them back cross-lots, very close to the way they'd come. "Our sentries spotted you earlier today, so we knew you were in the area. We don't draw attention to ourselves if we can help it. If travelers don't bother us, we don't bother them."

"Do you see many people on the move? We didn't see anyone on our way here, and we haven't run across any other large groups." Naomi looked at Martin, raised her eyebrows in question, and he nodded. "We came from Woodland Park, but we came on hiking trails. When I went through Manitou last spring, Highway 24 was pretty dangerous. We ran into trouble. So we avoided it this time around."

"That was probably a good idea. We stay away from there, or anywhere the traffic stacked up. There are people all over I-25, from what we've heard, scavenging those vehicles." He shrugged. "Makes sense, if you think about it. People packed up their valuables, or what they thought would be useful, then tried to leave. Better rate of return with the vehicles versus looting houses."

He gave them a wry glance. "I managed investments, before. Guess I still think that way. Anyway, to answer your first question, no. We don't see many travelers. Maybe we'll see more, now that spring's here, but I don't know. Seems like people are hunkered down, just trying to survive."

Martin spoke. "We heard there was a gang here, pretty violent group." The air fairly crackled with his intensity as he watched Ed for a reaction. "Know anything about that?"

Ed stopped walking and returned Martin's scrutiny for a long moment. Then, he shifted his gaze to Naomi, squinting, pondering. Whatever he saw satisfied him, because he started walking again, his battered hiking boots setting a swift pace. "You asked before, and I was glad you didn't pursue it, at least not in front of Samuel. He was with that group, and whatever terrible things you've heard, the reality is worse."

Ed walked on in silence for a few paces, then shook his head. "I will never understand, not if I live to be a hundred, the evils some folks are capable of. We've got quite a few people with us who slipped away from that group, and when they first started coming in with their stories, we thought they were making it up. But then Samuel came in. I actually knew him from the time before, which is rare these days. We went to the same church, which was how he ended up down this way. He and his family lived up in Briargate, on the north side. There were fires up there, he said, and they lost their home. Heard there was some kind of group in Memorial Park, so they went there."

Ed fell silent again. The only sounds were the crunch of their boots and the muffled clop of the horses' hooves. Then he sighed, a deep, sad sound. "They took his daughter. Raped her, until she was dead. He couldn't do anything – they said they'd kill his son if he tried. She was fifteen. And he had to watch her die. He left, when he knew there was no hope. They'd moved on to another girl. It's what they do. I'd appreciate it if you don't ask about it in front of him – it breaks him. He's not right in the head, not all the way."

"Who is?" Naomi murmured. It took her a few seconds to realize Martin had stopped. When she turned, she couldn't hold back a gasp. There wasn't even a hint of color left in his face. "Martin? What is it? Are you hurt?"

His eyes were glassy when they met hers. His legs wobbled, and she rushed to his side, wrapping her arms around his waist. "Here, here, let's get you down. Just sit right here and rest a minute." She looked up at Ed. "My canteen, tied to my saddle – could you get it?"

Ed hurried to help, and Naomi crouched down, lifting Martin's hat from his head and smoothing a hand over his forehead. He was clammy with sweat but didn't seem to have a fever. He reached up and caught her wrist suddenly, squeezing so hard she yelped. A deep breath shuddered into him, and wheezed out. "Oh, no. No, no, please."

He stared at her, blinking, as if coming out of a faint. "I don't know what happened," he rasped. He looked around, re-orienting himself. "I was walking along, listening to Ed, and all of a sudden I was gone. I could smell smoke, there was a bonfire. Men. They were laughing, and..." He shuddered. "I'm gonna be sick."

He heaved and heaved. Naomi rubbed his back, murmuring, then wet a handkerchief with water from the canteen and handed it to him. He scrubbed it over his face, which was already warming back to its usual tan. His eyes, though, were hollow. He got to his feet, swayed, then leaned on Shakti and forced a smile at Ed. "Naomi's been threatening to poison me. Maybe she finally made good on that."

"Hmm." Ed narrowed his eyes. "You folks are different, too. Changed."

Naomi and Martin looked at each other. "Yes," Naomi said. "You, too?"

"Not me." The corner of Ed's mouth kicked up. "My wife always said I couldn't catch a hint with a butterfly net. She'd have changed, if she'd survived, I'm pretty sure. But lots of us are different. Psychic, some call it. Intuitive is what others say. We don't really have a name for it yet."

"Neither do we," Naomi said. "It's accepted, then, in your group? We can talk about it openly?"

Ed blew out a long breath. "Well, that could get tricky. There's something you should know about our group before you're in the middle of it." He looked at Martin. "You okay to go on?"

Martin nodded. They started walking again, though at an easier pace, and Ed went on. "I'm a Johnny-come-lately to the group. I stayed in my home as long as I could, but water got to be an issue. I cleaned out all the bottled stuff for at least a mile around, collected rainwater, but we had a really dry fall. I remembered Bear Creek then. It's amazing what you don't know about the resources where you live, I'll tell you what. I decided to check it out. I made three or four trips, hauling water home, before Isaiah made contact. He's the leader of the people that have gathered there, and I guess you'd call him a visionary."

Ed's smile was just a touch sardonic. "He's a very spiritual man, though he wasn't in the time before, he claims. He says God told him we are the Chosen Ones of the New Age. His words – not mine. Anyway, he also claims that God gave him a vision of a new heaven on Earth." Ed gestured ahead of them, at the rocky ridges and foothills. "And it starts right here."

"So it's a religious group?" Martin's voice had returned to full strength. "A lot of rules?"

"Just one: Follow the teachings of the Bible. Old and New Testament." He sighed again. "I was a religious man in the time before, and though God and I have a thing or two to sort out, I guess I am still. But bringing back 'an eye for an eye' doesn't feel like the answer to me. I'll be real honest with you both and say I get uncomfortable. Fanaticism is a slippery slope. It's too easy to justify any action you want to take when you believe even your shit is sanctioned by God." He grimaced. "Profanity is frowned upon, did I mention that? It's been a trial."

"Why do you stay?" Naomi asked.

Ed shrugged. "I don't have anywhere else to go. I lost my whole family, at least the ones here in the Springs. No way to get in touch with my people in Texas. Like I said, I'm a Christian man, so I won't take my own life, not that I haven't prayed to God to do just that. I make the best of it, speak up when I can, try to keep my head down when it's prudent. If it goes too far, though, I'll go. Some already have."

He reached to ruffle Hades' ears, and they beamed at each other for a moment, doggy grin meeting weather-worn smile. "Maybe I'll find myself a buddy and just head out for Texas. Spencer died a few years ago, and my wife didn't want another. She had in mind we could travel, if we weren't tied down. But I sure miss a dog around, I sure do."

Martin spoke. "So should we admit that we've changed, as you say it, or not? What's the story with that?"

Ed pursed his lips, considering. "I'd keep it on the down low." His eyes twinkled. "My grandson used to say that. Sure miss him. I'm choosing to believe he's alive and well in Texas. Anyway, Isaiah insists that all psychic or intuitive information has to pass through him before it's shared or acted on. He says there are no clear examples in scripture where inward guidance alone was sufficient to know God's will, and intuition can only be trusted if a person is aligned with God's will."

Martin's voice was hard. "And he decides that. Who's aligned."

"Yep."

Martin and Naomi exchanged a long look, and Naomi was certain he was thinking what she was: Maybe they should just move on, find somewhere else to camp for the night.

She smiled brightly at Ed. "If you change your mind about Texas, you'd be welcome in Woodland Park." Martin shot a sharp glance at her, but she ignored it. "It's a good community. One of our leaders used to be a youth pastor, but he doesn't push his religion, and our other leader is a witch."

Ed blinked. "Really? One of those Wiccans or some such? What do you know."

They had reached the edge of the neighborhood overlooking the area surrounding the Bear Creek Nature Center. Ed paused, shading his eyes with his hand and scrutinizing the soaring rock ridges above. Naomi and Martin followed his gaze, watching as two bright red flags appeared on adjacent ridges, apparently run up far-away flagpoles. Ed took a mirror from his pocket, flashing a pattern of signals at first one flag, then the other. After a few moments, the flags descended. He waved, and on they went.

"Sentries," he explained. "Red flag means someone's moving into our territory. Yellow for people farther away. We signal when we're coming in and they lower the flags, but people will be on the lookout just the same. Everybody watches for flags, even the little kids. We've got six sentries at all times, stationed at the high points and on the buildings along Lower Gold Camp road. You can see the downtown area real well from there, which is where the gang's at. They don't leave their territory except for raiding parties and patrols, but if they ever come in force, we'll be ready."

"You plan to fight back, if that happens?" Martin asked.

Ed shook his head. "No. We'll hide. Back in the hills, in the woods. Isaiah insists on drills, even in the middle of the night sometimes. It sticks in my craw – I believe we should defend our homes – but from what I've heard, we'd be pretty mismatched." He made a face. "Can't turn an investment manager into a Ninja, no matter how many Chuck Norris movies he's watched."

He paused again, looking between the two of them. "I suppose there's one last thing, before we're caught up in the crowd. You two married?"

Naomi coughed, and cursed her easy blushes. "Ah. No. Why?"

"I'm sorry to embarrass you and it's none of my business, but unmarried folks aren't allowed to spend the night together. They've got dorms, so to speak, for the singles – houses, one for the men and one for the women. They'll want to put you up in those. So if you want it to be different, you best decide now."

Martin and Naomi exchanged another speaking look. His grin held just a hint of ferocity as he reached out to hook an arm around her neck, hauling her to his side. "Thanks for the heads-up, Ed. Mrs. Ramirez and I appreciate it."

Naomi shoved at his side, but he wouldn't budge. "Your last name is Ramirez? How did I not know that before?" She shoved again, harder this time. "And why should we pretend? What difference does it make?"

"We're not going to be separated. Not in an unfamiliar place." He let her go, but gave her an exaggerated wink – for Ed's amusement, she was sure. "Don't worry, honey, I'm not going to insist on my marital rights tonight. Pretty tired and all."

"You're hilarious." She gave Ed a dry look. "Okay. So we're Mr. and Mrs. Ramirez. Anything else we should know?"

"Just keep the cussin' under your breath and do as the Romans do. I'll stick close. You'll be fine."

They started to see more and more people the closer they got to the nature center. People would pause what they were doing, their eyes flickering back and forth between them and Ed, more curious than wary. Naomi returned a few friendly nods, constantly scanning, but she wasn't picking up anything threatening. People here were engaged in the same tasks that had become work-a-day in Woodland Park: gardening, gathering fuel, hauling water. By the time they reached the front doors of the nature center, they were being trailed by a half dozen slightly grubby kids, all of whom had their eyes glued to the animals.

"Pets aren't allowed," Ed explained in a low voice. "They consume too many resources." He raised his voice. "You kids leave these animals be, you hear? If you're good, maybe this nice lady will introduce you later."

They tethered the horses, Naomi put the dogs on a stay-and-watch, and they went inside. Ed introduced them as Martin and Naomi Ramirez, and they nodded and smiled their way around the room, Martin keeping his "good old boy" persona firmly in place.

Isaiah was a surprise to Naomi; she'd expected a fairly young man, long of hair and wild of eye, but the "visionary" was a slim, balding man with coke-bottle thick glasses. He took them off as he reached to shake their hands, and it wasn't until his eyes met hers that she understood. She stifled a startled yelp, and Martin's hand closed on her elbow, squeezing in warning. She slid a glance at him, and he shook his head slightly, waiting until they'd moved away to whisper low. "I felt it, too. He's packing some punch, but I'm not sure what."

They didn't get a chance to talk about it, or anything else they learned or observed, until hours and hours later. There was a communal meal at the nature center every night. People were free to attend or not as they chose, but word of the visitors spread and the place was a madhouse. Everyone wanted to hear about their travels, and two people asked after family in Woodland Park, though the people they described weren't familiar to either Martin or Naomi.

Through it all, Martin stayed in almost constant contact with Naomi – a hand on the small of her back or holding her elbow, an arm looped around her shoulders. He joked and laughed, more gregarious than she'd ever seen him, and after the fourth time he referred to her as "the little wifey," she slid a hand to his side and dug her fingernails in just enough for him to feel it.

When he looked down at her, she batted her eyelashes and dug in a little harder. "You're enjoying this way, way too much."

His grin was slow and irresistible. "You have no idea."

After the meal, Naomi supervised some visiting time between the kids and the animals while Martin made the rounds with Ed, gathering information. He was vibrating with excitement when he rejoined her. "They've got a couple of Zero Motorcycles – electric, totally silent. They use a generator to keep them charged up for emergencies. Isaiah has given us permission to use one, as long as we take one of their men with us. Ed has already volunteered. We can get a look at the gang tonight, in the dark, try to get an idea of what we're up against, maybe start to get an idea of their numbers."

Naomi gazed at him and swallowed hard. "What about the animals?"

"They can stay here. There's a woman here who used to keep horses. She can't wait to get her hands on them. And the dogs should be fine."

"Okay." Her throat clicked audibly as she swallowed again. "Okay. I can do this."

Martin put his hands on her shoulders and squeezed, what she was finally coming to recognize as his version of a hug. "I know you don't want to do this, but if we're careful, there should be very little danger. They don't post a night watch, from what everybody says. Typical street gang – relying on their rep to do half their dirty work." He squeezed again. "I'm not leaving you alone here. I don't distrust them, but I don't trust them either. We stay together."

The plan was to rest until just after midnight, then take off on the bikes. Martin and Naomi were given a tiny bedroom in a charming little log home, and even though it was twice the size of the tent they'd been sharing, Naomi felt painfully awkward as soon as the door shut behind them. Martin nudged her in the ribs as he edged past her, dropping their saddlebags on the bed. "Relax, Mrs. Allen. You're safe."

"How did you know my last name was 'Allen?'"

"It was on your mailbox at the house." He sat down and pulled his boots off, groaning as he reclined against the pillows. He patted the bed beside him, speaking through a giant yawn. "C'mon, my little wifey. We really do need to rest, even if we can't sleep."

Naomi lay down beside him and stared at the ceiling, mind whirling like a dervish. "I've been thinking, and we should take Persephone. Her senses can tell us a lot, through me."

"That's a good idea. The big guy won't like it," he yawned again, and stretched, settling deeper into the pillows. "But he'll have to lump it. What do you think the story is with that Isaiah? I couldn't get a read on him. Guy's shut up tight."

"I don't know – it wasn't until I met his eyes that I felt it. Sort of like a combination of Jack and Layla, now that I think about it. And something else. Something that could be...dark."

"I know what you mean. He's not there yet, but it could go either way."

Silence fell between them, a total silence unbroken by the house sounds Naomi was used to – the hum of a refrigerator, or the rumble of a furnace. She missed outdoor sounds, as well as the *feeling* of nearby life, and she desperately missed Hades and Persephone. They were staying with the horses in a nearby make-shift stable, and though Naomi could reach out to all of the animals whenever she wanted to be sure that all was well, she missed the warm, solid pressure of Hades curled against her side.

"I miss Persephone."

Naomi grinned in the growing dark, and turned her head on the pillow to look at him. "I was just wishing for Hades."

Martin was gazing at her, his forehead set in pensive lines. He cleared his throat. "I'm sorry. I just wanted to say that, from earlier. At the school."

Naomi frowned. "Why say it now?"

"I understand some things better now. I saw where you lived, what a perfect family you had. You had a beautiful life, with all your pretty things and everything just so. I could see that, even though your house was trashed. I guess it made me realize how much harder it must be for you than for the rest of us to adapt. You know. To the way things are now."

Naomi propped herself up on an elbow, looking at him with narrowed eyes. "I feel like I should be insulted but I can't put my finger on why. Everything you say is true. It was a beautiful life, and I loved it." She let her eyes go unfocused, thinking. "It was a sheltered life. Scott kept me safe, and he handled most of the unpleasant stuff, I see that now. He was the one that was prepared for this life, and it's only because of him that we made it. I never wanted to be involved in his prepper stuff – I didn't want to think about it. I never dreamed things could go this wrong."

She settled back against the pillows, sighing. "If I could have, I would have just stayed hidden, there at the house with Macy. I'd be holed up at the cabin now, if not for Piper. I'm not here because I'm brave. I'm here because I have to be here."

"That's what people never get about bravery. In combat, I saw grown men become infants. They literally fell down on the ground, curled up and started to cry. And I've seen those exact same men run through heavy fire to rescue another Marine, or cover their unit's retreat even though they're wounded. Bravery isn't something that you have. It's a choice you make, every day, to get the job done."

Again, silence fell between them. After a while, Martin reached out and picked up Naomi's hand, lacing his fingers through hers. "I was afraid to show you compassion today, because I thought you might fold. You were right on the edge of it. I didn't want you to decide to go back. I know it's selfish of me, I know it would make perfect sense for you to wait for Piper at the cabin, but I'm glad you're here. I can't think of anyone else I'd want watching my back."

Well. When this man came up with praise, he sure did it right. In the dark, Naomi's cheeks pinked with pleasure. "I'd say 'Glad to be here,' but we both know that's not true. I'll do my best to keep doing my part."

"My wife committed suicide."

It took a moment for the low, strangled words to sink in. Then, she squeezed his hand. "I figured. I'm so sorry. That must have hurt you so much."

"Losing Michael wrecked her. I wanted to die, too, when he did. I get it, now, when people say it hurts to breathe – it really does. But I had Gracie and Benji to live for. And her." His hand was kneading hers, almost to the point of pain, but she didn't think he even knew it. "She quit. We were supposed to be partners, to help each other, and she just quit. I know I have to forgive her, but how do I do that?"

If there was an answer to that question, Naomi didn't know what it was. So she just held his hand, letting her presence speak her comfort. They dozed like that for hours, until a soft knock at the door roused them both. Their host, a soft-spoken middle-aged woman, stuck her head in the door. "Ed's here. He says it's time to get ready to go."

They laced boots and donned warm jackets in silence, arming themselves with only their pistols. The rifles wouldn't be much use at night, and if this went wrong, wouldn't help them much anyway. Naomi's heart was beating so hard, her hands shook with it. The dogs were both awake when she went to retrieve Persephone from the stable, and Martin was right: Hades was emphatically not happy to be left behind. Naomi crouched down, holding his head in her hands and gazing into his sad eyes. "I love you, my beautiful boy. You need to stay. Stay and guard the horses. We'll be back soon, I promise."

His whine was so piteous as she walked away, she turned around to reinforce the *stay* and *guard* commands with a stern, mental imperative. He settled down onto his belly, grumbling and grousing, but she was sure he would obey her. Martin and Ed were waiting with the motorcycles; seeing them, her nerves ratcheted up another notch.

"Another first," she muttered, handing Persephone to Martin. "Is this different than the ATV?"

"More lean on the corners, but we're not planning on speed," he tucked Persephone into his jacket, then mounted the bike. "And they're not built for two, so snuggle up, sweetie-pie."

Naomi slid on behind him, stabilized Persephone, and they were off. She closed her eyes; they probably weren't even going 15 mph, but at night, with nothing but light from the almost-full moon to navigate by, it felt like warp speed. They slid through neighborhoods and across open spaces, taking the route Ed and Martin had planned out earlier. First to the south, to cross I-25 where the interstate arced over Tejon and Nevada, the only route Isaiah's group knew to be relatively safe. From there, they headed due north, weaving through silent neighborhoods.

Naomi kept her senses locked on Persephone, and long before they neared the gang's stronghold, her stomach was rolling. They stopped on the outskirts of the downtown area, and Martin looked back at her. "Anything to report?"

"Too many people, terrible living conditions. A lot of human waste. Fire. Big, from the amount of smoke." She hesitated, concentrating. "Alcohol. Blood."

Martin squeezed her hand and Persephone in the same motion, a mini hug. "Anything else, before we head in?"

"Fear." She gazed into his eyes, which were black in the moonlight. "So much fear. I've never felt anything like it." Her voice shook. "Persephone thinks we should go home and pop popcorn instead."

"We've got this, honey." He pressed back against her for a moment. "We sneak a peek, then we head home, most riki tik."

"Whatever you just said. Let's just get it over with."

They parked the bikes between buildings on Boulder Crescent and slipped into Monument Valley Park at the south end, walking north along the creek, letting the noise of the water cover the sounds of their passage. As they approached the blaze of light, Martin put his mouth near Naomi's ear.

"Don't look at the lights," he said, his voice more vibration than sound. "You don't need to see what's happening, and it'll preserve your night vision. If we have to get out fast, you're leading the way."

Naomi nodded, and felt a fraction of her fear ease. More than anything, she'd been terrified of seeing things she could never forget. It took just under half an hour to creep to their destination, a clump of trees bordering the tennis courts just to the southwest of Washburn field. Naomi's heart was pounding so hard and fast, it was vibrating Persephone, who was quivering inside her coat.

My God, they were so close, so close. Her legs were shaking with the need to run. Rock music blasted under the sounds of hundreds of people, and it was so hard not to cover her ears. Augmented by Persephone's senses, she could separate out other sounds from the cacophony: screams, shrieks, cries of pain. "It'll be over soon." She mouthed the words without sound, but it comforted both her and Persephone. "Soon. Soon."

Martin turned her so she faced due west, speaking directly into her ear. "Watch our backs. Do not turn around. Nod if you understand me."

She nodded, and he turned, pressing his back to hers as he and Ed watched through the binoculars they carried. Naomi closed her eyes for a moment, reaching for calm concentration, and finding it. She opened her eyes again, watching and feeling, keeping them safe. Persephone's night vision was so much better than hers, the moonlight slipping through the sparse spring leaves looked more like weak sunlight. A steady wind from the west pressed the tops of the trees rhythmically and had the added benefit of directing the disturbing scents from behind them away. Naomi focused on the shifting shadows, watching for movement that shouldn't be, feeling her racing heart slow a bit.

Until the smell hit her. A corpse. Garlic. Pepper. What the hell? A low whine quivered out of Persephone; through the combined perception that enhanced Naomi's senses, the little dog's instinct to *run* nearly overwhelmed her. She squinted, eyes darting, ears straining, nostrils wide open. Then, a rustle that shouldn't have been, a shadow that shouldn't have moved. Her pistol was in her hand, rock steady, but her voice wobbled like a sob.

"Martin. There's someone here. Right here."

Martin spun, and tucked his arm alongside hers, pistol sighting where hers was. "I can't see," he whispered. "How many?"

"Just one." She strained, *feeling* with all her ability. "Yes, just one."

Then, a shadow separated from a tree ten yards in front of them, and a tiny voice said, "Daddy?"

FOURTEEN
Piper: Walden, CO

Months of waiting, months of planning, and it all came down to today. To this moment. Piper lit an entire book of matches, cupping it in her hand until the initial flare and hiss was over, then crouched to tuck it in a pile of kindling. She watched until fire snaked along the lines of accelerant she'd spread, watched until she was sure the wind had caught the fledgling fire in its arms and would run with it. Then, she ran herself. Smoke chased her all the way back to the tree-top sentry stand.

Up she scrambled, to watch and wait. This was her only opportunity, and timing was everything. If she alerted the others too soon, they might be able to put the fire out. Too late, and they wouldn't make it out. An unusually warm and dry spring had accelerated her plans. Typically, June, July and August were the most likely months for wildfires, but who knew what the mercurial weather in Colorado would bring? Rather than risk a wet summer, she would act now. The wind had been blowing steadily out of the northwest for days, and they hadn't had measurable precipitation in six weeks.

Besides, her mother was on the move – she could *feel* it – and the implications of that were going to push her off the edge her toes were already hanging over.

She didn't let herself think about it during the day, but at night, the questions scrolled through her mind over and over, like a song she couldn't get out of her head: Why would she leave the cabin? Had something happened to her father, or Macy? Why would she leave the cabin? Why?

She'd been star-gazing the first time she became aware that the bond-line connecting them had shifted, subtly, to the east. That night, she'd convinced herself that maybe an equinox had occurred, which might explain her disorientation in relation to the stars, but she'd looked it up the next day. The tiny passage in the antiquated Encyclopedia Britannica Ruth kept in the clinic didn't contain much information, didn't explain whether or not the appearance of the stars would change with an equinox, but it was clear on one thing: The vernal equinox occurred in March. They were solidly into April. She had double-checked that, too.

As the days went on, the shift became more obvious, and Piper became more frantic. She was having trouble eating and was reduced to dozing in fitful starts, tossing and turning. She had tolerated the waiting before, because she'd been secure in her belief that her family was safe, stable, waiting for her at the cabin. Something had changed, and she needed to know what. She had to get to her family. Now.

So anxious was she to not jump the gun, she very nearly waited too long. She had stacked this deck with meticulous attention to detail, had waited until she was assigned watch in this area, had watched the skies, had hidden the can of kerosene here last time she'd had this duty. She'd thought of everything, and made everything happen. As she scrambled down the tree and sprinted through the forest, it occurred to her that it would be the ultimate victory for Brody if she died after so much careful planning. The thought gave her feet wings, and she flew into camp with smoke billowing only a half mile behind her.

Straight to the mess hall she ran, to ring the bell. "Fire!" She bellowed the word with as much wind as she had left. "Fire!"

People started to appear, and Piper kept shouting, kept ringing. "Get your bug-out bags and get to a vehicle – it's on top of us! Go, go, go!"

In minutes, the camp was mobilized – good old military training – with the exception of the patrols: Levi and Ethan to the west and Brody on his own, in the southeast. All part of the plan. If everything went her way, the fire might eliminate the last stumbling-block for her. They roared out of camp in the jeeps Tyler kept ready for just such an emergency, and the noise and speed were disorienting after over a year of foot-travel. Jenny was crying, struggling, screeching something about her babies' graves, and Aaron was trying to hold onto her, his face slack with shock. Piper turned away from them, allowing her lip to lift in a sneer. She was looking forward to seeing the last of both of them. In the front seat, their son Caden was nearly buried in a pile of bug-out bags and supplies. All three vehicles were similarly loaded down.

Elise and her kids, though new to the group, had been some of the first to respond. Piper knew her instincts about them had been solid. Elise's face was tight with worry, no doubt for Ethan, but Sam and Becca wore the cool, watchful looks that were typical of them both. Becca had taken Piper's long-ago advice, and passed among them as a boy. Other than Piper, only Ethan and Brody knew the truth. Her head turned and her eyes met Piper's as they bounced down the rutted drive towards the main road, and Piper gave her an encouraging thumbs-up, which was returned.

She and Ruth were bringing up the rear, with Max at the wheel. Their jeep was crammed with supplies from the clinic, supplies they'd been able to pack in under three minutes thanks to advance preparation. No matter what the future brought, Piper doubted she'd ever again be caught without a bag of essentials that could be grabbed in a matter of seconds, one of the many things she'd learned in the last year, and one of the few positives.

Now, it was all changing. From here on out, everything would be different.

By prior arrangement, they headed for the emergency rendezvous, a warehouse on the south end of the town of Walden the locals had been warned to leave alone. In the wake of the plague, the town's population had fallen to just over 20 people, but it was nearly triple that now, with refugees from Denver swelling their numbers. As they roared through the town, people were starting to step outside, pointing to the northeast, faces lined and tight with concern.

Piper crossed her fingers that the winds wouldn't shift and burn out the town, but if it did, que sera. If you lived in the mountains of Colorado, you'd better be ready for wildfires. Their compound was tucked in a forested area along the Michigan River, a few miles northeast of the town proper, and the river itself might act as a fire break if the winds cooperated. At least their compound had been located there, she corrected herself. Rather than waste her time worrying about the fate of the town, she should be concentrating all her hopes on the total destruction of the place they'd called home. If there was enough left to rebuild, she was screwed.

They pulled into the weedy parking lot by the warehouse just as a series of distant booms sounded. Tyler shut his jeep off and got out, eyeballing the black smudge that had joined the billow of white. "There go the propane tanks," he announced. A few minutes later, another deeper boom. "And there goes the gas. Shit."

Piper closed her eyes and bowed her head for a moment, light-headed with relief. If the fire had reached the tanks, the compound was certainly burning. She had to blink away tears when she opened her eyes, and bite the insides of her cheeks to keep her jaw from quivering. Tyler unlocked the warehouse, and they transferred their gear inside, then settled in to watch the smoke and wait for the patrols to come in. If they came in.

By late afternoon, the fire had swept well to the south, and appeared to have diminished as well. Tyler and Max took one of the jeeps to see if they could get into the area and check on the situation. They returned an hour later with grim faces, as well as with Levi and Ethan, who were so smoke-blackened it was hard to tell who was who. Not even half an hour later, Brody walked in, equally filthy, his eyes like arctic ice in his dirty face. Those eyes picked through the group until they found her, and locked on. After what felt like an eternity of scrutiny, he nodded, then went to get a drink and something to eat.

Okay, then. Okay. She was going to have to do this the hard way.

The compound, Max reported, was a total loss. "Nothing but smoking logs," he said. He looked decades older, almost frail. "Some of the cabins to the north might be salvageable – we didn't check all of them – but all the main buildings are totally gone, as well as the cabins to the southeast. The fire is still smoldering in spots – if we go back in, we need to be watching for the wind to change. It could flare back up any time. In my opinion, there's no need to take the risk. It's all gone."

Silence met his words as the group absorbed the information. Then Jenny started to cry again, her wet sniffles the only sound in the room. Piper looked around, analyzed bond-lines and noted where people were standing. All was exactly as she expected.

Phase one of her plan was complete.

On to phase two.

"We should go to Woodland Park." She said the words just like she'd practiced them, with quiet, calm conviction. She waited until everyone but Jenny had looked up – Jenny was irrelevant – then went on in a matter-of-fact tone. This was the most reasonable idea in the world. She needed them to believe that. "My family has a cabin on Carrol Lakes, and my dad is a prepper. There'll be supplies, at least enough to get us started while we regroup."

She'd thought long and hard about revealing that information, but when they left this place, the greatest threat this group posed would already have been eliminated. That was phase three.

People were exchanging looks now, shoulders were shrugging, and when their faces turned back to her, they were open. Curious. Interested in learning more. It was all she could do not to leap in the air in victory. She dug her nails into her palms and went on. "It's about 200 miles south of here. If the roads are open, we could make it in a day, if we take the jeeps." She looked at Jenny and Aaron, and did her best to fake compassion. "Some might rather stay here, settle in Walden."

"Why wouldn't we all stay here?" Max asked. Behind him, Ruth nodded. "Awfully long way to go for some supplies that may or may not still be there. And some of us weren't exposed to the plague back in the beginning, those that got to the compound early and didn't share nursing duties for Levi's dad or Jenny's kids. I know we're hearing that it burned itself out, but it could resurface. Safer just to re-establish right here, maybe over by the reservoir."

Piper lost a wager with herself – she'd bet Ruth would be the first to suggest that plan. Again, as she'd practiced, she shrugged and looked down. "I would like to know if my family is still alive. I know some of you have family you're wondering about." She made eye contact with Adam, then Ethan, and both of them nodded their understanding. "It would ease my mind, to know they're okay."

Throughout her carefully planned recitation, she'd avoided making eye contact with Brody. She had taken a calculated risk; he might take this as forcing his hand again and deny her suggestion just to teach her a lesson. She could feel him watching her now, his eyes pressing into her skull relentlessly. Against her will, her eyes jerked to his, but the contact told her nothing. His face was immobile, unreadable. Without looking away from her, he spoke.

"We'll stay the night here, then make our plans in the morning. Adam, you're on first watch with Elise. I'll take second. Piper, you'll be with me."

Piper nodded, but a chill of warning skated down her spine. Was that suspicion in his eyes? Or was she just being paranoid?

She busied herself with the tasks of settling in, but couldn't shake the chill of foreboding. Conversation was subdued as they suffered through a dinner of MRE's, and Piper quietly worked herself into a state of panicked despair. They weren't going to bite. It made more sense, to stay here; she knew that. She was going to have to implement plan B, which meant walking out of here on her own, as soon as an opportunity arose. Much as she hated to admit it, the thought made her weak with terror. She knew what could happen to a woman on her own in this changed world, and as awful as her situation was, she was certain it could be worse. Before she could force herself to start working out the logistics, Elise sat down beside her.

"We're in. Me and Ethan, and the kids." She smiled. "He told me, how you spoke up for us. And I've never forgotten your advice that first day. I owe you." She shrugged. "Besides, I've always loved Woodland Park. My husband and I used to take the kids camping down on Rampart Reservoir, and we always stopped for breakfast at the Hungry Bear on our way out. Did you ever have their Cranberry Nut French Toast? God, it was to die for."

Piper's eyes were suddenly swimming with tears. She tried to say something, but her throat felt like it had swollen shut. Finally, she just nodded, swallowing. Elise smiled again, squeezed her hand and headed out to stand watch with Adam. Piper looked around. Tyler nodded at her – he'd be in, she was sure of it, and Adam with him. Max and Ruth were huddled with Jenny, Aaron and Caden. No way Jenny would leave the graves of her children, and Max had never really stopped taking care of the little bereaved family. Ruth would stay with Max. And Levi would stay with his sister; weak as she was, she was the only family he had left.

It was all coming together. Just one thing left to take care of.

Nobody slept well. At midnight, when she and Brody rose to take their watch, the single cavernous room was still restless with murmurings and rustlings. Caden cried out, apparently in a nightmare, and was shushed by his mother. In a far corner, a low light illuminated the smooth young faces of Sam and Becca as they played cards and waited for their mother to come off watch. Ethan lay on a sleeping bag nearby, but his eyes, too, were open, the bright white bond-line that had connected him to Elise since the first day they met glowing steadily. Piper and Brody pulled on outerwear and armed themselves, then stepped out into the night to relieve Adam and Elise, both of whom were drooping with spent adrenalin and fatigue.

The night was clear and cold, bright with a fat, full moon, and the wind had risen to a steady, insistent whine. In the distance, orange light rose and fell as the fire pressed southward, and the smell of smoke, though fading, was still pronounced. When Piper started towards her position on the north side of the building, Brody caught her elbow.

"We need to talk."

Piper's heart started pounding. She tried to pull her elbow free, but Brody's hand was like an iron cuff. He steered her towards the parked jeeps, letting her go when they were sheltered between two of them. They stared at each other, and Piper felt like she couldn't move, frozen by his eyes. If she so much as twitched, she'd give herself away. A thousand years later, Brody spoke.

"Do you have anything you want to tell me?"

She nearly laughed. Her mom had always offered her that out, and she'd never once taken it. Let him make his case. She wasn't going to stick her head in a noose. "No."

Another eternity of locked eyes. Then, he reached into his pocket. He pulled out a familiar baggie, filled with powdered sulfur tuft mushrooms, and set it on the hood of one of the jeeps. A charred book of matches joined it. Finally, he removed the syringe and tiny glass vial of morphine that should have been hidden in the lining of her personal go-bag. He held up the last, and though the corners of his mouth tilted up, it was not a smile.

"If the overdose didn't kill me, the anaphylactic shock would have."

Piper didn't think; she just reacted. She had her pistol out and pointed at his face before her heart beat one more time. It wanted to wobble, and she clamped down on her nerves savagely, steadying her arm through sheer force of will. "How long have you known?"

"From the beginning." He didn't seem to notice the pistol pointed at his face. To her shock, the bond-line flared between them, as bright as she'd ever seen it. He set the syringe and vial beside his other damning evidence and let his hands hang at his sides. "I knew from the first moment I saw you. This is the path. It always has been."

It took her a moment to process the import of his words. Her arm wobbled again, and she brought her other hand up to steady her wrist, as her mother had taught her. *Not a good time to get sloppy,* her mother's voice intoned, and once again, she nearly burst into hysterical laughter. Of all the times for her mother to break her silence.

"Are you saying you see the future? That's how you've changed, like my bond-lines and Tyler's thing with the cards, or Ethan's intuition?"

"I see possible paths. Likely paths."

That would explain a lot, she realized. Why he was such a brilliant tactician. How he'd blocked her so completely, way back in the beginning, using Noah's death and the reactions of the group to trap her. But it didn't explain a few very important things...

"Why are you telling me this? And while I'm asking, if you could see all this, why didn't you stop me? The mushrooms. Or the fire. Why let those things happen?"

"I had my reasons."

For the first time ever, she gave him her very best Piper eye-roll. "Really? If that isn't the most lame, fakey-fortune-teller answer ever, I don't know what is. Isn't it a little too late to be cryptic?"

He smiled. A real smile, the first she'd ever seen on his face. It was transformative, a boyish grin that tilted rakishly at the corner and lit his eyes. She blinked, taken aback. And in that moment, he acted.

The pistol was jerked out of her hand, and his fist closed on the front of her shirt. He jerked her forward, until they were nose to nose. His calm expression was so much more terrifying than anger would have been.

"Let me tell you how this is going to happen: You're going to get your escort to Woodland Park. I will be part of that escort. And for your information, if I should die under unexplained or suspicious circumstances, both Tyler and Adam have been instructed to kill you. We served together, in Afghanistan. You can't compete with that bond. They won't even hesitate."

As he talked, he systematically disarmed her, stripping her of her rifle, the knife strapped to her wrist, the one strapped to her ankle, even the one hidden in an inner pocket of her coat. Piper was so frozen with fear, she couldn't make a move to stop him.

"Just as you planned," he continued, "Jenny and her family will not accompany us. Neither will her brother, or Max, or Ruth. We'll leave one of the jeeps with them, and the rest of us will go on in the other two." His eyes fixed on a distant horizon she couldn't see. "We'll make it to Breckenridge before we run into trouble. We'll have to leave the jeeps there. We'll walk a couple of days – two? Three? It's not clear. But we'll find other transportation, and we'll be in Woodland Park inside a week."

She stared at him, transfixed in spite of her terror. "What a terrible thing." The words surprised her when they came out of her mouth, but she found she meant them. "How awful, to be able to *see* like that. I feel sorry for you."

The look on his face. She would never be able to find words to describe it, though she'd spend the rest of her days trying, when the memory of this would come upon her. Anguish. Love. Desperation. Adoration. Despair. He was a twisted, broken monster of a man, and in spite of her hatred, she wondered for the very first time what had made him that way.

Then his expression contorted into something she was more familiar with; seeing the heat, the burn, made her stomach roll in greasy waves. He stripped her outer jacket off with rough hands, then shoved her back a few paces and lifted his hands, twitching his fingers at her.

"Fight me."

She shook her head numbly. "I won't."

He stepped in close and put a hand on her throat, fingers hooked just beneath her skull on her spine, thumb on her chin. "Fight me," he said hoarsely, "Or I will snap your neck. What will happen in Woodland Park doesn't require your presence. Not anymore." Again, his eyes fixed on a faraway place it was his burden to see. "I'm not sure if it ever did."

Out of the ashes of her plans, a desperate phoenix soared. If he felt like he no longer needed her, she could walk away. *Would* walk away, find a way to get to Woodland Park ahead of them, warn the people there...

"I'll find you. If you leave. Know that." He shoved her again. "Fight me."

What was there left for her to do? She fought.

FIFTEEN
Grace: Colorado Springs, CO

Grace felt her father step into the doorway of the bedroom, but kept her eyes shut. He spoke to the woman with the silver and blonde hair, his voice a low rumble. "She's still asleep? Why is she sleeping so much? It's been three days." His voice rose steadily, until it was hard not to wince. When her dad got cranked up, it was best just to hunker down and wait for it to blow over. "You know what, I don't care how she feels about seeing the doctor. I'm going to ride over to the nature center and get him, something's not right –"

"Hush."

And just like that, he hushed. Grace almost raised her eyebrows, remembering just in time that she was supposed to be sleeping. She wasn't clear on what the relationship was between her father and this woman, but she had never, ever known him to be successfully hushed. Not by her mother, and certainly not by his second wife.

She sensed movement and slitted her eyes, watching the woman rise and move towards her dad. Their low voices mixed and tumbled as they moved down the hall, leaving her alone. Grace took a deep breath and opened her eyes, turning her head to stare at the window.

By the light, it was late afternoon. She stretched and rolled onto her side, letting her eyes travel around the room, which was done in shades of neon, predominantly hot turquoise. A teenaged girl's room. Maybe a college student's, she thought, noting the graduation tassel hanging from the shelves that looked like things were missing – gaps where books or pictures should be. Whoever she was, she was probably dead, so it didn't really matter.

She heard someone coming back down the hallway and thought about closing her eyes, then sighed. She'd hidden long enough. Time to take the next step. The silver-blonde woman stepped into the room, and smiled to see her eyes open.

"You're awake." She sat down on the edge of the bed, keeping a respectful distance. "I'm Naomi, a friend of your dad's. Do you remember?"

A kaleidoscope of images flashed by: the bonfire, her dad crushing her in his arms, hurrying, hurrying, almost to the point of running, splashing sometimes in the creek, motorcycles that made no noise, then so many voices and too many lights. She was pretty sure she'd shut down right about then. "Not much. Where are we?"

"My old house. This is my daughter Piper's room. There are people nearby, good people, but your dad wanted to bring you here. He felt like it would be safer. He's just outside, watering the animals. He's not very good at sitting, so I keep giving him chores to do so he'll stop pacing." She winked, and started to stand. "I'll go get him."

"Wait." Grace wasn't ready to see her dad, wasn't ready for his questions, for the way he always knew things even if you didn't tell him. "Is your daughter dead?" She grimaced. "I'm sorry. I don't know...how to ask. I'm not used to being around people...in a normal way, I guess."

"It's okay. You'll figure it out. Your dad has been telling me how smart you are." The woman smiled again. Her eyes were so kind, and so sad. "Piper's alive. I'm trying to find her. My little Macy died, not quite a year ago. She was ten."

"My little brother died, too. Benji." It was the first time Grace had spoken of him since they'd left Limon. "He was twelve. Him, and my mom. My step-dad, too."

Naomi's face fell into lines of sorrow. She looked down, swallowing hard and shaking her head. "Your dad will be so sad to hear." Tears made her eyes bright when she looked back up. "Do you want to tell him? Or do you want me to?"

Grace's mind went completely blank. She felt her heart accelerate, her breathing quicken. "I don't... I don't know..." What was her problem? She'd been living by her wits for weeks now, and a simple question made her hyperventilate?

"Hush, now."

The gentle command worked on her, just as it had worked on her dad. The woman – was she supposed to call her Naomi? Or Mrs. Something? – took her hand, rubbing and patting. Grace felt a deep calm suffuse her, a sweet peace. Why, she was like Quinn. Of the Earth. At the thought of Quinn, though, her anxiety came roaring back.

"Uhm, you know what?" She sat up experimentally, and was pleased when the room only wobbled a little bit before settling down. "I've got to go...run an errand."

It was a ridiculous excuse and she knew it, but she needed to check in on Quinn and the baby, make sure they were still safe. Had her dad really said it had been three days? She'd been gone too long, far too long. And she needed to regroup, think about how to achieve her remaining goals. She wasn't sure how her father would fit into all that, but she'd figure it out. She swung her legs over the edge of the bed, and noticed for the first time that she was wearing different clothes: Soft fleece pajama bottoms covered with little yellow chickens wearing glasses, and a bright yellow pajama top emblazoned with the words "Brainy Chick." She looked around, more than a little panicked.

"What happened to my clothes? I need those clothes." She noticed then how clean her hands were, and lifted them to touch first her hair, then her face. Both squeaky clean. This time, her voice sounded panicked. "I need those clothes – they're how I get close to the gang without people getting close to me. And my stuff – I need to go get my stuff, my pepper and –"

"Grace. Gracie, listen." Naomi captured her twisting hands. Again, Grace felt the grounding effect of her, the pull towards calm stillness. "I know you've been on your own for a while, but we've got you now. Your dad and I. You don't need to go back to that gang, not ever. We're going to take you home, to Woodland Park. Just as soon as you're up to it, we'll go."

Her puzzle lay around her in a million pieces, unfinished, ruined. A sudden surge of rage burned the back of her throat like acid, and she struggled to hold it back, struggled and failed. She lurched to her feet, staggered, and ended up clinging to the curiously empty bookshelves. "I'm not ready to go! I can't! This is something I have to do, do you get that? Only I can do this!"

Naomi rose to her feet, and somehow, said just the right thing. "I know how tight you've had to hold on. I know you're not ready to let go yet. And that's okay." She let her words sink in for a moment, then spoke again. "You need to eat something. No matter what you decide to do, you'll need your strength. How about if I get some soup and fruit, and you can fill me in on what you need to do, and how we can help?"

Grace's shoulders dropped a fraction. Again, she thought of Quinn. Whenever she had gotten upset, his voice had sounded just like this woman's, reasonable and low. Without making a big deal, Naomi helped her sit back down on the bed, fluffing some pillows behind her back and tucking the bright quilt around her quivering legs. She smiled at Grace, but there was a break in her voice when she spoke.

"I've missed babying my girls, tucking them in, just being a mom to them. I appreciate you letting me fuss."

Grace nodded, leaning back against the pillows. Her eyes drooped for real this time, and she had fallen into a light doze by the time Naomi returned with a bed tray table. She waited until Grace had scooted up, then set it across her lap.

"It's just canned vegetable soup and a fruit cup, I'm afraid. I hope you like peaches." She snapped a cloth napkin open and laid it gently on Grace's chest to protect her pajamas. "We're a little short on groceries, or I'd make something homemade. If this stays down, there's plenty more, so just say so."

Grace swallowed the saliva that had pooled in her mouth at the first fragrant waft of steamy soup. "This is wonderful. I haven't eaten this well in a long time," she said. "Thank you."

Naomi nodded, then moved to sit in a nearby rocking chair, swaying gently to and fro as Grace ate. She made herself take it slow; since she'd left Quinn, she'd rarely had more than a single meal a day, sometimes less than that. Naomi had been right; the food settled both her stomach and her mind, infusing her with strength and helping her think more clearly. She felt like her head was finally attached to her shoulders again, instead of floating away.

When she finished, she set her spoon down and sighed. "That was so good. Thank you," she repeated, and again Naomi nodded. She took the tray and moved it to the hot pink student desk at the foot of the bed. Then, she sat back down in the rocker.

"Grace," she said softly, "Where's your baby?"

Her head went woozy again. "I, uh. I'm sorry. What did you say?"

Naomi rocked on calmly, her face as gentle as her voice. "I cleaned you up when we got back here. Washed your hair and your body, put you in clean clothes." She traced a finger from her belly button downwards. "You have a dark line on your tummy. It's called 'linea negra,' and it often comes with pregnancy. Also, your breasts are still leaking milk. I saw that you had them wrapped really tight."

"Does my dad know?"

"I haven't said anything to him yet, but yes, I think he does know, on some level anyway." Naomi didn't move towards her, but Grace felt a wave of warmth and caring surround her. It was like basking in sunshine. "Did the baby die?"

"No, I, uh…" She was having enormous trouble stuttering out even simple words. "I can't, that is, I don't want to…talk about it," she finished in a rush. "I can't talk about it. But can you help me? There's something I need to do."

"If I can, I'll help. When your dad learns that Benji is gone, he'll want to get you to Woodland Park as quickly as possible, to safety." She turned to look at the window, her expression faraway. "We were going to go on to look for my daughter Piper, but she's on her way. I thought maybe I was just imagining it, but this morning, I was sure." She turned back, and for the first time, Grace realized what a pretty lady she was. Her face was glowing with joy. "My daughter's on her way here. I can *feel* her, and she's getting closer. But that probably doesn't make sense to you, does it?"

Grace narrowed her eyes. "You're talking about the psychic thing, right? The gang was always looking for people who had changed. And…somebody I knew said he was different now. He could do this thing with plants, feel what their properties were, and so on. Are you different, too?"

"I am. So's your dad. What about you?"

So much easier to talk about this than the baby, though Grace didn't doubt they would circle back. She had a feeling this woman was tough to distract. "I'm not sure. I've always had this thing, where my brain forms a picture, even if I don't have all the pieces. And I can memorize huge chunks of information after hearing it just once."

She paused, thinking about how to put into words what she sensed. It was fun to talk about this, and her words flowed more and more easily as her enthusiasm grew. "But I think it isn't fully realized in me yet. Maybe there are different levels in different people. Maybe I'm still evolving. It'll be interesting to see."

Naomi smiled wryly. "Your dad was right. There's nothing wrong with your brain. You're going to love my Piper. She's brilliant, too." Then, she circled back. "Grace, why were you with that gang? They weren't holding you prisoner, were they? Were you escaping when we found you? We've tried and tried to imagine the circumstances, and we haven't come up with an explanation. Will you tell me?"

"Are you going to tell my dad?" She couldn't seem to get away from that question, could she?

Naomi's lips firmed, and her eyes were stern. "You're asking me to keep a lot of secrets."

"I'm afraid." Grace closed her eyes, and groped for words. "I'm afraid of what he'll do if he knows. It's just for the best."

"You want him to stay safe. They hurt you, and you don't want him to go off, looking to hurt them in retaliation."

"Yes!" That wasn't it, but it worked a whole lot better than the truth. "It wouldn't change anything. It's over and done. I was with them, because I was trying to get information. I wanted to do the right thing, to make up, see? To make up for it. For –" She gestured vaguely at her stomach, and Naomi frowned in confusion. Grace shook her head and tried again. "I knew how to get close to them, because of before. I could listen and learn things about their plans, learn how their group was structured, their social framework, things like that."

Her brain saved her then, kicking her up to the analytical level that had been her sanity for the last month. "If we understand the group's underlying ideology, analyze their sources of support and power, we can strategize ways to destroy them. So they can never hurt anyone, not ever again."

Naomi was still staring at her, but there was something that looked like awe in her eyes now. "Criminy, Grace. Where did you learn all that?"

Grace shrugged, pleased to have her intelligence recognized. It had been so long since she'd gotten a pat on the back for being smart. She couldn't believe how much she'd missed it. "I love history and social studies," she said. "And I did a term paper on the methodologies of non-violence. I think some of the concepts could work." She looked down modestly, tracing a finger along the seam in the quilt, and couldn't resist sharing. "The teacher gave me an A+ on it."

"I'll bet he did." Naomi's voice was so soft, and there were tears in it. Grace looked up to see her rubbing at her mouth, trying to hide the quiver there. She smiled, but some of the tears spilled free. She wiped at them and heaved a deep, shaky breath. "I'm sorry, honey, it's just that you're breaking my heart a little bit. It's a mom thing. Nothing for you to worry about." She sighed again and fixed Grace with a look that would not be distracted. "Grace, you need to tell me who the father of your baby was. I'm pretty certain I'm putting together what happened to you, but I need you to tell it all out, as much as you can. Then we can decide together what to tell your dad."

And just like that, Grace was slammed back down into the place where words wouldn't come, where stuttering was the best she could produce. "I...it's just that I don't...it doesn't really matter, see?"

Naomi moved to sit by her on the bed. Up close, Grace could see where grief had cut lines in her pretty face. The older woman picked up her hands and held them so delicately, like they were baby birds. "How about if I tell you what I think I know, and you can tell me 'yes' or 'no.' You can just nod or shake your head, if that's easier. Shall we try?"

Grace nodded. Over the next few minutes, Naomi talked, and Grace responded, yes or no. Naomi had guessed so much of it, it wasn't that painful. Not until they came to the whereabouts of Grace's baby did they hit a roadblock.

Naomi frowned. "I don't understand, honey. I know your baby is alive, but where is it now?" She swallowed, but kept her tone gentle. "Did you abandon it? It's okay to tell me, it really is."

"No." Grace closed her eyes, and felt exhaustion pull her towards sleep, but she needed to finish this. She opened her eyes again, and said, "Quinn. He's a boy from home – we traveled together from Limon. He saved me." The words came easily now, to her intense relief. "He helped get me away from the gang. He took care of me and kept us safe. He delivered the baby. She's with him."

"That's where you want to go, isn't it? You left them, to spy on the gang, and you want to go get them, take them to Woodland Park with us."

"Yes." The word came out as a sob. Grace clutched Naomi's hands, and felt the awful remorse rise in her chest like the swell of the tide. "Yes," she sobbed again. "We need to go get them. I shouldn't have left, but I had to go. I had to, and I have to tell him how sorry I am!"

Sobs tore out of her, faster and faster, until the torrent would not be stopped. She curled on her side and cried out a year's worth of grief and fear, cried for her mom, for her baby brother, for the gaping loneliness where Quinn belonged, for a baby girl who had been born of violence and pain. And she cried for herself, for the terrible things she hadn't even known about until they'd been done to her.

Dimly, she heard the bedroom door open, heard her father's worried voice, felt his big hand cup the back of her head. She opened her swollen eyes to see his face, almost unrecognizable, twisted as it was in pain. "Gracie," he rasped, "Tell me how to make it better, sweetheart, and I will. Just tell me how."

She reached her arms up, and he sat down beside her, scooping her close to cradle her in his strong, strong arms. She pressed her face to his chest and just breathed him in, the scent of childhood, love and safety. The terrible tightness in her chest eased, the endless need to watch her back, to sleep with one eye open and both ears on. She dropped into sleep to the murmur of his voice, the slow circling of his hand on her back.

Afternoon slid into night, and she drifted in and out of sleep, rousing to eat again, sometimes hearing the murmur of their voices, sometimes just listening to the beat of her dad's heart as he held her. Only once did she wake to find him gone, in the early gray of morning. Naomi was there, humming a soft lullaby, her pretty hands stroking Grace's butchered hair. Grace rolled onto her back and raised her own hand to touch the uneven, choppy mess self-consciously. Fresh tears slid free.

"I had to cut it," she said. "I did a terrible job on purpose. It looked so bad it made me cry, isn't that dumb? After everything else?"

"Not one thing dumb about it." Naomi reached up to touch her own hair, smiling ruefully. "I just avoid mirrors. My stylist would have a heart attack if she could see me now. When we get home, I'll see if I can clean it up if you like, or maybe Layla could try. You're going to like her, I have a feeling. Your dad went to take care of the horses. If you're up to it, we'll start for Woodland Park today. We've got gear to camp with if you get tired. What do you say we get you up and see how steady you are?"

Grace sat up, and the room didn't wobble at all. Naomi hovered close by as she used the bathroom – they had rigged up a bucket similar to the one Quinn had improvised for use as a toilet – then came back to sit on the edge of the bed while Naomi searched through the drawers and closets. "Piper is bigger than you, but we'll find something that works. Do you have a favorite color?"

Why the question made her cry again, Grace couldn't begin to explain. Naomi looked up at the first wet sniffle and moved to pat her back matter-of-factly. "Honey. I'll tell you what I always told my girls: Tears are like rain. They help you grow, so just let them fall." She crouched down so she was at eye level. "Do you like dogs?"

Grace sniffed again, thinking of the dog pack she and Quinn had always been on the lookout for. "I used to. Why?"

Naomi smiled and rose, going to the bedroom door. She spoke to someone outside in the hallway. "No, Hades, not you, you're too much of a tank. All right, you can come in, but you're going to lie down like a gentleman, got it? Persephone, why don't you go see if that beautiful girl over there would like to meet you?"

Grace's eyes widened when the biggest Rottweiler she'd ever seen stepped into the doorway. He cocked his head at her, whined, then looked up at Naomi, who just pointed at the floor. Grumbling, he curled up right where she had indicated, watching with liquid eyes as a golden fairy-like dog danced across the room, her tail a wagging blur.

Through her tears, Grace smiled. "Oh, she's so cute!" She held her arms out, and the little dog leaped into them, quivering with delight. Grace laughed. She actually laughed, and it felt so, so good.

"That's Persephone you've got, and this is Hades," Naomi said. She moved to crouch by the big Rottweiler, who pressed into her stroking hand. "This guy can be overwhelming, but he would never, ever hurt you. His heart is a great golden thing, isn't it, my sweet boy?"

Grace held Persephone up, who licked the end of her nose and made her laugh again. "Ruler of the Underworld and the girl he tricked into marriage." She kissed Persephone's bright head between her butterfly-like ears. "How could you fall for that pomegranate thing? Wasn't it a little obvious?"

She looked up, and Naomi was once again watching her with a hint of awe. "You're kind of like a living, breathing encyclopedia, aren't you?"

Grace cuddled Persephone close, marveling at how good the warm weight of her felt in her arms. "My brother used to call me 'Groogle.' My name, plus 'Google.'"

"I remember." Her father's voice. Grace looked up, and he was standing in the doorway, smiling at her in joy and in sorrow. "Naomi told me, about Benji and your mom, and Wayne. I'm so sorry you had to go through that alone, sweetheart." Before Grace could wonder what else Naomi had told him, Persephone struggled free of her arms and raced across the room to launch into her dad's arms. He caught her and bent his head to kiss her just where Grace had.

Naomi moved to sit beside her on the bed, speaking low. "It's okay. He knows some things, but not all. He also knows that you're not ready to talk about some of it yet. We'll just take it slow, okay?" Then, she inclined her head towards Martin and Persephone, who was now licking his chin in frantic adoration. "Don't feel bad. Persephone was mine, until your dad came into the picture. If he's in the vicinity, I'm chopped liver."

Martin set Persephone down, and she scooted back to Grace's lap, curling into a tiny, snuggly ball. Grace stroked her soft fur, threading her fingers carefully through the drape of her ears. "It feels so good to hold her. Like a –" She'd been about to say, "Like a baby," but her throat closed up. There was a beat of silence, then her dad spoke.

"She feels like a baby, doesn't she? I thought so, too, the first time I held her. It was a comfort to me. Still is." He looked down at the floor, then spoke to his boots. "I lost your step-mom, Grace, and little baby Michael."

Grace leaned into Naomi. "Daddy. I'm so sorry." She re-oriented around this information. "So it's just you and me left. Just us."

Martin looked up, and his eyes touched Naomi. He smiled crookedly. "No, sweetheart. Not just us. Now, you three are a real pretty picture and all, but we're wasting daylight. Gracie, did Naomi tell you we'd like to ride out today? Do you feel up to it?"

Grace nodded, then buried her face in Persephone's fur to hide. "There's somewhere we need to go first. Something we need to do." She shook her head slightly, remembering that she didn't need to keep her secrets alone anymore. "We need to go to Garden of the Gods – well, Rock Ledge Ranch, really. There are people there we need to take with us."

She could feel them looking at each other, and the silence was thick with unspoken words. Then, her dad spoke. "Can you tell us a little more?"

Grace could feel the effort he made to invite the information rather than demanding it, and it made her heart clutch with love for him. Her pushy, demanding Marine dad had mellowed right out. She looked up, peering through Persephone's ears. "It's Quinn Harris. And..." She couldn't speak of the baby. Not yet. She'd cross that bridge when she came to it. "Do you remember? His family lived just to the north of us, that ranch with all the boys?"

"You were dating William."

Grace nodded, but didn't elaborate, not on any of it. William's death. Why she had traveled from Limon with Quinn, but wasn't with him now. The identity of the other person she had alluded to. She didn't need to. Her dad just nodded, and started re-working his plans. "All right, if that's what we need to do, it's done. We've got three horses. We'll have to share, with one of us walking, I guess—"

"There are horses there. Quinn's Koda, and a little mustang named Kava that was at the ranch when we got there. She's a sweetie." Her dad didn't need one bit of this information, but it was information she could give. "There are supplies, too, if we need them. We canned a bunch of stuff from the garden last summer, we had a really bumper crop of tomatoes and green beans, it was crazy..."

She let her voice trail away. Her dad was watching her with a worried frown, and he folded his lips in on themselves to keep himself from asking any one of the hundreds of questions he must have. Grace stood up, then knelt to put Persephone on the floor. "I feel really good. I'm ready to go. Just let me get dressed."

She ate breakfast while her dad and Naomi ferried supplies to the basement, where there was a hidden storage room, Naomi explained. Apparently, they'd been provisioned for a much longer trip, and they were planning to leave most of it behind. Grace would be riding the pack horse, an Appaloosa named Pasha; they'd included a saddle for her in their gear, planning on bringing kids back with them. By the time she finished eating, they were ready to go.

They rode out, accompanied by brilliant sunshine, stopping first to say goodbye to the group at the Bear Creek Nature Center. Naomi hugged a man named Ed, promising to see him again, and Grace's eyes swept the crowd automatically. A pair of teenage boys were staring and nudging each other. When her eyes met theirs, they both grinned and puffed up, like boys do. She dropped her eyes, folding her arms around herself. She could hardly remember a time when she would have grinned back.

When they reached Old Colorado City, Grace took the lead, winding them through one of the many paths she'd memorized, stopping them constantly to check their back trail and listen. They stopped at her last hidey-hole, and her dad followed her inside. She emptied out the grubby backpack she'd been using, taking only the dog-eared, precious manuscript, and they were on their way again. On the edge of the park, she insisted they stop for the count to 1,000. She could feel Martin and Naomi looking at each other again, talking about her without words, but she didn't care. This had to be done properly.

Instead of climbing the ridge, Grace led them straight into Rock Ledge Ranch, her heart pounding. Pasha picked up on her energy and broke into a trot, then a canter. Grace let her go, exhilarated, and rode into the tiny clearing by the cabin ahead of her father and Naomi. She slid out of the saddle by the small, circular corral, and looped Pasha's reins around one of the logs. Then she ran to the cabin.

"Quinn! Quinn, it's me, Grace!" She didn't want to startle him by bursting in, and hesitated at the door. She heard her father and Naomi ride up, and for the first time, she noticed how still everything was. Too still. Her whole body started to shake. "Quinn? Quinn, please answer me!"

She shoved the cabin door open. Empty. Cold. Deserted. Her breath started coming in sobbing gasps. She ran back to Pasha and hurled herself onto her back, wheeling her to ride for the barn and the Chamber house, praying, praying. At the barn, she found all the stables and stalls empty – the goats and sheep were grazing out in the open field, and the chickens had likewise been released from the coop. The horses were nowhere to be seen.

And she knew before she burst into the kitchen at the Chamber house, before her frantic eyes had darted around, noting the layer of undisturbed dust. Her father stepped into the kitchen just in time to catch her when her legs crumpled underneath her.

They were gone.

SIXTEEN
Jack: Woodland Park, CO

The crackle of the radio yanked Jack out of a dream filled with water that burned. He jerked upright, looking around in confusion until he realized he'd fallen asleep at his desk again. So much to get done, so many changes coming, so many decisions to make. The radio crackled again.

"Jack, this is Thomas. Come in."

Jack fumbled for the radio, clearing his throat, still froggy when he spoke. "This is Jack. Go ahead, Thomas."

"Jack, we've got a young man here you need to talk to. We're at location Juliet. He's asking for Martin, and he has an infant with him. Over."

Jack swung to the map. Location Juliet was near the old middle school, at the junction of Rampart Range Road and Maplehurst. It marked the most likely point of entry for travelers coming in on one of the dirt roads. He keyed the radio. "Do I need to bring Rowan with me? Over."

"Negative. She looks to be in really good shape." Instead of "Over," Jack distinctly heard Thomas coo something like, "Aren't you? Yes, you are!" He shook his head.

"I'll be there in five minutes. Out."

The cool morning air washed the rest of the sleep from his brain as he zoomed towards the middle school on his ATV, though flashes of dream images continued to haunt him: flaming water lighting a dirty, night-time sky, and of all people, his sister, punching through that wall of flame in a boat that burned all around her. Jack scrubbed a hand over his head, as if he could rub away the unsettling images. He hadn't seen Caroline in years and did his best not to think of her. Even before the plague, he hadn't been sure whether or not she was still alive.

He pulled up at the checkpoint and took a moment to take it all in. Thomas was cradling a dark-haired infant in his hands, smiling and making exaggerated facial expressions at her. The baby appeared for all the world to be chatting right back, cooing and gurgling, her dark eyes serious in her tiny face. Nearby, two horses were cropping at the springtime grass, one of them saddled, one of them loaded down with gear, including a brightly colored crib mobile that sprouted crazily from the top of the rolls and bundles. And a few feet from that, a teenage boy was...milking a goat? The boy looked up as Jack shut the ATV off, and Jack revised his assessment: a boy in years, yes. A man, judging by the experience in his eyes and the maturity Jack could *feel* emanating from him.

Thomas tucked the baby in the crook of his arm and walked over, tilting his head in the boy's direction. "Jack, this is Quinn Harris." The young man nodded but continued with his task. "He's originally from Limon, he says. He traveled to the Springs with Martin's daughter, Grace, but they got separated. Ran into trouble with that gang Anne told us about." He tilted the baby up, and she gazed at Jack with ancient eyes. "And this young beauty is Lark. Quinn said he helped the mother give birth, but she didn't make it."

Jack's eyes narrowed. A thread of disbelief ran through Thomas' words, and at the mention of the mother, he *felt* a spike of betrayal surge in Quinn. There was more here than met the eye. There was also plenty of time to sort it out. He smiled at Quinn.

"You're welcome here. I take it you'll need a place to stay where you can keep the animals near?" He gestured to the goat. "I assume she's the baby's food supply."

"Yes." Quinn stood, and ran a hand down the nanny goat's neck, murmuring to her. She pressed into him for a moment, bleated, then trotted over to join the horses in their grazing. "Lark stays with me, too. She's mine."

Jack and Thomas exchanged a quick glance; neither had missed the fierceness in young Quinn's declaration. Jack smiled again. "Of course. We wouldn't take her from you; that's not how we operate here. There will be plenty of help with her, though, if you need it."

Quinn nodded, and Jack felt *relief* surge and settle in him. He walked to the horses, and poured the goat's milk carefully into a container hanging from the pack of supplies. Thomas returned the baby to him when he was finished, and Quinn deftly tucked her into the sling across his chest.

Jack looked at Thomas. "I'll take him to the church and send someone to bring Ignacio in. We'll see if he and his daughter can put Quinn up, at least for the time being."

He looked at Quinn. "While we're waiting, we can have our healer check the baby, if you like. You, too, if there's need."

"I'm fine, but I'd like her to look at Lark." He rubbed and patted the baby's back as he talked, swaying in the age-old dance of a parent trying to get a baby to sleep. "She had a rough start. She wouldn't take any of the formulas I found." A storm cloud passed over his features. "The mother nursed her once, but then she was gone. If not for Alice and her milk, we'd have been sunk. Huh, bunny?"

As if in reply, the baby's arm shot out of the sling to pat against the front of Quinn's t-shirt. He picked her tiny fist up and kissed it, and the *love* binding them was a tangible, visible thing. Again, Jack and Thomas exchanged a look. Strange, the way Quinn had phrased the information about the mother: "She was gone." Definitely more there than he was telling, but until Jack had a reason to push the young man, he wouldn't.

Quinn remounted his horse, and they caravanned in with Jack leading the way. People were out and about now, and they stopped to stare at the newcomer and his menagerie. Jack glanced back, noting that Quinn's face was burning a dull red, his eyes fixed on the back of Jack's ATV. He didn't appreciate the attention, that was for sure. When they arrived at the church, Layla's class was in the meditation garden, though Layla was nowhere to be seen. They were working with Carla, helping to prepare the ground for the fledgling herbs and vegetables they'd been nurturing as a class project.

Jack shut the ATV off, and Quinn dismounted, moving to hold his big quarter horse by the bridle. "Is there somewhere I could water them? We've been riding since before dawn."

Before Jack could answer, a squeal pierced the bright morning. "Oh my god, is that a goat? She's so cute!"

Karleigh led the charge. As the entire class abandoned Carla to converge on them, Jack *felt* a spike of pure panic from Quinn. The baby startled into wakefulness, going from peaceful sleep to screeching banshee in less than a second. Huh, Jack had just a moment to think. She was sure sensitive to her young protector's feelings. Interesting.

He stepped in front of Quinn and held his arms wide, shielding the boy from the charging herd. "Could you guys chill it? In case your ears are stopped up, let me point out that you woke the baby." Over his shoulder, he muttered to Quinn. "Don't worry, I can hold them off. Just keep breathin', buddy."

He *felt* Quinn relax a little, even when Karleigh met Jack's words with a much softer though no less excited squeal. "Oh, he's got a baby with him, too! Can we see?"

Jack fixed the group with a stern glare. "Take it down a notch, all of you." He met Karleigh's eyes. "You especially. Why don't you tell me how he feels about this onslaught?"

Karleigh's eyes went unfocused for a moment, then her expression dropped into sheepish, apologetic lines. "I'm sorry, Pastor Jack," she mumbled. "I didn't think."

"Don't tell me, tell this young man." Jack stepped to the side. "His name is Quinn, and if you don't mob him, I'm sure he'd be pleased to meet all of you."

Karleigh stepped forward. "It's nice to meet you, Quinn. I'm sorry we all came at you like that. We haven't seen someone from the outside in a long time, and we – I – got a little too excited." Her eyes fell to Lark, who had subsided into little complaining noises against Quinn's neck. "Is she your daughter?"

"She is now." *Pride.* Quinn tucked the baby in the crook of his arm to show her off, looking at her instead of the other kids. "Her name is Lark."

Coos and cries of delight met his pronouncement. Quinn's face was still flushed, but he seemed to be holding his own, especially with the baby and Alice the goat acting as buffers. Jack moved to where Carla was watching, and cut right to the chase.

"Where's Layla?"

Carla frowned at him. "She's been out most of the week. Owen said she hasn't been feeling well. Anne and I've been keeping the kids busy – there's always plenty for them to help with. I thought you would have known."

It was Jack's turn to frown. "I haven't been taking the kids to the gym. We've just got so much going on. Water issues, which I'm sure you're aware of. There's talk of moving the whole community to Carrol Lakes, with Naomi." He *felt* for the link that was always open to Layla, but hit her wall of ice instead. He rubbed at the sting in the center of his chest; she had a little push-back going on with her defenses these days. "And with Martin gone, there's just a lot of extra."

Carla nodded and accepted his excuses; Layla would have recognized them for the half-truth they were. The real truth was that Jack had been avoiding contact with any of the women who shared leadership of this community; Layla, of course, Rowan and Verity as well. He'd had all he could stomach of their honesty and opinions. His duties had multiplied since Martin left, and he'd made the absolute most of that excuse, putting in monster long days, working at whatever tasks needed doing, taking refuge in constant motion.

Unfortunately, though, the luxury of avoiding Rowan was no longer his. He left Carla monitoring Quinn and the kids and went to his office to radio Rowan as well as send a runner out to Ignacio's ranch. When he returned, Quinn had unloaded and picketed his animals in a shaded patch of grass, and some of the kids were just lugging in buckets of water for them. Viola was smiling down at little Lark, who was kicking on a blanket in the same patch of shade. Some of the younger kids surrounded them, and some had returned to helping Carla.

The older kids, Karleigh, James, Ben and Dylan, were all grouped around Quinn, who once again looked like he'd prefer to sink into the ground. Karleigh was smiling up at him through her eyelashes, twisting a lock of her dual-toned hair around her finger, her expression reminiscent of a love-struck Disney fawn. The boys were all eyeballing the newcomer with varying levels of hostility, depending on their relative fondness for Karleigh. Jack bit the inside of his cheek to keep from grinning. Lord, he loved these kids. He had missed them, so much.

"Pastor Jack!" Karleigh scooted towards Quinn, gesturing for Jack to join their circle. "Quinn came from out on the plains – he said the city is totally dangerous, that there's a gang that does all kinds of horrible things!"

"I heard," Jack said calmly. What was romantically dangerous to Karleigh made *misery* bleed from Quinn. She had no idea how fortunate she'd been, and Jack prayed she'd never have to learn. His heart hurt for this young man, whose very energy spoke of his gentle nature. He held his hand out, gesturing to Quinn. "If you'd like to bring the baby inside, we can get you some food. Rowan should be here shortly."

Quinn ducked his head, hurrying to gather Lark, as well as the container of goat's milk, a bottle and a diaper from the depths of his supplies. He nodded and mumbled goodbyes to the kids, oozing *relief* as he followed Jack into the cool darkness of the church. Jack spoke as they walked, headed for the library.

"They're good kids, but they can be overwhelming." Quinn nodded, and Jack went on. "Most of them have been here since the start of the plague. Dylan and Evie were in Cascade, but they've been with us for nearly a year. None of them were on their own for long, if at all." Another pause. "I take it you and Grace weren't so lucky?"

"No." Quinn cleared the hoarseness out of his voice. "I lost my whole family. Gracie did, too, but she didn't know about her dad. I was sure glad to hear he made it. I just wish..." His voice trailed off, and the roiling emotions that Jack *felt* from the quiet young man were as complex as they were powerful: betrayal again, and disappointment, but also admiration, friendship, and a deep and abiding love that belied his youth.

They settled into the library to wait for Rowan, and when Judy arrived with a tray of food, Jack offered to hold Lark while Quinn ate. As she had with Thomas, she cooed and chatted in response to his baby talk, but even when she beamed her gummy baby smile, there was something in her eyes that made Jack's heart ache. Rowan came bustling in a few minutes later, and Jack settled into a chair to watch as she examined the baby, asking Quinn questions about her birth, her eating and sleeping patterns. Jack curled his fingers over his lips to hide another grin as he listened to Quinn discuss the infant's bowel movements with great seriousness and authority. He was going to like this young man very much. He was sure of it.

Exam finished, Rowan took a few moments to tickle Lark's plump little legs, smiling when she was rewarded with a gurgling coo. "She's fit as a fiddle, Quinn – you've done a great job. You let us know how much and what kind of help you want with her. No one goes it alone here."

Quinn's shoulders slumped, and he heaved a great sigh. "I'm so glad. I was so worried about her. I couldn't stand to see her suffer, or die. It wasn't her fault she..." He folded his lips into a tight line over the words he'd been going to say, then went on, "Anyway, there's been too much death."

"That's for sure. And there's nothing that brings more hope to a community than a healthy new baby. One day, little girl, I'll introduce you to my nephew, Oliver." Rowan scooped Lark up and tucked her against her body, expertly slipping the nipple of the bottle between her lips. The baby curled towards her, eyes already drooping. "If you like, Jack and I can babysit while we wait for Ignacio.

Maybe you'd like to take a break, visit with the other kids for a while?"

Just the thought made Quinn's whole body radiate *alarm*. Jack spoke. "Or maybe you'd like to take a few minutes to yourself, get cleaned up, that sort of thing?"

Quinn looked like he was about to refuse, then cocked his head to the side, considering. Jack felt the *longing* in him for a minute, just a minute or two to rest, to put it all down. This young man had been carrying heavy burdens, alone, for too long.

"Well, I could probably use a quick wash. I can't smell me, but after a few days on the trail, I'm sure you can." He moved to stroke a finger along Lark's forearm. Even though she was nearly asleep, her mouth curved in a brief, milky smile. "Are you sure?"

"Go." Rowan waved him along. Jack led him down to the church basement, showed him where the water was stored and where to dispose of it after he was done, supplied him with toiletries and a clean towel, then left him to his own devices. By the time he returned to the library, Rowan was curled in one of the wing chairs with her eyes closed, the baby sleeping on her chest. He was about to sneak back out when she spoke.

"There is nothing that knocks me out faster than a sleeping baby. Little Oliver and I have taken some excellent naps together." She slitted her eyes and gazed at him. "Quinn seems like a good kid. It was hard for him to leave this little girl, even I could feel that. There's something he's not telling us about the baby, though."

"Yeah, I got that, too. If I *felt* any kind of threat from him, I'd push it."

Jack settled in the other wing chair and stretched his legs out. Rowan's eyes were shut again, though he could *feel* she wasn't sleeping. She was relaxed, her guard was down, and it wasn't in any way ethical to probe her for information right now. He probed anyway.

"So, I'm glad to hear Layla's starting to feel better..." He let his voice trail off conversationally, and pitched it just so – friendly concern, just making idle chit-chat, nothing more.

"Is she? Well, then you know more than I do." Rowan snorted, but didn't open her eyes. "She's blocking me with that 'wall of ice' thing she does. Says I don't need to be worrying about her, with everything else I've got on my plate."

"Mmm." He kept his tone light, in spite of his intense concentration. He couldn't quite get a handle on Rowan's emotions. She was both *concerned* and *excited*. "Well, she does have a point..."

Rowan sighed. "I suppose. Pregnancy isn't an illness, after all, but she is older and it's been a rough start. I'm glad she finally told you."

There was no longer any air in the room. Jack couldn't suck enough in to even attempt a reply. And yet, he'd known, hadn't he? Before he'd even asked, he'd known.

"Why, you sneaky bastard."

Jack looked over to see Rowan glaring at him. The baby stirred on her chest, suddenly whimpering and discontent, and Rowan patted her gently even as she hit him with enough *anger* to punch the wind out of him, if he'd had any wind to give. She opened her mouth to give voice to that anger just as they both heard the foyer door open and Ignacio's voice.

"Hello in the church," he called.

Still glaring at Jack, Rowan called back. "We're in the library."

A moment later, the rancher appeared in the doorway, holding his battered cowboy hat in his hand. His face lit up when he spied Lark, and he tiptoed over to stand by Rowan's chair. His eyes flickered between Rowan and Jack. Even someone with zero intuitive ability could read the murderous look she was blasting him with, but Ignacio was no fool. He kept his attention on the baby, reaching out a brown, knotty forefinger to stroke the baby's forearm, just as Quinn had done.

"I heard there were some folks with animals that needed a place to put up. Is she with them?"

"She is." Rowan eased to her feet and smiled briefly at Ignacio. "Would you like to hold her? I've got to be on my way. I can lay her down on her blanket, if you'd rather —"

Before she had even finished speaking, Ignacio was carefully gathering the sleeping baby from Rowan's arms, tucking her against his chest and murmuring when she stirred. He patted her little back with his big, work-weathered hand, and in his face, Jack saw the agony and joy of his memories.

Ignacio closed his eyes, but moisture leaked out anyway. He laid his cheek against Lark's head. "They're small like this for the blink of an eye," he murmured. "You should always hold a sleeping baby, every single minute you can." His chest lifted in a shuddering sigh, and his face twisted for just a moment. "Before you can't hold them anymore, not ever again."

Rowan squeezed his shoulder. "Thanks for helping them, Ignacio." Then she knifed Jack with one last glare. "You and I will talk later. Bet on it."

Jack didn't answer. He watched her gather her things and leave, watched Ignacio bounce and sway around the room, but he couldn't seem to form words, or even a thought, other than *Layla is pregnant*. It beat in his head, rhythmic and relentless as a heartbeat, all-controlling, over-riding everything else.

Quinn returned, and he had to focus all his concentration on keeping the words from coming out of his mouth. He introduced Quinn and Ignacio, helped Quinn repack his horses, and saw them on their way, and still those words grew in his chest, pressing on his heart and lungs until he felt like he had to gasp for each breath of air.

Layla is pregnant.

They were the first words he thought when the radio crackled again later that evening, followed by Thomas' excited voice informing him that Martin and Naomi were back and that they had Martin's daughter with them. He knew he should go to them right away, explain about Quinn, find out what they'd learned, but he couldn't devote enough of his mind to the task to accomplish it. In the morning, he told himself. In the morning, when he could think.

Dreams again, awful dreams. His eyes shot open to early morning light, and the damn words came at him again, like torpedoes: *Layla is pregnant.*

He didn't snap out of it until mid-day, when an awful *knowing* overrode his preoccupation and drove him out of his office. He headed towards the foyer, his footsteps gradually picking up speed until he was jogging. Something was *wrong*. Something very close. He and Judy nearly collided in the foyer, and in her face, he saw the same trepidation that was making his heart pound and his palms sweat.

She wrung her hands, peering out the glass doors. "There's something...I don't know what it is..." Judy saw possible paths, and had always maintained a pragmatic, "what will be, will be" attitude about it. Jack had never seen her this distraught and sudden terror for his community iced his spine. "Something or someone is coming," she continued in a rush. "It's...big. Bah! What a stupid word! Significant. I don't want to say 'bad,' but..."

"I know."

Movement outside caught Jack's eye. He crouched, peering out the glass front doors, and what he saw sent fire and ice chasing along every nerve in his body. He caught Judy's wringing hands and stilled them. He ducked his head to lock eyes with her, *commanding* her to calm, swift obedience.

"Slip back to my office and radio Naomi at her cabin. If she doesn't answer, try Martin's." His eyes swung back to the people gathering in front of the church. "Tell her Piper's here."

SEVENTEEN
Everyone: Woodland Park, CO

Naomi flew down the road, careening around curves, sliding on gravel, clinging to the handlebars of the ATV with sweat-slick palms. While she drove, she swore. When she had run through her limited and mostly G-rated repertoire, she started all over again. She was simultaneously terrified and filled with the kind of joy that kept making her breath catch and hold.

Piper was here.

Naomi had known – she had *felt* for days how close her daughter was. When she, Martin and Grace had arrived in Woodland Park, she'd been frantic to get to the cabin, sure she'd find Piper there. Disappointment had been a dull ache in her chest through the long, restless night. Finally, she'd dragged a blanket into Macy's room to sleep near at least one of her daughters, something she hadn't done in months. The dogs had curled up just outside the open door, unsettled and anxious, and beyond them, Ares had stalked back and forth, yowling his disapproval.

God, the animals. She had just left them when the call had come in on the radio, had just slung her rifle across her shoulder, bolted out the door and jumped on the ATV. She took a moment to connect with all three of them, sent a pulse of love and reassurance along that connection and nearly skidded into the ditch. She yelped and corrected, then renewed her concentration and zoomed on.

A crowd had gathered in front of the church when she pulled up. She shut down the ATV and scrambled off, craning to see over people's heads. She was about to start shoving her way through when the stillness of the group registered. She paused, looked around, and felt the first chill of foreboding slip icy fingers down her spine.

Guided by an instinct she couldn't explain and didn't need to, she hurried to the far edge of the crowd and started slipping along it. There was something dangerous happening here, something that involved her daughter. She slid a hand along the rifle strap crossing her chest, and kept creeping along, though something, some unknown dread, dragged at every step she took. She could hear voices now, a low murmur. Then, she saw Piper, and every muscle in her body locked into stillness.

Oh, her beautiful hair! All cut off, shaved so close, Naomi could see the tender scalp underneath. A bruise on her temple, another darkening her jaw. Naomi's eyes ran over and over her daughter, and the ice that had touched her spine spread now to her arms and legs. A deep shaking started in her gut and spread as well.

Her awareness expanded to take in the rest of the newcomers, four of them that she could see. The strangers were bristling with weaponry and armored with protective gear, all of them displaying at least two visible firearms. Warriors, Naomi realized, as their collective menace rolled over her body and sizzled a warning along her nerve endings. The hair on her scalp and nape prickled and rose. The shock of that realization was followed by another, like a punch to the center of her chest.

Piper was one of them.

It was all there to see, in the way she held her weapon, the ease with which she carried the well-worn gear, the way her eyes scanned ceaselessly, the ready stance on the balls of her booted feet. Her daughter had become something new. Something Naomi didn't recognize.

She couldn't move. What was happening? What should she do? Was Piper in danger? Why were these people here, and what did they want? Jack was speaking to one of them, a big man with the coldest eyes Naomi had ever seen. Even from this distance, Naomi could *feel* the tension of the exchange. Andrea and Paul, who were always on sentry duty together, stood among the strangers, faces locked and grim.

Her eyes flew back to Piper. How did she fit in with all of this? Around her, she could feel the stir and shift of the crowd, the touch of more and more eyes. People's gazes were starting to flicker back and forth between her and Piper – the resemblance was unmistakable. Any second now, Piper would see her. What should she do? Naomi had imagined their reunion so many times and in so many ways, but never this. This was a nightmare.

A second before his hands locked under her elbows, she *felt* Martin's presence. She clutched at his supporting arms, and looked up at him. "I don't know what's happening," she whispered. "What do I do? I don't know what to do."

Martin's hard eyes flicked over the group, analyzing. "Andrea and Paul as hostages and shields," he said, his low voice as grim as their faces. "Jack, too, if they decide to go there. They're outnumbered, but it doesn't matter. Not enough of us are armed, and they've got automatic weapons. Training, too, by the looks of it." Then, his hands tightened almost painfully on her elbows. "She sees you, Naomi. Piper is looking right at you."

Naomi's eyes snapped back to collide with her daughter's. The whole world rolled and wobbled, and in spite of it all, in spite of the danger and uncertainty of the situation, something in her chest burst with incandescent joy. She pulled in a deep breath, but she couldn't engage her voice.

"Piper." The word was a silent movement of her lips.

"Mama." Piper's lips moved just as soundlessly. Her face was joy, fear, shock and love, all at the same time. For the space of three heartbeats, she just gazed at her mother. Then her eyes shifted to Martin, and her brow furrowed in confusion. Her gaze darted around the crowd, and Naomi could see her breath coming faster and faster. Through the bond, she could *feel* Piper's increasing desperation, her denial. When her eyes returned to her mother's, asking the unimaginable question, Naomi shook her head. She fisted a hand over her heart, and shook her head again. *No, my baby. Daddy and Macy aren't here. I'm so sorry.*

Piper dropped to her knees, and everything happened at once.

The big man snapped a command, and the strangers' weapons snapped up, ready to fire. He started to move towards Piper, but Naomi ripped free of Martin's restraining hands, stumbling, falling, crawling the last few feet to her daughter. Piper reached for her at the same moment, their arms locked around each other, and the last year of Piper's existence blasted through Naomi like a gale-force wind: hate, grief, violation, betrayal, loneliness, fear, pain, pain, pain.

Naomi's breath came in gasping sobs. Her eyes lifted to the big man staring down at her as she held her broken daughter, his eyes as ice-blue and cold as glaciers, and she *knew*. She *knew* everything. She disengaged Piper's arms gently and took her baby's beautiful, battered face in her hands, kissing her forehead, her eyes, her cheeks. "It's okay my honey, my sweetheart, my love. Everything is going to be all right."

She rose to her feet, un-slinging her rifle in the same motion, and sighted point-blank on the big man's face. She did not hear Piper's cry of warning, did not see all the weapons snap to point straight at her heart. The big man's face relaxed, and his eyes closed momentarily, as if in relief. When they opened again, they were filled with calm acceptance. He dropped his hands to his sides, palms facing her, and closed his eyes again. His expression was peaceful. Naomi snapped the safety off and slid her finger to the trigger.

"You're here! At last!"

Golden curls and a pair of sparkling blue eyes appeared right in front of Naomi's rifle. Verity's eyes crossed as she looked at the end of the barrel. "Thanks, Naomi, but I've got this from here."

Martin's arm clamped around her waist, his hand around the barrel of her rifle, which he wrenched upwards. He dragged Naomi backwards with him. At the same moment, Jack stepped to Piper's side, lifting her to her feet. He, too, backed towards the crowd, half-dragging, half-carrying Piper. His eyes snapped to the men still pointing their weapons at them, and he barked a command that resonated with *power*.

"Lower your weapons!"

As one, the men's weapons wobbled and dropped. Under other circumstances, the shocked expressions on their faces might have been comical. Naomi let go of her rifle, twisting and fighting to free herself of Martin's grip. Other people stepped forward to help him, and she fought as she'd never fought in her life, writhing, panting, kicking, intent only on getting to the big man. She would kill him. She would feel his blood hot on her hands for what he'd put her daughter through. When Martin's arms banded around her, locking her arms into immobility, a scream of rage exploded from her, burning her throat.

The big man didn't even look up. His eyes were riveted on Verity, his expression bewildered. "I don't understand," he said, his low voice barely audible. He looked up, looked around, then frowned back down at her. "It's not supposed to happen this way. This isn't what I saw." His eyes swung to Naomi, to Piper, back to Naomi.

"This is not what I saw," he repeated, his voice edged with what sounded like fear.

"Surprise!" Verity's voice rang out joyously. She clapped her hands like a child, her laughter rising like chimes. "You were planning to commit suicide by Naomi, right? Ha! Gotcha! I can't take all the credit, though. It was Uriel's idea." She glanced at Naomi and leaned to speak confidentially. "Just so's you know, we don't encourage her to shoot living things. It messes her up, and we love her. So, sorry. You do have a Plan B, don't you?"

The big man was starting to regain his composure, though his eyes were still darting around. "What I see always happens," he said to Verity, "Always." His head dropped, and he growled the words at her. "I wanted it to happen!"

"Well, too bad, so sad. This isn't where you die." She stepped forward, and folded her delicate little fingers around his big, hard hands. His head snapped up, and he stared all around, his expression a mixture of fear and awe. People in the crowd stirred and shifted – many of them knew exactly what he was seeing – and Verity's voice lifted, clear and bell-like. "This is where you start to live."

☙

Piper clawed up out of the grief that wanted to close over her head. Day after day of increasing anxiety, of wondering what would happen when they reached Woodland Park, of agonizing over the fact that she was escorting this danger right to them, and now this.

Daddy. The sky was suddenly so big, and there was nothing sheltering her from it. The safety she'd thought to find here, she would never find again. And, oh, sweet *Macy.* Sweet baby sister, never to feel those soft arms or see that sly smile again.

Blackness fluttered along the edges of her vision, and her heart was beating so hard she felt it falter in her chest. She tipped her chin up, gasping for air, and forced herself to rise up and out of the abyss where there was no father, no sister. She couldn't do this now, could not give in to the luxury of grief. She had to get between her mother and Brody, had to, right now.

She pushed away the pastor's supporting hands. Naomi was still fighting to free herself from the tall man who held her, her eyes glued to Brody, an expression in them Piper could never have dreamed she'd see: killing rage. Piper didn't try to break the man's grip, just wrapped her arms around both of them and held on.

"Mom, stop." She pressed her forehead to her mother's, willing her eyes to focus on her instead. "Mom, you need to stop. It won't help. It won't change anything." Still, nothing. "Mama, please, I need you. Please."

That did it. Naomi's eyes met hers. Her struggles eased, then stopped. Piper took her mother's face in her hands and kept their foreheads pressed together until the mother she knew was back in those eyes. The man dropped his arms and took a step back, giving them room. Naomi's hands came up to clutch at Piper's wrists. She braided their hands together between them, squeezing Piper's fingers so hard it hurt, and gazed at her with joy and sorrow brimming in her eyes.

"I'm so sorry, baby. Daddy tried to warn me. He saw. He told me what would happen. God, I wanted him to be wrong." She reached up to touch Piper's face, then to cup her cheek, a gesture from so long ago. Piper closed her eyes and leaned into the caress. With her eyes closed, she could sink into the familiar comfort, the warm essence of her mother. With her eyes open, she was overwhelmed.

She had looked right past her twice, had even craned to see around her. The bond-line had been strong and true, but Piper couldn't believe what she was seeing. Everything soft had melted from Naomi's bones, leaving behind someone Piper didn't know. She dropped her head to her mother's shoulder, lifted her arms and locked them around Naomi's lean back, grieving for the plump softness.

Naomi squeezed back for a moment, then took Piper's shoulders and eased away. Her eyes darted to Brody, and Piper saw the killing rage flicker again. "We need to finish this. Then we can go home, to the cabin." Her mother looked up at the tall man who'd been holding her. When she spoke, her voice was level, cold, practical. "He needs to be put down. I'll do it, if no one else can."

"Jesus, Naomi." The man scrubbed his hands up over his head. "Jesus, you can't mean that. You don't know what you're saying."

"We don't do that. No matter what they've done, we're not going to become that." The pastor spoke – youth pastor, had he said? Jack? Piper had hardly glanced at him, she'd been so anxious to spot her mom. He stood between Brody's men and the crowd, as if he would protect them from this threat single-handedly, and though his next words lacked the imperative punch from before, the *command* that vibrated underneath was unmistakable. "But it's time for you to leave."

Piper watched as Tyler, Adam and Ethan exchanged glances, uncertainty in their expressions. Brody was still focused on the tiny blonde woman who appeared to be not altogether sane. She nodded at the pastor's words, shrugging apologetically. "He's right, I'm afraid. No room at the inn."

"Wait." Piper spoke on instinct. "Elise and the kids." She nodded at Ethan. "They're traveling with him. I want them to stay."

Ethan met her gaze. "If they stay, I stay."

Piper stared him down. "You didn't help me when you could have. You knew, and you didn't help."

Ethan's face tightened, but he didn't drop his gaze. "I knew." He confirmed. "And I didn't help. I'm not proud of it."

If he had scrambled with excuses or asked for pardon, she'd have condemned him with the rest. As it was, she turned away. "It's not up to me. These people will have to decide."

The pastor spoke over his shoulder without looking away from the men. "Martin, I'd sure like your input here."

The tall man stepped forward and met Ethan's gaze. "What do you want?"

Ethan blinked, caught off guard by the question. He looked at Piper, looked around at the crowd, then laid a hand in the center of his chest. The bond-lines connecting him to Elise, Sam and Becca flared. The three of them were waiting on the outskirts of town, but for a moment, they seemed to shimmer in front of Piper's eyes, conjured by the depth of Ethan's love. Ethan looked at Martin and spoke simply.

"I want safety. To be with Elise and keep the kids from harm. To be a part of a safe community, and do my part. That's all."

Martin gestured at his weapon and gear. "Our community isn't much like yours, I'm thinking. Are you willing to abide by what we're trying to build here?"

"Yes."

Martin glanced at Jack. "He believes what he's saying."

Jack was silent for several long moments. Then he nodded. "For now, you and your family can stay," he said to Ethan. His voice hardened as he turned to Brody. "The rest of you have to go. Now."

Verity looped an arm through Brody's and began to stroll with him away from the church, chatting away about someone named Gabriel and the symmetry of little souls or some such. Piper had never seen him look like this, like a dazed sleepwalker. Adam and Tyler followed behind, both of them looking equally shell-shocked. It took her a moment to register the import of what was happening.

He was walking away. Just like that, without a fight.

And he was leaving her here.

Her eyes narrowed. What was the catch? He had to be maneuvering for tactical advantage; Brody would never capitulate like this, not unless it played in the long game.

Oh, God, just the thought made cold fear curdle in her stomach.

He stopped, then, and turned back to face her. His eyes. Would she ever be able to forget them? The corner of his lips twitched humorlessly, and he spoke to her as if they were alone. "You were supposed to be the death of me. I saw it."

Piper closed her eyes. To be so used, in his machinations and agendas. She had no idea what beat in his heart that he could have walked this path out, thinking it would be his end. When she opened her eyes again, he was gazing down at Verity.

He gently disengaged himself, and said something to her. She answered back, and whatever she said made the bond-line linking him to Piper flare into full brilliance. He shut his eyes for a moment, then spoke a low command to Adam and Tyler, turning away without looking at Piper again. She watched him go, the familiar, smooth grace of his movements carrying him away, and waited for the bond-line to dissipate. It didn't.

Martin spoke to Andrea and Paul. "You guys okay?" They nodded. "Do you feel up to following them, just to be sure they head out of Dodge?"

Andrea spoke for them, as she usually did. "It would be our pleasure," she spat, baring her teeth. "Bastards, sneaking up on us like that. Sorry, Jack."

The pastor brushed her apology aside, and spoke to the assembled crowd. "Okay, let's get back to life as usual, but stay sharp. Like Andrea said, they snuck up on us, and we can't let that happen again. Check in with your neighbors, just make sure everyone is accounted for and informed about what happened here. We'll let you know what changes we'll need to make in response." He lifted his hand in benediction and blessing. "Stay safe."

As the crowd dispersed, he turned to Martin. "Can we go inside and start talking this out? Where's your daughter?"

"She's at home, sleeping. I have some time, but not much. I want to be there when she wakes." He turned to look at Naomi and Piper, still standing with their arms banded around each other. "Well, you two might be mistaken for sisters if we got your mom to agree to a buzz cut. I'm Martin."

"I gathered." Piper nodded at Verity, who was a half dozen yards away. Was she actually dancing? She was. "Who the hell is that?"

"Her name is Verity." Martin scrubbed a hand over his head. "She's a little hard to explain. And I'd say that you get used to her in time, but that's not actually true. She's, ah, what you might call a 'free spirit.'"

Behind her, she heard the pastor snort and mutter, "If by 'free spirit' you mean 'complete nut-job,' then sure." He coughed, then lifted his voice. "Piper, I'm Jack, in case you didn't gather that, as well."

Piper turned, and for the first time, their eyes met. An arc of pure white light sizzled and snapped at the contact; her ears buzzed and crackled as if a naked electrical wire had just gone live. Her jaw dropped, and she goggled at him for an eternity of seconds.

Jack took a step towards her, then a step back, and though it was obvious he wasn't seeing what she was seeing, it was clear the connection had staggered him, too. He squinted at her, and shook his head in denial.

Piper wasn't so polite. "Oh, *hell* no."

ℂℂ

Jack shook his head a second time and retreated another step. He knew that face, knew those eyes, from dreams he had done his best not to remember. She was part of it, part of the awful darkness that pressed on him from the future, and yet...and yet...

"She's part of the light, too. Nifty, huh?"

Verity's voice, right in his ear. Herculean effort kept him from leaping away in an undignified scramble, though he couldn't suppress a whole-body twitch. He stepped away from her and spoke as calmly as he could manage. "Verity, I'd rather not have your input right now, if you don't mind. We've got things to discuss, and Martin needs to get back to his daughter."

"What did you say to him? To Brody?" Piper snapped the question at Verity, and Jack winced. Nothing good ever came of demanding information from Verity.

To his surprise, though, Verity sighed and went to stand by Piper and Naomi, close, but not touching them. She gazed at the younger woman for long, long moments, her eyes liquid with compassion. Then she lifted her hand, and as slowly and gently as if she were stroking a wild animal, ran her palm over Piper's shorn head. Piper's eyes widened, then filled with tears.

"Who are they?" she whispered, looking around her. "So beautiful."

"They're always with you. They always have been, always, though you weren't always able to feel the comfort of their presence. Your path, beloved Piper, has been such a difficult one. It's time to rest, to grieve, and to prepare for the next part of the journey."

Naomi stirred, tightening her arms around her daughter and glaring at Verity. "She's done with her journey. She's home."

Verity lifted her other hand and laid it on Naomi's cheek. All three of them seemed to glow for a moment, and mother and daughter both closed their eyes, their heads tilting together. When Piper's eyes opened again, Verity smiled at her.

"I told him even sleeping souls can be awakened by the Divine, that no heart is ever dead. He serves the Light, just like I do." A final stroke of Piper's head, and Verity stepped back. "It's something you needed to hear, too, and now I've told you. Rest and heal, sweet Piper. When you're ready, we'll speak again."

She turned and caught Jack's eye, waggling her eyebrows. "Told you she was no Rebecca of Sunnybrook Farm. Hubba hubba."

He felt Piper's eyes on him, *felt* her confusion, her embarrassment, and her feelings became his, as if his shields didn't even exist. Heat lifted from his neck to his cheeks, and he closed his eyes, undone. To blush, now of all times. "I'm praying, Verity, that when I open my eyes you'll have gone on your way, wreaking havoc and inciting mayhem somewhere else. Anywhere else."

He counted to ten, and to his astonishment and gratitude, she was nothing but a pirouetting shape in the distance when his eyes opened. "Dear God. That actually worked."

"What was that?" Piper's voice was hoarse, urgent. "When she touched me, I saw…"

"Archangels." He said it so she wouldn't dither around, trying not to. "Can't explain it. Wouldn't even try."

He left the rest of what Verity had said alone. There was no sense in trying to explain that, either. Martin was standing off to the side, watching all three of them with speculation in his eyes. When their eyes met, he tightened his mouth, trying not to grin.

"Interesting," he commented. "Look, I know you want to debrief, but I've been gone too long. Andrea and Paul will see them on their way, and we can meet later. I'm sure Piper and Naomi would like to go home and settle in, too."

"Of course." Jack looked at Naomi. She was gazing at her daughter, eyes running over and over her face like caressing hands. Every once in a while she leaned to kiss her forehead or her cheek. Piper was leaning into her mother's embrace, eyes closed, her bruised face so young. "Why don't you radio me when you're ready."

Naomi nodded without looking at him. She retrieved her rifle, and she and Piper returned to the ATV, walking with their arms locked around each other's waists. They zoomed off, Martin took his leave, and Jack was left to stand there alone.

Not knowing what else to do, he headed back inside. He spoke to Judy briefly, returned to his office and stared at the schedule he'd been working on without seeing it. Then, he laid his head down on his desk and prayed, throwing his heart open.

"Take this cup from me," he whispered. "Beloved Father, I'm begging. I don't want her. I don't want the path she'll walk. I want..."

Layla. He couldn't say it out loud. God, he missed her so much. He missed her laughter, her intelligence, her ridiculous spells and the torment of being around her, knowing she had given herself to another. He missed even that. The agony he'd slept and woke with, the misery of knowing she was pregnant, seemed so irrelevant now. Funny, how simple his relationship with her seemed, now that he'd looked into Piper's eyes.

EIGHTEEN
Piper: The Cabin on Carrol Lakes, CO

Piper gazed down at the lump in the bedding that used to be her baby sister, at the tuft of fading, strawberry-blonde hair, so carefully braided and tied with an array of pastel ribbons. Naomi reached out to touch one of the ribbons tenderly.

"For Easter," she said, as if that explained it. As if that made sense.

They had been home for three days, and this was the first time Naomi had allowed Piper in this room. Now she knew why.

She looked at her mother out of the corner of her eye, so afraid of what she might see. It took her long moments to work up the courage to actually turn her head for a good look. Naomi's face was serene. When her eyes lifted from the mummified remains of her daughter, there was clarity in them. Sanity. Piper couldn't make it make sense.

"Mama, this is not okay."

A frown line creased between Naomi's eyebrows. She straightened the covers over Macy, trailed her fingers over the bright braids, and spoke. "We'll see you later, honey. Sleep tight." Then she led Piper out of the bedroom and shut the door. "I'd rather not talk about it in front of her."

Piper pressed her hands over the cold dread that sat like a rock in the pit of her stomach. Before she could try again, Naomi looked up, and again, Piper was struck by the calm sanity in her gaze.

"I know it's not the healthiest thing. I couldn't stand the idea of putting her in the ground." Naomi shuddered. "I couldn't smother her in the cold, dark dirt. I'd have gone crazy." Her eyes sparkled so much like the old Naomi, Piper felt tears start into her own eyes. "And if that wasn't an invitation for a pot shot at your old mom, I don't know what was."

"Mom, she should have..." What? A "proper" burial? Since when had Piper ever concerned herself with what was "proper?" She stumbled on. "She should be put to rest. This doesn't feel right. For her, or for you." Then, a terrible thought occurred to her. "Oh, my God. Do you have Daddy here, too?"

Naomi laughed, actually laughed – as if *that* was crazy, but keeping Macy's corpse tucked in Piper's old bed wasn't. "No, my girl, I do not." She held her hand out. "Let's walk outside. It's a beautiful day."

They headed down to the lakeshore and strolled, arm-in-arm, along the path worn by Naomi and the dogs on their rambles. The big Rottweiler Naomi had introduced as Hades plowed into the lake, sending up a mammoth spray of water, then waded out to shake all over them. He trotted away, grinning a huge, doggy grin, and Naomi's face was young with relaxation and love as she watched him.

"He's such a clown. They say you can love many dogs in a lifetime, but there'll be one special dog, one animal you connect with in an extraordinary way." She nodded after the sniffing Hades. "Pretty sure he's mine."

"Mmm." Piper had never shared her mother's rapport with animals, though she didn't mind having them around. Other than her joy in watching her birds, she'd leave the critters to Naomi. They walked on in silence for a few moments, and before she could think of how to return to the subject of her sister's remains, Naomi did it for her.

"When Macy died," she had to swallow hard to get past the word, "I probably wasn't totally...in my right mind. I don't remember much. I didn't eat, didn't wash. I just stayed beside her. I barely took care of the animals. I was so afraid to leave her. I still feel that way, though I've gotten a better handle on it. I know she's gone, Piper. I can't *feel* her anymore, either her or Daddy, the way I could before."

They'd spent hours discussing the changes people had gone through – so much easier to talk about that, than some of the other things that needed to be spoken of. Confessed. Piper didn't tell her mother, but she was still waiting for the bond-line connecting Brody to her to disappear. On and on it went, steadily glowing, hatefully strong. Several times, Piper had caught herself trying to brush it off, a gesture of both irritation and fear. She could not yet bring herself to analyze what the steadfastness of his bond-line might mean.

For the moment, she was content to rest in the safety of her mother's love, to enjoy the new peace between them. They touched easily now – no more grudging hugs or flinching away from Naomi's frequent gestures of affection – and it felt like they were getting to know each other from a brand new place, without all of the old resentments getting in the way. The plague had done for them what time and maturity on Piper's part would have done before. She could see and appreciate that now.

Naomi spoke again. "I didn't bury Daddy, either. I couldn't." She smiled a sad smile. "I have it on good authority he was happy with my solution, but that's a story for another time. It comforts me, to have Macy near, to care for her body and talk to her, and why is that wrong? I've thought about it, and here's where I stand: In the time before, we used to pump our dead full of chemicals, then seal them in an air-tight, multi-thousand dollar casket, all so they'd decompose more slowly once we'd buried them. How did that make any more sense than what I've done with your sister?"

"Well, geez, Mom." Piper couldn't help grinning at her, though an under-current of worry remained. "When you set out to justify something, you do it up right." They both chuckled. Then Piper squeezed her mother's hand where it was looped through her arm. "If you need to keep her like that, I'll get used to it. I just...need you to be okay."

And there was the crux of it. It really wasn't about burial practices or the right-or-wrongness of mummification. She just needed her mother to be stable. Reliable. Sane. All the things she'd been in the time before. Piper, too, had been thinking, and she'd recognized some truths about herself.

All her life, she'd pulled and tugged and yanked, always anxious to take the next step away from both her parents, especially her mom. In the time before, it had been a hostile thing; if there was a way to be different from her mother, she'd found it. So many of her beliefs and interests had evolved from her "anti-Naomi" stance, and it made her sad, now.

Her mom had never tried to stifle or discourage her. She'd tried to share the things she was interested in – things Piper saw as "too domesticated" to have value – but otherwise, even though it hurt her sometimes, even though she made no secret of the fact that she wished they were closer, she'd supported her daughter as she'd gone her own way. Together, her parents had been the solid bedrock from which Piper had launched herself. She didn't realize how much she had relied on that stability until half the bedrock was gone.

And while Piper was sorry for the years of conflict, she also recognized that she and her mother were fundamentally different. Naomi was a nester, a creator of homes. People like her formed the basis of communities. Piper was a seeker. A traveler. The urge to strike out for parts unknown was an innate part of her. She yearned constantly for independence, for growth, for change. That yearning was still there – she could feel it, a restless murmuring in her heart – but she shushed it, recognizing as well her need to be still, to heal.

A grating croak in a nearby tree made both of them look up, and Naomi laughed a welcome. "You! I thought you'd abandoned us."

Piper shaded her eyes with her hand, and saw a huge raven, head cocked and eyes bright, gazing down at them from the lowest branch of a nearby Cottonwood.

"You've got bird minions, too," she said. "I am so not surprised. I watched my birds every day, when I was with..." She still hadn't figured out a comfortable way to refer to Brody's group, so she just abandoned the sentence and started another. "I loved the Cedar Waxwings and these big guys the best. Ravens are highly intelligent, did you know? As smart as the great apes, some researchers think."

"Well, this fellow sure is. I call him 'Loki.'"

"Norse God of Mischief. Nice. Have you mind-melded with him, like you do with the dogs?"

"Only a couple of times, and only on his terms, but yes. You should see the way he sees colors – I don't even have words to describe it." Naomi looked up at the sun and sighed. "We probably ought to think about some lunch before we head to town. Are you sure you're okay with this?"

Piper shrugged. "It's no big deal." They were supposed to meet with Jack, Martin and some other key members of the community this afternoon to talk about Brody and his men, as well as discuss changes in the community's security as a result of the confrontation that had occurred. "If Jack gets pushy, I'll just shove right back."

Naomi laughed. "You can't know how many times I thought of you when he hit me with his twisty words and sly tricks." She patted Piper's hand fondly. "He thinks he's quite the manipulator, but he's got nothing on my girl."

They'd discussed Jack, of course, and many other members of the community, including the strange and compelling Verity and the absent Layla. Her mother was worried about the latter; apparently, she was pregnant, and wasn't having an easy time of it. "She was so kind to me," Naomi had said. "We'll get in touch with Owen, and see if we can drop in soon. Maybe take them some soup or some cookies."

Her words had made Piper smile. Plague or not, some things were ever the same. They ate a simple but beautifully presented lunch of tuna on crackers and the last of the canned fruit. Naomi talked about her plans for building a greenhouse so she could grow and preserve food year-round, which she hoped to trade for meat when the dogs weren't successful at bringing in game. She had told Piper about her single attempt at hunting, as well as Martin's unhappiness with her decision. They hadn't discussed Martin much at all, which suited Piper just fine. She was still coming to grips with her father's absence, and she sure wasn't ready to see someone take his place. Of him, Naomi would only say. "He's a friend, and a good person to have at your back." It was all Piper wanted or needed to know.

They finished their lunch and headed out to the ATV, leaving the dogs behind for this trip. Piper had insisted she could walk the distance – it still shocked her that her mother regularly did – but Naomi was equally insistent. She needed to baby, to nurture, to protect, to coddle. For the time being, Piper was content to let her, but soon, she would need to remind Naomi that she'd survived a great deal on her journey home, and could certainly handle a four mile hike, among other things.

She thoroughly enjoyed the ride into town, watching the familiar scenery flash by, the giant boulders and cool green pine forests, the fresh, spring-scent in the air of growing things and melting snow. They pulled up to the church just as Martin and his daughter were arriving, also on an ATV.

Martin nodded at Piper, then fixed his dark, intense eyes on Naomi's face, analyzing. After a moment, he smiled. "You look about ten years younger than the last time I saw you. You girls been up there playing 'beauty spa?'"

Naomi narrowed her eyes at him, then slid a sideways glance at Piper. "Never quite an insult, but not a compliment, either." Then, she smiled at Martin's daughter, her expression tender. "Hi, Grace. How are you, sweetheart?"

Grace's lips lifted, but it wasn't really a smile. "I'm fine, thank you." Her dark eyes, so like her father's, shifted to Piper. "I stayed in your room." She fingered the sweatshirt that bagged on her skinny shoulders, and Piper was startled to recognize it. "And this is yours. Thank you."

"You're welcome." Piper lifted a hand to her throat, then to her mouth, hiding a sudden tremble. Her mother had told her what had happened to Grace, of course, but Piper hadn't expected to feel such an instant rapport, such a need to protect. She recognized the ghosts in Grace's dark eyes and wanted to banish them for her, to wrap the younger girl up in vibrantly-colored sweatshirts and warm safety.

"It looks good on you," she said unsteadily, working hard to keep her tone light. This traumatized girl didn't need her big emotions. "That color works better with your dark hair than with my, well –" She rubbed the top of her head. "With what *used* to be my hair."

Grace grimaced, and touched her own choppy hair. "Mine is such a mess," she said, then looked at Naomi. "I don't suppose you brought scissors with you?"

"I can find some." Naomi smirked at Martin. "All three of us can play 'beauty spa,' after the meeting. In fact, if you don't have other plans, you should come up to the cabin. I can cut Gracie's hair, you could stay for dinner and visit with Persephone. She's been pining for you, I'm afraid." Then, she looked quickly at Piper. "Is that okay with you? I'm sorry, honey, I should have said something to you first…"

"It's cool, mom." But it gave her a twinge, the thought of others invading their safe cocoon. To hide it, Piper smirked at Grace, falling back on a little old-school snark. "It'll be just like play-dates when I was little. My mom had to bribe kids to be my friend then, too. So, Grace, if you're nice and do everything I say, I'll let you play with my Barbies, but only the ones with the chewed-up feet."

Naomi's familiar huff and soft, admonishing, "Piper!" gave her comfort. It was good to know her mom's buttons were all where she'd left them.

"You were one of those, huh?" A little smile, a real one, played around Grace's mouth. "I was never much into Barbies. I don't suppose you have Trivial Pursuit? Or Monopoly?"

"We have 'Horseopoly,' which is almost the same thing. My sister –"

Piper's words strangled in her throat. She squeezed her eyes shut tight and fought against the rising swell. *Macy*. Oh, little sister. The grief kept coming like this, like a slap out of nowhere. She didn't know which was worse, this, or the sudden bouts of overwhelming fear, the terror that woke her in the night, or froze her in the middle of some mundane task, her body suddenly clammy with sweat, her hands shaking uncontrollably. She felt a light touch, feather-soft, land on her forearm. Opening her eyes, she met Grace's gaze.

"I know." The younger girl said simply. "My little brother, too. You stop forgetting after a while, and that makes it easier." She paused a moment. "I'm sorry about your dad."

Piper nodded, and rubbed at the center of her chest where the ache was easing into something she could manage. "I think I knew, on some level," she said softly. "I couldn't tell where they were, like I could with my mom. And I think you're right — it will get easier when I stop expecting them to be here." She blew out a huge breath of air, then led the way towards the church. There was refuge in motion. "Let's get this show on the road, people. Grace has challenged me to a game of Trivial Pursuit when we get back to the cabin."

They walked together into the cool, dark church. Jack and Ethan were already in one of the conference rooms, along with a woman Piper hadn't met yet. Her eyes flickered over Piper, lingered on the fading bruises, and narrowed. She strode over and stuck her hand out.

"I'm Rowan. You couldn't be anybody but Piper. You're the image of your mom."

"Nice to meet you. I've heard a lot about you." Piper could analyze, too. She'd never seen anything like this woman's bond-lines – there were too many to count, all of them surging and fading, only to pulse again, according to a rhythm too complex to identify. "You're the healer."

"Ack." Rowan made a face. "If you say so. I prefer 'Physician's Assistant,' which was my title before, but nobody listens to me." Her eyes probed Piper's face, then seemed to go unfocused. "How are you sleeping?"

Piper blinked, and almost asked how she'd known. Then, she remembered what Naomi had told her about this woman. "Better last night than the first two."

"Nightmares?"

"Yep."

"If they get worse or if you start avoiding sleep, let me know. We don't have medication, but we have some herbs that can really help. Your appetite's okay?"

Piper smiled. "My mom could make dog food appetizing if she had to. No problems there."

"Good. If the other symptoms get worse – the sudden shakes, the anxiety – just be sure to ask for help." She reached out and squeezed Piper's arm, the gesture both matter-of-fact and comforting. "You're safe. We've got you."

She returned to her seat, and Piper moved to take a seat as well, refraining from voicing the thoughts Rowan's words conjured. She was safer, that was certain. In just the few days she'd been here, her body was already responding to the alleviation of stress; both physically and mentally, her strength was surging. Other than the nightmares and the occasional bouts of severe anxiety, she hadn't felt this stable and solid on her feet in over a year.

But absolute safety was a fairy tale she didn't believe in any more. None of them should.

They were joined by a man named Thomas, as well as the sentries from the other day, Andrea and Paul. They all took seats at the table, including Grace, which was surprising. Piper nodded at Ethan, and in Jack's general direction, but avoided meeting the young pastor's eyes. That white arc of light was something she would rather not think about just yet. Easier to do that than to convince herself it didn't mean what she feared it meant. To keep her eyes busy, she started analyzing bond-lines, instantly fascinated by what she learned.

The kaleidoscope between her mother and Martin was to be expected, even if she'd rather not dwell on it. She moved on quickly. Vibrant green and pink bonds between Martin and Grace, touched with purple and white – what she'd come to think of as the "good parent-child relationship" colors. Ethan's bonds to Elise and the kids were as strong as ever, and tentative bonds were already forming between him and the people in this room.

Jack's bonds were as multiple as Rowan's, but different. Where Rowan's were what Piper thought of as "mutual" – a two-way bond – Jack's were primarily one-way, like the bond linking Brody to her. This community was clinging to him, but other than a few sputtering bond-lines, he didn't feel a reciprocal connection. She saw the exception when her mother asked about Layla.

"She won't be joining us, I'm afraid. I spoke to Owen this morning, and he said she's been resting a lot, just taking it easy. They're hoping the morning sickness and other issues will settle down soon, and we can have our teacher back."

His voice was completely level, and not even a hint of color warmed his face to betray what he was really feeling, but zowie, this Layla sure lit him up. He was like Brody, Piper thought – exceptionally skilled at hiding what he was feeling or thinking from others. Without her ability, she never would have suspected, but as it was, she sat there enjoying the show. When he spoke of Layla, the whole rainbow of colors flared, all of them, though a deep, throbbing orange predominated. Poor guy, he really had it bad for another man's pregnant woman. It made her wonder if she'd imagined that arc of white light. It had been an exceptionally stressful situation...

As if he could feel her attention, Jack glanced at her. The moment their eyes met, it crackled between them again, white light accompanied by a hissing, buzzing, pop. She'd been half expecting it, and it still made her jump. Jack winced and looked away. Okay, so she hadn't imagined it, but the jury was still out as to what it implied.

Jack looked at Thomas. "You want to fill everyone in on what happened with our visitors, so we can get started?"

Thomas nodded. "Andrea and Paul followed them all the way into Manitou Springs. They weren't trying to be discrete, and they're sure the men knew they were there. They camped on the outskirts of Manitou that night, then headed into Colorado Springs. We don't know where they went after that."

Andrea spoke. "Paul was picking up some pretty bad stuff. He said it wasn't safe to go on. We backed up the pass a ways and watched for the rest of that day and part of the next. They may have circled around another way, on one of the hiking trails, but they didn't double back the way they went."

Ethan spoke. "I don't know what the plan was, beyond Woodland Park." His eyes touched Piper. "Brody Sanders – he was the big guy, the leader – didn't speak about anything beyond this objective."

"Was that usual?" Martin asked. "He only shared short-range goals, rather than speaking of long-term strategy?"

"Yes." Ethan and Piper answered at the same time. Ethan gestured for her to go ahead, and Piper swallowed. She would rather have just listened, but she'd jumped in.

"No one ever knew what Brody's long-term strategy was, but you can be sure he had one. Everything he did was calculated for tactical advantage." She glanced around, and groped her way forward carefully. "After we were burned out, he revealed that he'd changed. People here have changed, my mom says, and it's okay to talk about?"

Rowan answered. "More okay with some than with others, but yes. An increase in intuitive abilities, primarily, which manifests in several different ways, depending on the person. Really strong in our kids. I'm documenting whenever I have a chance. You've changed? Will you say how?"

Again, Piper looked around the room, wondering what the best strategy was here, or if the revelation would be used against her somehow. Then, she shook her head. This wasn't Brody's group. "I see bonds between people, as color and light. I studied sociology in college. Social dynamics and relationships have always fascinated me. It's as if I can *see* what I could only theorize about before."

Around the room, heads were nodding. "Cool," Grace murmured. "Useful."

Piper nodded at her, and went on. "In any case, Brody suggested that he could…" She paused, because it sounded so hokey. "He said he could see the future. Possible paths, he said. I think he came here expecting to…" Again, she had trouble speaking of it. She looked at Ethan for help, and he obliged.

"That blonde woman, that Verity – she made it sound like he came here to die." He didn't look at Piper this time, and she appreciated his discretion. Her business didn't need to be everyone else's. "He had some things to atone for. Some things I knew about, and who knows what he carried with him from his life before, or from his time on active duty."

Briefly, silence fell, as people digested the information. Then Martin looked between Piper and Ethan. "There's a gang, para-military or ex-military, we're not sure which, operating out of Colorado Springs. We don't know much about them, except that they're extremely violent. They control a significant portion of the Old North End, and they have in excess of a thousand people living in their territory and cooperating with them. How likely is it that this Brody would seek to join them?"

Ethan was the first to answer. "I couldn't venture a guess. Brody doesn't need people, not like most of us do. He doesn't ask for advice or input. He just commands. He doesn't make friends, and he doesn't seem to need them. He wouldn't join, unless he had a reason to."

"And he wouldn't join as a subordinate," Piper added her input while staring at the table top. The very idea of Brody in command of such a large group made her suddenly light-headed. "He would take over, for a specific reason, with a specific goal in mind."

"There are somewhere between 10 and 15 men in positions of power, as near as we can tell," Martin said. "Is he capable of staging that kind of coup, with only three men?"

"Yes." Ethan and Piper spoke the word in unison. "Absolutely," Ethan added.

Silence, again. Then Thomas spoke. "We can't know what this Brody and his men will do, but we can talk about what we have to do. A handful of people walked right in here, and if they'd wanted to, they could have taken this community over with a few automatic weapons and some hand grenades. We're likely to be facing a similar situation when that gang decides the grass is greener up the pass."

Andrea and Paul were both nodding at his words, and his voice picked up speed and strength. "We have to train more defenders, and find a way to secure our perimeter. We have to be able to fight fire with fire. When they come at us in force, we need to be prepared to fight for our homes and families, for what we're trying to build here."

"That'll never work."

Grace's soft voice took a moment to register on everyone. Thomas' face darkened, and though he didn't quite bluster, his irritation was obvious. "Grace, I know you 'studied' them and all, but you should let us do the talking here. You don't have the experience to –"

"If you try to meet violence with violence, this community won't survive." Her voice was still soft, but there was something commanding in her quiet tone. "I may not have experience, but I do know that in such a conflict, the side capable of being the most violent will win. My dad says there are less than a hundred people here, which means they outnumber us at least ten to one. Many of them have military training, and they have the munitions from Fort Carson at their disposal."

From under her sweatshirt, she pulled a thick, ragged stack of papers that had been rubber-banded together, dark with row after row of neat handwriting. "Some of the information's here, some of it I haven't had a chance to write down yet." She shot a sideways glance at her father, who was staring at her. "Dad, there are parts of this you shouldn't see. I just...I don't want...please? Could you trust me on this?"

Martin nodded slowly. "For now, honey. If that's what you want."

Grace went on. "I'm not saying all this because I'm a pacifist, or because I believe in the ideology of non-violence from a religious perspective. I'm just saying that when you analyze the resources available to both sides, when you look at it from the perspective of incompatible interests rather than 'war,' it's the most effective method, given the circumstances." She looked around, shrinking a little from the incredulous looks, and scratched her nose. "Unless we could just nuke 'em. That would work, too."

"Holy shit, Grace." Piper was the first one to regain the power of speech. "Brilliant much? How old did you say you were?"

"Seventeen." Grace scratched her nose again, using the gesture to hide a tiny smile of pleasure. "I did a paper. It got an A+."

And just like that, Piper's heart broke. How in the world was this wisp of a girl advocating for non-violence, after what she'd been through? Piper knew without doubt that she could never have been so level-headed in Grace's place. Given the chance, she'd call hellfire and brimstone down on Brody's head, then dance on his smoking corpse.

Piper looked around the room. "She's onto something, here. I don't have her knowledge, but I have read some papers by Sharp, and Roszak." She looked at Grace, who nodded her recognition. "Non-violent action as a means to fundamentally transform a society. Man, what I wouldn't give for the internet right about now. We need to understand the methodology of using non-violence against a violent regime, how to undermine and possibly deconstruct their power base –"

"Hold the phone." Andrea spoke. "Are you seriously suggesting we just sit here, and let them roll right over the top of us while we hold hands and sing 'Kumbaya?' Because I, for one, would rather go down fighting. If they shoot, we have to shoot back, or we're dead."

"Dead is dead, no matter how it happens." Grace's soft voice again. "If you use a non-violent approach, there's a chance you could end up killed. If you try to shoot it out with a superior force, there's an even greater chance you'll die. It's not about being passive and submissive, it's about choosing how you'll engage in the conflict. I don't have all the answers, but I know there are ways to disrupt or destroy established behavior patterns, to create alternative beliefs in a populace. The key is in there somewhere. I just need time to figure it out."

Jack hadn't spoken throughout the exchange, but he did now. "Grace, your dad has been saying something much like this for months, although he's a bit easier to understand." He smiled at her. "I can see where you got your smarts from. We need to work with this idea. You and your dad are both right when you say we can't outfight them." He looked at Andrea and Paul, who were wearing strikingly similar mutinous expressions. "I know it's not how we've been trained to think – our society loved stories where the underdog triumphed against all odds. But that society is dead now, and we need to think in new ways. Does that make sense?"

Paul nodded, while Andrea just shrugged. Thomas chimed in then. "I think she's got some good ideas – she really has a point about dead being dead – but we should still talk about defense, so we can't be so easily blindsided. Maybe we should talk about moving again. Up by Naomi."

Piper glanced at her mother, who didn't seem surprised. "They're not my lakes," she said.

Jack nodded again. "We need a count on the houses and cabins and a community meeting to assess people's willingness to relocate. As a stop-gap, let's look at the schedule and increase our presence on the perimeter." He looked in Piper's direction but managed to not meet her eyes. "Can you look at Grace's documentation and see what can be gleaned, maybe work with her to fine-tune some of her ideas?"

Good move, Piper thought – and delivered with just the right tone. Her mom might dismiss this youth pastor, but from what she'd seen, he had some skills. "It would be an honor," she answered, and saw again Grace's tiny but real smile.

"Unless there's something else, then?" Leading the way, Jack rose.

Around the table, chairs scraped back, all except Martin's and her mother's. Martin stayed where he was, one arm locked across his body, gripping his elbow with knuckles that were white. The other hand, Piper now saw, had a similar white-knuckled grip on her mother's hand. She glanced between the two of them, waiting until the room had emptied out to ask, "What's wrong?"

Her mother just shook her head and let Martin hang on. His eyes were shut as he clearly fought to control some overwhelming emotion. Beside him, Grace stood, shifting uncertainly. She put a tentative hand on his shoulder. "Dad? What's the matter?"

He looked up, and his face just broke. "You're eighteen," he gasped. "Gracie, honey, you're eighteen. Your birthday was in November." He brought his hands up to cover his face. "I'm sorry. I'm so sorry, I just need a minute, honey. You go on with Piper. I just need a minute."

Naomi looked up at Grace. "It'll be okay, sweetheart. He's having a 'Daddy' moment. Piper, would you guys like to meet us outside by the ATVs? You can tell

Grace all about how often I embarrassed you with my weepy ways."

Piper nodded, and looped her arm through Grace's. "She was terrible. School plays, sporting events, you name it, she bawled." She winked at her mom as she steered Grace out the door and hoped it took any sting out of words she didn't want to sting, not anymore. "You should have seen her at my high school graduation, my God, we should have bought stock in Kleenex..."

They met Jack hovering in the hallway. Piper touched a finger to her lips, and the three of them walked silently to the outside doors, then stepped out into the bright warmth of a beautiful day.

"Is he okay?" Jack didn't try to exclude Grace, but the question was clearly directed at Piper.

She tilted her head, a gesture that conveyed her uncertainty. "Are any of us okay? Something hit a vulnerable spot. My mom'll help him sort it out; she's really good at that sort of thing."

Jack hummed an affirmative sound and turned to Grace. "You were a junior, when the plague hit, is that right?" When Grace nodded, he smiled. "When you and Piper are finished with your document, are you interested in joining our other students? Our teacher, Layla, would love to meet you. You could study independently, maybe even help with instruction with the other kids. I get the feeling school was something you really enjoyed and excelled in."

Grace shrugged and looked down. "I loved school. But...I don't know if I'd fit in with the other kids. Not after...everything." She looked sideways at Piper. "Maybe I could study with you? My dad says there's a library here with a crazy librarian who thinks she's Buffy the Vampire Slayer."

"I'd love to study with you, as long as I'm here." Piper blinked. Both Grace and Jack were looking at her with questions in their eyes, and it was her turn to shrug. "I mean, yes. I'd love to study with you. I enjoyed school, too, and this librarian sounds like someone I've got to meet."

Martin and her mother emerged from the building, then, and Grace nodded politely at Jack. "It was nice to meet you."

He nodded back, the smile on his face warm. Her mom had said he was at his best with the kids, his most real, and it looked like her observation had been correct. "Likewise, Grace. I look forward to you being a part of us."

Piper and Jack watched as Grace joined her father, who appeared to have settled back into his "tough guy" persona once more. Piper turned to offer a similar goodbye and found Jack watching her with layers of speculation in his eyes.

"Do you have plans to leave, then?"

Piper maintained his gaze, ignoring the crackling bond-line. "I'm not sure why I said that. Habit, maybe. When I finished high school, I couldn't wait to get out on my own. I guess I'm just not used to the idea of living with my mom again." She wrinkled her nose as a thought occurred to her. "Hey, just for the record, this does not make me a boomerang kid. The circumstances were extraordinary."

Jack's lips twitched, and for just a moment, humor touched his eyes. "That's what they all say."

Piper turned, ready with a smart-ass rejoinder, but when her smiling eyes met his, the bond-line flared into something she'd never seen before, an opalescent rainbow that nearly blinded her. When she could see again, the look on his face made the words die on her lips.

"I don't want this," he whispered, and she got the feeling he wasn't talking to her. "I did not ask for this. It's not what I wanted."

Piper looked away, stung without really knowing why. "Who gets what they want anymore? Adapt, like everybody else." She walked away without looking at him again. "See you around."

She started for the ATVs, then changed her mind, giving in to the restless, irritated energy that was suddenly making her skin twitch. "I'm going to walk it," she called. Before Naomi could voice the protest Piper knew was coming, she waved her off and turned to set her feet on the road. "I got this, Mom."

NINETEEN
Jack: Woodland Park, CO

Jack hadn't known. That would always bother him, that he had not known the minute he heard Rowan's voice on the radio.

"Whatever it is, can it wait?" Jack put his finger on the list he was working his way through, keeping his place. "We got nine more refugees from the Springs this morning, and I'm having trouble figuring out where they can go. Half the town has already moved to Carrol Lakes, but nobody has kept track of which half. Just give me fifteen minutes. Over."

He went back to what he was doing, only half-listening for her reply. When it came, she was crying. "Jack. It can't wait. Come now." She sobbed, and that was when he knew, even before she said, "It's Layla."

He would never remember the trip to Layla's cottage. He found Rowan there on the front porch, pacing and wringing her hands. She ran to him before he even shut off the ATV. "You have to talk to her! Use that thing you do! *Make* her listen!" She grabbed his arm and shook it. "I could be wrong – I don't always have to be right – I don't want to be right!" She ended on a wail.

Jack swung his leg over the ATV and gripped Rowan's arms in return. "Tell me what's happening."

Rowan's breath was heaving, and she fought to control it. "Ectopic pregnancy – the embryo attached outside the womb." Her eyes went unfocused. "In her fallopian tube, or maybe on one of her internal organs, doesn't matter. It ruptured. Jack, it ruptured." Her face twisted. "I should have insisted on seeing her! I would have *seen*, there are drug treatments or maybe we could have figured out how to use the laparoscopic equipment. I'm not trained, but...but..."

She went down, right there in the dirt, just curled up on the ground. Jack went down with her. He held onto her arms with hard hands. "Rowan, what do you need me to make her do?"

"Make her stay! Just...make her..." Her head tilted to the sky, and she wailed the words, at him and at the heavens. "Please, just make her stay here, with us!"

He shook her, gently at first, then harder. "I can't help you if you don't tell me what to do. What's the treatment? What do we need to do to save her?"

"There's nothing we can do." Rowan's eyes were dull when they lifted to his. The frantic energy was gone. "If we'd caught it earlier, maybe emergency surgery. But it's too late. She's bleeding to death, internally." Tears filled her eyes and began a steady coursing down her cheeks. "I *knew* as soon as I saw her. I *knew*."

"No. Unacceptable." Jack hauled her to her feet and began dragging her towards the cottage. "You're not infallible, Rowan, none of us are. You tell me what to *make* her do, and she'll do it, by God. There has to be something.

They used to operate on the battlefield, for the love of Christ. There has to be something!"

Rowan didn't try to resist him. She let him drag her along, her body heaving with hopeless sobs, until he gave up and just dumped her on the porch. Leaving her there, he wrenched open the front door and ran through the familiar house. When he saw her, pale and bloated under a canopy that rioted with jewel-like colors, he *knew*, too.

He slumped against the door jamb, suddenly terrified to take another step. He hardly glanced at Owen, who was sitting in a chair by the window, arms clutched around himself, rocking in dazed silence. Behind him, he heard the front door open, and a moment later, Rowan brushed by. She went to Owen and helped him to his feet, murmuring softly as she led him from the room. He went with her obediently, already lost to shock and grief.

Then, Layla's eyes opened, and Jack's legs turned to water. *Death* was in her eyes, *death* all around them. The spirit was not malevolent, nor cruel, simply inexorable. Somehow, he took the last few steps and dropped to his knees beside the bed, reaching to gather her cold, clammy hands in his own.

"Please," he said brokenly, a prayer to her and to God at the same time. "Please, anything you ask. Tell me what to do. Tell me how to stop this."

"You know better." Her voice was a thread of sound. Her breath was coming in rapid, shallow puffs. "Stay with me until it's done. I'm cold. I'm scared."

"Layla." Her name came out as a sob. He lifted her, as gently as he could, grimacing when even his careful movements made her moan in pain. He sat down on the bed, cradling her in his arms as a father would hold a child, tucking the blanket in around her. Something that had been imbalanced in him shifted back to center. Something that had been *wrong* for a long, long time. "I'll stay with you. Whatever you need, you only have to ask."

Layla tilted her head back, and he supported it in the crook of his arm. With all pretense between them gone, they gazed at each other. Finally, Layla sighed, a feather-soft sound. Jack had to strain to hear her words.

"I don't know who she is, the one who's meant for you." She paused to breathe for a moment, then continued. "But I've known for a long time that it wasn't me. I'm part of your path, but not in the way I thought I wanted."

Hearing this would kill him. "You shouldn't try to talk. Save your strength."

Her lips lifted in the ghost of a smile. "For what, exactly?"

How long they stayed like that, he did not know. He stroked her hair, her back, her arm. He comforted her when her eyes filled with fear, rocked her when she seemed to doze. Rowan came in and watched them for long moments, eyes swollen and mouth trembling. She walked to the bed and leaned to kiss Layla on the forehead, cradling her face in her hands with such tenderness. She kissed Jack as well, pressing her lips to his head fiercely.

As the morning light brightened into afternoon, Jack heard a change in Layla's breathing. He tilted her head back again to look at her face, and *saw* the darkness that was even now falling over her. She stared up at him, eyes already luminous with the light of the next world, and her lips moved. Jack bent his head close, and she repeated her request.

"Psalms. The 23rd." Her lips formed the last word, but no sound came out. "Please."

Jack lifted his head, and clenched his jaw as he stared down at her. The funeral Psalm. She had told him, when he lay recovering in this very bed, that she loved the Psalms. He had never asked her why.

Pitching his voice just so, speaking so that his words wrapped her in comfort and love, he gave her what she asked for. "The Lord is my shepherd, I shall not want..."

She listened until he finished. "Jack."

He would never forget the way she said his name that last time, the soft exhale of it. She lifted her arm, and curled it around his neck. He closed his eyes, and bent his head to nestle in the curve of her throat, giving himself a glimpse of what might have grown between them had they taken a different path, passion and friendship and cherishing. Then, she turned her head and brushed his lips with hers, first and last kiss. Forgiveness. Farewell.

Only when he was sure she was gone did he give her his heart of hearts, from the Song of Songs. "Love is as strong as death, its jealousy unyielding as the grave. It burns like blazing fire, like a mighty flame."

For the rest of his life, he would be grateful for the time he had alone with her then, for the terrible intimacy of it. He settled her in the bed and straightened her nightgown, gently touching the soft curve of her belly where her tiny child had been lost, too. He stroked her hands as he folded them neatly over that curve, knowing he would never admire their graceful elegance again. Never see her lips curl into a smile. Never see her lovely dark eyes snap with the spark of life. Finally, he brushed and arranged the silk waterfall of her dark hair, making sure every strand was just so. In the still moments that followed his ministrations, he felt her absence so keenly. That which had been Layla, the spirit that had been housed in this cooling flesh, was gone.

On the curly, wrought-iron table by the window, hundreds of charms dangled from a vase holding willow branches. Jack reached out to touch one, then another, remembering his anger over her tribute to their dead, his fear of her wicked ways. How petty that seemed now. How close-minded. Beside the vase sat her well-worn Tarot deck, and he slipped a card off the top and into his pocket without looking at it.

He left the bedroom and didn't have to speak the words. Rowan was seated with Owen at the kitchen table, trying to get him to eat some soup. Jack met her eyes and shook his head. Beside her, Owen howled, and Jack's heart ached with the misery of this quiet, strong, gentle man, who had lost both mate and child on this terrible day.

News of Layla's death went through the community with the speed and devastation of the plague. People gathered at the cottage to support Owen and to honor Layla with their memories and their grief. Jack moved among them, offering what comfort he could, but he was just going through the motions.

Part of him was numb. The other part stood back, looking at the faces of the people around him and really understanding for the very first time what they had suffered in the wake of the plague. These people had lost husbands, wives, children. They'd had the fabric of their lives shredded; their losses had left gaping holes where loved ones used to be. Jack had lost people he'd loved, students, friends and distant parents, but he hadn't lost a part of his life. Not until today.

The sun was setting when he finally returned to the church, the last warm rays sliding through the stained glass windows of the sanctuary to gild a small figure curled on the steps leading to the pulpit. Verity's head hung low and her eyes were closed, but tears flowed steadily, tears she wiped away with delicate flutters of her hand. Her sorrow enraged him.

"You dare to cry for her?" His voice was an angry rasp as he strode up the aisle toward her. "You, who speaks with angels? You could have stopped this! You could have intervened, could have told Rowan before it was too late! Her death is on you, Verity!"

Verity's head lifted slowly, and when her eyes met his, terror froze him into stillness. Her face was terrible to behold. "Her death is on *you*," she said, and her voice resonated with the same *power* he saw glowing in her face. "It has been written, a soul contract, since the two of you were in the time before time. I knew it, the very first moment I saw you together. Her death was part of a pact you made before you were ever born."

Her shoulders slumped, and once again, she was just Verity – there was more light around her than around others, perhaps, but right now, she was just a small, grief-stricken woman.

"I loved her," she said softly. "For more than the Divine's purpose. I loved her as a friend. She understood and loved me, and believe you me," her voice was broken and rueful. "That is a rare thing."

Jack's legs just went out from under him. He slumped down onto the steps beside Verity, feeling boneless. "What do you mean, she died because of me? What pact?"

Verity sighed and closed her eyes for a moment. "Forgive me," she murmured. "I spoke in grief and anger, and it was selfish of me. I said more than I should have, because I wanted to hurt you." She looked up at the glowing colors cast by the stained glass windows, and smiled through her tears. "It was a joyous homecoming. So many of your former students, the kids you both loved, were there to greet her. Her parents – they wouldn't speak to her in this life, but that's all mended now." Verity sniffed, and scrubbed her nose along her forearm. "She will be so missed, but she's home now. Home."

"Verity." Jack waited until she looked at him, then opened his hands and his heart at the same time, knowing she would *see* what was in him. "I have never understood you, and I know you know that. You get a kick out of it, I get that, too." Tears swarmed up, and he let them go. "But I need you right now. I need to understand this, and I think you're the only one who can help me. I don't know how I'm going to keep breathing without her."

Verity scooted over until she could lay her head on his shoulder. Jack looked around, watched layer after layer of angel's wings cradle them both, and shut his eyes when she started talking.

"The first spirit I saw was my brother's," she said softly. "He got in our dad's way, when my dad came after me. I went into foster care after that, and Allister went with me. He stayed with me for years, until I'd learned what I needed to learn. Then he went to be with the One." She reached out to hold Jack's hand. "So I know how it feels, to be the one left behind. To feel like it's your fault."

Jack turned his hand over and laced his fingers with hers, returning the comfort. "What did you need to learn?"

"That all souls are eternal. That love goes on and on, forever. That those among us who appear to be evil are often the most self-less servants of the Divine. He died so I could go on and walk my path with that understanding and knowledge. It was our soul pact."

Jack rested his cheek on her head and felt fresh tears well up. "And my pact with Layla? Why did she have to die? What did I have to learn from that?"

"To shatter." Verity lifted her head and gazed at him, wisdom of the ages deep in her eyes. "You've been hurt before, Jack, but you needed to break. 'The wound is the place where the Light enters.' Rumi knew. All spiritual warriors are broken. Only through the break can the wonders and mysteries of this life enter us."

Jack turned his head to gaze up at the stained glass windows. "I'll never know, now, how she came to love the Psalms. Was she my soul mate, Verity? Am I meant to be alone, always?"

Verity returned her cheek to his shoulder. "Our society is so limited when it comes to defining 'soul mates.' On a different path, she might have been your lover, and you might have grown into the kind of closeness you're thinking of. But 'soul mates' can be so much more broadly defined. Friends can have such a relationship, so can parents and children, brothers and sisters. That connection can be found in so many different ways. Great love isn't limited to romantic love. My brother was my soul mate. I missed him so much when he went on, and I miss him still, but we'll be together again." She slanted her eyes up at him, and he saw just a wisp of the irreverent buoyancy that was her natural state of being. "At the risk of weirding you out, he completed me."

Jack smiled at her, wondering if he'd ever feel this in tune with her again, knowing somehow that it didn't really matter. "In a completely socially-acceptable, non-incestuous way, of course."

She smiled back, and he wondered how he could never have seen it before, the sorrow that lay, always, beneath her joy. "Now you're getting it."

She left him, then, but the angels stayed. Jack sat there for hours with their wings wrapped around him until the moon's cool light replaced the sun's glow in the stained glass. Then, he slipped through the dark silence of the church to his small room. By the light of the hurricane lamp on his bedside table, he changed and readied for bed, slipping his hands automatically into his pockets, only then remembering the card he'd taken. He slid it out of his pocket and gazed down at it.

On a brilliant yellow background, a man strode out on a journey, a stick with a bundle tied to it over his shoulder, face lifted confidently to the sky. A little white dog danced joyfully at his heels, and at the bottom, in bold capital letters, were two words: "The Fool."

Layla's scent circled around him, and her soft laughter ghosted through the room. He felt her lips brush his cheek. Then, she was gone. Jack sat down on the edge of his bed and didn't know if the sounds coming out of him were laughter or sobs.

TWENTY
Grace: Woodland Park, CO

Grace watched the community grieve, and wondered what was wrong with her. She got it intellectually of course; this Layla, whom she'd never met, had been beloved. She'd been a leader, a teacher, a friend to everyone here. But so what? Millions, maybe billions of people had died. Why was this woman worthy of such an outpouring, when so many had slipped from the planet virtually unnoticed? Why should their little corner of the world come to a dead stop, so one woman's life could be remembered, when no one but Grace knew the day and hour of her own mother's death?

She kept these observations to herself, of course, and stayed on the fringes of the crowd. So much less privacy now, than in the time before. She didn't know how accurately her thoughts and feelings could be detected by these people, and she wasn't going to take any chances. There was so much that must be kept secret, so many thoughts that needed to be hidden, and the effort of maintaining what Naomi called her "shields" – a term the departed Layla had used, apparently – was exhausting.

Only in the company of Naomi and Piper could she relax a little. Naomi knew the worst, and though she never spoke of it, Grace was sure Piper had suffered a similar ordeal. All the signs were there to see, in the occasional sudden shaking of the older girl's hands, the ease with which she startled, and the way Naomi's worried eyes followed her daughter whenever Piper wasn't looking. It was an unspoken bond between them, an awful sisterhood. Grace had spent a lot of time with Naomi and Piper in the last weeks, and her growing affection for them both was one of the few assurances she had that she could still feel, like normal people did. Still, there were things she didn't want known, things she didn't want to talk about, not even with them.

There had been a service in the church, and the crowd had now moved outside to observe Layla's burial in a corner of the meditation garden. At the front of the group, Jack was speaking, surrounded by Layla's former students, most of whom were crying. The crowd shifted, and Grace caught a glimpse of Quinn. He was standing beside a man who looked like he'd been cut from the earth itself, weathered and brown. Probably the man he lived with now, a rancher, her father had said. It was the first time she'd seen Quinn since Rock Ledge Ranch, and her eyes raced to catalogue the changes.

He was dressed in clean clothes that were just a little too small, his shirt stretched across the bulk of his shoulders. He'd put on healthy weight from what she could see, and someone had trimmed his hair. His back was to her, and over the top of his shoulder, she could just see a small round head adorned with a fluff of dark hair. She forced her eyes away then, afraid to see more, only to have them drawn back again, like a lodestone to true north.

Three times, she looked away, and three times, her eyes returned. Finally, she gave up, filling her eyes with both of them.

Her father had asked if she wanted to see Quinn - he knew they had traveled from Limon together, that they'd been neighbors – but she had declined. She had longed to see him, but when presented with the possibility, she couldn't stand the thought of meeting his eyes. So she'd lied to her father. Too painful, she had said, clothing the lie in truth. He made her think of William, her dead boyfriend. Made her think of home. Her father had watched her in silence for a long time after she'd made up her excuses, too long a time. But he'd turned away without pressing her about it. The silences between them had grown longer and longer lately, and while Grace appreciated how hard he was working to respect her need for time and space, she also wondered how much longer they could go on like this.

"Outside looking in, huh?" Piper's voice made her jump, and the older girl reached out to steady her. "I'm sorry. I didn't mean to sneak up on you."

"It's okay." Grace looked down at her feet and forced her eyes to stay there. "It would be easier if we had met her, I guess."

"I guess." Piper was silent for a moment, scanning the crowd. Grace knew she was watching her bond-lines, something she never seemed to tire of. Then Piper turned her head, staring at her with narrowed eyes. "I'm going to apologize for prying, but I don't really mean it. What's with you and the kid with the baby?"

Grace's head went light, and the stuttering started. "I, uh, that is, he was my neighbor, but..."

"Jesus, Grace, take a deep breath." Piper reached out and cupped a hand under Grace's elbow. "I really am sorry. I didn't mean to upset you. Just keep taking deep breaths, okay? My mom will skin me if you pass out."

Grace did as Piper instructed, breathing until she felt the feeling return to her face, and the lightheadedness ease. "I'm sorry. You surprised me, that's all."

Piper gazed at her in silence for a few minutes, then sighed. "Here's the thing – and tell me if you get lightheaded again, okay? Other people are going to figure it out, Grace. It's more than the changes in people, the intuitive stuff, though that would be enough, if others can *see* or *feel* bonds the way I do. But honestly, I knew the minute I saw her. It's her eyes." She looked back at Quinn and the baby, then returned her gaze to Grace. "Her eyes are your eyes, exactly. So sad and so smart, at the same time." Another pause. "Is he the father?"

"No." Grace stared into a middle distance without seeing. The information rose out of her without her volition. "I don't know which one was her father."

She sensed Piper's stillness, then heard her sudden, indrawn breath. "The gang," she whispered. "Holy fucking hell, Gracie. Does your dad know?"

Grace shook her head no, still staring, wondering what the ramifications of this would be. Piper was silent for a long time. She still had a hold on Grace's elbow, and the contact felt good, stabilizing. Then, her hand tightened, and she tugged gently. "Grace, I need you to look at me. I need to understand something."

Grace complied, and found herself pinned by Piper's intelligent scrutiny. "What?"

"I need to know what your plan is, and don't tell me you don't have one. I've been through something similar to what you went through, and you can talk about the efficacy of non-violent methodology all you want, but I know better. You're not advocating non-violence because you've forgiven them. It's part of a larger plan. And there's a reason you haven't told your dad." She let go of Grace's elbow, but rather than dropping her hand, she stroked Grace's arm. The tenderness on her face highlighted how very much she resembled her mother, but on Piper, the expression was blended with a warrior-like fierceness. "You can trust me. I want to help you."

"I don't want help." This time, Grace paused, giving herself time to make a conscious decision before she started talking. "I have to do this alone. I won't endanger anyone else. It's why I left Quinn, and it's why I didn't tell my dad. I don't want anyone telling me what to think or feel. I don't want them telling me what to do or not do, or worse, doing it for me." Rage boiled up out of her gut at the very thought, burning her throat and chest with the acid of hate. "I'm going to do it myself. And before it's over, they'll *know* it was me, they'll know I outsmarted them before I destroyed them. As far as I know, I'm the only girl who ever got away from them. I'm the only one who survived. This is my duty, but it's also my right. I earned the right to do this on my own."

Piper stared at her, measuring, and Grace returned her gaze steadily. She might never recover from what had happened to her; she knew that on a cerebral level. She might be broken beyond repair. But she could do this for herself. In the same master stroke, she could exact her vengeance and protect this community, including her tiny daughter and her Quinn.

Finally, Piper nodded. "You did earn it," she said quietly. "We've both earned the right to demand our pound of flesh. I don't know if I'll ever get the chance to take mine, but I'm not going to stand in your way when you claim yours. Just promise me something." Her eyes went unfocused, in the way Grace had learned meant she was watching the bond-lines between people. She placed a hand over her heart, then closed it into a fist, and Grace blinked in surprise when she felt an answering tug in her chest. "Just remember that many people care about you, and that enough of the good ones have died."

"I'll remember."

Around them, the crowd shifted and started to break up, voices rising in soft murmurs. Apparently, the service had ended. People gathered in clumps of twos and threes, talking in quiet tones, many of them weeping. Grace craned her head around, but she'd lost track of Quinn. Probably for the best. She knew she'd have to speak with him eventually, but she had no idea what might come out of her mouth when that day came.

Piper stood on her tiptoes, waved, then looked at Grace. "My mom's waiting. I need to go. One more piece of advice, though: If you want to keep your plans to yourself, you're going to want to avoid that Verity. I don't know what her deal is, exactly, but it's some spooky shit. She'll *see*, I'm certain of it." She caught Grace's hand and squeezed, and for just a flicker, Grace thought she saw the bond connecting them, a vibrant blue-green line of light. "Take care."

Grace squeezed back, then watched her go. Piper and her mother were now the keepers of Grace's greatest secrets. She thought about that, as her eyes scanned the crowd, looking for her father. Piper wouldn't interfere or try to stop her, of that she felt certain. Naomi was another story, though. She needed a contingency plan, just in case Piper inadvertently let something slip. Her mind was already working out the details when she turned around and nearly ran into Quinn.

He stood there, taller than she remembered, cradling the baby in his arms. He didn't say hello, didn't nod, or try to pretend that this was an ordinary meeting. He just gazed at her, his eyes traveling over and over her face and form. Long moments passed before he sighed, a deep broken sound. "You're okay. I had to see, with my own eyes."

"I'm okay." She would never know how she got the words out. "And you? You're all right?"

"Yes."

Grace squinted, trying to keep her eyes on Quinn. Then, she gave up.

The baby's nape looked so soft, and her little cheek was flushed. She rested against Quinn's chest, nearly asleep, her eyes drifting shut only to snap open, then drift again. Her little pink mouth pursed and bloomed like flower petals, perfectly curved. She was dressed in a dainty white eyelet dress trimmed in pink ribbon, her chubby little legs and feet bare. One of Quinn's arms was curved under her little rump; the other hand patted her back rhythmically.

Grace's voice was the thinnest wisp of sound. "What's her name?"

"Lark."

"Like the bird. Your favorite." She returned her eyes to Quinn, and the tears in his eyes cut her in two. "I checked on you. Every couple of days, I watched. To make sure you were safe."

"I know. I felt you." Quinn shrugged to wipe his tears on his shoulder, as unashamed of and easy with his emotions as he'd always been. "When you didn't come back for so long, I decided it was time to go. I thought you were..." He couldn't finish the sentence, and didn't need to.

"Quinn, I...I..." She couldn't make herself say the words. They were so puny, compared to what she was feeling.

"Please don't say it." Quinn ducked his head, hiding his eyes from her. "I'm the one who's sorry. I never should have moved us. The cabin was so small and dark. I read about it – about what happens sometimes after..." He tilted his head towards Lark. "You know. You should have had light. We should have stayed where you were comfortable. There were a lot of things I should have done better. I don't blame you for leaving."

He thought she'd run away because the cabin wasn't good enough? He thought *he* should have done better? Grace thought about what she'd become after she'd left them, the filth, the snot, the rags. She touched her shorn hair, and bit her lip until she tasted blood to hold back the awful laughter that wanted to burst from her throat.

"Quinn, no. It wasn't that." She wanted to say more, so desperately, but her throat sealed tight over the words. She shook her head, blinking over and over, concentrating all her energy on just holding it together.

"Well." He turned to leave. "I just needed to see you were okay and to let you know that I won't tell. Not anyone. Take care, Gracie."

"Wait!" The word was so hard to force out, like screaming in a dream. She looked from Quinn, to Lark, and back at Quinn. "What's going to happen? With her, I mean?" Her throat tried to tighten again, and her voice sounded strangled. "I should be doing something. I should be...helping."

Quinn turned back to face her fully. He swelled to his full height, his arms tightening around the baby, who started to squirm and fuss. In this moment, his face held nothing of the boy, as hard as a man's. "She's mine," he said. She could never have imagined his voice so cold. "I don't hold it against you that you ran away, Gracie, but Lark is mine now. You're not going to take her away from me."

He stared her down for a moment, then ducked his head to whisper his shushing magic into Lark's ear and walked away without another word.

Grace stood there, eyes fixed on nothing, as people continued to mill around her, talking, comforting each other, crying and laughing. Sharing their lives. It all seemed so theoretical to her. From afar, she watched Layla's students gather around Quinn, the younger ones making over the baby, two older girls making over Quinn. Grace watched them flirt and giggle, and felt a thousand years old.

"Gracie?" Her dad touched her arm. "Honey, are you okay?"

She barely glanced at his face. "Tired. Can we go home?"

"Of course."

Their path took them right past the group of kids, and Grace kept her face averted. Her breathing had almost returned to normal when she felt it: Someone was watching her. She turned, but it wasn't Quinn. Over his shoulder, Lark's round, dark eyes regarded her steadily. Her footsteps faltered, then stopped.

Piper had been right: The baby's eyes were so filled with sorrow and knowledge, they made Grace's heart ache with every beat. Somehow, she was sure, little Lark knew: Grace wouldn't ever give up, wouldn't rest or know peace, until every single man that might be her father was dead and gone from the Earth.

TWENTY-ONE
Naomi: The Cabin on Carrol Lakes, CO

Naomi buried her daughter on a soft summer day in late May, though she didn't think of it that way. Life, she had learned, was a mind game. What you thought you couldn't bear, you could. All you had to do was look at it from a different perspective.

So she didn't bury Macy's fragile corpse in the cold, dark, suffocating ground; she tucked her into the warm, cradling arms of Mother Earth, surrounded by friends who had become family, supported by her living, breathing daughter. The surging, flaming *life* that was Piper warmed and comforted her as she took the awful and necessary step.

She had invited those people from the community she felt closest to: Martin and Grace; her old neighbor, Ed, who had arrived in Woodland Park just a few days after their return, accompanied by a scruffy mutt he called "Rosemary;" Rowan, Ignacio, Jack, and after some internal back-and-forth, Verity. All of them had come, bringing specially prepared food. Even Verity had brought a remarkably delicious and beautiful salad of mixed baby greens and edible spring flowers. Naomi had cleaned and polished the cabin and had decorated with whatever she could find and transform into something festive. She was determined that this celebration of her daughter's life would be as vibrant and beautiful as Macy had been. So old wrapping paper bloomed into garlands and wreaths, pine cones were scented with cinnamon and displayed in pretty baskets, and spring flowers were harvested for miles around to be arranged in sparkling jars and pretty glasses. She had a few photos of Macy here at the cabin, and these were lovingly displayed on the mantle.

The night before, Piper had helped her lift Macy's body onto a fresh sheet, one she'd brought from the house years ago, printed with brightly-colored unicorns and rainbows. At home, Macy had graduated to bedding more suitable for a serious cowgirl, with realistic horses and lassos, but she'd never outgrown her love of these soft, whimsical sheets. For the last time, Naomi carefully combed out her bright hair, braiding it and tying ribbons that matched the cheerful colors of the shroud, clipping the prettiest braid to keep. Finally, she neatly stitched the sheet closed around Macy, tears flowing to blur her work and dampen the material. Piper sat beside her until the task was finished, reaching out occasionally to pat her sister or adjust a wrinkle in the sheet for her mother.

They kept vigil by Macy's body through the night, arms wrapped around each other, speaking occasionally of favorite memories, letting tears come when they would, remembering Scott as well. Naomi was sure she *felt* both of her lost ones just before dawn, when Piper had fallen into a doze. She had closed her eyes, reveling in their presence, almost able to hear their voices. They had faded, together, just as the sky outside the cabin was warming with the dawn, leaving Naomi filled with grief and peace.

Martin and Hades had helped her dig the grave under Naomi's favorite pine tree on the ridge, and Grace and Piper had lined it with blankets, creating a soft nest. The girls had talked quietly throughout the process, discussing burial rituals from other cultures, analyzing the underlying social implications of sky burials versus cremation, and Naomi's heart had filled to bursting with love for these two brilliant young women, finding in their intellectual discussion support and defense of her choices, reassurance that she wasn't any more crazy than the next bereaved mother.

Not one person she'd invited had expressed surprise or dismay when she carried Macy's shrouded body from the cabin herself; she was certain she had Piper to thank for preparing the way there. Her daughter had steadied her on one side, Martin on the other, and once at the gravesite, Ignacio had helped her take the last steps and lower Macy's body into the Earth. Ed had shared some memories, then Rowan. Finally, Jack had offered some verses from the Bible and a short sermon. Though his exact words were lost on Naomi, the cadence of his voice comforted her.

Now, hours after the gathering at Macy's graveside, after they had all worked together to carefully cover Macy in Earth, tender handful by handful, after they had eaten together and honored the passage of her lovely girl, Naomi watched the group from the cabin window. She had cleared away the dishes from their feast so the others could enjoy a board game on the picnic table outside, and she stole these moments of solitude to just breathe and observe.

Pictionary was the game, and the teams made her smile in amusement. In the time before, these people would probably never have met, much less gotten to know each other. Now she watched as Piper and Grace bickered over Piper's painstakingly slow drawing method; as Ignacio and Rowan quietly and competently won round after round; as Ed laughed good-naturedly over Martin's inability to draw even a stick figure recognizably. Verity had set herself up as keeper of the timer, as well as judge and jury when disputes occurred. Only Jack didn't actively participate. Seated a few feet away in a wooden lounge chair, he looked over at the action occasionally and smiled, but more often than not, his attention was fixed on some distant point, over the lake and far, far away.

Layla's death appeared to have changed Jack profoundly. He was softer and stronger, broken and at peace in a way Naomi had never known him to be. Unlike most of the rest of the community, he hadn't relocated to a place on one of the eight Carrol Lakes, though there were other exceptions. What had once been one scattered community was evolving into two smaller, tighter ones. Ignacio remained on his ranch with his family, which now included young Quinn and baby Lark, and a significant number of the survivors had moved to cluster near his place. Verity stayed with her greenhouses. Martin and Grace had claimed a cabin just a little way down the shoreline from Naomi, though they hadn't moved yet. And although the community center had shifted to one of the large houses on Aspen Lake, Jack stayed on at the empty church. Naomi suspected he wanted to be close to Layla, something she understood all too well. He continued to offer his leadership to the community, continued to work with their youth, but his heart of hearts had left them when Layla died.

Beside her, Hades rested with his head on his paws, eyes closed, though she could *feel* he wasn't sleeping. The big dog hadn't left her side for a single moment today, watching her with adoring, worried eyes, pressing close to warm her when grief wrapped cold arms around her. By contrast, Persephone had attached herself to Grace, much to Martin's dismay. He had managed to coax her into his arms a time or two, but only for a few moments. Then her sturdy little golden body would squirm to get down, and she'd scamper to Grace's side, ears perked adorably. She was curled in Grace's lap even now, dozing while the game raged on around her.

After a particularly boisterous round, Martin rose to his feet. Through the open window, Naomi heard him appeal to Jack to take his place. "Ed deserves better – you're a man of God – have some mercy!" Jack capitulated, and Martin headed towards the cabin, joining her inside moments later. He came to stand by her at the window, his shoulder just brushing hers.

"You okay?"

"I am." She turned her head to smile at him. "I really am."

He leaned into her shoulder for a moment and smiled back. "Good."

They watched the group for a while, both of them snorting with laughter when Verity leaned over to press her palm to Piper's head, causing her pencil to fly with speed and precision over the notepad. Grace shrieked "Mount Rushmore!" and both girls leaped into the air, fists raised in celebration of their first victory while the rest of the players voiced their protests to the serene and unapologetic Verity.

"Is it cheating, if angels are involved?" Martin asked.

"That's a Jack question, though I doubt he'd appreciate you asking it." Naomi walked away from the window. "I'll brew some tea and take them out some cookies."

"Nothing like some of your cookies to settle a dispute." Martin moved to help her, filling the kettle and hanging it over the low coals in the fireplace while Naomi arranged cookies on her prettiest tray. She plucked the flowers that hadn't been eaten from Verity's salad, tucking them in among the cookies, then looked up to find Martin watching her.

"I know it's been a hard day, but it seems like you're enjoying yourself, too."

"I am. It feels good to host people again, to have a gathering and have things all special and nice." She fussed with the cookies, feeling suddenly shy. "It must seem frivolous and ridiculous. But Macy would have loved this. She and I had so much fun, planning and preparing for her birthday parties every year. She always picked the theme, and we'd make decorations, prepare special foods, the whole deal. This is the perfect way to remember her."

"It doesn't seem either frivolous or ridiculous," Martin said gruffly. "Why do you always think you know what I'm thinking?" He was quiet for a moment. "Why did you finally decide to do this?"

Naomi looked up and met his gaze. "I'm not sure if I can put it into words. I needed Macy with me, where I could see her and touch her, before Piper came home. I knew people would think I was nuts, if they knew, and I really didn't care."

"I knew, and I didn't think you were nuts." Martin adjusted the kettle to a lower height over the coals and stared at the rising steam as he went on. "People do what they need to do. When my wife and son died, I was so scared of seeing their bodies...change...I buried them as fast as I could. The ground was still frozen solid, and I was out there, pouring boiling water on it so I could hack a hole deep enough."

Naomi felt the tug of his sad memories in her own heart, not at all surprised that he had known about Macy, not needing to ask him how. She drifted back to the window, where the game had segued into a drawing lesson, delivered by Ignacio. Naomi smiled, watching his quick brown hands dance over the sketch pad as competently as they handled horses. He turned the pad around, and both Rowan and Grace grinned in delight, Rowan exclaiming, "It's us! How did you do that, with just a few lines?"

Ignacio bent to show them, and as Martin joined her, she found the words to answer his question. "I buried her for Piper's sake. Not because it was freaking her out – though it was."

She smiled for a moment, then let the smile fade. She went on slowly, feeling the importance of her words, for herself as well as for Martin. Grace's secrets weighed heavily in her heart, and she dreaded the day he would need to learn this for himself. "I buried her because I needed to show Piper that you can let go of the past and go on. That it's our job to let go and go on, and remember the people we loved and lost. If I can let go of someone I loved so much, she can let go of the hate she's feeling. She can let go of that man, and what he did to her. I felt like I needed to show her the way."

Martin's warm hand captured her wrist, then slid down until his fingers laced with hers. Together, they watched the people that had become family to both of them enjoy the beautiful May warmth and each other's company. Naomi felt a space inside her chest relax and open, a warmth alongside the ever-present ache of loss. What an amazing thing the human heart was, able to heal and grow and love from the ashes of heartbreak. These people had become so beloved by her, a feeling that was only enriched by the sure knowledge of how fragile and fleeting life could be.

Martin made a thoughtful sound. "Jack is a thousand miles away. He's been like that all day; have you noticed?"

"I had noticed, yes. He's missing Layla." She pressed her hand over the protective amulet her friend had given her, which would always hang around her neck now. Macy's bright braid was coiled inside, next to the stones and herbs Layla had chosen for her protection. "We're all missing her. She left a space no one else can fill, and it feels unbalanced and strange, without her."

"I know what you mean, but it's more than that." His sharp eyes didn't leave Jack. "I get the feeling he's thinking of leaving. He hasn't said anything, and he's not shirking or anything like that, but he's making sure others are in place to back him up, you know what I mean?"

"Mmm. I do."

But it wasn't the distance she, too, could already *feel* growing between Jack and the rest of them that concerned her. It was the far-away drift of her own daughter's gaze.

Martin's suspicions about Jack were confirmed less than a week later, when word buzzed through the community that he would, indeed, be leaving. Ed brought the news when he came to help move Martin and Grace to the cabin near Naomi. He arrived bright and early with Ben hitched to a small wagon, which was loaded with supplies and a few sentimental belongings from the house Martin had shared with his small family. Naomi went out to nuzzle and love on Ben while Martin and the girls started ferrying loads into the cabin she'd been scrubbing since dawn.

Ed leaned on the side of the wagon, lifting his grubby baseball cap to swipe at his forehead. It was unseasonably warm for the end of May, and Jose, their weather forecaster with the "intuitive knee," was predicting a hot, dry summer. "Jack told the kids first, as I understand it, yesterday afternoon. He didn't want them to hear it from anybody but him and wanted to answer all their questions, James said."

When he'd arrived from the Springs, Ed had been invited to share living quarters with James, one of Jack's youth group kids from the time before, and James' dad.

The three of them now lived near Ignacio's ranch, and the fit seemed to be a good one. It was a toss-up as to which one of the three adored Rosemary, Ed's scruffy side-kick, more. Her affection wasn't in question, though. Even now, she sat at Ed's feet, panting and gazing up at him with worship in her snappy brown eyes. Ed let his hand drop to her head, absently ruffling her spiky ears. He waved Martin over to join them, then went on.

"From what James said, Jack has a younger sister he lost touch with years ago, well before the plague. He told the kids that losing Layla made him realize how precious people are and how quickly they can leave us. He needs to try to find her. Told the kids he didn't stand by her when he should have, and he needs to ask her forgiveness."

Martin frowned. "Where is she? Does he have any idea?"

"They grew up in Wisconsin, but last he knew, she was somewhere in Michigan. Ran away from home when she was just a teenager, he said." Ed shook his head, and smiled crookedly. "And this is where it would have sounded weird, a year or so ago. Jack said she was always trying to tell people she could see ghosts. When she was younger, their folks would get after her for lying and telling tales. But she kept insisting, and as she got older, she started to act out. Drugs, alcohol, and the like. James said Jack cried when he told them this part. Said he felt responsible for not believing her, for not helping her, when she must have felt so scared and alone. Said he believed her now, and he couldn't live with himself if he didn't try to find her and tell her so."

Martin spoke again, his mind as always going to the practical needs rather than the emotional aspects of Jack's story. "When is he planning to go, did he say? Naomi and I were supplied for a much longer trip when we left here, and he's welcome to whatever of our supplies he can use. Is he going alone?"

"I'm not sure. James didn't say. Making such a long trip alone would be difficult as well as dangerous, though. He's not a fool, from what I gather. I imagine he'll look for someone willing to travel with him."

Cold fingers danced down Naomi's spine, and she frowned, unsettled by the warning. "This could trigger an exodus," she said. "So many people have lost touch with far-away family and loved ones." She looked at Martin. "It feels like everything is about to change again."

He nodded. "It does." He turned his gaze to Pikes Peak, where snow still lingered in spite of the warm spring. "He's not going to want to delay; that's a journey of 1,200 or so miles. On horseback, riding steady, that's at least two or three months, maybe more, depending on water sources. He might be smarter to try for abandoned vehicles, once he's well past the Springs, if he can get them to start after this long."

Ed nodded, and they fell into a discussion of the practical considerations that Naomi only half-listened to. Why the chill down her spine? Cold foreboding was creeping along the edges of her heart, and she didn't understand why. Ben whuffed and butted her gently in the chest, and she took a moment to *connect* with him and steady herself. His great and generous heart, as always, filled her with wonder even as it calmed her. She leaned into his side, breathing in his dusty scent and absorbing his strength until the girls had emptied the wagon and Ed was ready to go. After she had waved them on their way, she spent the rest of the day helping Martin and Grace settle into their new home.

She made up beds for both of them with sheets she'd freshened on the clothesline, and gathered fresh flowers for both their bedside tables. She had brought over some of Macy's books for Grace, stacking those on her bedside table as well – Harry Potter and Anne of Green Gables were good companions, no matter how mature and brilliant you were. Grace's tiny, real smile told her she'd hit the mark, and even Martin seemed to genuinely appreciate her homey touches, though he faked a giant sneeze when he saw the flowers she'd put by his bed. All four of them sat down to a celebratory dinner of vegetable and rabbit soup – the rabbit supplied by Hades, a feat he'd been rapturous over. After dinner, she and Piper left the pair to settle in, walking home in the chilly spring twilight.

By unspoken agreement, they went the long way, strolling along the edge of the lake. Loki the raven shadowed their steps, flitting from tree to tree and croaking occasionally to remind them he was there and to annoy Hades. Persephone had stayed with Grace, a shift in allegiance that was so obvious and so right, Naomi couldn't feel sad about it. Persephone had always gravitated to those that needed her most – first Martin, and now his daughter. Besides, as much time as they all spent together, Naomi would hardly have time to miss her tiny golden self.

A stiffening breeze stirred soft ruffles on the water's surface; the weather was changing, Naomi was sure, but she was reluctant to go inside just yet. Piper had been uncharacteristically quiet all day. The news of Jack's departure had made her frown thoughtfully, and Naomi had caught the same frown on her face over and over as the day went on. It was there now, as they stood on the edge of the lake together, arms linked.

As Naomi watched, Piper reached up to brush at the center of her chest, and the question Naomi had been wanting to ask for a long time left her lips. "Why do you do that? Does it have to do with the bond-lines you can see?"

Piper's lips tightened, and she didn't answer right away. Just when Naomi thought she wouldn't answer at all, Piper took a deep breath. "Brody is still connected to me," she said with sharp quickness, as if she were ripping a bandage off a wound. "And I don't know why. I can't get the bond to go away."

Just like that, the tranquility of the evening evaporated like steam in the heat of Naomi's rage. Beside her, Hades surged with aggressive movement, chest swelling as he bristled to his full height. He barked once sharply, before subsiding into a growl that rose and fell in rumbling menace. Loki screeched a grating alarm and flew off, disappearing into the gathering dusk. Piper swung startled eyes to her mother, and Naomi's lips curled in a snarl.

"I should have killed him when I had the chance."

"Mom, no." Piper turned to face her, gathering their hands together in a bouquet of fingers she clutched over her heart. "Mom, no matter what, I don't want that." She gazed at Naomi as if weighing a great decision, then spoke words that Naomi would never be able to forget. "I killed a man. In cold blood. I executed him."

Naomi's first reaction was denial. "No, you didn't. You couldn't have. It's not in you, to do that."

"It is in me. And at the time, I was not sorry. Not at all."

Piper's face was tight with both fear and defiance, and Naomi recognized the look from a thousand confrontations when she'd been younger: Piper would make an announcement designed to hurt or shock her mother, dropping her words like bombs, then wait with both glee and fear to see what the results would be. Until this moment, Naomi had never understood it. Of all the things she and Piper had struggled with, this had been the hardest. Now, Naomi saw through the defiance to the desperate need for reassurance. Piper needed to know that no matter what she said or did, she would be loved. Naomi's heart cracked at the realization; how could she not have seen this years ago?

Tears stung her eyes as she lifted her hands to Piper's cheeks, cradling her face and leaning to kiss her forehead and nose, just like she'd done when Piper was a prickly, independent little girl. "No matter what happened, I love you. It might frighten me, and I might wish it had been different, but not one thing you've done can change my love for you. Not ever."

"Mama." Piper sobbed once, and leaned to press her forehead to Naomi's. They stayed like that until Piper leaned back, wiping her cheeks. She began to talk, telling the story in a flat voice, not trying to justify or rationalize, explaining the decision she'd come to, the actions she'd taken, and the unexpected results. Her eyes held echoes of the desperation she'd felt when she turned to look at Naomi. "It makes me sick, to remember. I *saw* all of his bond-lines snuff out, even before he was dead. And he *knew* it, Mama. He knew how alone he was, and he was so scared. I did that to him. It was worse than putting that gun to his head and pulling the trigger."

She gazed out over the lake, where the setting sun painted the rippling water orange and pink. "We're not made to be alone," she said. "Humans need each other, in so many different ways. But what we haven't figured out yet is that when we hurt each other, we hurt *ourselves.* Literally, Mom. Killing Josh killed a part of me."

Piper turned to look at her, and Naomi recognized the stubborn set of her face. Her daughter was drawing a line, and she would not be moved from it. "I won't have that for you. No matter what, I won't let you kill Brody for me. I'm telling you right here and now that it would hurt me worse than anything I can imagine, what that would do to you. Because I *know*, Mom. And I will never be able to forget."

Naomi tried to keep her voice calm, in spite of her racing heart. So much easier, to feel that killing rage instead of the cold terror that gripped her now. "The bond – does it tell you how close he is, or where?"

Piper's eyes turned to the south-east. "He's in Colorado Springs, I'm pretty sure. He moves around some, but it *feels* like he's got a home base." Her eyes went unfocused. "Maybe in the southern part of the city, which makes sense. He'd be interested in getting his hands on whatever's left of the supplies and munitions on Fort Carson."

"Okay. All right." Naomi forced the chaos of her thoughts into order. "We need to leave, then. We need to put distance between you and him. We can talk to Ignacio, see if we can take Ben and maybe Pasha, and –"

"Mom."

And that was when Naomi knew. All of it came together, like one of the puzzles Grace talked about: the cold foreboding, her daughter's far-away gaze, the sense that change was upon them. Piper turned to gather up her hands, and spoke the words Naomi already knew she was going to say.

"When Jack leaves, I'm going with him."

If you enjoyed the first two books in the
Colorado Chapters series,
the final book in the triology,
The Journey is Our Home
is available for purchase!

Please share a review on the retail website of your
 choice or Goodreads - or both! Reviews help other
readers find new books, and help indie authors rise
in the ratings so we can play with the big kids.

If you would like updates on my future projects, you
can find me on Facebook at Kathy Miner Books,
contact me via email at kathyminerwriter@gmail.com,
check out my website at www.authorkathyminer.com
or sign up for my monthly newsletter. So many legal
ways to stalk people these days...

Thanks so much for reading!

Turn the page for a sneak peek at
chapter one of The Journey is Our Home!

The Journey is Our Home

Kathy Miner

ONE

Naomi: Woodland Park, CO
July

For the third time, Naomi set the log on its end and centered the axe head on it. She tightened her shaking hands until the axe stopped wobbling, pictured Martin in her mind, lifted the axe into the air, and tried to do as he did.

Didn't work.

The axe glanced off the log again, jarring her shoulders and back, and Naomi discovered she was snarling. Out loud. From where she'd put him on a stay fifteen safe feet away, Hades whined. For once, she didn't pause to reassure the big, watchful Rottweiler, to send love. She had nothing left to give Hades, couldn't comfort him, because she couldn't comfort herself.

Piper was gone.

She, Jack and the other travelers had zoomed off shortly after dawn this morning, waved off by the entire community, the sound of their motorcycles a shocking roar in the soft, rosy morning. Everyone, even the elderly and those with tiny infants, had gathered to see them off. Jack had been their leader, and although he'd spent the last several months delegating his responsibilities and had grown steadily more distant from everyone since Layla's death, he had led them through the early days following the plague and he would be missed.

No one had stepped up to take his place yet, and there was a shifting, anxious restlessness in the community as a result. Jack's responsibilities could be divided and shared, but who would lead them? Who would they look to when danger threatened and swift decisions were called for? Who would speak for them, as more and more outsiders found their way here? Naomi was acutely aware of the collective anxiety and was equally aware of how often eyes turned to her now, how often people asked her the questions they used to take to Jack.

Today, though, she couldn't care less.

Today, her only surviving child had once again struck out on her own. But unlike that long-ago, other-life day when she and Scott had moved Piper into the dorms at the University of Northern Colorado, she couldn't call to chat, to hear her daughter's voice and know she was safe. Couldn't Skype, couldn't hop in the car and make the two-hour drive to see her. Couldn't turn her attention to Macy and Scott, filling the empty ache with the rest of her family. Today, she was alone. No longer wife, no longer mother. Just taking the next breath hurt more than she could believe.

She might never see Piper again. Her daughter had disappeared into the morning mist and might never be back. There had to be somewhere to go with the emotions boiling in her chest, the regret making her heart boom, the grief making her vision ebb and pulse with light. Something she could do, some way to let it out. Back at the cabin, she'd cleaned everything there was to clean, rearranged every room, and then put it all back the way it was in the first place. The harder she worked, the harder she tried to not think, the more frantic she felt.

She had refused to join the rest of the community to see them off, turning her face away from Piper's goodbye this morning at the cabin, refusing to *feel* the tears her daughter had been choking back. Fifteen minutes later, she'd been running, running as fast as she could manage with Hades on her heels. Piper had taken the ATV, and when Naomi finally arrived on the edge of the gathering wheezing, staggering, breathless, she'd heard the collective call, the voices raised in fare-wells and safe-journeys, the startling roar of the bikes. Too late. People stared at her wild self, at her halo of snarled hair and the tears she couldn't stop, and a few of them tried to approach her, to offer comfort. She had snarled at them, just as she was snarling now.

Too late. Too late to kiss her daughter's soft face one last time. Too late to give her the protective amulet she'd fashioned, patterned on the one Layla had given her last spring. Too late to wrap every bit of love and mother-energy she had left in her broken-down heart around her girl, as if that would have made a difference. As if anything would make a difference. Her daughter was heading into a violent, desperate, unpredictable world. She may as well have jumped off a cliff.

Naomi centered the axe head on the log again, glaring fire at it, then swung the axe up and brought it down with all her strength. It bit this time – bit deep and stuck. She jerked at it, then jerked again, yanking and cussing.

"Naomi! What in hell are you doing?"

She ripped the axe free and swung around. Martin was standing beside Hades, hands propped on his hips, face dark with irritation. He took a half-step back when she turned, his eyes widening slightly, his body falling into a defensive posture. Oh, the gratification of that. The ferocious satisfaction his wariness brought her. Hades tensed as he picked up her mood, shifting into a silent crouch, his body taut with the potential of menace. Naomi hefted the axe, saw Martin's eyes flicker to it, to Hades, then back to her, and she exulted.

"Show me how to do this," she snapped. "Now."

Martin's eyebrows rose slowly. He stared her down for a handful of heartbeats. Then, he moved to join her. "First, put the log lower, on the ground – here, on this bed of wood chips so you don't damage the axe head. You need your full range of motion, to make up for what you don't have in upper-body strength. Feet apart. Hands apart." He accompanied his words with nudges of his own feet and hands, and then pointed at a crack on the log. "Hit it right here."

She listened to every word he said and did exactly as he told her, striking the log precisely, feeling the axe head sink deep again. Amazing, how much easier it was. Martin grunted approval and helped her lever the axe head free. "Again. Same spot."

She split the log on her second strike, and he set up another without a word. They fell into a silent rhythm, broken only by the "chunk" of her axe and the increasing huff of her breathing. She lost track of the number of logs she had split by the time he reached for the axe.

"That's enough for now."

He took hold of the axe, but Naomi refused to let it go. As she'd worked, the burning in her gut had eased, replaced by the burning in her arms and shoulders. Her stomach clenched at the thought of stopping. Stopping meant thinking. "I'll finish the pile."

"No, you won't." He popped the axe out of her hands with maddening ease. "Best way to get hurt splitting wood is to keep working when you need a break."

She grabbed at the axe, missed. "I don't need a break." She grabbed again, and felt the snarl boil up her throat once more. "Give it back to me. I said give it back!"

"Naomi."

She looked up. Exasperation and a sad knowing on his features this time. As soon as their eyes met, the dam broke.

"I didn't say goodbye!"

The words wailed from the depths of her. Dimly, she heard him sigh before he maneuvered her to sit on one of the large, un-split logs. Huge, tearing sobs felt like they'd rip her chest apart, but she couldn't begin to stop them, rocking back and forth with the force of her misery. Martin up-ended a log beside her and sat, letting her cry it out. Not until she was swiping at her streaming nose and hiccupping brokenly did he touch her, his big, warm hand landing on her shoulder and squeezing. She looked up at him through swollen eyes.

"Well. I bet you won't make a dumb-ass mistake like that again, will you?"

The old, soft Naomi would have been crushed and outraged, cut to the bone. The hardened thing she'd become barked out a laugh and shrugged his hand off her shoulder. She shook her head, lifting her t-shirt to scrub the tears and snot off her face. "Thanks, Martin. You always know just what to say to make me feel better."

She tipped her head back and stared at a summer sky so blue it looked like a painting. A steady, increasing breeze picked up the wisps of hair that had escaped her braid; there was monsoon energy in the air in spite of the blue sky. Before the day was out, she was sure, they'd have thunderstorms. Where would Piper and the others take shelter, she wondered? The tears welled up again. She let them flow this time, gentle cleansing instead of violent catharsis.

"The ironic thing," she said to the sky, "is that I've been acting just like her. Just like Piper used to act when she was a teenager. Not talking to her unless I had to, refusing to look at her." Her throat tightened up, but she kept choking the words out. She needed to get this out. "I thought she'd see how hurt I was, that she'd change her mind about going. Or about letting me go with her."

"You could have gone with her. If you had really wanted to go, she couldn't have stopped you."

"No, she couldn't have. But she didn't want me to go."

She swallowed and turned her face away; no need to remind Martin of the words Piper had hurled at her. He had been there when she'd done it. There had been plenty of witnesses to that mother-daughter throw-down.

They had been gathered at the church to begin working through the practical details of the travelers' departure. Weeks before, the call had gone out in the community for people willing to travel with Jack and Piper. Ed, their former neighbor, had been the first to volunteer, showing up to the meeting with his scruffy dog at his side.

"Maybe I'll swing down to Texas after we get Jack settled," he had said. "See if I've got any family left other than Rosemary, here." At the sound of her name, Rosemary had lifted adoring eyes to Ed's face, and his hand had dropped to rest on her head. "As long as I can bring my best girl, I wouldn't mind seeing what's going on in the rest of the world."

To everyone's surprise, Owen Weber had also stepped up. Layla's death and the loss of their unborn child, so soon after the loss of his wife and children in the plague, had brought the quiet giant of a man to his knees. His eyes had been haunted, hardly lifting from the floor as he spoke in a voice rusty from disuse. "I can't stay here. I have people in Minnesota. Might be I'll head there when we've found your sister, Jack. But I can't stay here."

Naomi had glanced nervously at Jack, but if he was feeling anything other than compassion, he didn't let it show as he nodded his acceptance. The meeting had progressed with a discussion about mode of travel, and as opinions were offered and expanded on, Naomi had been aware of the ever-increasing tension emanating from her daughter, a tension that had been building steadily since Piper had announced she'd be leaving.

They had argued about that, of course. Naomi had said everything she could think of to dissuade her, but Piper would not be moved. Eventually, Naomi had been forced to admit her daughter's reasoning was sound: Piper wanted to put distance between Brody and her, wanted to help Jack find his sister, wanted to expand on the historical record she'd started during her time with Brody's group and start creating connections between the scattered communities, like theirs, that had to be out there.

Naomi had come to understand those reasons, especially the first of them. She had also assumed she'd be going with them, and began to plan accordingly. As the weeks had passed, though, Piper had grown increasingly tense whenever Naomi spoke of the trip, increasingly silent. Naomi had ignored it. Deep inside, though, she had known what those silences meant. Piper had confirmed her fears, breaking in as Naomi had been lobbying for travel on horseback.

"Mom, stop!" Piper's words had burst out of her, and she had closed her eyes for a moment before going on in a calmer tone. "It's not going to happen. I should have said something sooner, but I didn't want to hurt you. You're not going with us."

It had taken Naomi long, breathless moments to get her voice working. "I am going," she had insisted. "Of course I'm going, Piper. I have to. We just found each other again."

"I know, and I'm sorry. But we need to travel as fast as possible on the way there, and horses just aren't practical. You've never driven a motorcycle, and –"

"I can learn! I learned to ride a horse, didn't I? I'm not like I was before, Piper. I'm stronger now, more fit, and I –"

"Mom, I don't want you to go!" Again, the words had erupted out of Piper, and again, she had modulated her tone, meeting her mother's eyes steadily. "I'm sorry it hurts you, but I don't want you to go."

An awful silence had followed Piper's quiet words. The reactions of the others had been telling: Jack, Ed, and Owen had all looked down. Naomi could *feel* their respect and their sorrow for her pain, but none of them spoke up in support of her. Martin's eyes had been steady on Naomi's stricken face, and his hand had found hers under the table. He had known this was coming, Naomi realized. Whether he had guessed or Piper had told him didn't really matter, because he didn't argue with Piper, either.

"It's not...I just..." Piper had hemmed and hawed in very un-Piper-like fashion, and Naomi had *felt* the swooping roller-coaster of her emotions: terrible guilt warring with a powerful yearning. For freedom. From her. "Mom, this is just something I need to do on my own. I just need...some space. Some distance from...everything."

Naomi had risen from the table where they had all been seated. Too hurt to feel angry. Too frightened for her daughter to feel humiliated. Martin had started to rise with her, but she'd stopped him with a raised, shaking hand. She had left the room without another word.

Preparations had gone forward without her input or involvement, and the confrontation had never been spoken of again. Until now.

Martin handed her a handkerchief before she could swipe at her face with her t-shirt again, and she took it, murmuring a thank-you. Somehow, he always had a clean handkerchief, even now, when laundry was a much more difficult chore than in the time before, and people were becoming accustomed to going about daily life much grubbier. Naomi blew her nose, then returned her eyes to the sky, wishing she could pull that cool blue inside her and soothe her heart with it.

As hurt and frightened as she had been by Piper's decision, she was still a good mother. And a good mother did not smother, stifle, coerce or manipulate her children. Not ever, not even in these times. "I could have gone with her. You're right. I could have insisted on following her or guilt-tripped her into staying."

She looked at Martin, feeling empty and angry and lost. "But then what? Do I follow her around for the rest of our lives? Do I cling to her forever? Refuse to let her go? When it was time for her to go to college, she couldn't wait to get away, to get out on her own. She hasn't changed, and she never will. Piper has been walking away from me since she took her very first steps."

"She loves you. You know that."

Naomi heaved a deep sigh. "I do. And it's not an angry thing anymore, thank God. But Piper is a seeker. She has a gypsy's soul. The plague, everything she went through – none of it changed her basic nature. She is who she is. I could feel how excited she was to go, all tangled up with her guilt over leaving me." Her throat tightened. "I miss Macy, so much. She was a homebody, like me. Scott and I used to joke that we had one of each. Piper started asking for her own apartment when she turned 16, and we'd have been nudging Macy out on her 30th birthday. Now, I don't know who I am. I don't know who to be without being a mom to my girls."

Martin snorted softly. "So. Empty nest syndrome on steroids, then."

Again, he surprised a bark of laughter out of her. "Yeah."

A soft, chuffing bark drew Naomi's attention, and she turned to meet Hades' worried gaze. Unless she was in physical danger, he stayed where she put him, though it distressed him terribly to see her cry. Naomi clicked her fingers twice, releasing him from the stay, and he shot to her side. The big dog pressed close, rumbling softly in contentment under her stroking, scratching hands. As always, contact with one of the dogs calmed and comforted her.

She looked around for perky, golden, butterfly ears and bright eyes, blinked in surprise at the impressive pile of wood she'd split, then looked at Martin. "Where's Persephone?"

"With Grace."

He looked away as he said it. Naomi frowned. She'd been so caught up in the boil and turmoil of her own feelings, she'd been oblivious to all else. Her frown deepened as she examined his familiar profile, seeing the subtle lines of strain that only someone who knew him well would see, *feeling* the undercurrent of distress in him.

"What's wrong?" Worry made her words sharp. Martin's daughter, Grace, had become so precious to her. "Has something happened? Is Grace okay?"

"She's fine. She's at the library with Anne, like always. She'd sleep there if I'd let her." But he still wasn't looking at her.

"Then what are you so worried about?"

He did look at her then, a sideways glance of annoyance. "It can wait."

"If something's wrong with Grace –"

"God, this intuition thing can be such a pain in the ass," he muttered. When she started to argue, he glowered at her. "I said it can wait. You've got enough with Piper leaving today. I'm trying to be sensitive here."

"Oh. I see." To her amazement, she felt the corners of her mouth twitch, and a laugh bubble up. She set it free, then laughed again when his frown grew darker still. "Come on, Martin, you can't blame me for not catching on. When have you ever worried about being sensitive before?"

"A guy can try."

He looked gruff and embarrassed, and Naomi felt her toes edge closer to a cliff she'd been sneaking up on for some time now. As always, the realization sent her into nervous motion. She stood up and stretched, feeling the pull of new muscles in her neck, shoulders and arms. In the time before, the sensation would have dismayed her; she'd have headed straight for some ibuprofen and a heating pad. Now, that ache meant strength to come, a new skill learned, and she had learned to love it.

"I guess I'd better stack this. If you help me, I've got some herbal tea Verity gave me chilling in a jar, down in the lake."

"Herbal tea from Verity? That could be dangerous." Martin stood up and started helping her stack. "Does it have mind-altering properties?"

"Just a blend for relaxation and calming, she said." Naomi frowned, considering. "Guess if we start seeing angels, we'll know she lied."

"Any cookies to go along with it?"

A smile lifted her mouth again, and this time, her heart. Martin might be blunt, plainspoken to a fault, and sparing with his compliments, but he was forever angling for her cookies, and his praise of them was extravagant. It stroked her ego and satisfied her nurturing soul. Small moments of joy. Breath by breath. This was how to survive now.

They worked until the newly split wood was stacked, and then took a break to sit side-by-side in the Adirondack chairs Naomi had set up under a huge old cottonwood tree. Naomi produced the promised tea and the gingersnap cookies she'd baked yesterday with mixed intentions, half-planning to send them with Piper, half-planning to eat them all herself in an orgy of self-indulgent self-pity. This option was better. She'd splurged and traded for some of the spelt flour Ignacio had just started harvesting and grinding, and the result was delicious. She closed her eyes and leaned her head back, listening to Martin hum appreciatively as he munched, enjoying the peace of the summer morning.

With her eyes closed, she could *feel* Piper, her bright and burning girl, there in her chest. Hades pressed against her leg and laid his big head in her lap. She curved an arm around him, using the comfort he gave her to send a pulse of love and apology along the connection between her and Piper. Experimentation over the last couple of months had taught them that Piper might not get the message right away, at that exact moment, but it would be there waiting for her when she chose to focus on the bond. It wasn't the goodbye Naomi should have given her, but it was better than nothing.

A rustle overhead, followed by a series of low, chuckling notes, made her open her eyes. The raven she called Loki perched on a branch just a few feet above them, glossy black feathers sleek and handsome. He cocked his head inquisitively at her, eyes darting to the last cookie on the plate. She picked it up, broke it into pieces, and stood. "I'll share. But it'll cost you."

She reached up, and felt a thrill when he took a chunk of cookie without hesitation. It had taken her weeks to get him to take food from her hand. She fed him several more pieces, then withheld the last. "Your mission, should you choose to accept it, is to keep tabs on Piper." She focused on Piper, on her bright hair and way of moving, on the sound of her voice and the lilt of her laughter, then offered the impressions to Loki and imagined him watching her daughter. Loki ruffled his feathers, head tilting from side to side in interest. As always, she could *feel* his intelligence and curiosity, could sense the surprisingly sophisticated structure of his mind. "Just report back to me from time to time. I'd really appreciate it."

"Do you really think he can understand what you're saying?"

Martin's voice startled the young raven. Loki launched off the branch with an irritated "Kraa!" and flapped away, flying low over the lake and disappearing into the trees on the far ridge. Naomi watched him go, then sat back down. "No, I don't think he understands my words. But he may understand my intent." She smiled wryly. "Not that it'll do much good. Even if he did follow Piper and keep an eye on her, I don't speak raven."

She changed the subject. "So, I'm pretty sure you had something other than 'teach a crazy woman to chop wood then listen to her cry' on your to-do list this morning. What am I taking you away from?"

Martin shrugged, and she detected frustration in the movement. "Not much. Thomas and I need to talk. He wants to increase our perimeter security, and I don't think there's any way to do that. Not here, anyway. The area is too wide-open, and there aren't enough of us to pull off the patrolled boundaries he has in mind."

"He's still angry about Piper and her group walking in and taking control."

"Yeah, he is. We're more prepared for that scenario now, but he still thinks we could mount a defense against a larger hostile force, and I think it's dangerous to think that way. Our best chance is to clear out if we're faced with superior numbers and fire power. We need bolt holes, places we can shelter and hide until the danger passes. Thomas and I need to reach a meeting of the minds on it so we can have a community meeting and give folks instructions."

"Hmm." A frown creased the skin of her forehead. "We've lost so much. It's understandable folks would want to stand and fight, defend what little we have left."

"Understandable, but stupid. It's not worth it to die defending things that can be replaced. Food and shelter are important, but people are irreplaceable."

"I agree." She raised a stern eyebrow. "But telling people they're stupid isn't a good way to get them to listen to you or to do what you want."

Martin made an impatient sound. "Sugar-coating it wastes time. I say it like I see it. You know that."

"I do. That's why you should let me do the talking when the time comes. You and Thomas get your ducks in a row, and I'll talk at the community meeting, let people know what the recommendations are. They need to know we understand, and that the choice will ultimately rest with them whether to hide or stand and fight, but we can't take care of each other if we're all dead."

Martin's lips lifted. "You're plenty blunt yourself, in case you didn't notice."

"You've rubbed off." It felt so good, to focus outside herself and her heartache over Piper. "Do you know how Rowan's doing with Quinn and that medicinal herb garden? Or where Alder's at with his solar panel project?"

They talked for the better part of an hour, discussing ideas and problem-solving. Now that people were starting to come to grips with the fact that life would never return to the way they had known it, it was time to look to the future, time to think beyond basic survival. People all over the community were starting to buzz with excitement over the projects that were taking shape, and the collective energy that was beginning to build was one of innovation, determination and hope. These people would probably never see another open gas station, but how could they adapt vehicles to run on alternative fuel? Before the plague, the green movement had been thriving in Colorado. Many homes in the city already had solar panels installed, and Alder was determined to salvage and install panels on every occupied home before snow fell again. And the world-wide-web might not be resurrected in their lifetimes, but how could they collect, organize and preserve the knowledge they were already in possession of?

Grace and Anne were knee-deep in the latter project, working together every day to gather books from the community, add them to the library's collection and catalog them. Alder had installed a solar panel array to run the lights and a single computer at the library, but Anne was also creating a physical card catalog to back up the digital files. Some of the older teens were helping with the project, though Naomi had heard rumblings of problems there. Grace shared her father's predilection for straight-talk and had very little patience with the giggling frivolity of the other teenage girls, especially the ones who persisted in casting Bambi-eyes in Quinn's direction.

Thoughts of Grace and Quinn made her slip a sideways glance at Martin, wondering at his earlier disquiet. Had he started to suspect that the solemn-eyed baby girl with Quinn was Grace's daughter? As always, the secret weighed heavily on her heart. Not for the first time, she regretted promising Grace she'd keep it.

Since the Woodland Park survivors had split between Carroll Lakes and Ignacio's group on Turkey Creek, weeks could go by without the whole community coming together. Even at the larger gatherings, Quinn was adept at avoiding Grace, and, therefore, Martin. It was possible Martin hadn't gotten a clear look at the baby, who resembled Grace to a startling degree. But what if he had? If he asked her straight out, Naomi had decided, she would tell him the truth. He would be furious, Grace would be furious, but Naomi would not lie, and not just because Martin would *know*. That baby was his granddaughter. He had a right to be a part of her life.

Naomi had watched Quinn from a distance, little Lark perched in the crook of his arm, shadowed by the young tweens who had arrived with Piper's group – Elise's twins, Sam and Beck. Like Grace and Quinn, Elise's children had seen things children shouldn't see on their journey here. If Piper hadn't told Naomi that Beck was a girl – Becca – she wouldn't have guessed. The three had become inseparable, and didn't mingle with the Woodland Park kids. Naomi wished there was a way to reconcile the tension between the two groups, but she suspected only time and experience would resolve the situation. The kids here had lost loved ones, had suffered the loss of the life they knew, but the kids from the outside had experienced the violence and depravity of a world in transition. Quinn and Grace, Sam and Beck, would be forever marked by what they had seen and survived.

Martin gave a mighty stretch, then looked over at Naomi. "Why so quiet all of a sudden?"

She blocked the guilt that wanted to rise – too easy to detect in these times, and she didn't want to explain herself. "Long night. Tired."

"Naomi." He waited until she looked over at him. "People are looking to you to take Jack's place. You know that."

Naomi rolled her eyes. "They should be looking to you. You had command experience in the Marines. The only thing I ever led was a PTA meeting."

"You can trot that self-effacing shit out all day long, it's not going to change anything. Résumes and past experience don't mean squat. People are starting to trust what they *feel*, more and more, and this community's instincts are pointing at you."

He was right, and she didn't need him to tell her this. Nor did she want to talk about it. Not today. They sat in silence for long moments, listening to the wind build into small gusts, watching birds flit about the business of a summer day, ripe and in full bloom. Then Martin slapped his thighs and stood up. He held his hand out to her.

"What do you say we go get drunk?"

She snorted and swatted at his hand, squinting up at the sun. "Get drunk! It's not even noon!"

"Total breakdown of society, Naomi. Those rules no longer apply."

She gazed up at him, at his outstretched hand. Then she stood up and took his hand, knowing it put her toes on the edge of that cliff. Exhilarating. Terrifying. "I've never been drunk."

Surprising Martin was a rare thing, but she'd managed it. "You're shittin' me."

"Nope. Not unless 'tipsy' counts."

"It certainly does not. You are way overdue, then. Rite of passage." He laced his fingers through hers and squeezed. "And I happen to know where a bottle of whiskey is that has your name on it."

Naomi wrinkled her nose. Whiskey. Probably pretty different from the white wine she had occasionally enjoyed in the time before. "I thought Rowan confiscated all the alcohol for her tinctures."

"She thinks she did. What she doesn't know, and all that." He gazed down at her, then tugged her a little closer. "Are you going to faint again if I tell you I plan to kiss you one of these days, sooner rather than later?"

Naomi's heart gave a great and painful lurch. "I'm not sure. Probably not before. Maybe after."

"Hmm. That could work in my favor. C'mon." He pulled her along, moving towards her cabin door. "You can settle the animals, then –"

He broke off. His head snapped around, scanning the skies, his forehead creasing in concentration. "What the hell?"

She heard it, too – a deep, steady "thump-thump-thump" she hadn't heard in over a year. The sound seemed to be coming from everywhere. She and Martin stepped farther into the clearing by the cabin, turning in circles with their heads tipped to the sky.

The helicopter seemed to explode from behind a ridge, the heavy throb of the rotors a surreal battery against their ears. It was flying low, coming at them fast.

Martin shoved Naomi to the ground, crowding her against the cabin wall. She reached out and snagged Hades around the neck, yanking him to her side. Martin watched until the helicopter was almost on top of them, then spun around, covering his face with his arms, shielding Naomi's body with his. It flew close overhead, buffeting them with air, dirt and noise.

When it had passed, Naomi staggered to her feet. They stood together in the clearing by her cabin, watching the helicopter continue north, then swing in a wide arc and head due east. Not until it was no longer visible did Naomi find her voice.

"My God! Where do you think it came from?"

Martin's face, so young a moment ago, so old now, remained tipped to the sky as he answered. "Fort Carson, I'd bet. It was a Black Hawk." He spared her a bleak glance. "That whiskey's going to have to wait, honey. We need to get everyone together. This changes everything."